D1643467

L
L'

0241 115949 2346 7E

The Man Who Was Saturday

BY THE SAME AUTHOR

Novels
Angels in the Snow
The Kites of War
For Infamous Conduct
The Red House
The Yermakov Transfer
Touch the Lion's Paw (filmed as Rough Cut)
Grand Slam
The Great Land
The St Peter's Plot
The Memory Man
I, Said the Spy
Trance
The Red Dove
The Judas Code
The Golden Express

Autobiographies
The Sheltered Days
Don't Quote Me But
And I Quote
Unquote

Under the pseudonym Richard Falkirk
Blackstone
Blackstone's Fancy
Beau Blackstone
Blackstone and the Scourge of Europe
Blackstone Underground
Blackstone on Broadway
The Twisted Wire
The Chill Factor

The Man Who Was Saturday

by

DEREK LAMBERT

(with apologies to the memory of
G.K. Chesterton whose man was Thursday)

WOLVERHAMPTON PUBLIC LIBRARIES
W.M.
LOCATION
RESERVE STOCK
CLASS NO. GB
0241 115949 2346 7E
INVOICE No. HY 850295 CHECKED

HAMISH HAMILTON
London

First Published in Great Britain 1985
by Hamish Hamilton Ltd
Garden House 57-59 Long Acre London EC2E 9JZ

Copyright © 1985 by Derek Lambert

British Library Cataloguing in Publication Date

Lambert, Derek
  The man who was Saturday
  I. Title
  823'914[F]   PR6062.A47

ISBN 0-241-11594-9

Printed in Great Britain by
Richard Clay (The Chaucer Press) Ltd,
Bungay, Suffolk

'. . . for life is a kind of Chess, in which we have often points to gain, and competitors or adversaries to contend with, and in which there is a vast variety of good and evil events that are, in some degree, the effect of prudence, or the want of it . . .'

Benjamin Franklin

To Roger and Lise.

OPENING

Chapter 1

Kreiber peered into the black wound in the river ice and in the light of a kerosene flare saw the face of a young man peering up at him.

He wasn't surprised because nothing surprised him when he had been nipping steadily at the vodka bottle, but he was intrigued, so intrigued that he scarcely heeded the footsteps behind him.

Probably another fisherman who had left his hole carved in the frozen curve of the River Moscow to pick his way through the darkness to cadge some bait.

The footsteps slithered, stopped.

Kreiber continued to stare at the reflection of the young man whose face occasionally shivered into rippled particles in the iced wind blowing in from Siberia.

A face from the past.

My face.

Kreiber, packaged against the cold with felt and newspaper and a fur hat with spaniel ears, took a long pull of *Ahotnichaya*, hunter's vodka, and smiled sadly, almost paternally, at the young warrior, armed to the teeth with ideals, that he had once been.

Twenty years ago a girl who had crossed the wall from East to West Berlin had espied those ideals and sunk sharp teeth into them. A refugee was what she had claimed to be; a recruitment officer seeking Western brains was what she had proved to be.

'Look at the decadence around you,' she had fumed to Kreiber, nuclear physicist, harnessing awesome powers to preserve peace. 'Look at the capitalists, hedonists, wheeler-dealers and neo-Nazis. Do you think they give a *pfennig* for humanity?'

And so persuasive was her tongue, so compliant her

3

WOLVERHAMPTON
PUBLIC LIBRARIES

magnificent body, that, reversing the trend, he had trotted from West to East of the divided city and thence to Moscow, losing the girl in transit, only to discover that in Russia there were those who didn't give a *kopek* for humanity.

A long time ago. At forty-five he was now an old man in a still-alien city finding contemplative pleasure in long night-watches beside the black hole in the ice threaded with a line and tackle.

Taking another nip of firewater, he winked at the Kreiber he had once been. 'Don't worry,' the wink said, 'we'll show them yet.' He warmed mittened hands against his charcoal brazier and found strength from it.

The man in the long black coat stood directly behind Kreiber, eyes glittering in the holes in his grey wool mask.

A fish attracted by the kerosene flare tugged Kreiber's line and the young face in the water disappeared in the commotion.

Kreiber pulled; the fish pulled. A fat lunch there judging by its strength, probably bigger than anything the other anglers hunched beside their flares and charcoal braziers had caught. Not that he would ever know: they didn't discuss their catches with the foreigner who fished alone on the fringe of the ice-camp.

The fish gave a little. Kreiber slipped, kicking the brazier. A charcoal ember fell hissing on the ice. But his quarry was firmly hooked. Maria would cook the fish in butter and he would wash it down with a bottle of Georgian white.

An aircraft, red light winking, passed high over the fishermen engrossed beside their black troughs on the outskirts of Moscow. Kreiber wondered if it was flying to Berlin.

The man in the black coat pinioned Kreiber's arms from behind, twisted one behind his back. He wasn't excessively strong but Kreiber was vodka weak. Kreiber began a scream but it was cut out by a sweet-smelling rag pressed hard against his mouth.

He kicked backwards, lurched forward, pain burning his trapped arm. He let go of the line and thought ludicrously: 'The one that got away.'

He was propelled, feet slipping, the last few centimetres to

4

the edge of the neat round abyss that he had cut that evening. Beside him the line ran out as the fish dived.

A dreamy fatalism overtook him. The other anglers, he supposed, were too far away or too deep in their reveries to notice anything untoward. In any case you don't tangle with a foreigner's problems.

How about a last slug of *Ahotnichaya* to dispatch him glowing from this life? With his free hand he tore away the hand from his mouth but his plea for a last nip was a rubbery mumble.

Cold ran up his legs. His feet splashed. He was paddling in a lake in the Grunewald in West Berlin. Pressure on his shoulders, down, down.

He inhaled water as, with the girl at his side, he crossed the border from Capitalism to Communism never to return.

Bitch!

He began to fight, thrashing the black water with his legs, clawing at the terrible pressure above, but dragged inexorably down the ice-tube by water-logged newspaper and felt.

He managed to grasp the edge of the ice. Crack. He heard the bones in his fingers snap as heavy boots stamped on them. Crack. Still he held on, not feeling pain anymore, just the cold of the grave.

Boots, kicking, pushing, grinding. Broken fingers uncurled. Why?

Then he gave up the fight.

Gently, almost gratefully, he slid into the darkness to join the young man he had seen in the light of the flare, realising in the end that he had been beckoning him.

Gazing at Kreiber's alabaster features in the open coffin in the Institute for World Economy and International Affairs, Robert Calder was nudged by an elbow of fear. How accidental had the deaths of any defectors been? How natural the causes?

In front of him in the queue in the entrance hall Kreiber's maid, Maria, built like a wrestler, sobbed enthusiastically. She moved on, sniffing into a scarlet handkerchief, Calder took her place directly above Kreiber's shuttered stare.

5

According to the post mortem Kreiber's blood had been lethally charged with alcohol. Another Friday night drunk. Another statistic.

Calder, legal brain blunted but still cynical, didn't quite buy that. Kreiber's capacity for hunter's vodka had been phenomenal and he had been an experienced ice fisherman.

Bowing his head, Calder examined the face that had been spotted two days after his disappearance peering from beneath thin ice between reflections of the cupolas of the Kremlin close to Bolshoi Kammenyi Bridge. They had been ennobled by the mortician but beneath the cosmetics you could still trace wandering lines of indecision.

At least, another defector could trace them. Calder touched his own face. The lines, dye-stamped by doubt, were as indecisive as Kreiber's. And yet according to the photographs, his features had once been strong, almost fierce, as he strode the campus, climbed Capitol Hill; even as he crossed the divide between Washington and Moscow.

Kreiber, you sad sonofabitch, what happened?

The elbow of fear sharpened.

He left the coffin and joined the group of mourners, mostly defectors who worked at the Institute, waiting to depart for the cremation. The coffin, marooned in the echoing lobby, seemed to be pointing at them.

A blade of cold reached him through a crack in the inner doors of the entrance. Outside, the chilled February breeze nosing through streets still winged with soiled snow would be an executioner – a winter funeral usually dispatched some of the bereaved to their own graves.

Maria was there, stuffing her mouth with sugar-coated redcurrants which she fished from a cracked plastic shopping bag. And Fabre, the French defector, creased tortoise face bobbing above the moulting collar of his topcoat, and Langley, the Canadian, one time ice-hockey star and sexual athlete, and . . . a girl Calder didn't recognise.

She had grey eyes and her black hair, released from the fur hat she carried in her hand, made an untidy frame for her

6

winter-pale face. Langley, of course, was talking to her but he didn't seem to be making much of an impression.

'She's the new girl in Personnel,' Fabre informed Calder, lungs making rusty music as he spoke. 'She keeps our files in order.'

So she was Surveillance. A pity. But you couldn't blame her: she wouldn't have any choice.

'Attractive,' Fabre judged, 'in a distant sort of way,' vowels in his English theatrically Gallic.

Distant? Perhaps. When cornered by Langley. But Calder detected a challenge in the set of her eyes and mouth. Her nose was, perhaps, a little too assertive but, having had his own broken in a locker-room brawl at Harvard, he was sensitive on the subject of noses.

Fabre, losing Calder's attention, turned to Maria. 'A merciful release,' he said in cassette Russian, bobbing his head towards the coffin. Startled, Maria stopped chewing. Red juice trickled down her chins like blood. But Fabre didn't give up that easily. 'He died for a good cause.'

Maria turned her back on him: the only cause she knew anything about was earning enough money or horse-trading enough merchandise to keep the stew bubbling on the stove. Any other causes unsettled her: they sounded official.

Despite his misgivings, Calder smiled at her. She regarded him suspiciously for a moment, then grinned. It was spectacular, that grin, shining here and there with steel teeth, and it banished Calder's foreboding. Maria delved into her bag and produced half a dozen white-powdered redcurrants cupped in one hand. She handed them to Calder who chewed them slowly; they were delicious, sweet and sharp. He glanced up and saw the girl from Personnel smiling at him; it was positively unseemly – any minute now they'd all be rolling in the aisles.

Fabre said coldly: 'This is a funeral not a burlesque.'

Calder was saved by the doorman who, as the last of the mourners trailed past the coffin, herded by a KGB sheepdog in a square-shouldered topcoat, let the cold in. Whoosh, it entered

7

snapping and Calder buttoned up his grey Crombie (Blooming-dales and still wearing well) as the girl put on her fur hat, tucking in her hair with long fingers.

He wondered how much, being in Personnel, she knew about him.

As the red-draped coffin, destined for Donskoi Monastery, was carried down the outside steps by six pall-bearers, their breath smoking with exertion, Maria dug him in the ribs. 'Come.' She licked red juice from her lips with the tip of her tongue.

But he didn't follow her into the blue and white coach, doubling up as transport and hearse, along with the other forty or so mourners. Instead, although he had no intention of attending the last rites, he followed in his black Zhiguli.

He parked the small car in Donskaya Square and waited in it while the coffin and wreaths and red cushion bearing Kreiber's three Soviet decorations were carried into the monastery, stone walls surrounding the five bunched domes of the cathedral still plastered with old snow. The corpse would be burned immediately, ashes flown to West Berlin in an earthenware casket adorned with a sprightly hammer and sickle. In the final reckoning both sides would be seen to be commendably decent. What harm could a few cinders do?

Through the exhaust fumes billowing past the windshield Calder picked out the defectors among the mourners following the coffin. American, British, German, French, Dutch, Canadian, Scandanavian, Australian . . . known to the KGB as The Twilight Brigade.

Twilight. . . . How many of them, trapped between day and night, between dog and wolf, had wondered, as he had done, about the deaths of their fellows?

Donald Maclean, British diplomat and partner in a celebrated defection in 1952, who had died in March '83, ostensibly from cancer. Could he have been slipped a few spoonfuls of Brompton Mixture, alcohol, cocaine and heroin? It was said to dispatch patients singing.

Be fair. Even if the mixture had been prescribed it could have

8

been on compassionate grounds. After all it was prescribed in the West freely enough.

And Guy Burgess, Maclean's partner in espionage and homosexual lush, who had died in his sleep in 1963 in an iron bed in the Botkin Hospital. He had died from booze. But, of course, the simplest way to hasten the death of an alcoholic is to inject him with alcohol.

When Maria and the girl – was she the reason he had driven to Donskaya Square? – had been hustled into the monastery by the shepherd from State Security, Calder drove onto Lenin Prospect and headed for the centre of the city. Tomorrow, he promised himself, such neurotic fantasies would be banished for ever. Unless another defector died too accidentally or too naturally or too soon.

If in doubt consult Dalby.

Calder arranged to meet him late that afternoon beside the waterless fountain at the entrance to Sokolinki Park. You could safely trade indiscretions in Sokolinki's lonely pastures of snow and belts of silver birch thick with silence.

When Calder arrived on Friday night boozers were already gathering, tilting bottles of vodka bought legally or paid as wages or distilled by the friendly chemist on the corner of the block, banding together in case any of them collapsed, easy prey for teenage muggers.

Hands deep into the pockets of his Crombie, fur hat worn with a jauntiness he didn't feel, Calder roamed between the burgeoning drunks and the pavilions remaining from international exhibitions. The cold crisped his nostrils.

No sign of Dalby. But, like the Russians with whom he mixed more compatibly than most defectors, he wasn't noted for punctuality. From the very beginning of his banishment from Britain he had managed to adapt. Calder envied him.

'Good evening my dear fellow.'

Calder spun round. Dalby still managed to surprise; that was thirty years of espionage for you. He was smiling benignly. Although the slanting lines on his face had settled into pouches

Dalby, now in his seventies, still looked like an urbane pirate. He wore a peaked cap instead of a *shapka*, challenging the cold to take off his ears.

He squeezed Calder's arm. 'Come, let's take a walk.'

They walked down one of the avenues that had once rung to the harness jingle of aristocratic coaches; on either side the snow had been packed hard and bright by children at play and cross-country skiers, but they had departed for the night and loneliness was settling.

Calder glanced at the fountain. He saw a figure detach itself from the boozers and strike out towards the avenue.

'Is he there?' Dalby asked.

'I didn't know you had a watchdog.'

Dalby chuckled. 'Not me, my dear chap. You.'

Sokolinki was derived from the Russian for falcon because falconry had once been practised in the park and Calder felt the scissored nip of sharp talons. 'I wasn't aware I was being followed.'

'You wouldn't be, would you? Not if your watchdog is a pro. And the comrades are very professional in these m . . .matters.' Paradoxically, Dalby's occasional stammer refurbished his authority.

'How did you know I was being followed?'

'Let's just say I've acquired a certain prescience over the years.'

No one quite knew what those years had entailed. But as he had been in the top echelon of British Intelligence it was safe to assume that he had blown great holes through many Western spy networks.

But he doesn't know what I know. The knowledge gave Calder an edge over the enigma that was Austen Dalby; it also scared him. He was about to look over his shoulder again when Dalby, gripping his arm, said: 'Don't.'

'Why would they want to follow me?'

'You would know b . . . better than me. After all, you're from another generation of . . . let us say idealists. Perhaps you know secrets to which I couldn't possibly have had access.'

Did he – could he – know?

10

Calder directed the conversation into safer waters. 'Idealists? A cosy euphemism.'

'Then how would you describe us? Traitors?'

'There isn't a tag,' Calder said. 'We merely followed our convictions. We had our own sets of values but they weren't necessarily idealistic.'

'Values . . . you make Moscow sound very different from London or New York. Is it so different?'

'It's different all right,' Calder said. He half-turned his head with exaggerated nonchalance. The crow-like figure was alone on the avenue. Perhaps he was just a lone walker – parks could be the most desolate places in the world.

'Mmmmm. Outwardly, perhaps, but what about the equation?'

Always the equation. Vodka in the Soviet Union versus drugs in the West. Scarcities versus surfeits. Spartan flats versus chic apartments. Full employment versus unemployment . . . .

Dalby who, like most defectors, tilted the equation in Moscow's favour, said: 'Here a police state, in the West freedom. Such freedom. A g . . .gutter press that incites violence, encourages promiscuity. A political system hellbent on self-destruction. I sometimes wonder which is the CIA's greatest enemy, the KGB or Congress.'

When they reached the birch trees and the silence made conspirators out of them Dalby said: 'All right, out with it. Kreiber?'

'He looked so . . . puzzled. Even in death he seemed to be saying, "Now what the hell was that about?" '

'I should imagine everyone thinks that before they meet their maker, defectors, priests, gangsters.'

'I doubt whether they ask themselves if they've wasted their lives by taking a wrong turning when they were too young to understand.'

'Don't they? I wouldn't be too sure about that.' Ice-sheathed twigs slithered together like busy knitting-needles. 'But that isn't what you really want to talk about, is it?'

Calder said abruptly: 'Do you figure it was an accident?'

11

'Kreiber? Why not? He had enough alcohol in his blood to fuel an Ilyushin from Moscow to Berlin.'

'He'd been fishing from that hole in the ice all winter. He wasn't likely to fall in.'

'People can die falling over their own doorsteps.'

'There was blood on the rim of the hole.'

'Sharp stuff ice, especially in minus twenty degrees.'

'And bruising on one arm.'

'You don't fall down a well without touching the sides.'

'It must be wonderful to be so sure of everything.'

'Why doubt? We're here. There's not a damn thing any of us can do about it. Let's enjoy our elected way of life.' Dalby tore a strip of paper bark from a thin tree and began to shred it.

'And Maclean?'

'Cancer, surely.' Dalby threw tatters of bark into the air. 'Ah, you mean euthanasia. A possibility,' he admitted. 'Compassionate people, the Russians. Just listen to their choirs.'

'And Blunt?'

'Poor old Anthony? He hadn't even defected.'

'He was blown,' Calder pointed out. 'And he died within three weeks of Maclean.'

The American newspapers, part of the material analysed by Calder and his staff at the Institute, had given a lot of prominence to Blunt's death. Queen's art adviser and Establishment figurehead, he had been exposed in 1979 as a one-time Soviet agent and died four years later.

'Aren't we being a little m . . . melodramatic? Paranoic even? Blunt died from a heart attack.'

'They can be faked.'

'True.' Dalby knew about such things. 'An injection of potassium chloride, usually into the main vein in the penis where it isn't readily detectable. It alters the ionic balance between potassium and sodium and the heart febrillates. If the body isn't found for five or six hours the potassium chloride isn't detectable. But who would want to kill poor old Anthony? He wasn't of any use to anyone any more.'

Somewhere a twig cracked.

'I guess I'm getting morbid,' Calder said.

'Positively funereal. Anthony wasn't neurotic. He would have been tickled pink to think that he was buried on Spy Wednesday – the Wednesday before Good Friday when Judas asked how much he would be paid to betray Jesus.'

'Okay, I'm stupid.'

'Not stupid, you just listen too much to Institute gossip.'

'You're right, let's get out of here. I'm purged.'

As they emerged from the wood the figure on the avenue turned abruptly and began whistling to an invisible dog.

When they reached the fountain Calder asked: 'Why weren't you at the funeral?'

'I find my enjoyment elsewhere,' Dalby replied. 'I don't read obituary columns either.' Smiling, he pointed at a group of tipplers who had begun to sing *The Sacred War* – 'Arise enormous country, Arise to fight till death' – and said: 'I was once asked by a fellow traveller from London with bum-fluff still on his cheeks why Russians drank so much. Do you know what I told him?'

Calder shook his head although he could have hazarded a guess – Dalby's contempt for naïve Communists from the West who, like penguins, gulped every morsel of doctrine tossed to them, was well-known.

'I told him, "Because they like to get drunk." '

They shook hands, confessor and penitent. Behind them park and sky were a black-and-white print. And chords of sadness could be heard in the strutting voices of the vodka choir. Compassion? For whom? Themselves?

Briskly, Calder walked to his Zhiguli outside Sokolinki metro station. Kreiber, Maclean, Blunt . . . stupid! He put the car into gear and drove down Rusakorvskoe Road towards the Sadovaya, the highway ringing central Moscow.

The Estonian at the wheel of the battered cream Volga who had been keeping Calder under surveillance in the park gave him a five-second start before following.

Chapter 2

March 8th. Women's Day in the Soviet Union.

From the ice wastes of the north to the deserts of the south, from mid-Europe across eight time zones to the Pacific, women reigned in the country comprising one sixth of the world's land masses.

In fretwork villages becalmed in Siberia, in the splendid dachas of the privileged outside Moscow, men made love with unaccustomed tenderness, dressed the children, cooked dinner, washed the dishes and bought carnations at ten roubles a blossom.

Beaming, Mother Russia loosened her stays and relaxed. Until the following day when the men became goats again. Or so the feminists asserted.

On a platform in a wooden hall that smelled of resin and carbolic to the south-west of Moscow near the Olympic Village on Michurinsky Prospect, the girl from Personnel was poised to make just such an assertion. As it was her first speech, apprehension fluttered inside her like a trapped bird.

While the introductory speaker, mannish and indignant, barked hatred of all men, Katerina Ilyina nervously smoothed her blue woollen dress, fashionable but not provocative in case it upset the clucking hens in the audience.

Svetlana Rozonova, sitting on the chair beside her, patted her hand. 'Don't worry, you'll slay them.'

Contemplating the forty women listening impassively to the speaker, Katerina thought that was extremely unlikely. If, like Svetlana, you were leggily tall with wild blonde hair and didn't give a damn what people thought about you then, yes, you could slay them.

Katerina shifted on her rickety chair. It creaked so loudly

14

that the speaker turned and glared. The trapped bird beat its wings with renewed agitation.

It was daunting enough making a first speech but when you knew that three women had already been expelled from the Soviet Union for promoting the same cause . . ... Like her they had been loyal to their country, like her all they had wanted to do was improve the lot of its women. Their expulsion had been wicked and it had sharpened the protest within her.

From her vantage point in the hall in which a stove was burning incandescently in one corner, Katerina surveyed her small band of rebellious womanhood. The turn-out was disappointing but what did you expect with an icy breeze still at large? Come the thaw and the women of Moscow would unfurl their banners of feminism.

The women were mostly young but there were one or two of the older generation among them padded with *valenki* boots and heavy coats, scarves folded on their laps.

Svetlana, wearing a wolfskin coat bought in Vladivostok by an Aeroflot pilot – when you were employed by Intourist as a courier you had such luck, not when you worked with foreign defectors – nudged her. 'That one over there who looks like a maiden aunt. KGB – bet you five roubles.'

The maiden aunt, pepper-and-salt hair combed into a bun, was writing busily in a blue notebook. 'No bet,' Katerina whispered. Through a window she could see the fur hat and bulky shoulders of a militiaman. Ten policemen to control forty women. What did they expect, an armed uprising?

The speaker sat down. Katerina stood up. The bird's wings beat inside her. 'Good luck,' from Svetlana. The faces had become a blur, stationary white moths.

When she opened her mouth the bird flew out. Her voice rang and words bore little resemblance to the ones she had rehearsed. She astonished herself. This Katerina Ilyina was a stranger. She crumbled her notes into a ball and dropped it on the floor.

'Today is Women's Day and today your man will be kind and charming. Perhaps he has already prepared the breakfast,

15

bought you a carnation . . . . How very considerate of him. Perhaps even now he is making the beds, queuing at the gastronom . . . .' She paused with the cunning of a seasoned orator. 'Wouldn't it be wonderful if he did just one of those things for the other 364 days of the year?'

Some women smiled at such an improbable vision. That was the trouble: too many women were indulgent; their plight was a radio and TV joke alongside absenteeism from work and graft.

Katerina hurried on. 'They say we enjoy equality with men. *They* being men. All right, there is equality during the day when you and your husbands are both at work. But what about those long evenings after work. Is there equality then? Well, is there?'

A few heads shook.

'While you scrub and sew and cook they enrich their minds in front of the television and refuel the inner man with firewater. What sort of equality is that? How can they talk about emancipation when fifty-one per cent of the work force are women? When eighty-three per cent of all doctors and health workers are women? When seventy-four per cent of all teachers are women?'

'And what are you?' a tough-looking woman wearing a red shawl demanded.

'An adviser,' Katerina retorted. My first heckler, she thought. 'A seeker of women's rights. Your rights,' pointing at the woman. She felt quite capable of handling her. 'Sad, isn't it, that Soviet women are still cowed, yes cowed, by the fear of pregnancy. Not because you don't want children,' hastily, 'because every woman wants children, but because you can't afford them. Granted a mother is given twelve months off work after she's had a baby. But if she wants to continue giving the child the care it needs she loses her job. And what does the State do about that? It provides facilities for abortion, that's what. Only the other day I read about a woman in Kiev who had fifteen . . ..'

The woman with pepper-and-salt hair scribbled furiously.

16

The heckler in the red shawl shouted: 'Tell her old man to buy some goloshes.'

A few women smirked at the reference to sheaths spurned by most men because the latex was so thick that it spoiled pleasure. For the first time Katerina faltered. Smut she hadn't anticipated. Then she decided to invoke it. She was amazed at her adaptability.

She said resonantly: 'In a truly liberated society there won't be any place for remarks like that. Sex isn't dirty, you know. Smut is merely a by-product of suppression.'

There, that should put paid to the potato-faced heckler. If she wasn't interested in the movement why had she come? A paid trouble-maker?

Svetlana clapped her hands. 'Hear, hear!'

Face screwed up with fury, the heckler rose to her feet and pointed a stubby finger at Svetlana. 'I bet she's fitted a few goloshes in her time.'

Svetlana had this effect on some women. Innocently she reminded them of girlhood dreams never fulfilled. Once she had worn a mini-skirt in the Arbat and women had leaped from doorways bunching their fists.

This time no one smiled and that might have been the end of it if Svetlana had allowed the heckler to get away with it; but that wasn't Svetlana's style. 'What can she know about sex?' she asked Katerina in a penetrating whisper. 'Except on a very dark night.'

The heckler planted her hands on her hips. 'Night,' she proclaimed, 'is for the modest, daytime for the shameless. There are some,' glaring at Svetlana, 'who don't care whether they see the sun or the stars when they're lying on their back.'

From the other side of the hall came a voice: 'Sit down you with the face like a boot.'

Svetlana was rising to her feet but Katerina restrained her; sometimes she was wiser than her friend. What I need, she thought, is a rallying cry. She flattened her hands against her audience. 'By arguing among ourselves we are playing into the hands of the male chauvinists.'

17

Chauvinist *pigs* in the West. But Katerina didn't feel that way about them: she liked men's company. It was injustice that angered her.

The heckler, now under attack from her neighbours, finally sat down and Katerina moved triumphantly onto divorce – its alarming popularity – and the plight of the housewife with children abandoned by a husband for a rival down the assembly line.

She had intended to finish as she had started with an ironic reference to Women's Day. Instead she heard herself saying: 'The Revolution was supposed to have given women equality. It failed. Now another Revolution is under way. Women of the Soviet Union arise, you have nothing to lose but your chains!'

Desultory clapping. Well, there was surely nothing wrong with adapting Marx. Or was there? At that moment the militia moved in, three of them in long grey coats, from a door behind the platform.

Hands on the pistols at their hips, they stood beside the speakers menacing the audience.

Tossing her blonde hair, Svetlana said: 'Hallo boys, and what can we do for you?' while Katerina shouted: 'Go on, shoot us.'

A fourth militiaman materialised, a tired-looking officer who needed a shave. He addressed the meeting. 'Leave quietly by the door over there,' pointing at the exit by the stove, 'and you won't come to any harm.'

Svetlana blew him a kiss.

Katerina, still raging, turned to the audience. 'Take no notice of him: it's Women's Day.'

The officer nodded to a militiaman with a Tartar face and pock-marked skin. He clapped one hand over Katerina's mouth and trapped her flailing arms with the other. Svetlana hit him on the head with her handbag before she, too, was pinioned.

More militiamen came onto the stage and Katerina thought: 'This is monstrous, the way foreigners see us.' She bit one of the Tartar's fingers. He swore but didn't release his grip; oddly there was something gentle about his strength.

Two militiamen jumped from the stage, jackboots exploding

18

puffs of dust on the floorboards. The women backed away knocking over chairs.

The officer shouted: 'Take it easy, don't panic. No action will be taken against you.'

Katerina continued to struggle but the Tartar's arms were steel bands. The hand clamped to her mouth smelled of onions; perhaps he had been preparing a Women's Day supper before being called out to put down a riotous assembly of female hooligans. Beside her Svetlana was vigorously kicking her captor, young with fat cheeks, with the heels of her magnificent boots.

The militiamen on the floor advanced steadily but placidly on the women. Regaining some of their dignity, they turned and made an orderly exit.

As the door opened the breeze brushed sparks from the glowing stove.

When the women had all gone – all, that was, except for the scribe with the pepper-and-salt hair – Katerina and Svetlana were released.

'Well done, comrade,' Svetlana said to the officer. 'A great job, terrorising a handful of women. Guns against handbags. They'll make you a Hero of the Soviet Union for this.'

The officer regarded her impassively.

While the Tartar sucked his bleeding finger, Katerina, fight gone out of her, said: 'So what are the charges?'

They had several to choose from, the officer told her in his tired voice. Creating a breach of the peace, holding an assembly without permission, inciting violence. And how about hooligan behaviour for good measure? But he made no move to arrest them.

The exit door banged shut tossing dust and woodshavings against the stove.

The scribe mounted the platform and showed the officer a red ID card. He nodded and departed with his men.

'After all, it is Women's Day,' she said, smiling at Katerina and Svetlana. 'And now may I see your papers, please?' She smelled of lavender water.

They showed her their blue work passbooks and internal

19

passports containing their *propiskas*, their residential permits.
The woman studied them cursorily, as though confirming what
she already knew.

'And now,' Svetlana said, 'may we examine your identifica-
tion?'

'If you wish.' The woman dug in her handbag again. The red
ID was militia, not KGB; that was something. 'You know, my
dear,' she said to Katerina as she replaced the ID, 'I agree with
everything you say but not with the way you say it.'

Svetlana said: 'What you mean is you don't agree with
freedom of speech.'

The woman tut-tutted. 'Come now, let's be realistic: this is
the Soviet Union not outer space. We can't allow public protest
can we? That's a phenomenon in the West.'

Svetlana buttoned up her wolfskin with exasperated
precision. 'Without protest we shall achieve nothing.'

'But, my dear, a lot has been achieved without your
assistance. You have no idea, when I was a girl . . . .' Perhaps,
Katerina thought, she had lost her man in the Great Patriotic
War when twenty million souls had perished. 'The point is that
your goals must be achieved with subtlety. Nothing wrong with
feminine wiles, is there?'

Katerina said: 'Do you really believe that we are better off
than we were?'

'You must know that. Your life-style for instance. Clothes,
entertainment, your relations with young men . . . . Why in
my day we would have been shot for less.'

'Then why,' Katerina demanded, 'can't we speak our minds
in public if we have such liberty? Why do the police have to be
called in?' She could still smell onions on her fingers.

'I am merely advising you, nothing more. Just as an elder of
your family might warn you.' She smiled wistfully. 'A maiden
aunt?' She touched Katerina's arm. 'I do hope you'll take my
advice, my dear.' Apparently Svetlana was beyond redemption.
'If not . . . .'

She didn't finish the sentence. They all smelled smoke at the
same time.

The fire was behind the stove. A tongue of flame snaked out

from behind it, licked the stripped pine wall, fell back and returned to gain a hold. Resin crackled and spat.

The 'maiden aunt' took command. 'Quick, the sand buckets.'

But the buckets were empty.

The flames leaped onto another wall. Smoke rolled towards the platform.

'You,' to Katerina, 'call the fire brigade. You,' to Svetlana, 'get water from the rest-rooms.' Grabbing a twig broom she jumped from the platform and advanced on the flames.

Katerina ran into the street. There, thank God, was a telephone kiosk. But when she reached it she discovered it had been vandalised. She ran around an apartment block, found another, dialled 01, fire emergency.

By the time she got back to the hall it was a bonfire. A crowd had collected and Svetlana and the 'maiden aunt' stood among them, snow melting at their feet. Sparks and ash spiralled into the grey sky. As the roof caved in the crowd sighed.

'Happy Women's Day,' Svetlana said to Katerina.

'So, what did you make of the maiden aunt?' Katerina asked as they made their way to Vernadskogo metro station.

They had answered questions from a fresh detachment of militia, signed statements and finally been allowed to leave the smouldering wreckage.

Svetlana said: 'She showed us the yellow card.' Her pilot was a soccer fanatic, Moscow Torpedo. 'Beware the red card next time. That means we'll be sent off,' she explained in case Katerina didn't share her new wisdom. 'Be warned, Kata.'

'But why wasn't she tougher with us? Why aren't we locked up? After all we'll be held responsible for burning the place down.'

Svetlana, hair escaping from her red and white woollen hat, glanced at her wristwatch and lengthened her stride, long thighs pushing at the wolfskin; she was hours late for a date with the pilot. 'Odd, isn't it? Let's count our blessings.'

They passed a snow-patched playground in front of a new pink apartment block. Children were playing at war, Soviets against Germans. The Soviets were winning again.

'What do you think will happen now?' Katerina asked.

'God knows. But take care, pussycat, take to your lair for a while.'

'I can't, it would deny everything the Movement stands for.'

'Then get ready to spread the good word in a labour camp. Or outside the Soviet Union.'

Katerina thrust her hands into the pockets of her old grey coat, even shabbier than usual beside the wolfskin. 'You forget things have changed since Tatyana Mamonova and the other two were expelled. There are letters about the plight of women every day in the newspapers.'

'Whining letters, vetted letters. *We're* inciting revolution. The Russians have had one of those and they don't want another. If the Kremlin thinks we really pose a threat we'll be hustled into exile and there won't be a whisper about it in the media.'

'But there would be in the West.'

'So? Far less harmful than a forest-fire of protest in the Soviet Union.'

Katerina knew she was right and the knowledge saddened her. She was a patriot, didn't they understand that? Of course they did, the final deterrent. The Motherland, don't betray her. That's why we put up with so much: it was something foreigners, confusing Country and Party, would never understand.

A man passed carrying a bunch of tulips, holding them like a baby to protect them from the breeze.

'But,' Katerina protested, 'we're doing this for Russia, for her women . . . .'

She remembered the old joke. Four men sitting in a bar nipping vodka. 'Where are your women?' asks a Western journalist. 'The working classes aren't allowed in here,' replies one of the tipplers.

Things were changing, it was true. Five hundred of the toughest job categories had been designated Men Only and unmarried mothers were getting more money per child. But equality? It was light years away.

As they approached the metro station Katerina said

22

anxiously to her friend: 'But surely you aren't thinking of quitting?' It was unthinkable.

'Why not? We won't get anywhere.'

'Not you!'

Svetlana turned and faced Katerina. 'Well, not until they do something about those goloshes.'

Laughing, they slid five-kopek pieces into the slot in the turnstile and ran down the warm throat of the metro station.

Katerina had worked at the weekend updating the files on the defectors so she had a free day. In view of events that morning she thought it might be her last free day for a long time.

On the way home she broke her journey to pick up some Caspian caviar that Lev Koslov, her boss, had promised to supply for the party that evening.

Koslov was a past master at obtaining *defitsitny* goods. The only drawback was that he expected rewards – a pinch here, a fumble there. So far she had eluded his inquisitive fingers but a two-kilo tin of glistening black pearls, as rare these days as swallows in winter, that would take some evasion. At least he wouldn't be able to come to the party: today being what it was he would have to dance attendance on his wife.

When she entered the tiny office she shared with Sonya Ivanovna the first thing she noticed on her desk was a vase of mimosa, a cloud of powdery yellow blossom that smelled of almonds. Koslov making his play! Under the vase was an envelope.

Katerina slit it with a paper-knife. The note inside said: 'Enjoy *your* day.' It was signed Robert Calder.

Katerina leaned back in her chair and stared at an avuncular Lenin on the wall. Since she had seen Calder at Kreiber's funeral she had wondered about him.

Like the rest of her flock at the Institute he was a traitor and therefore contemptible. But Calder displayed qualities a cut above the rest of the turncoats. A sense of humour for one thing; she smiled as she remembered him stuffing the sugared redcurrants into his mouth, like a guilty schoolboy. And there was strength in his face that hadn't quite gone out to grass.

Why had a man like Calder deserted his country?

It bothered her.

It also bothered her that she had come to work in this futile place. She had only been here for a month but already it depressed her. The legion of lost souls sifting foreign journals for insights into their country's policies. Eyewash. The KGB grabbed shifts in policies before the policy-makers shifted them.

So why had she applied for the job? Come clean, Katerina Ilyina, *blat*, the influence that accompanies position. Bottom-of-the-scale *blat*, perhaps, but already she had a few perks – tip-offs about consignments of luxury goods in the stores, the promise of a one-roomed apartment of her own, the passbook that asserted she was someone to be reckoned with, a hint that one day she might be allowed to travel abroad.

With her gift for languages, English, French and German, she had romped through the academic interviews. What occasionally bothered her was the way she had weathered all the other interrogations. Why hadn't her involvement with the feminist movement damned her? Could they possibly understand that her belief in the rights of women was not a contradiction of patriotism? She doubted it.

The knock on the door startled her. It was probably Sonya returning from one of her furtive perusals of Western magazines, eyes shining behind her spectacles at the discovery of some new and wonderful decadence. Presumably she had knocked in case Koslov was seeking his rewards.

Katerina called out: 'Come in,' and Calder walked in.

He seemed to fill the room.

He said: 'I wanted to make sure you got the flowers.'

She touched the saffron blossoms. 'I got them, thank you, they're beautiful. But . . . .' She had only spoken to Calder twice since the funeral.

'I'm glad you like them.'

'I love all flowers. Muscovites are like that – they see too few of them. Soon we'll see snow flowers.'

'Snow flowers?'

'In the winter people fall and die from exposure. The snow covers them and they are lost until the thaw. When the snow melts they're found perfectly preserved . . . . Is anything the matter Comrade Calder?'

'No, nothing.' Calder smoothed the frown from his forehead with his fingertips. 'I think I prefer mimosa. I suppose it comes from Georgia.'

'Probably. Somewhere in the south, anyway. Have you seen much of the Soviet Union, Comrade Calder?'

'Don't you know?' His smile tightened.

She skated over that one. 'Do you feel you've been accepted?'

'People have been very kind.'

What sort of an answer was that?

'Why don't you come to a party this evening?' she said.

Chapter 3

Spandarian was a Georgian and therefore a schemer and on the afternoon of Women's Day he was scheming busily in his office on 25th October Street.

On his desk were eight buff dossiers, dog-eared and stained from frequent perusals, and one eggshell blue folder, relatively unscathed.

Thoughtfully, stroking his luxuriant moustache and pulling on a yellow, tube-tipped cigarette, he picked up the dossiers in turn and scanned the latest computer print-outs inside them.

He didn't touch the blue folder.

A knock on the door and his secretary, Yelena, cheeks as bright as a wooden doll's, came in carrying a glass of lemon tea brewed in an electric samovar in the outer office. Spandarian slugged it with Armenian brandy.

He gestured out of the window at the grey sky drooping over Red Square. 'A typical Moscow day.' He sipped his fortified tea.

'Spring is just around the corner,' she said brightly. 'March the eighteenth, *Maslennitsa*.'

Madame, he thought, you delude yourself. There was no way winter in Moscow would be locked away that early; in any case *Maslennitsa* was a country festival. But all Muscovites were the same: they couldn't accept the slightest criticism of their capital city.

That was because they were Russians and still believed that the Russian republic *was* the Soviet Union. Didn't they ever pause to consider the other fourteen republics? The hundred or so ethnic groups speaking different languages? Moldavians, Uzbeks, Armenians, Georgians . . . . Didn't they ever cast their eyes to the sun-drenched south, peer down the Golden Road to Samarkand?

But soon they would have to face reality. Admittedly Russians accounted for more than half the 260 million or so inhabitants of the Soviet Union but the combined populations of the other republics were overhauling them, particularly with virile Georgians multiplying like rabbits. Then the Slavs in the Kremlin would have to tread warily.

'You're looking very smart today,' he told Yelena. He couldn't quite muster 'attractive' even though it was Women's Day. But he had bought her half a dozen pink carnations flown in from Tbilisi – at a knockdown price because he was Georgian.

'Thank you, Comrade Spandarian,' bright cheeks bunching. She was severely built and the rouge gave her a clownish air.

Spandarian finished his tea and dismissed her. '*Adlobt*.' He spoke Georgian whenever he could. 'That will be all.'

When she had gone he lit another yellow cigarette and stared through the window at the clustered cupolas and spires of the Kremlin. The Politburo was meeting there tomorrow; thirteen strong and not a Georgian among them. It was enough to make Stalin turn in his grave. Nine Russians, two Ukrainians – the Russians had to pay lip service to the fifty million restless souls in the south-west – and a couple of minority republics.

But with the appointment of Mikhail Gorbachev as Party Leader, the old order was changing. Out with the aged roosters, in with the young hawks. And who better placed to lead them one day than an up-and-coming Georgian KGB department chief?

Spandarian, head of the department responsible, within the Second Chief Directorate, for the defectors in Moscow, smiled crookedly at the gilded baubles across the square.

He closed his eyes and the baubles became a bunch of purple grapes freshly washed and glistening in a bowl in the restaurant at the top of the funicular climbing Holy Mountain in Tbilisi. He was eating *lobio*, beans in walnut sauce – his mouth watered – and drinking red Khvanchkara, the wine that Stalin, the most wily Georgian of them all, drank. Beneath him sprawled the city, cobblestone streets teeming with gangsters and girls with beckoning eyes, cafés filled with conspirators, perfumed air rustling with money and intrigue.

No, there was no one better equipped to scheme his way to the secretaryship of the Communist Party than a devious Georgian. Why in Tbilisi the name of Otari Lazishvili, Godfather of the 'sixties who had swindled the State out of two million roubles and lived like a Rockefeller, was revered alongside Stalin's. Recently the Kremlin had decided to purge the Georgian Mafia. Fat chance.

Spandarian saw himself as part Stalin, part Beria – Stalin's police chief and executioner – part Lazishvili.

But a much more polished schemer than either Stalin or Beria. Stalin, God rest his soul, was only a cobbler's son and when Beria wanted a woman he pulled her off the street! Spandarian, who was forty-two, belonged to an aero club and flew his own plane in Georgia, favoured sharp suits, had his wavy brown hair cut by a barber imported from Tbilisi, jogged and enjoyed modern music and read contraband *Playboy* magazines. The naïve sometimes asked him how he got away with it; the answer which he never supplied was simple – he had too much on his bosses and, for that matter, the granite-faced old men in the Kremlin.

27

Just the same he had to succeed at the job in hand. Fail, like a five-year plan, and you were doomed whatever clout you possessed. Spandarian opened his eyes and met the gaze of the ubiquitous V.I. Lenin regarding him shrewdly from the wall of his sumptuous office. Then he picked up the fattest file on the leather-topped desk, opened it and began to read the computer summary.

ROBERT EWART CALDER
Born April 5, 1946, Mt. Vernon, Boston.
Height: 1.8 metres.
Educated: New England prep and Harvard.
Profession: lawyer.
Specialisation: member of legal team advising Secretary of State.
Marital status: divorced.
Progeny: one son, Harry, by ex-wife, Ruth.
Recreations: baseball, sailing and chess!

Spandarian wondered if the computer had added the exclamation mark unprompted.

Character: determined but resolution undermined by adolescent ideals exacerbated by death of brother in Vietnam.
First approach: second year Harvard. At Elsie's, Mt Auburn St. (A whorehouse, Spandarian had surmised at first. In fact an establishment selling king-size sandwiches to students).
Progress: finally suborned third year – Cross-Ref 8943XA, Infiltration US universities.
Grading: *B* but promoted when posted Washington.
Value: inestimable until blown.

Spandarian speed-read the rest of the summary. Reactions to Soviet life-style, sexual inclinations, companions, ideological stability, veracity of information brought from Washington . . . .

28

He paused, feeling the last sheet between his fingertips. What information? *Value: inestimable* . . . . What the hell did that mean? To his Georgian mind in which every highway was a maze, the lack of definition jarred.

Ever since he had taken over the department Calder had bothered him. The apartment on Gorky Street, the dacha, the air of impregnability that he carried with him like a briefcase full of secrets . . . . Spandarian suspected that Calder possessed knowledge that had been denied to him and that was insufferable.

Which was why he had mounted Grade 2 surveillance on the American. Grade 1 as from now, following Dalby's report that he had expressed doubt about the manner of Kreiber's death and was generally expressing disquiet.

And today Calder had made his own contribution to that surveillance. Mimosa indeed! Spandarian picked up the eggshell blue folder and peered into the life of Katerina Ilyina.

Chapter 4

The Kremlin – *kreml*, fortress – is the hub of Moscow, more so than the seats of government of most capital cities. Driving into town there is no escape from it, the great avenues converging on it like the spokes of a wheel.

Around this fabled triangle of palaces, towers and cathedrals and around the old town of Kitay-Korad lie seven squares hemmed by a belt of green boulevards which are linked in the south, beneath the Kremlin's walls, by the River Moscow. After the boulevards, and the next layer of assorted development – Czarist baronial, Stalinist wedding-cake, 1980s' functional – comes the Sadovaya, the Ring, the city's broadest highway, and finally a roaring motorway that girdles Greater Moscow as the *Périphérique* girdles Paris.

Katerina Ilyina lived on a spoke of the wheel, Leningradsky

Prospect, leading to Sheremetievo Airport and, eventually, Finland.

When he crossed the Sadovaya, Calder pulled into a side road to consult the map Katerina had drawn. She would never make a cartographer: she even managed to make Leningradsky, as wide and straight as a runway, look like the trail of some demented insect. Past the Bolshevik sweet factory, she had said, not far from the Dynamo stadium.

He compared her effort with a printed map; it wasn't much better. Cars swooped past on the avenue, phantom-quick in the moonlight. Across the street a dewlap of snow hung from an old wooden house, one of the few left in this area, old teeth among new dentures.

Why had she invited him to the Women's Day party? There were a number of possibilities, most of them unwelcome; those that were welcome were unlikely.

Why had he sent her the mimosa? Easier. She was an injection of impetuous youth into the Institute, that fount of futile endeavour, and he wanted to share it. (The defectors reminded him of Dickensian clerks.)

Apartment block 33. There it was on the insect trail. He read the name of the side street under the dewlap of snow. Raskovoj. He was almost there.

The block was white and square with a children's playground and thinning lawns scattered with a dandruff of snow. There were several notices telling tenants what they should not do.

Calder took the elevator to the fourth floor. Party sounds came from the end of a long corridor that smelled of disinfectant. No. 41, that was where the action was.

Katerina opened the door. She was wearing a black dress cut provocatively but not shamelessly low, Baltic, probably, or one of Zaitsev's specials which never reached the stores. Her shoulder-length hair had been brushed until it shone blue-black. She wore an amber necklace, almost certainly Baltic, and her grey eyes challenged.

For one disturbing moment Calder saw himself through her eyes. Ageing – forty if he was a day. (He was thirty-eight). Tall and dark and defeated.

30

'Comrade Calder, come in.'

He handed her a bottle of pink champagne and walked into Baccanalia.

Rugs had been drawn back from the parquet flooring of the sitting room, dark lacquered furniture pushed flush with the walls. Television, potted plants and assorted chinaware were on high ground out of harm's way, a bed was doubling up as a couch. Guests crowded the small arena expansively.

'Can I get you a drink?'

Her English was almost perfect. Although he spoke near-perfect Russian he answered her in English. 'Are you sure you've got enough?'

The table at the end of the room was a distillery. A dozen different vodkas, Stolichnaya, Starka, Russkaya, Yubileinaya, lemon, pepper, hunter's – Kreiber's tipple, Calder remembered – caraway, the liquid gunpowder known as animal killer, and a few bottles of moonshine. The firewaters took pride of place. Among the other ranks were Georgian wines and Armenian brandies, Zhigulovsky beer, mineral waters, Limonad and the Soviet Coke, Sayani.

She smiled back at him, the smile at the funeral. 'I think we can manage.'

'Vodka then. Yubileinaya.'

'You're a connoisseur.' She poured him a shot of vodka and a glass of mineral water and pointed at the *zakuski*. 'You have to eat or the vodka burns holes in your stomach.'

Calder inspected the snacks. Glistening mounds of black, golden and red caviar, slices of smoked salmon, pickled mushrooms, gherkins, blinis, salamis and salads tossed with sour cream, brown and black bread.

He selected a couple of gherkins, tossed back the vodka, drank some mineral water and snapped his teeth into a gherkin.

'You've done that before,' she said.

'Many times.'

'We have a saying that drinking is the joy of Russia.' She drank some white wine.

'Then everyone must be very happy.'

'It's also a problem,' she said. 'Crime, absenteeism, divorce –

31

drinking is usually the culprit. Even children in the kindergartens have been found drinking alcohol.' She poured him another shot of vodka.

Calder noticed a stocky man, black hair needled with grey, pushing his way through the throng towards them. He skirted a poet tearfully reciting, stepped over two guests arm-wrestling on the floor and stopped beside Katerina. He carried himself like a soldier.

Katerina introduced him as her step-father. He clasped Calder's hand and crushed it. 'My name's Alexander,' he announced in Russian. 'Sasha to you. My home is your home and now you must drink or else I shall be offended.' He laughed hugely. 'And now a toast. Silence!' He waited until the only sound was the sobbing of the poet. Raising his glass he proposed a toast: 'To Anglo-Soviet friendship and our guest from the United States.'

For a frozen moment everyone stared at Calder. He sensed no hostility in the concentrated gaze. But what was all this about? He had left America five years ago.

The stares dissolved, heads tilted. There was some scattered applause.

Sasha tapped his throat with one finger. 'Pah, it is good to drink is it not, *Gaspadeen* Calder?' He refilled their glasses with Yubileinaya. 'Where do you live in America? I have only been to New York. With the choir, you understand.'

'Sasha was in the Red Army Choir,' Katerina explained and, turning her back to her step-father for a moment, whispered: 'I didn't tell them who you are.'

'Boston,' Calder said.

'Ah. I pahked my cah in Hahvahd Yahd. How is that?'

'Spoken like a true Bostonian,' Calder said in Russian. The vodka was beginning to reach his socks. He smeared caviar on a finger of toast and ate it.

'Sadly I had to return from New York before I could visit anywhere else. There was, ah, a little trouble . . . .' Sasha winked theatrically. 'But my voice stayed with me. Later I will sing to you.'

32

Katerina said: 'The kitchen first. Have you forgotten what day it is?'

'Ah, the most terrible day of the year. But if we don't play their little game, *Gaspadeen* Calder, then we shall be denied our creature comforts for the other 364 days of the year.' He winked again, with the other eye this time. 'Isn't that right, *dochka?*' He pinched Katerina's cheek and thrust his way back to the kitchen.

Katerina sighed. 'Another male chauvinist.'

Beside them the arm-wrestlers, hands locked, veins bulging from their necks, grunted. In another corner a young man with long pale hair began to strum a guitar.

'So I'm just visiting, huh?'

'I couldn't say you were a defector. My step-father wouldn't have let you in. And not a single person in this room would have raised his glass to you.'

'And you?'

Katerina sipped her wine. 'You won't find anyone in Russia who has much time for someone who . . . .'

'Betrayed their country?'

She shrugged. 'Deserted.'

'Then why did you invite me here?' He held up one hand. 'Don't tell me – you felt sorry for me.'

'Because you worry me. You know, you left the West because you were disillusioned. That *was* the reason, wasn't it? And now you seem to be disillusioned with the Soviet Union. I thought I'd show you what life here can be like.'

Calder gestured with his empty glass around the room. 'Your friends certainly know how to enjoy themselves.' It was the first time he had been inside a home like this; all the other invitations had been arranged – safe, tame, dull Communists. 'It's a bash.'

'Would you find people enjoying themselves like this in Boston?'

Here we go, he thought, the equation. There was no escape from it. He said: 'Sure you would.' In his shared apartment near Fenway Park in his long-ago student days, for instance.

The arm of one of the wrestlers almost touched the floor,

then sprang back again. The poet, to whom no one was listening, petulantly threw his glass against the wall.

A small woman with dimples and bright brown eyes said: 'Is this the gentleman you were telling me about, Kata?'

Katerina introduced her mother.

Her mother said: 'His glass is empty, Kata. Fill it with the demon. And don't forget to eat, *Gaspadeen* Calder. We have a saying in the Soviet Union. Food on an empty stomach makes a full grave.'

Calder had long decided that Russians made up their sayings on the spur of the moment. 'A wise proverb,' he said graciously as she handed him cucumber salad and sour cream on a side-plate.

'And what are you doing in Moscow, *Gaspadeen* Calder?'

Hurriedly, Katerina said: 'He's a writer. He's writing an article for an American magazine.'

'The *National Geographic*,' Calder said, looking Katerina straight in the eye.

'And how do you like our city?' her mother asked. 'Beautiful, no?'

'Noble,' Calder said. 'Especially the Kremlin and the metro stations. They put ours to shame.'

Creases of pleasure appeared at the corners of her mouth. 'We are very clean people, we Russians. Orderly *and* exuberant. Nothing by halves. And we look after our old people,' she added.

Why don't Intourist and Novosti introduce foreigners to people like this? Calder wondered. Instead visitors were forced to listen to actors reciting tired scripts, and taken to brochure showplaces instead of wooden villages clustered round a pump, to escape the dreaded condemnation: 'Primitive.'

Not that the West managed much of a PR job: most Russians still thought London was a nineteenth-century stew.

Katerina's mother said: 'Soon we will eat and see what sort of a mess our men have made of it,' sounding very indulgent towards male inefficiency. 'And you, Kata, what have you been doing with yourself today?'

Calder sensed maternal worry: at the Institute it was

34

common knowledge that Katerina was into Women's Lib. What surprised everyone was that she was allowed to keep her job.

Katerina told her mother that she had been to a meeting. She didn't elaborate and, although there was transparently more to it than that, her mother accepted the compromise and departed for the kitchen to see what sort of a hash the menfolk were making of supper.

'What sort of meeting?' Calder asked when she had gone.

'You know perfectly well.'

'The feminist movement?' Calder frowned. 'But why? I realise women get a pretty raw deal here. Divorce, abortion, exploitation . . . . But why do *you* care so much?'

She told him.

She was nineteen now, her father had left her mother when she was three. He met a girl at a summer camp on the Black Sea organised by the snow-plough factory where he worked and came home only to pick up his belongings.

The *babushka*, Katerina's grandmother on her father's side, left too and her mother had to quit her job as a waitress in the National Hotel to look after her daughter.

Her family helped financially and the State helped but she had to move into an apartment block of 'boxes' near the docks at Khimki Port. She got a job in a canteen there and paid a neighbour to look after Katerina during the day.

She tended to Katerina in the evenings and worked late into the night cooking and cleaning and mending.

A docker moved in briefly. He beat her up and stole her savings from under the mattress. Where else?

Her mother became bitter towards men. The bitterness was infectious.

Apart from visits from a family friend – 'Yury Petrov, a pirate,' Katerina said fondly – and an expedition to his home in Siberia this state of affairs lasted for thirteen years.

Then she met Sasha at the Central Soviet Army Drama Theatre on Kommuny Square and everything changed.

A miracle.

'He sang his way into our hearts,' Katerina told Calder. Her eyes were moist. 'A wonderful man.'

35

'But a chauvinist.'

'Beyond redemption,' she said happily.

'Don't you think the big-heartedness of Russian men outweighs their faults?' They were both speaking English now.

'You don't understand: it's injustice I'm fighting. I lived with it for thirteen years; it's part of me. Just as it's part of your Judy Goldsmith. When her father left home her mother lived for three years with *five* children in a chicken-coop. Now Judy Goldsmith is president of the National Organisation for Women, but I bet she still dreams she's living in a chicken-coop.'

'And you want to become president of something like that?'

'Doubtful, after what happened today.'

'The meeting?'

'I burned down the hall,' she said.

Sasha made his ceremonial entry from the kitchen carrying a dish of chicken cutlets and singing:

A circle for the sun
Sky all around
That's what the little boy drew
Carefully sketched on his paper
Wrote underneath the corner.

Sasha paused. Children had materialised from another room. They stood like a choir poised for song. Sasha winked at them. Piping voices joined his baritone:

Let there always be sunshine
Let there always be blue skies
Let there always be Mummy
Let there always be me.

Then everyone fell on the food. Chicken and meat dumplings and beef stewed with sour cream and borsch. The men, Katerina's mother admitted, hadn't made such a hash of it.

'So,' Katerina said, spearing a meat dumpling with her fork, 'do you feel as if you've been accepted?'

'Marvellous people.'

36

'That song – the chorus was written by a four-year-old boy. Sentimental people, the Russians.'

'What would Sasha do now if I told him I was a defector?'

'Throw you out on your ear.'

'Has it ever occurred to you that it can take more courage to defect than to stay in your own country?'

'You didn't defect,' she said, 'you ran away,' voice suddenly frosted.

The noise around him seemed to swell. Chink of cutlery against china, laughter, talk, the strummed notes of the guitar. The arm-wrestlers had called it a day, neither vanquished, the poet was asleep curled up like a bulky foetus. Sasha had his arm round the shoulders of Katerina's mother.

He thought: 'I'll never belong.'

He heard her voice distantly. '. . . told you my story. Isn't it time you told me what happened?'

He concentrated. 'Not yet. Not here.'

'Are you all right?'

'I think I drank some animal killer by mistake.'

Would Sasha really throw him out? Of course. The Red Army Choir rang with patriotism. The Twilight Brigade took a different view. Their motto was Samuel Johnson's: *Patriotism is the last refuge of the scoundrel.*

Calder felt like an island. He told Katerina that he was leaving.

'So soon?'

'Perhaps you'll show me more of your Moscow. The city foreigners never see. I remember as a kid on the waterfront in Boston there were some slot machines. You fed them a nickel and a tableau came to life. A circus, a rodeo, that sort of thing. That's the Russia foreigners see. Feed Intourists with hard currency and the tableaux come to life. But with you I have a passport . . . .'

'You have Soviet citizenship, an internal passport. You're free to travel.'

'You know that's not true.'

She gave a shrug, a dismissal. 'Perhaps one day . . . .'

37

Calder said goodbye to Katerina's parents. 'But the party's only just beginning,' Sasha objected. He sung a few bars of the *Volga Boatman*. 'The song all Americans know.' Calder braced himself for Sasha's handshake but it was limper this time, emasculated by firewater.

Calder left.

Outside the cold embraced him like an old friend and sent the vodka coursing through his veins. With a skull full of fancies he made his way on rubber knees to the Zhiguli in the parking lot.

The cream paint on the battered Volga that followed him shone silver in the moonlight.

When he got back to his apartment off Gorky Street Calder found Jessel from the American Embassy waiting for him.

Jessel, a New Yorker, was his link with the United States: he was one of Jessel's links with the Soviet Union. Jessel worked for the Commercial Counsellor. He was middle-aged with amiable features and a soft voice and thin, ear-to-ear hair. He didn't look at all like a spy and that was his strength.

He pretended to like Calder but from time to time Calder caught a frayed glance and he knew that Jessel was thinking: 'How can you have done it?'

To make things easier for themselves they played chess.

For Calder chess was his therapy. It gave him direction. He believed it to be the distillation of human behaviour encompassing prodigious foresight, petty opportunism, grand strategems, puny deceptions and glittering combinations that could fail because of a single unsighted flaw. Moreover chess was the honed product of centuries of trial and error, a diamond made of compressed genius.

Jessel, who had the key to the apartment, was sitting in front of a crowded chess board drinking bourbon.

'Make yourself at home,' Calder said.

'And where,' Jessel asked, moving a white pawn, 'have you been making yourself at home?'

'At a party.'

'Obviously. Whose?'

'None of your business.'

38

'That,' Jessel said mildly, 'is for me to decide.'

Calder took off his coat and *shapka*. In the kitchen he dropped ice-cubes into a glass and poured Narzan mineral water onto them. The ice-cubes cracked back at him. The vodka had made his tongue thick and unmanageable.

Glass in hand, he went back to the living room. Jessel had lit his pipe and rearranged the chess pieces in pre-battle order.

Calder gestured around the room with his glass. 'Clean?'

Jessel picked up the bag containing his electronic sweep. 'As a whistle. The comrades must trust you. What were you drinking, paint-remover?'

Jessel wasn't a great drinker. He took care of himself and jogged every morning along the banks of the Moscow River. He was tougher than his appearance suggested.

Calder said: 'You know better than that: they don't trust anyone.'

He moved to the window and gazed at the floodlit public gardens below. He enjoyed them. In summer they dozed dustily; in winter they radiated vitality as youngsters with polished faces skated exuberantly along paths hosed with water to convert them into canals of ice.

In fact he enjoyed the apartment near the monumental buildings of Gorky Street, the best bakery in town and the extravagances of Gastronom No. 1. Compared with the barrack-block flats occupied by most of the defectors it was a palace and attracted much envious comment. But then they didn't know what he knew. He was a VID, a Very Important Defector, and as such was entitled to a home isolated from the Brigade. He even had a wooden dacha in the country. Dalby was the only other defector with one of those.

Jessel said: 'You'd better take white. In your condition you need the extra move.'

'I can still beat you blind-folded,' Calder told him. In fact there wasn't much to choose between the two of them, although Jessel was the more cautious player, Calder finding it difficult to resist a potentially swashbuckling brilliancy without assessing it thoroughly. Patience was what he lacked. Jessel's careful intricacies had earned him the right to play in a few

39

minor tournaments in the Soviet Union and to spy in unlikely places. 'I'll take black,' Calder said.

P-K4.

P-K4.

Calder made his move standing beside the marble-topped coffee table and continued to patrol the living room; movement, he hoped, would help to sober him up. The apartment helped to settle him – he had grown into it and it was shabby like himself. Period Muscovite with sombre furnishings and a rich, balding carpet; but it did contain small glories such as carvings leafed with gold, a painting of Siberian pastures feathered with mauve blossom, a chandelier whose frozen tears had been washed with soapy water only that morning by Lidiya, his maid. Unlike so many members of the Twilight Brigade he hadn't cluttered it with bric-à-brac, the detritus of the abandoned West.

'Your move,' Jessel said.

'Knight to queen's bishop three,' Calder replied without looking at the board.

'You're very sure of yourself.' Jessel undid his button-down collar and loosened his striped tie.

'How many times have we played the Ruy Lopez before?'

'I might surprise you this time.'

'Surprise me,' Calder said.

A few minutes consideration, then: 'Your move again.'

'Pawn to queen's rook three,' Calder said, again without looking. The popular line these days, when vodka was your second and you had to play carefully.

Looking at the sparkling chandelier, he hoped he hadn't been too abrupt with Lidiya earlier that day. She had been waiting for him when he had returned from the Institute, normally docile features animated. Apparently she had joined a queue in Warna, the Bulgarian store on Leninsky, and bought a cherry-coloured dress with a flared skirt. Despite the fact that five hundred other women would be wearing the same dress she was delighted with her purchase and she was wearing it for him.

He was touched. 'Very pretty,' he told her.

She smoothed the skirt against her thighs. She had been

allotted to him when he first came to Moscow and she had served him well in the apartment, adequately in bed.

Respect had arisen between them although even now he didn't really know if she enjoyed the love-making: it seemed to him to owe a lot to a Western sex manual given to her to cater for a decadent American's appetites.

She was a lean woman with surprisingly large breasts. She was frankly plain and might one day look spinsterish, but there was a pleasing serenity about her and her brown hair curled prettily at the nape of her neck.

'Would you like me to stay?' she asked him but he told her no, he had work to do, and she departed ostensibly unperturbed, but you could never really tell with Lidiya.

The reason for the dismissal had been the invitation to the party from Katerina Ilyina.

Calder sat down at the coffee table and considered the Ruy Lopez developing on the board. He had little doubt that Jessel would move his bishop to rook four and that he would be able to produce a reasonable opening game by making copybook moves. By the ninth move they had progressed predictably to the Closed Defence. No dazzling variations tonight. Wasn't it Reti who had said that a player's chess style tended to be the opposite to his life-style? Tonight that made him a buccaneer off the board.

Calder moved his knight to queen's rook four. The Chigorin System still as popular as ever nearly eighty years after the master's death. When your own adventurous instincts were temporarily paralysed you could do worse than follow the father of the modern Soviet chess who had confounded the old Tarrasch school.

He said: 'How's Harry?'

Jessel said: 'Whose party was it?'

'A girl at the Institute.'

'The new girl who looks after the files on the defectors?'

Calder nodded. 'Harry?'

'He's fine. He's got a sailboat and he's hoping to take part in the Charles River Regatta in October.'

'He isn't sailing now, is he? It must be cold.'

41

'It's Boston,' Jessel said. 'He had a little accident the other day.'

Alarm spurted like acid. 'How little?'

'Very. He fell off his bicycle and grazed his knee.'

So why tell me? All part of the process, Calder assumed.

'He's still a Bruins freak of course,' Jessel said, moving a bishop.

Still? Harry was only eight. 'And Ruth?'

'Where was the party?'

Calder gave him the address on Leningradsky.

'Guests?'

'Her mother and father were there.'

'Step-father,' Jessel corrected him. 'Ruth's finally passed all her exams and got a job teaching handicapped children.'

Who would have thought it? Ruth, one of the flowers of Bostonian society, arrogance her birthright. He saw her shopping in Newbury Street: the street seemed to belong to her.

Jessel said: 'I presume this girl is *stukachi*.'

'An informer? If she catalogues our lives she must be. One in twelve Soviet citizens are supposed to be KGB contacts, aren't they? But I should think she's innocent enough. You know, merely passing on updated material to her superiors.'

'She's into Women's Lib isn't she?'

'You seem to know a lot about her.'

'Sure, I do my homework.'

Calder knew that Jessel had contacts other than himself inside the Institute.

Jessel said: 'Doesn't that strike you as odd? You know, that a dissident of sorts should be employed there?' He relit his pipe and blew smoke across the chess board; it smelled of autumn.

'Ours not to reason why,' Calder said.

Jessel stroked his long, sparse hair. 'Aren't you going to ask about your parents?'

Calder asked; he doubted whether they ever asked about him. His mother, perhaps.

'Your mother's fine. Your father had a stroke but he's going to be okay. Maybe a little speech impediment.'

42

Calder found it difficult to imagine his father's diction impaired. That magisterial voice saying grace before lunch -- Calder had never quite forgiven God for semolina pudding.

'How's my mother taking it?'

'Bravely. As always. It's your move.'

Calder stayed with Chigorin. Pawn to bishop four.

Somewhere a clock chimed. He stood up and walked to the window. The floodlights had been switched off but he could see the bluish radiance of the street lights on Gorky Park. He closed the curtains.

Jessel was frowning at the board. What was bothering him about Calder's play was his uncharacteristic conformity: it upset his own. Calder wondered how the party on Leningradsky was progressing. For the first time he had been accepted by Russians, but only because his presence had been a lie.

Jessel said: 'Is there still a lot of speculation about Kreiber?'

'The rumours have become facts. He committed suicide, he was dumped beneath the ice after being knifed in his apartment, he was a double – or should it be triple – agent, a rapist, a homosexual . . . .'

'He was a sad sack,' Jessel said, not quite touching his queen's pawn. 'So the Twilight Brigade is in disarray?'

'Alarm bells have been sounded, sure. *If* Kreiber was murdered then the comrades were clumsier than usual. That blood on the edge of the ice . . . .'

'And you, do you think he was killed?'

Calder shrugged. 'It's your move.'

'Do you anticipate any more deaths? No one thinking of trying to get an exit visa?'

'You must be kidding,' Calder said.

'Not even figuratively? You know, retracing their footsteps.'

'You think they'd tell me if they were? If they confided in anyone it would be Dalby.'

'Alas, he's not my pigeon.' Jessel moved. P-Q4 as Calder knew he would.

Calder sat down and tried to concentrate but the firewater had frozen in his veins and his head was full of ice. He looked at

Jessel who was examining his pipe the way pipe-smokers do, as if he had only just discovered it protruding from his mouth. 'I quit,' Calder said.

Jessel appeared mildly surprised; disconcerted never. 'You really put one on, didn't you?' His speech was a curious mixture of slang and protocol English.

'Do you mind if I go to bed?'

Jessel stood up. 'It's your bed.' He picked up his coat and Persian lamb hat from the sofa. 'Laura will be surprised to see me home so early.' Jessel was very proud of his happy marriage and tried to keep his home in one of the complexes reserved for foreigners as American as possible. Calder found his visits disconcerting, their purpose questionable; he tolerated them because Jessel kept him informed about Ruth and Harry. In the past he had tried to contact Ruth but his letters had been returned unopened and her telephone number was no longer listed. 'I'll be in touch. Any messages?'

'None.' There wasn't any point: he was his family's shame. He hoped Ruth had put antiseptic on Harry's knee.

Jessel let himself out of the apartment, closing the door softly behind him. Calder waited until he heard the clatter of the elevator gates, then went into the bedroom.

The phone shrilled as he was lowering his head gently onto the pillow. When he picked up the receiver he heard breathing.

'Hallo.'

The breathing was slow and measured.

'Who's that?'

Click.

He stared at the receiver for a moment before replacing it.

He laid his head on the pillow; above him the moulded ceiling spun like a dying top. He closed his eyes. He was playing chess with Stalin and he was losing. When Stalin called: 'Check,' he leaned across the board and pulled his shaggy moustache. It came off in his hand.

Chapter 5

The next to die was a fat Italian named Bertoldi.

He died, paradoxically, at a time of hope – the thaw. Moscow rang to the music of water. Dripping from dwindling icicles, plunging down drainpipes, frothing in the gutters. Listen carefully and you could hear the accompaniment – wet snow falling thickly from rooftops and, in green-blushing parks, tentative bird-song. On the river this April day the ice was on the move and in the streets Muscovites straightened up from winter. A time of hope. But not for Alfredo Bertoldi.

Since he had come to Moscow five years ago, blown, it was said, as financier for the Red Brigade, unsuspected for years because you expected Red Brigadiers to be young and fierce and Bertoldi was neither of these things, he had mourned. For pasta. For girls on the Via Veneto who wore nothing but fur coats and high heels. For Neapolitan songs. For God, Italian style.

Hopeless lamentations when, because you were a gangster rather than a fugitive keeper of secrets however cob-webbed, you were housed in a cramped studio in the foreigners' complex on Kutuzovsky Prospect, named after the field-marshal who sent packing another intruder, Napoleon.

Despite the lack of pasta Bertoldi perversely grew fatter on Chicken Kiev spurting with butter and black bread and *assorti* ice-cream which he bought even in minus 20 degrees. But it wasn't the healthy, baritone fatness of an Italian enjoying his sustinence: it was the bloated corpulence of the compulsive eater, the worrier.

His departure from this life of regret was spectacular. A few tenants were strolling in the courtyard of the barrack-block apartment blocks where foreigners – diplomats and journalists mostly – were housed together in the interests of surveillance. It was 10.35 am. The sun had already melted the temporary skating rink, tyres hissed excitingly on Kutuzovsky, even the two militiamen posted at the gates to check visitors were smiling.

Suddenly the windows of an apartment on the fifth floor were flung open with such force that the glass shattered. And there stood Bertoldi in a scarlet dressing gown. Later some witnesses were to testify, unofficially and without any degree of certainty, that they had observed movements behind the obese Italian; others were equally convinced that Bertoldi had stood alone.

What was undisputed was the manner of his fall. He seemed to float supported by the scarlet wings of his dressing gown. There was, it was asserted, a monstrous grace about his exit. His scream lasted from the window to the ground.

Such was his bulk that when he hit the concrete he spread. Within fifteen minutes the mess was cleaned up by militia and taken away in an ambulance.

A note was found in his cramped apartment. It was written on a picture postcard of his native Turin beside the remains of his last supper.

It said: *I can't stand this fucking life anymore.*

Chapter 6

Katerina always remembered Easter that year: it changed her life.

In the afternoon of the Saturday she went with Svetlana to a meeting of the feminist movement near the pink massif of Soviet Radio and Television on Piatnitskaya Street.

The purpose of the meeting was to establish some sort of order in the crusade. And to an extent it succeeded largely due, Katerina believed, to the call of spring. The lime trees were tipped salad green, *kvas* vans were in the streets, cotton dresses were beginning to blossom. 'Anything is possible,' the breeze whispered.

In a small assembly hall – 'Stone, this time,' Svetlana had insisted, 'in case of arson' – a committee was elected, a chairman appointed. Katerina was given a place on the committee with a responsibility to teenagers; Svetlana was charged with 'spreading the word across the length and breadth of the nation.'

'Just because I was going out with an Aeroflot pilot,' Svetlana said later when they were drinking lemon tea in a steely-bright cafeteria. 'Ah, well, it's only one sixth of the world's land surface – it shouldn't take long.'

'It's because you work for Intourist,' Katerina corrected her. '*Was* going out?'

'He was too keen that one,' Svetlana said.

Keen for what? Svetlana had never been sexually reticent. All she demanded was respect. And that, if you boiled it down, was all the movement wanted.

Beside them a crumpled-looking man was reading *Pravda*, starting at the bottom of a page where brevities of interest lurked and losing interest when he reached the exhortations to greater productivity and recriminations about absenteeism. The coffee machine behind the stainless steel counter hissed like a steam engine.

'He wanted to get married,' Svetlana explained when the hissing subsided. 'Can you imagine? Marrying a Russian is bad enough but a pilot . . . girls in Leningrad, Kiev and Archangel and the faithful wife waiting in Moscow to stir his borsch while he kicks off his shoes in front of the television. No thanks. Besides he was a goat.'

By which, Katerina assumed, she meant he was a selfish lover. The old school. The younger generation were more considerate, some of them.

'So who's taken his place?' Katerina asked.

'An architect. Lots of *blat*. Special pass for the third floor of GUM, dollars for the Beryozka shops, a Volga, hi-fi, video. He tells me he's got a dacha in the country too.'

47

'Obviously a very good Communist,' Katerina remarked.

The crumpled-looking man looked up from his newspaper and smiled.

'*And* he's not bad-looking,' Svetlana said. She sipped her tea. 'Not exactly good-looking.' The coffee machine hissed. 'But architecturally sound.'

'Does he know you're a defender of women's rights?'

'No, he wouldn't like that at all,' Svetlana said decisively. She searched in the pockets of her coat for cigarettes; to Katerina the coat looked suspiciously like part of an Aeroflot stewardess's uniform. 'And you, what have you been up to pussycat?'

Katerina wanted to tell her that Calder was taking her to midnight mass but she checked herself. The crumpled-looking man looked benign enough but you could never tell. 'Nothing much,' she said. 'The Institute's boring as ever. It reminds me of a literary treadmill. No one ever gets anywhere, they just keep turning pages.'

The crumpled-looking man folded his newspaper. He said: 'Enjoy yourselves while you're still young,' and was gone.

Pushing at her blonde, untamed hair with her fingers, Svetlana leaned conspiratorially across the table. 'So tell me, *kotik*, what have you really been up to? Consorting with decadent foreigners?'

When Katerina told her Svetlana was uncharacteristically solemn. 'Take care. It's always struck me as odd that we weren't prosecuted over that fire.'

'I don't see the connection,' Katerina said.

'Nor do I, but I suspect one.' Svetlana sipped her tea. 'Perhaps I've been reading too many spy novels. Too many videos . . . . Why not give the American a miss?'

'He's a Soviet citizen. I'm not doing anything wrong. Merely showing him the real Moscow. He bothers me,' Katerina added. 'He's not weak like the others. Just . . . .'

'. . . misguided?'

'Maybe.'

'So you're trying to prove to him what a great place the Soviet Union is? Are you angling for my job?'

48

'No chance,' Katerina said. 'I'm stuck with the Brigade.' She finished her tea, slid the oblong of hard sugar into her bag. 'Come on, let's get a breath of spring.'

But by eleven that night the air was chilled again. When Calder picked her up on Leningradsky he was wearing a top-coat and fur hat. Katerina's face was framed in sable, a second-hand gift from Svetlana's discarded pilot.

He drove to Bolshaya Ordinka Street, a discreet thoroughfare with a roll-call of churches, small houses and lime trees. She took him to a small pink and gold church. A crowd was packed around it and through the open doors they could smell Easter.

Spandarian's phone rang at ten minutes past midnight.

The girl beneath him swore.

Rolling clear, he picked up the receiver and asked brusquely: 'Well, are they there?'

'Affirmative, Comrade Spandarian.'

'Stay with them.'

Spandarian returned to the girl, the Estonian to the entrance to the church pausing on his way to lock the battered cream Volga.

Easter was mostly age. Burning candles smelling of the past and priests with grey beards and worshippers as fragile as autumn. But there was youth there, too, peering in from the godless outside and wondering.

Calder and Katerina eased their way through the militia-ringed throng to the back of the church where, with the rest of the congregation standing in a nave bereft of pews, they were entombed in candlelight, cocooned in the chanting of priests and choirs.

Time was the pendulum swings of censers, the diminishing of tallow-spitting candles lighting icons. The senses melted. The congregation was as one. Glowing, golden adoration filled this small House of God.

Feeling her warmth through her shabby coat, Calder wondered if Katerina, great-grandchild of a Revolution that

49

had invented its own religion, acknowledged the Resurrection of Christ. He wondered if he did.

As the priests walked three times round the outside of the church, searching for the body of Christ in the Holy Sepulchre, Calder saw wistful young faces in the crowd.

Walking back to the car, Katerina said: 'It's strange but that ceremony was more Russian than anything the Party has invented,' and Calder thought how ironic it would be if, innocently, he was becoming the instrument of her doubt.

Immediately she recanted. 'To think that there are more than thirty million churchgoers in the Soviet Union. There aren't as many accredited members of the Communist Party. Did you know that?'

He did. He also knew that the Party tolerated the Church because it was the ancient heartbeat of Mother Russia. A heartbeat, they hoped, that would soon falter and allow the young to worship at the altars of Marx and Lenin without Christian distractions. Unfortunately for the Party religion was said to be undergoing a revival.

One binge, one night of homage. What next? Sitting behind the wheel of the Zhiguli, Calder grinned into the night and didn't think about Alfredo Bertoldi at all. He drove back to Leningradsky with a flourish.

After the second phone call Spandarian lay, hands behind his head, staring at the reflections of himself and the dozing girl on the mirror on the ceiling. He decided he would make his move tomorrow, Easter Sunday.

Chapter 7

Resentfully, Katerina caught a bus to the Institute: it just wasn't the Sunday morning to squander in that futile place. Budding plants had pushed through the wet soil overnight.

River breezes fanned the late-sleeping streets. A tentative sun was finding the city's fragile graces.

Still, she only had to spend a couple of hours there preparing and allocating periodicals for the Monday return-to-work in the absence of the Study Supervisor who was recovering from a prolonged encounter with a crate of Ukrainian pepper vodka.

And then? It was a day for the first visit to the river beaches at Serebriani Bor or an excursion into the forest to see if mushrooms had begun to sprout among the damp remains of winter or a trip to one of the villages outside Moscow. But for that you really needed a car.

Calder had a car.

The bus, proceeding at a measured speed along the broad reaches of Leningradsky, reached Byelorussia Square. Here Leningradsky became Gorky Street where Calder lived.

The bus stopped outside the green and white stucco hulk of Byelorussia Railway Station. A young man carrying a shiny fawn suitcase climbed aboard and sat in the seat in front of Katerina. His brown hair was stylishly barbered and he wore a new blue suit cut with a discreet elegance that few Soviet tailors could manage. As the station served the west Katerina assumed he had arrived from somewhere like Smolensk or Minsk.

He turned and smiled. 'This time two days ago I was in Paris.' Paris! 'But I'm glad to be back.' That saved him, as far as she was concerned.

'Oh, really?' She stared out of the window. She was wearing her new lemon costume bought *defitsitny* in the Arbat and she knew she looked attractive enough; the young man was probably making a pass and she didn't object to that – the time to worry was when they didn't – but her mind was on Calder.

The bus headed down Gorky Street. Through the arcades to the right stood a huddle of old streets. Chekhov had lived there, and so had Chaliapin. She would like to show the house to Calder.

She tried to analyse her feelings about the big American. He was a challenge. She wanted to prove to him his wisdom in coming to Russia. Or his weakness. She wasn't sure which. Until she had met him she had been sure of her values. Now

51

they were presenting themselves for inspection. She wished he hadn't eaten those redcurrants at Kreiber's funeral.

'And where are you going to so early on a Sunday morning?' the young man asked.

'To work.'

'Really?' He considered this. His features were Slavonic but warm, peasant or intellectual, whatever way you chose to regard him. They were also vaguely familiar. 'And what sort of work is that?'

Her work was difficult to label: it invited elaboration. 'A waitress,' she said. Good enough for her mother, good enough for her.

'Where?'

'The Centralny.'

'Then I shall come and eat there.'

So he was making a pass. She tried to put a label to him. Paris . . . carried himself with unobtrusive style . . . accent, pure Moscow . . . son of some Kremlin *nachalstvo*? If so, why hadn't there been a Chaika at the station to meet him?

The bus passed the arch through which Calder lived. It had occurred to her that she might glimpse him but there was no sign of him, the sidewalk outside the arch occupied by a group of tourists trooping patiently towards Red Square behind their Intourist leader.

She picked up her handbag and prepared to alight at the National Hotel corner of Manezhnaya Square.

The young man took a card from a slim wallet and handed it to her. 'If you feel like coming along anytime . . . .' She slipped the card into her wallet without looking at it. As she made her way to the exit he called after her: 'By the way, you've gone past the Centralny.'

The atmosphere at the Institute closed in upon her. Furniture polish and cheap paper and the baked paintwork of the radiators. The bad breath of wasted endeavour.

Footsteps echoing, she walked past the empty, book-lined chambers to the spacious office of the Study Supervisor.

Outside stood sheaves of newspapers and magazines tied with coarse string.

She began to sort them into nationalities on a trestle table in the study. *The New York Times, Wall Street Journal, The Times, Daily Telegraph, Le Monde, De Telegraff, Bild, La Stampa* . . . . As always what astonished her was not the content of the papers but their freedom to print what they pleased. Editorials actually criticising the Government. Vistas of freedom beckoned slyly through screens of newsprint.

'But don't close your eyes,' she had been warned before she got the job, 'to the decadence you will find on those pages.' As if she could. Corruption, child abuse, rape, racism, industrial injustice . . . you name it. 'All encouraged by circulation-crazed newspapers and magazines.'

But don't we get our fair share of most of these evils in the Soviet Union?

Treason!

The biggest pile of papers was from the United States. A skyscraper of them. Calder was in charge of that section, analysing and indexing with a team of six other American defectors.

The Study Supervisor's phone rang. Katerina picked up the receiver, at the same time pulling out a drawer in the table. It was filled with cuttings from glossy magazines. The Study Supervisor apparently reserved the right to analyse the female anatomy of the West.

Katerina shut the drawer. She spoke into the receiver, giving the number of the Institute. 'Katerina Ilyina speaking.'

'My name's Spandarian,' said the voice on the other end of the line. 'It's about time we met.'

Although his fingernails were polished, although his hair was carefully waved and his moustache was a topiarist's dream, although his brown eyes were soulful and his brilliantine smelled of spices, Spandarian was a gangster. Katerina sensed this instantly. He was also a born interrogator, bandit brain and veneer, the hot/cold of the third degree.

53

He spoke melodiously but with a strong Georgian accent, fashioning flowers from some of his phrases. 'So, Katerina Ilyina, you want to save Soviet women. Has it ever occurred to you that they don't want to be saved? That, like Mother Russia herself, they merely want to endure?' He lit a yellow cigarette packed with black tobacco and blew acrid smoke across his desk.

'That's what the Russian male would like to think, Comrade Spandarian.' Her defiance pleased her: although few had seen him, the ruthlessness of the shadowy mentor of the Twilight Brigade was common knowledge.

'The Russian male? I am not a Russian, Katerina Ilyina, I am a Georgian. In Tbilisi we know how to treat women. We flatter them, court them, love them. But they know their place just the same and they are happy.'

Katerina had been to the Georgian capital once. And what Spandarian said was true. Up to a point. Women were treated extravagantly. But they were chattels just the same. Georgia would be a challenge. But first Mother Russia.

Spandarian said: 'Russian men are pigs.'

Katerina regarded him with astonishment, then found herself saying defensively: 'Some of the younger ones are learning; they are more considerate.' The young man on the bus, for instance.

'You are a true Slav, Katerina Ilyina. Already you are confounding yourself. If the young men are improving what is the point of your Cause?'

'Only some of them, the sons of the privileged.' *Privileged! What was she saying?* 'As for the rest . . . goats. And as for the Cause – equality, that's what it's all about. Just like Communism,' she heard herself saying. 'How many women are there in the Politburo, Comrade Spandarian?'

He didn't answer. Instead he picked up a light blue folder, finger and thumb feeling one corner as though he were rubbing an insect to death. He recited from it:

'Unlawfully convening a meeting; incitement to violence; incitement to treason; hooligan behaviour; indecency in a public place; arson. That lot,' Spandarian said mildly, 'could

54

put you away for the rest of your life. Or put you in front of a firing squad. Dissidents have been shot for less.'

Reeling, she queried 'Indecency in public?'

Spandarian extracted a typewritten sheet of paper from the folder and read the exchanges with the woman in the red shawl. 'Goloshes,' he said. 'Really!'

'I can't help what harridans in the audience say.'

'Your friend Svetlana Rozonova wasn't exactly reticent.'

'You wouldn't . . . .'

'We might.'

Spandarian stood up, walked to the window and stared in the direction of the Kremlin. 'Strange, isn't it, that the fount of Communism should look more like the ultimate altar of religion. All those cathedrals and churches . . . . The contradictions of revolution. Especially on Easter Sunday.'

Hot/cold. Her courage was trickling away. 'What do you want, Comrade Spandarian?'

The angular woman from the outer office brought them tea and biscuits. When she had gone Spandarian sat down and said in between sips of tea: 'You're a very patriotic girl, Katerina Ilyina.' She wondered about Spandarian's brand of patriotism. 'The spirit that won the Great Patriotic War.'

Katerina nibbled a biscuit; it tasted of aniseed; she sipped lemon-sharp tea to disperse the flavour.

Spandarian went on: 'You are very fortunate – you are in a position to help your country.' He dunked his biscuit in his tea and bit off the soggy tip.

Warily, Katerina asked him how.

He finished his tea and biscuit, dabbed the corners of his mouth with a red silk handkerchief and told her.

She had struck up a friendship with an American defector, Robert Calder. Nothing wrong with that. In fact the friendship must have been arranged in heaven – 'or whatever Arcadia awaits a good Communist' – because that was what provided the opportunity for Katerina to be of service to the Soviet Union.

All she had to do was observe Calder. Report on his moods, his thinking – party-line or otherwise – his habits. Encourage him to talk about the past – and the future.

Touch his soul.

'No!'

Spandarian lit another of his terrible cigarettes. 'When I was talking about the penalties involved in that disastrous affair on Women's Day I omitted one. You would be expelled from the Soviet Union. I would see to that.' The words rolled from his mouth in smoke.

So this was patriotism. Her beliefs shrank, tarnished.

Spandarian explained. 'To serve one's country one has to carry out acts that are sometimes distasteful. It's unfortunate but when you're dealing with unscrupulous enemies there isn't any alternative. Always remember that these acts are a means to an end – the survival of the Soviet Union.'

'No!'

'And is what I'm asking so distasteful? I can assure you that at the head offices of State Security in Dzerzhinsky Square and on the Outer Ring, they would be far more unpleasant. My duties are more . . . delicate. Perhaps that's why I am permitted such pleasant offices away from harsh realities.'

No. But this time she didn't speak.

'And don't forget Svetlana Rozonova,' he said.

Bastard.

'I'm not asking you to betray anyone. Just to keep a defector under observation.'

'Why is he so important?'

'That needn't concern you.'

She thought: So that's why I've been allowed to stay active in the women's movement *and* keep my job. Blackmail.

She felt soiled.

'Will you do it?' he asked.

'I'll think about it,' she said. *Give me time to think of a way out.*

'Think well, Katerina Ilyina.' Stroking his moustache, he stood up and bowed. For the time being it was over.

From 25th October Street she walked into Krasnaya Ploschad, Beautiful Square in old Russian, better known as Red Square. To her left the windows of GUM and, farther

56

away, the barley-sugar baubles of St Basil's; in front of her the Kremlin walls and the red-granite block of Lenin's Mausoleum where, in a glass sarcophagus, the father of the Revolution lay in peace. What would he have thought of the choice facing her?

She walked past the queue waiting on the cobblestones to pay homage to the embalmed spirit of Bolshevism and past the main entrance to the Kremlin, the Redeemer's Gate.

She was arrested three days later.

A bald man and a woman with a pale face slit by bright lipstick, both in plainclothes, called at the apartment on Leningradsky and took her in a black Volga to the women's section of the prison at 38, Petrovka.

They were courteous but uncommunicative. Katerina conducted herself with dignity but she wanted to weep.

The cell was painted dark green. It contained two bunks, one above the other, a scrubbed deal table and two chairs, a washbasin, a slice of red soap and a galvanised bucket.

The door shut with jarring finality.

She sat on the bed. Concentrate on the logic of it, she thought, otherwise you'll break. Humiliation. Question: why? Three days ago I was useful to them; suddenly I'm disposable, garbage.

A shiny cockroach as big as a thumb made a run across the wall opposite her.

She wondered if she would be expelled from the Soviet Union.

A key turned in the lock and Svetlana was pushed through the door.

She held out her arms and they embraced. Katerina felt courage pass between them.

Svetlana said: 'Let's call room service and have a drink.' She wore an emerald two-piece, a leftover from the reign of the pilot, and looked stunning. 'Are you looking forward to life in New York?'

'You think they'll throw us out?'

'We had one yellow card. This is the red.' She sat beside Katerina and put her arm round her.

From the corridor they heard scuffling. A woman with a Ukranian accent shouting: 'Get in there, you fucked-out old iron.' A cell door slammed.

'One of the girls,' Svetlana remarked. 'Railway station material by the sound of it. We're in good company Katerina Ilyina.'

The key turned in the lock. Katerina smelled spicy brilliantine. Spandarian came in carrying a document headed MINISTRY OF INTERNAL AFFAIRS.

He handed it to Katerina. 'Your expulsion order,' he said.

'But you said . . . .'

'That was three days ago, this is now.'

Svetlana stood up, a little taller than Spandarian. 'And mine?'

'Yours? Who said anything about you being kicked out?'

Katerina froze. To be expelled without Svetlana, that was worse than a death sentence.

Svetlana said: 'Listen you Georgian prick, if Katerina goes I go.'

Spandarian hit her across the face with the back of his hand but before she could throw herself at him an immense wardress invaded the cell and pinioned her arms.

'If you don't behave yourself,' Spandarian said mildly, 'we'll have to lock you up with the old whore next door.' He bowed to Katerina. 'Read this document and digest it. If there's anything you don't understand I'll be happy to explain. As we cross the border,' he added. He lit one of his yellow cigarettes. 'And now the contents of your handbag. A formality, you understand.'

He picked up Katerina's handbag and pillaged it. Compact, lipstick, crumpled one-, three- and five-rouble notes, a few kopeks, tissues, punished wallet, ballpoint pen. A nondescript mess.

Spandarian opened the wallet. Flipped through the plastic-sheathed ID cards hinged inside. A couple of ten-rouble notes, photograph of her mother and step-father at a camping site at

Adler on the Caucasion coast road, a few visiting cards and a couple of invitations. Spandarian examined one of these. Frowning, he asked: 'Where did you get this?' He was surprised, and that with Spandarian was a small victory.

Realising that it was the card the young man on the bus had given her and realising that Spandarian was impressed, she said: 'From its owner, of course.' She wished she had read the card.

'I wasn't aware you knew him.' *Him*. Who? Spandarian was patently furious that the name hadn't featured in the blue folder. Someone would fry! 'Have you known him long?'

'Since childhood.' They would boil!

Spandarian timed his revenge nicely. 'By the way, your mother and father – apologies, step-father – are quite comfortable in their jail.' He slid the invitation back into the wallet.

'You bastard. What have they done wrong?'

'Let's think. Harboured a known hooligan? How about that?' He gave a stage bow and walked out of the cell.

When he had gone Katerina allowed herself to cry. 'A good man . . . my mother, always hardship . . . . What right?'

Svetlana sat beside her again. 'Never mind, pussycat. They won't come to any harm. It's us they're gunning for.'

Me, Katerina thought. 'I never dreamed they would expel me without you.'

'Don't worry, I'll be there too.' And curiously: 'Who was that invitation from?'

'I don't know.'

'Come on, Kata, I'm not a Georgian bandit.'

'Honestly.' Katerina extracted the card from her wallet. 'My God!'

'Hand it over.' When she did Svetlana whistled. 'How did you get to know him?'

Katerina retrieved the card. It was an invitation to a pop concert. A personal one with the star's name embossed on the bottom right-hand corner. Leonid Agursky. Pop idol, sex symbol . . . . And I met him on a bus!

★ ★ ★

59

Spandarian returned the following day. Picking up the expulsion order, he said: 'You have read and understood it?'

'I realise I'm being expelled for preaching Leninism.'

'Ah, the rights of women. A worthy cause, Katerina Ilyina.' He stroked his moustache downwards and outwards. 'But you do understand the document?'

'I'm not an imbecile.'

'Good, good.' He was pensive for a moment; Georgian spice reached Katerina strongly. 'By the way you will be pleased to know that your mother and step-father have been released from jail. After all, why hold them? I'm sure you're not going to be a hooligan any more.'

He tore up the expulsion order.

Striding past Petrovka's shops in the direction of Sverdlov Square metro station, Svetlana said: 'So it's a different game from football. *Two* yellow cards and we're still on the pitch.'

'My parents . . . the son of a bitch.'

'We were being given the treatment,' Svetlana said. 'The expulsion order – a phoney.'

Judas counselled Katerina. *Would it really harm Calder if I processed what he told me and passed on innocuous trivia?*

'What I want you to concentrate on,' Spandarian told her later in his office, 'is Calder's state of mind, what he plans to do with the rest of his life. Any secrets he's kept to himself . . . .'

Why, she wondered, was Calder so important? She hoped she never found out.

Chapter 8

In summer mushrooms proliferate in the green and silver countryside outside Moscow as urgently as that short season itself. And armies of *gribniki*, mushroom-hunters, leave their sweating city in search of Little Foxes, Shaggy Parasols,

60

Caesar's Mushrooms, Horns of Plenty . . . . The fungi are eaten raw, cooked, pickled or salted; they are also measured with a fisherman's elastic rule and toasted exuberantly – brown vodka for the milk mushroom, pellucid and ice-cold firewater for a *russala*. The pastime is pursued exhaustively because there has to be a little exquisite suffering in most experiences; photographs of mammoth fungi are printed in the Press; doctors in hospital casualty departments stand by with stomach-pumps for the first imprudent *gribniki*.

At the Institute the Twilight Brigade went mushroom-hunting with qualified enthusiasm. Few of them had ever hankered after anything more exotic than the cultivated mushroom, on the other hand the younger recruits were keen to take part in anything characteristically Russian. It was all part of adapting, being accepted, and if long-serving members of the Brigade were sceptical about this they nevertheless accompanied the alien *gribniki* because there was not a lot to be said against supping a few grams of Stolichnaya in the cool of a birch forest.

In charge of mushroom-hunting was Mrs Lundkvist from Sweden. In fact she was in charge of most Russian-orientated pursuits managing through perseverance and unrelenting good humour to drum up support for her activities.

She was a once-beautiful blonde who was being remorselessly converted by the years into a matron. A decade earlier her husband had fled to Moscow bringing with him the secrets of Swedish submarine surveillance in the Baltic and his wife had followed him. The unkind asserted that if he had known this he would have stayed where he was and faced the music.

On this particular June morning Mrs Lundkvist, seated at the head of Table No. 5 during mid-morning break in the Institute canteen, was finding it difficult to sustain interest in mushrooms because another subject was vying for attention. A subject that is always discussed with animation in any expatriate society. Death.

Just as speculation about the death of Alfredo Bertoldi had begun to wane a Dutchman named van Doorn had disappeared.

Mrs Lundkvist, sipping lemon tea and speaking in English because she had long ago discovered to her chagrin that Russian would never be the *lingua franca* of the defectors, began to list to her audience the ten articles they would have to take with them into the country.

'Basket, waxed paper, tins, notepaper, stick . . . .'

Fabre, the Frenchman, said to Calder: 'Do you think he's still alive?'

'How should I know? It's not the first time he's gone missing . . . .'

'True. Once he meets the pretty boys outside the Bolshoi he seems to stick with them.' The nodding of Fabre's creased old face acquired an obscene air.

Dalby said: 'He'll be back.' As usual he spoke with nonchalant authority. He had retired from the Institute two years ago and had stopped by for coffee on his way to the Pushkin Museum.

'Unless he's dead.' The speaker was Langley, the Canadian who had been talking to Katerina at Kreiber's funeral. A bright young hope in the RCMP he had elected to stay in Moscow when the KGB had shown him photographs of himself with two girls which they planned to show to his boss and his wife unless . . . .

'Dead?' The slanting pouches on Dalby's face took up the question. 'Why should he be d . . . dead? You younger people do tend to be terribly dramatic.'

'Well he won't be the first this year,' Langley said defensively. He was thirty-ish and followed Western fashions as best he could, managing with his mussed fair hair and moustache to look like a shop-worn model for a cigarette advertisement.

'True. Natural causes, accident, suicide . . . . We all have to go some time you know. Even you.'

'A whole lot of people seem to have been going-some-time recently.'

'Coincidence, my dear fellow. Would you have preferred their deaths to have been staggered over the year?'

'I'll let you know,' Langley said, 'when van Doorn shows his face.'

Mrs Lundkvist said loudly: 'You must pick out mushrooms with care. Never, never experiment. Peasants will tell you' – Calder suspected that anyone outside Stockholm was a peasant – 'that there are ways of testing fungi to see if they are edible. Take no notice, consult the experts.' She laughed gaily. 'In this case me.'

'Do you really think,' Langley went on, 'that Bertoldi committed suicide?'

Dalby sighed. 'How many times have we been through this? There is no evidence to the contrary. He left a note, he was seen to jump.'

'Fall,' Calder said.

He was keeping his eye on the Russians coming into the canteen to see if Katerina was among them. He had been to the Maly Theatre with her the previous evening and he wanted to discuss the play – and to be near her. The Russians veered away from the corner of the canteen occupied by the defectors: that was alien territory.

'Very well, fall. That's what happens when you jump, I believe. Do you m . . . mean you still have doubts?'

'I believe nothing, disbelieve nothing.'

'A rather negative philosophy, don't you think? But then you have had other things on your mind . . . .' The pouches took on knowing angles.

'Lucky bastard,' Langley said.

'I wish I were younger,' Fabre remarked. If he were, his tone implied, Calder wouldn't stand a chance.

'Be careful, Bob,' Dalby said. 'Be very careful.'

Mrs Lundkvist said: 'Did you know mushrooms contain more protein than other vegetables?'

China broke behind the metallic food counter. Heads swivelled. A young man with burning cheeks knelt to pick up the pieces.

Katerina was wearing a blue linen dress. It was simple but to Calder she looked like a model in *Vogue*. Her black hair had been cut shorter for summer; her face was still pale because, unlike most Muscovites, she didn't abandon herself to the sun; as usual the tilt of her head challenged, but she was also looking for him. She found him, smiled. The smile warmed him. He felt younger, looked it. He had even taken to jogging with Jessel along the river bank.

'And very strong in Vitamin B,' Mrs Lundkvist said.

Calder bit into a biscuit coated with pink, lacquer-hard icing. However much younger he looked he was still too old for her. Why did she bother with him? This sometimes worried him during the night. At other times he awoke with a flash of light and there smiling at him from a Polaroid photograph were Ruth and Harry. At the racecourse at Suffolk Downs. In Fenway Park. On the manicured lawns of his father's house – he could hear the feathered patter of the sprinklers. Harry then only three, his face happy with trust.

Then a page in the photograph album turned and there again was Katerina Ilyina. Riding the ferris wheel in Gorky Park with Robert Calder. Moscow spread beneath them. Trust on Calder's face just as there had been trust on Harry's. Harry had been betrayed.

'Did you hear me?' Dalby's voice intruded. 'We seem to have lost you . . . .'

'And I know where he was,' said Langley without quite leering.

Fabre's head bobbed.

'As a general rule,' Mrs Lundkvist said loudly, 'beware of fungi with thin stems. Our friends call them *poganki*. Ugh!' She shuddered, swishing greyish blonde hair across broadening shoulders. 'And beware the Avenging Angel. And the Death Cap, of course. It smells of honey, the brute.'

At the word *death* she rekindled group interest. For a moment, unaccustomed to undivided attention, she was nonplussed. Then, adroitly, she used it.

'But that's not for another two weeks of course. Even that's very early for mushrooms but I seem to have a way of finding their haunts. Tomorrow Russian classes. Saturday, ballet lessons for the girls.' Not one of them under forty, Calder thought. 'Tuesday, a minibus trip to the diplomats' beach at Uspens-koye.' The foreign diplomats will love that, Calder reflected; generally speaking they disliked defectors even more than the Russians. 'Bridge on Wednesdays as usual. And chess – but there I bow to my superior. Over to you, Mr Calder.' She smiled winningly.

Before the advent of Katerina, Calder had intended to organise a chess tournament. No longer. 'Chess as usual on Thursday. Here in the recreation room.'

'Nothing more, Mr Calder?' voice seeping with disappoint-ment.

Calder shook his head and Langley murmured: 'The lucky sonofabitch has other recreations in mind.'

Katerina was sitting beside Lev Koslov, her plump and moist boss, and her colleague, Sonya Ivanovna, a fair-haired girl with the naked gaze of someone who has just removed their spectacles. Calder caught Katerina's gaze. She nodded gently.

Fabre lit a French-smelling cigarette. 'Poor old van Doorn,' he said. '*C'est très triste*.'

Dalby, rippling fingers through his soft grey hair, said: 'I think you've all summoned the Reaper a little prematurely.'

'The gays stick together,' Langley said. 'I'll give you that. Outside creed or colour.'

'Until they're warned off,' Calder said.

Van Doorn, wistful features jaded, walked up to the table and said: 'Can I get anyone another coffee?'

At 4.38 that afternoon Calder, brooding on the death of Bertoldi, entered the vision of a sniper peering through the telescopic sights of his rifle.

Calder, being a creature of habit, was a gift to a marksman. Every weekday afternoon after finishing work he walked home through Pushkin Square. A dead duck if you had a good vantage point. And what could be better than the big grey building where *Izvestia* projected luminous news flashes?

To make sure that neither his aim nor concentration were

disturbed the sniper had asked his boss for authority to extinguish the neon lights flickering around the window where he had mounted his tripod.

Calder, head down, approached the cross-hairs of the sight. He looked up once, features registering mild surprise at the absence of news, then returned his gaze to the pavement.

The sniper, waiting until Calder was separated from other pedestrians in the great square containing the Rossia Cinema and the Pushkin Monument, stroked the trigger of the rifle. On the other side of the street from Calder an ambulance kerb-crawled, stretcher-bearers waiting to pick up the body before anyone realised what had happened.

4.39. Calder was clear of other pedestrians, in the centre of the cross-hairs.

The sniper's finger tightened on the trigger.

4.40. An indignant George Sokolov, corpulent Director of Illuminated Intelligence, who had taken a day off to attend his daughter's wedding, punched the button that switched on the news. Lucky that he had been astute enough to make a surprise return. Heads would roll.

Huge letters burst into radiant light around the marksman. US BLOCKS DISARMAMENT TALKS. Dazzled, he lowered the barrel of the rifle.

He peered through the telescopic sight once more but of Calder there was no sign.

Lately Calder's reading matter had diversified. In addition to airmailed newspapers, *The New York Times, Washington Post* . . . and magazines, *Time, Newsweek, Fortune* . . . he was being given books to analyse, among them a few novels. Even espionage, always well-thumbed en route. Le Carré in particular. 'Any idea who Smiley's based on?' Calder had been asked by a junior Soviet analyst.

Well he didn't know that. But if he had told the analyst what he *did* know the analyst would have retreated stunned. In fact his knowledge was shared only at a rarified level. Two, three heads of KGB directorates at the most. Spandarian wouldn't know. He doubted whether the Secretary of the Communist Party knew.

Monday, Tuesday, Wednesday . . . such beautifully simple codenames. But who was Saturday? That he had never known.

As he made his way through the Institute to his office the following day Calder, stooping slightly, glanced into the book-lined chambers of specious deduction on either side of him. Scandinavian, Mid-European, Australasian – a surprisingly large section – Great Britain, Central America, South America . . . .

What did the Soviets make of all this dubious speculation, much of it wildly concocted the way students contemplating an incomprehensible examination paper fill a sheet of paper in the hope of getting at least something right? Shredded it, probably. The Twilight Brigade were only given these duties to give them a sense of importance.

He was now directly above Katerina's office. The new, younger Calder straightened his stoop. What had she asked him last night in the interval? 'Do you ever feel you want to return to the United States?' That was it. 'Not any more,' he had replied. What a tantalising relationship. No sex. Was she really attracted to him? It was difficult to accept. Thirty-eight was young enough, but to a girl of nineteen an elder. Worse, a traitor.

So why did she profess to enjoy his company?

Come on, Calder, it's not unknown for a young girl to be attracted to an older man.

He was still tormenting himself when he pushed open the door bearing the words, white on black, ROBERT E. CALDER, DIRECTOR OF UNITED STATES STUDIES, and sat at his desk.

Sunlight peering through the slatted blinds made quivering tiger stripes on the green metal surface. He could hear traffic, the whine of a high-flying jet. He felt detached, suspended.

'Do you ever feel you want to return to the United States?'

If he blamed anyone – other than himself, that was – he blamed Holden.

All those golden words, those shining ideals over the chess board. While Calder's elder brother, Dean, was away fighting Holden talked.

And, boy, could he ever talk. Lean and crisp and outraged, he dispatched INJUSTICE snivelling into the wilderness. Bostonian privilege, Capitol Hill corruption . . . anti-black prejudice, American intervention in Vietnam . . . .

Off with their heads.

But although Gary Holden was an orator he was no Bobby Fischer. So to add piquancy to his inevitable defeats at chess at the hands of Calder, his junior, he invented a game within a game.

Beneath each other's major pieces they stuck tabs naming personalities they considered to be particularly obnoxious. So you didn't know the identity of your own rook or bishop until it was captured. Hitler, Churchill, Henry Kissinger, Al Capone, Doris Day . . . even Donald Duck made a guest appearance.

Calder who regarded chess as intellectual poetry – he subsequently became more practical – condoned such levity in deference to Holden.

Holden was in his third year at Harvard while Calder was still being prepared for that august campus. But their families on Beacon Hill had been close for more than a century.

When Dean went to war Holden became Calder's mentor. And if Calder's father noticed that he had been usurped he didn't protest; with one telephone call he could have stopped Dean's call-up but, by enlisting, Dean had defied him and his voice at the end of the dinner table became an echo that lost itself in mountains of outrage.

Dean came home from Vietnam once during that heady period. He was highly decorated but his medals were tarnished with disillusion. He spoke of carnage and the slaughter of innocents and the brutalising of youth, but mostly he spoke about futility. 'A war we can't win and everyone knows it but we go on fighting to feed Washington egos.'

Dean was main-lining drugs too.

And Vietnam became the spearhead of Holden and Calder's crusade. They took part in demonstrations, they even joined a far-out left-wing society in Cambridge.

The intoxicating round of protest continued until a couple of days after Holden graduated. Until he sold out.

Chin cupped in his hands over the chess board in Calder's den, he explained why. Protest was a part of maturing, no less worthy for that. It was youth's contribution to democracy.

Hand poised above a belligerent white queen, Calder said: 'What is all this shit, Gary?'

Leaning back fingering his striped college tie – Calder had never seen him wear one before – Holden elaborated. At a certain age you had to abandon dissent otherwise you became an anarchist. 'We don't want anarchy, we want equality.'

'Who got to you, Gary?'

'No one got to me, for Chrissake.' Holden tugged at the knot of his tie. 'I have to earn a living, you'll grant me that. So my old man came up with this job in Washington.'

'Conservation?' Calder asked without hope – that had been part of the crusade too.

'Pentagon.'

The crucible of Vietnam.

A pause.

Then: 'I'm very pleased for you, Gary.'

'Honest?'

'Sure.' Calder picked up the queen.

'Then you won't mind me asking you a couple of things. You know, I may have been a little indiscreet. Maybe you could forget some of those indiscretions.'

Calder moved the queen. 'Check-mate.'

'Do you still have the membership cards for that society we joined? You kept them, remember?'

'I have them.'

'Do me a big favour and destroy mine.'

'Sure thing, Gary.'

Moving the queen briskly and unnecessarily, he knocked over Holden's black king. Picking it up, smiling fiercely, he

showed Holden the name underneath it.
   LYNDON B. JOHNSON.

After the earnest young man had approached him three years later at Elsie's, on Mt Auburn Street, Calder blamed his subsequent actions more on Gary Holden, already going places in Washington DC, than on the Viet Cong soldier who had cut his brother in half with a burst from a submachine gun.

Drunks at dusk, joggers at dawn.
   As first light explored the peaceful city – night barely an intermission at this time of year – Calder struggled to keep up with Jessel as they loped through Krasnaya Presna Park.
   Close by a pilot boat pushing its way along the river towards the canal linking the docks with the Volga dispatched rippled messages to the waterside. Calder smelled the burnt-paint breath of the ship's funnel and the mossy odour of the deep brown water.
   'Don't overdo it,' Jessel warned. 'Not at first. Stop here if you like.' His breathing was regular, stride rhythmical; only the ear-to-ear strands of hair were in disarray.
   'Don't worry about me. Got to get fit.' Calder whose chest ached shaved his words to save breath.
   'I don't have to ask why.'
   Jessel seemed to increase his stride, the bastard. It was the third week that Calder had accompanied him and each morning the stress got worse instead of better. But he stayed with him. Ahead lay the oasis in the self-inflicted suffering, the bench where Jessel rested.
   Heel and toe, heel and toe. Other joggers ran with them, against them, some wearing shorts but most, like himself, in blue track suits.
   'So how is Katerina Ilyina?' Jessel asked.
   'She's okay.' He was panting like a thirsty dog.
   'She seems to be showing you the city. You're a lucky guy. Not many of us get to see the genuine article.'
   'Perhaps you don't try hard enough.'
   'Bullshit. You're being given the treatment. Why?'

'Old-fashioned charm?'

The bench was a hundred yards away. Pray God he didn't collapse before he reached it. On the grass he noticed a crumpled heap of blue; jogger or drunk left over from the night before, you could never be quite sure.

Swallows dipped over the river pecking arrows in the water ahead of the pilot boat.

Fifty yards. Three middle-aged men in blue flopped onto the bench. And Jessel would never share a bench, part of his training. Another hundred and fifty yards before the next casualty clearing station. He'd never make it. A legacy of booze and cigarettes and eroding self-pity. He continued to run on bending knees.

'There,' said Jessel, sitting down. 'Relax. Breathe deeply.' He smoothed his hair. 'We'll take it easy going back.'

Calder sucked in night-cooled air. Around him the city, an early riser, was waking in the timid light, lime green on the horizon. Lights stuttered into life on bleak-walled apartment blocks and the spike of the Ukraina Hotel wedding cake reached for the last stars, and soft sparks fell from an acetelyne welder on Novo-Arbatsky Bridge and the air smelled of new bread. Soon the sleep-drugged pulse of the city would quicken as the serpentine heads of trains nosed out of the great stations, burrowing into European Russia, plunging south to the Orient and north to the Arctic and east to the Pacific, and swarms of Muscovites, blooming in the fragile sunshine, poured into buses, trolleybuses, collective taxis and metro trains to take them to their five-year plans.

For the first time Calder felt affection for the city that had rejected him. He knew why.

When his breathing had steadied Jessel asked him if Katerina had asked any pertinent questions of late.

'Pertinent to what? I mean what the hell could I know that would interest her?'

'Questions about yourself?'

'No,' Calder lied. 'And how's Harry making out? No more falls?'

'He's fine, just fine. Taken to sailing.'

71

'Does he ever ask about me?'

Jessel shook his head. 'You know something? You squeeze much more out of me than I ever get out of you. You're supposed to be filling me in on Twilight Brigade gossip. Who's screwing who, that sort of thing.'

'Who's thinking about re-defecting?'

'That sort of thing.'

'How's Ruth?'

'Where is Katerina Ilyina taking you next?'

'To a concert.'

'Cosy.' Jessel stretched. 'Ruth's okay. The handicapped children love her apparently.'

They had planned another child. A girl, they'd hoped, but if it had been another boy they would have loved him just as much, so they had said. A long time ago. 'Maybe three,' she had said, 'I've got child-bearing hips.' And short red-gold hair that skipped in the breeze coming off the ocean and well-muscled, tennis-playing legs which she braced against adversity and grey eyes that gazed with astonishment upon deceit.

'And my father?'

'Always last, huh? He's well enough except for the speech impediment. He'll always have that. But he's lucky, I guess – he's got your mother.'

So she's come into her own at last, Calder thought. Affection for her family had always been governed by her husband's rules.

Jessel said: 'A friendly word of warning, Bob. Be careful of this girl. She's what, twenty years younger than you? Hasn't it occurred to you that she might have ulterior motives? Information?'

'What information, for Chrissake?'

What I know they know. But not many of them. Intelligence operatives made it their business to spy on each other – they couldn't help themselves – and a lot of KGB executives would be neurotically curious about his privileges. Spandarian . . . .

Jessel said: 'How about breakfast?' and when Calder looked

72

surprised: 'Laura's in Helsinki with the kids,' as though they were far enough away from contamination.

The kitchen of Jessel's apartment, near the steam-shrouded, open-air swimming pool, was all-American; an imported electrical showroom that operated at half-strength because the UPDK electricians couldn't get the parts.

Jessel poured orange juice, made coffee, fried ham and eggs. In his castle he seemed much more menacing, soft-shell camouflage removed and hung on a hook.

Sitting at the breakfast bar, he prodded his knife at Calder and said: 'I want you to tell me what the hell's going on. You've got a tail, you know that?'

'I guess we all do from time to time. Don't you follow Russian defectors in the States?'

'You've got one all the time. Even jogging just now.'

'I hope he managed to keep up with us.' Calder was surprised at the thoroughness of the surveillance; there was an ominous determination about a dawn shadow. He knifed his egg and watched the yolk spread from the wound. 'How do you know he wasn't tailing you?'

'He drove up behind you. All ready in his tracksuit. He'll be waiting outside.'

'Doesn't that worry you? That State Security knows you've been visited by an American defector?'

'Why should it? They know you want to keep tabs on Ruth and Harry. They hope you might pick up a trick or two from me. After all you *are* working for them. And now they have a go-between.'

'Katerina?'

'Don't kid yourself, you're not God's gift to a girl of that age. Now you tell me – what are they after?'

'There's nothing to be after.' Calder smiled at Jessel through the steam rising from his coffee. 'This apartment . . . .'

'Is clean. You're safe. Is there anything you want to tell me?' Wary lines at the corners of his eyes like sparrow's claws.

'Nothing.'

The claws sharpened. 'Don't leave it till it's too late . . . . They don't put a tail like that on you for nothing. And they

73

don't simultaneously fix you up with a swallow.'

Swallow, KGB parlance for female plant, seductress, whore. Could anyone be less like a swallow than Katerina? He almost felt sorry for Jessel, snared inescapably in suspicion.

He pushed his plate away, yolk congealing. 'Take it easy,' he said. 'Don't get too paranoic about surveillance or one day you might find yourself staring into a mirror.'

He drove to Byelorussia Square. Katerina lived to the left down Leningradsky. He smiled into the driving mirror: his eyes were clear and there was a sheen to his skin. He picked up a pack of cigarettes, returned them to the glove compartment unopened.

He turned right down Gorky. 7 am. The first metro trains would be prowling the city's bowels; above ground traffic was sparse but picking up, his tail among it. So? A black Zil, curtains primly closed across the rear window, sped down the reserved centre lane towards the Kremlin; that was privilege for you. Calder crossed Pushkin Square, passing through the ring of green boulevards, and parked the Zhiguli outside his apartment block.

He ran a finger along the compact's dusty flanks. It was coated with summer dust. A rouble fine on the spot for a dirty car. Not so long ago the possibility of such fussy retribution would have irritated him; not today – he determined to hose down the car.

In the apartment he opened the heavy drapes to let the day come in, drank a glass of Narzan water. Then he lay down on the sofa and fell asleep.

He was awoken at nine by Lidiya. She had purchased croissants at Gastronom No. 1 and she brought them with a dab of white butter, a glass of apple juice and coffee on a tray.

'Jogging again?' She shook her head reprovingly. 'You should have a medical.' She belonged to that generation – but only just – that still expected their menfolk to eat hugely, spend their leisure hours in the bath-house drinking beer and eating salted fish and exercising in abrupt bouts of athleticism or sex.

This morning she brought him a small pot of African violets.

They were on the coffee table beside him, placed there gently while he slept. They made him feel guilty.

Since that first party at Katerina's home he hadn't made love to Lidiya. Did she feel slighted, hurt? He had no way of knowing. He didn't want to wound her; on the other hand she might be relieved that she was no longer expected to go to bed with him.

'Thank you for the flowers,' he said.

'I didn't know whether to buy carnations or violets. Then I thought, the carnations will die soon like our summer but these will live throughout winter.' She touched the mauve cups, each containing a jewel of water.

Did the violets symbolise her desire for permanency? Russian women believed implicitly in symbolism. And superstition. Yesterday a sparrow had flown in the window and she had screamed. When Calder had managed to let it free she had explained that a bird inside a home was an omen of death.

Her scream had been all the more startling because she was normally so composed.

'And how's Yuri?' he asked.

She would have dropped him on the way to the apartment at Work-Polytechnical Middle School No. 28. Yuri was eleven years old; he was a Young Pioneer – an Octobrist before that – and one day he would join the Komsomol. He looked very much like Lidiya's husband who had died in an accident on an ice-breaker on the Volga and he was her life.

She smiled the wondrous smile that visited her when she spoke about Yuri. 'In good spirits. I told him last night that he can go to summer camp. I shall miss him but he has to learn to be independent.'

She began to dust the table. Splinters of coloured light from the chandelier played at her fingertips.

Sipping his coffee, Calder looked at her fondly. She didn't look like the mother of an eleven-year-old boy. She looked unfulfilled. Placid features, slim body settling into angles; only the surprisingly full breasts gave any hint of sensuality.

Calder remembered their firmness in his hands.

Why didn't she ever ask why he no longer wanted her?

She straightened up, a patch of coloured light shifting on her face like moving water. And he had the answer: she knew why.

Chapter 9

The sniper couldn't believe his luck: Calder was going to trade in his car.

That meant that when he left the field on the south-west limits of the city he would have to drive down a steep hill towards Simonovskaya Quay on a fat curve of the Moscow River. Above the final descent was a ledge of rock curtained with creeper, a sniper's dream. A bullet through Calder's head and the car would plunge into the river. Much better than Pushkin Square.

Mikhail Boldin followed Calder's Zhiguli in his old, souped-up Moskvich. He was twenty-two years old with a cleft chin, and brown eyes; his eyes always surprised strangers who expected them to be ice-blue.

On the back seat of the grey Moskvich were three rifles sheathed in khaki canvas. He had licences for all three. Two he used for shooting bear and deer in the game reserves of the Caucasus; the third he used for homo sapiens. It was an old Mosin-Nagant M1891/30 fitted with a PE telescopic sight. His grandfather had used it at Stalingrad in the Great Patriotic War when he and a crack German sniper had stalked each other in the pitiless streets of the besieged city. A vendetta within an epic. Boldin's grandfather, catching a flash of winter sunlight on the barrel of the German's rifle, had won.

The rifle had been handed down to Boldin's father, also a sniper in the Red Army, and finally to Mikhail, a marksman in another sort of army.

Calder's Zhiguli began its climb to the bartering field. Boldin wondered what sort of car he intended to buy. An old American limousine, perhaps, abandoned by a long-departed diplomat, to remind him of the country he had deserted. Boldin enjoyed killing traitors.

The impulse to trade in his travel-worn Zhiguli had seized Calder over lunch. Sitting in a café near the Institute eating blinis and drinking beer, he had stared out of the window at the black compact parked at the kerb and been ashamed of it.

In the States automobiles had been his one indulgence. He had owned a Mercedes and a Stingray. In Moscow he had ceased to bother about cars as he had ceased to bother about many things.

Suddenly he wanted to impress a girl.

As a foreigner he could have bought a new car within a few days. But as a Soviet citizen it could take two years. So the only solution was to meet the *spekulyanty* in the bartering field.

He drove there the following morning, the first Saturday in July. On the horizon a summer storm was gathering irritably; thunder grumbled, lightning blinked. He had once been advised never to buy a car in the rain because the water polished the bodywork with false promises; well, if the storm broke he would also be selling a car in the rain.

He parked on the edge of the balding grass. Most of the cars looked as if they had come to die but among the terminally ill were a few glossy fledglings, the property of the true speculators who had bought them *defitsitny* and would sell them at a criminal mark-up. But all the cars would be sold: to own a car however senile was to have made it in the Soviet Union.

A swarthy man with garlic breath wearing a white shirt and black trousers approached him. A Georgian, Calder guessed. Uzbek as it happened. He offered Calder four thousand roubles for the Zhiguli. Calder laughed indulgently. Five thousand. Calder settled for six. They drove down a cul-de-sac to clinch the deal out of sight of informers sent to the field to try and make sure State-controlled prices were observed.

That would take half an hour, Boldin calculated.

He bought a glass of *kvas* from a stall on the edge of the field. A few heavy drops of rain fell in the dust at his feet.

He drank thirstily. It was the most refreshing drink in Russia and being fermented from rye bread, the most nutritious and he couldn't understand why anyone bothered with beer or spirits.

The bruised clouds inched nearer. Lightning forked the sky. Thunder chased it. A crack of thunder just as he pulled the trigger wouldn't be unwelcome, he reflected.

And now the purchase. Calder had made six thousand roubles from the sale of the Zhiguli and he had brought five thousand and a wad of dollars with him. It was the dollars that would count; they were the pass-keys to luxury.

He approached a speculator wiping spots of rain from the windshield of a white Volga. He peered at the dashboard: seven hundred kilometres on the clock: it could have been re-wound but the car, the pride of Gorky assembly lines, smelled new.

The speculator who wore black boots made of soft leather and wrap-round sun-glasses assessed Calder. 'Roubles or dollars?'

'Both.'

'Okay, we do business.'

They drove to the end of the cul-de-sac for a test drive.

Watching them depart, Boldin calculated: three-quarters of an hour. He was no soft touch, that bandit in the shades.

He drank another three kopeks worth of *kvas*, then climbed into the Moskvich and drove in second gear to the bottom of the hill.

He parked it out of sight on the quay. He put on a fawn raincoat and, taking the Mosin-Nagant from the rear seat, began to climb the wooded slope to the ledge of rock.

When he reached it the clouds burst. Raindrops splashed ankle-high. Serpent tongues of lightning flickered across the rooftops of Moscow. Thunder cracked overhead. The wet dust had a primeval smell about it.

★   ★   ★

Calder drove the white Volga away from the field with pride. He hadn't felt like this about a car since he had bought the Stingray. The Volga was no Stingray, no Mercedes come to that – too inflexibly practical – but impressive on the streets of Moscow. He touched the controls lovingly. Then, peering through the swotting windshield wipers, he began his descent to the river.

Calder, observed through the telescopic sight, was smiling. Pride of ownership. So he would die happy.

Boldin took first pressure on the trigger of the Mosin-Nagant mounted on a collapsible tripod. He wanted to hit Calder as he was level with the ledge. He would slump to the left pulling the wheel and the car would careen into the river.

Fifty metres.

Boldin was vaguely aware of scuffling behind him but his concentration was everything, the concentration known only to hunters of men. He checked his breathing.

Twenty metres.

The barrel of the rifle that had shot a German marksman more than forty years ago in Stalingrad moved fractionally to the right.

The rain sluiced down.

Lightning.

He pulled the trigger as the thunder cracked.

As the man behind him threw himself at him. The bullet ricocheted off the mudguard. The Volga swerved, straightened, accelerated.

Boldin rolled clear of the tripod. 'What the fuck . . . .'

The Estonian driver of the battered cream Volga kicked him in the crotch. In the ribs. In the face. Then he rolled Boldin off the ledge and watched his body splash into the puddles below.

Chapter 10

Spandarian who normally schemed, raged.

How could the Executive Action Department have been so shit-stupid? Muscling in on his territory, seeking a slice of the glory – that, being a Georgian, he could understand.

But the crudeness, that was beyond belief. For two years he had been controlling the life-spans of the Twilight Brigade, assessing through surveillance when they might be entering the menopause of defection, contemplating re-defection even. And he had acted accordingly, helped by an accomplice whose identity would never be suspected.

Accidents and natural causes, those were *modus operandi*. Nothing to deter a potential defector with a shopping bag full of secrets. But who would want to make the crossing if he thought a bullet in the head might be his ultimate reward?

After the phone call from the Estonian, he vented his anger first on a girl named Nina. Standing in front of him shimmying into a green dress, she asked him for money. Fifty dollars – dollars! – to buy some mink ear-rings she had seen on sale in a *beryozka* shop. He hit her across the face with the back of his hand and told her to get out.

When she had made a tearful departure Spandarian prowled the living room of his apartment in the Arbat caged by his fury.

Even though it had been a balls-up by the Executive Action Department – sabotage, kidnapping and assassination – of the First Chief Directorate – some of the stink would rub off on him. Why, for instance, had he failed to accomplish what the Executive Action Department had attempted?

Why? Because he hadn't yet ascertained whether Calder had reached that dangerous state of re-assessment, that was why. In fact on the face of it it seemed, according to Katerina

Ilyina's reports, that Calder was coming to terms with his life in exile.

Not that he necessarily bought that: the girl might be protecting Calder. There was also another factor to consider: Calder's love affair with Russia might owe a lot to his feelings for her. If that liaison ended Calder would either slump back in the rut or make a run for it. But before that happened he would make sure that, through the girl, he discovered why Calder was treated like a VIP.

You had to be a Georgian to understand such subtleties, to manipulate men's lives. It was through just such inspired manoeuvering that Spandarian intended one day to take his place at the helm of the Politburo.

And he had no intention of allowing some moron in the Executive Action Department, obsessed with blood letting, to prejudice his chances.

The rage subsided.

Think, Spandarian, you whose Chechen ancestors once terrorised the dizzy heights of the Georgian Military Road dispatching any marauding Slavs from Muscovy back to St Petersburg.

He lit a cigarette and poured himself a shot of Armenian brandy.

Adapt. The attempt on Calder's life had been incredibly clumsy. Since when did you set up an assassination without first making sure that you weren't being followed yourself? He would have to make sure the Chairman of State Security appreciated his own finesse. He would have to show him how it should be done.

How? Patience. That would come. Natural causes or accident . . . brilliance whichever.

Spandarian poured himself more brandy and thoughtfully stroked his moustache. One aspect of the Calder shooting attempt particularly bothered him. Why had the Executive Action Committee wanted to kill Calder?

He walked to his office. It was Saturday afternoon and the crowds in the hot streets were festive. He assumed it was some sort of commemoration day: it usually was. Merchant Navy Day the other day, Fisherman's Day coming up.

Queues waited thirstily for *kvas* and cherryade and ice-cream. Soldiers and sailors led their girls towards the parks; plump women fanned themselves with copies of *Pravda* – someone should draw up a list of the uses to which it was put; children fidgeted in front of ancient monuments; a couple of fugitive toy balloons floated high over the Kremlin.

Spandarian strode briskly down Kalinin Street. He would make two protests. One to the head of the Second Chief Directorate which contained his own department, the other to the head of the First Chief Directorate which ruled the Executive Action Department – if anyone ruled that gang of cut-throats.

And make sure both protests were brought to the Chairman's notice.

Spandarian was currently making a study of the Chairman for his own coercive files. Since the one-time Chairman Yuri Andropov had been made Soviet Supremo and died in harness there had been several changes in the leadership of the KGB.

The latest Chairman was old. Weren't they all? But he was astute and apparently honest – in Spandarian's view a bizarre qualification for the job – and dedicated to stamping out corruption in his clandestine legions massed across the Soviet Union and the globe.

In his office Spandarian called on his computer to refresh his memory about Dmitry Kirov.

Age 71.

Formerly Director of Central Committee liaising all Communist parties.

Joined Party 1934.

Fought as guerilla behind German lines in Great Patriotic War.

Member of NKVD and MGB prior to re-organisation as KGB.

Married, two children.

Vices –

82

Spandarian sighed as the green letters on the computer screen quivered negatively. Give me time and I'll fill in the blank.

He pressed the remote control button and another chapter in the Chairman's life appeared. Foul-ups that could be traced directly to him. Even they were pretty thin on the ground. But they were a beginning.

The red telephone on his desk rang. He picked up the receiver. The voice on the other end of the line said: 'Dmitry Kirov speaking.'

The dachas of the *nachalstvo*, the élite, lie around the hamlet of Zhukovka twenty miles from Moscow. It is a lovely, untroubled place where men climb from big black limousines to change their identities. In summer it smells of pine and river-water; in winter it smells of cold, a comforting knowledge when you are playing with your grandchildren in front of a log fire.

It was to this settlement, suspended in time on the banks of the Moscow, that Spandarian came that afternoon at the request of the Chairman of the KGB. To observe protocol he had collected his own driver, but as they drove deeper into the sylvan heart of privilege his Volga seemed more and more prosaic. This was Chaika country, any minute now they would be in Zil territory.

Twice they were stopped by militia. His red ID hauled up a couple of salutes but they weren't as snappy as they would be if he had been in the back of a Chaika or a Zil. One day, comrades, one day.

Kirov's dacha was surrounded by a tall green fence. Two armed guards stood at the entrance. They logged Spandarian, let him pass.

Kirov was standing at the door of the dacha, a wooden palace. Two spaniels panted at his feet. He looked avuncular, a family man who couldn't possibly know what the inside of a KGB mental home, where dissidents were broken with aminazin, reserpine and sulfazin, looked like; couldn't visualise a Siberian labour camp where frost-bitten prisoners lived like vermin.

He was tall and trim. There were warrior lines on his face.

83

His nose was a prow. His eyebrows silver. He walked with a slight limp, a German bullet at Smolensk. He clapped Spandarian on the shoulder: they might have been comrades at arms. What did he want?

'I thought we'd take the dogs for a walk,' Kirov said. 'Get some summer air.'

They walked towards the river, dogs snouting in pale woodland grass. Sunlight on water sparkled through the pine trees.

Kirov pointed at a clearing rucked with old earthworks. 'Know what they are?' And without waiting for a reply: 'What's left of the trenches we built to defend Moscow against the Hun. But he didn't come this way. I'm not going to have it smoothed over. It's a reminder and we need reminders, people like you and me.'

Spandarian who had no idea why he should be reminded of the last war didn't answer.

'We need to be reminded of the threats that surround us. A long border is a vulnerable border. Throughout our history it's been violated. It must never happen again.'

The paranoic side of the Russian Slav, Spandarian thought. The complex seeded in history that accounted for the mistrust of foreigners, the over-reaction to arms threats.

'I should have thought your wound was sufficient reminder,' Spandarian ventured.

'That was a long way from here. This is Moscow. The Germans almost took our capital.'

Your capital, Spandarian thought, not mine.

'And when I look at those old trenches I realise that everything I do is justified. I am charged with containing our enemies inside and outside the Soviet Union. But I forgot, you're a Georgian. Perhaps these things don't matter so much to you?'

Oh no you don't! 'I'm a Soviet citizen first, a Georgian second.' Spandarian's tongue was thick with the lie.

'I always thought it was ironic that Georgians should have rallied to the flag to fight the Germans and been exiled by Stalin to Kazakhstan for their pains.'

84

I am being tested, Spandarian realised. Why? 'And yet Stalin is still venerated in Georgia. That's an indication of the strength of Georgian character.'

They reached the river-bank. One side of Kirov's estate was a Japanese print. Men of power finding lonely therapy fishing in calm waters.

Kirov threw a stick and the two spaniels raced into the water for it. Ripples chased each other towards the anglers. No one would protest.

Kirov said: 'A wily Georgian . . . . We need people like you in State Security. Particularly in your specialised domain. The Twilight Brigade – velvet gloves, eh, Comrade Spandarian?'

So finally, through a circuitous route, they were getting to the point. He had been assessed and for the moment found adequate. Now was the time to take the initiative.

'You're absolutely right, Comrade Kirov,' he said, 'and as you appreciate how delicate my responsibilities are,' playing his line as carefully as one of the anglers downstream, 'you will understand my feelings' – not anger, that would be overplaying his hand – 'when I learned that the Executive Action Department had trespassed on my territory.'

Silence, apart from a lot of splashing and panting from the dogs. *Trespassing*. Too strong? Perhaps it had been Kirov's decision to shoot Calder.

A brown and white butterfly tripped its way across the water.

Finally Kirov said: 'I owe you an apology, Comrade Spandarian.' Unbelievable. 'Let me explain.'

Kirov revealed that he had discussed Calder with the head of the First Chief Directorate. A mistake. The director had in turn discussed it with the head of the Executive Action Department which was his responsibility. The head of the Executive Action Department had interpreted this – 'Perhaps the discussion was oiled by a few grams of firewater' – as an order to eliminate the American. Stupid. Especially the way the assassination attempt had been carried out. Spandarian shouldn't worry: he had every right to have Calder shadowed, every right to have forestalled interference.

Spandarian said: 'With respect, Comrade Kirov, you must

85

have implied to the head of the First Chief Directorate that Calder should be eliminated. Why?'

'Implied, perhaps. But in no way did I authorise him to take the matter into his own hands. Regrettable, most regrettable . . . .'

Kirov made no attempt to answer the question; instead he threw another stick for the dogs. A white steamer rounded a curve on the other side of the river. Kirov shaded his eyes above his hawk nose and stared at it. The decks were crowded with passengers. The good citizens that Kirov was protecting.

The dogs returned and showered the two men with water.

Kirov threw the stick again and said: 'Your methods would have been far better. We shouldn't assassinate defectors in broad daylight. Who would ever defect again?' Not even Kirov could have guessed the identity of the subtle executioner; the knowledge soothed Spandarian. 'By the way, Bertoldi, it was suicide, wasn't it?'

Spandarian said it was. An unfortunate occurrence that had increased the incidence of death in the Twilight Brigade beyond his estimates.

'The five-year plan?' Kirov smiled thinly. 'I'm afraid you will have to revise your estimates, comrade.'

'Calder?'

'In certain matters my predecessors have been far too lax. Too trusting.' You had to admire Kirov's capacity for not answering questions. 'In the case of Calder, for instance. You have been assessing his mental state?'

'A routine process, Comrade Kirov.'

'Quite. But there is a possibility that he might renege?'

'There's always that possibility with a defector. Once a traitor always a traitor.'

'Traitor? They think they're idealists.'

'Traitors in my book,' Spandarian said.

'How soon can you kill him?'

Shocked, Spandarian stopped walking. He lit a cigarette. 'Can you tell me why?' He waited for the answers to the questions about Calder that had plagued him since he took office.

'How soon?'

'Subtlety, that is the essence of my job. Why I was given it, I believe.' Kirov should write a treatise on the art of evasion, Spandarian thought.

Impatiently, Kirov said: 'Let me put it this way: I want Calder dead and I want him dead as soon as possible. I understand the need for subtlety as you put it. That's why I'm giving you twenty-one days – in the interests of burgeoning defectors all over the world. But if you can't do the job *subtly* within that time then I shall hand the job over to the Executive Action Department. If you succeed then there's another job waiting for you – head of the First Chief Directorate. A well placed stepping stone, eh, Comrade Spandarian, to the chairmanship of State Security and ultimately to the Politburo which is where, I understand, you have your sights set upon.'

For the last time Spandarian asked: 'Why?'

'That's quite simple. As far as the Soviet Union is concerned Robert Calder is the most dangerous man in the world.'

Chapter 11

It was Katerina's birthday, she was twenty and Calder was thankful because now he wasn't quite so old. While she attended a women's rally he went shopping for a present in the open-air animal market.

Rabbits, guinea pigs and white mice twitched whiskers at him. Pigeons pulsed their throats and canaries sang about freedom. Tiny fish hung in jam-jars of water like irridescent pendants. Puppies of dubious parentage yapped beside peerless aristocrats.

It was a puppy that Katerina wanted. In the apartment on Leningradsky? he had queried. Why not? Every other apartment was a kennel – at the end of the corridor the Litvaks had a puppy which seemed to be developing into a St Bernard.

Just the same Calder looked for a puppy without elephantine potential as he pushed his way through the elbowing crowds past breeders, dealers and gypsies.

But his thoughts weren't entirely with puppies. It was Saturday, a week since the incident outside the car mart. According to Jessel the dent on the Volga could have been made by a flying stone.

'And the gunshot?'

'You said yourself there was a thunderstorm overhead.'

'It sounded like a shot to me.'

'How would you know? You said it coincided with a crack of thunder.'

Calder wavered. But he had felt an impact. Had swerved. He wished he had stopped and investigated. But stop is what you don't do when you think someone is trying to put a bullet through your brain.

Dalby had been more scathing than Jessel. 'If they wanted to kill you they would have brought in a pro, a marksman. The bullet hit the wing of your car. Some m . . . marksman.'

'Perhaps he was distracted.'

'KGB snipers don't get distracted.' They had skirted two lovers lying among the birch trees in Sokolinki Park. 'You're getting neurotic about death. Kreiber falls into a hole in the ice in a drunken stupor, Bertoldi jumps out of the window, Maclean dies of cancer . . . . You must have been disappointed when van Doorn turned up after his couple of gay days.'

Calder hadn't pursued it. He glanced at his watch. A week to the minute when he *thought* he had felt the impact. Had glimpsed death.

He bought a puppy with a brown nose.

The rally was held two miles from the animal market on the scimitar-shaped island south of the Kremlin formed by the Moscow River and a drainage canal dug in the eighteenth century to divert flood water.

The idea was to meet outside the gardens in Bolotnaya Square where Pugashev, who led a peasant revolt against the

Czar in 1785, was executed, and march down Ossipenko, named after a woman pilot killed in an accident in 1939. An inspired choice. Embryonic Bolshevism *and* feminism. Katerina's choice.

But Katerina had lost her zest for the movement because she knew she was being allowed to protest only if she continued to pass on information about Calder. And that was no protest at all: it was miserable compromise.

But, she reminded herself, that was no reason to abandon feminism. Their crusade was no less worthy because of private torment. Look at those banners unfurling in the sunshine EQUALITY FOR WOMEN and WE'VE NOTHING TO LOSE BUT OUR APRON STRINGS.

Svetlana said: 'Your heart doesn't seem in it these days. Is there anything wrong, pussycat?'

'Nothing.' Katerina tied the blue silk scarf that Svetlana had given her for her birthday round her neck. The mannish looking woman who had spoken the day they razed the assembly hall was winding up. At last. The hundred or so women gazing at the fountains in the gardens shifted impatiently. They had come to march.

'Are you in love with this Calder?'

'Don't be ridiculous. He's twice my age. And he's a defector.'

'Weak you mean?'

'I don't mean anything of the sort,' and was annoyed with herself for answering so hotly.

Svetlana, a Nordic vision in saffron, smiled, cat-like.

Then they began their march, a small rehearsal of things to come. This time they had been given permission and militia in summer uniforms walked beside them. Across the river they could see the spires and the Great Palace of the Kremlin.

Despite everything Revolution began to stir once more in the soul of Katerina Ilyina as they marched over the drained marshes where the market gardens of Muscovy had once flourished.

What right had men to use women?

She smiled fiercely.

Svetlana smiled back. 'That's better,' she said.

The march passed off without incident. Katerina was quite disappointed.

To celebrate her birthday they drank pink champagne in Katerina's home while the puppy sniffed its way around the living room.

'To the best daughter in the world,' Sasha cried emotionally. He flung his glass against the wall and apologised to his wife.

Katerina's mother shook her head sorrowfully. A true Russian, the shake implied. Incorrigible. To Calder she said: 'This must be a very long article you are writing.'

'The *National Geographic* is very thorough.' Calder looked at Katerina; she looked away.

Sasha raised his glass again. 'To the *Geographic*. May your article go on for ever.' This time he didn't throw his glass. 'So what do we call the dog? Kata?'

'It's a boy,' Calder said.

'Then we shall call it Nicki,' Sasha announced for no apparent reason. He began to sing.

On the way to Leonid Agursky's concert Calder and Katerina saw a couple of gutter drunks being tossed into a van bound for a sobering-up station. Only yesterday *Izvestia* had been pontificating about alcoholism and absenteeism. It had also contained an item about two drunken teenagers who had knifed each other in Gorky Park.

Inside the concert hall on the Lenin Hills Calder felt old again. All around him in the dusky, light-spangled atmosphere he could see Youth.

Katerina held his arm; she must have sensed that he had grown old again. She said: 'You're looking very smart tonight, Robert.'

Not young! He was wearing a short-sleeved shirt striped in red and blue and a pair of flared slacks from long ago. She wore Levi jeans and a pink blouse. He could see her nipples through the cotton.

Agursky was good, no doubt about it. Apparently Katerina

90

had met him on a bus; she had attended another concert and he had invited her to this one and told her to bring a friend. He was Ukrainian and he sang folk songs in a voice that yearned for his land. He also sang pop – the songs of David Tukhamov, the Jewish composer who wrote *Farewell Moscow* for the 1980 Olympics, and old Beatles' numbers. He also recited Yevtushenko. Calder felt Katerina's hand tighten on his arm; he suspected she was a little in love with Agursky.

The applause was prolonged and wild. After three encores the spotlight and strobes were dashed and Calder and Katerina went to the dressing room.

Agursky was drowning in sweat. 'Happy Birthday,' he said to Katerina and gave her a bottle of Chanel. 'From Paris. I had it with me the day we met.'

She kissed him on the cheek. 'What were you of all people doing on a bus?'

He grinned. 'There weren't any taxis.'

There was warmth and strength in his high-cheekboned face, Calder thought. When Katerina introduced them Agursky said: 'I shall be going to New York in the winter. Perhaps we can meet? I shall be very lost there.'

'Not for long,' Calder said. 'Not you.'

'But we can meet?'

'I hope so,' Calder said.

'I hope you didn't mean that about seeing him in New York,' Katerina said later over dinner in the Praga Restaurant on Arbat Street.

'It would be kind of tricky, wouldn't it?'

'You've never told me about leaving America. About your wife, son . . ..'

'You mean you don't know?'

'Some of it. Yes, I know some of it. But not the inner truth: the way you felt.'

Later in his apartment he told her. Starting with the letter he received from his brother, Dean, in Vietnam.

'It was full of spent passion. Passion for his country, for the

91

great crusade, for a future floodlit with promise. A passion that had become a haemorrhage in a distant country. By the time I received the letter he was dead.'

There were tears in Calder's eyes. She sat beside him on the sofa.

'Not that any of this is any excuse: I'm just telling you how it was. When Dean went to war a friend called Gary kind of moved in. He'd always been around, I guess, but when a void suddenly appeared there he was. Dear old Gary. But could he talk, could he ever talk. If he'd been a Kremlin PRO the whole world could be Communist today. Golden words, shining words, persuasive words. He was at Harvard, I was a kid waiting in the wings, easy meat. I often wonder why he bothered. Perhaps he was rehearsing his speeches for the day he made it. Then he sold out. To everything that had outraged us. To the Pentagon, would you believe.'

'And you?'

The cries of children prolonging dusk in the public gardens reached them through the half-open window. The apartment smelled of evening and carnations.

'I met another persuasive tongue. A lonely man in a sandwich parlour called Elsie's. He could talk, too. But he was more practical. He made *sense* out of everything. No dreams. He talked about Dean's death, the pointless deaths of thousands of other kids. I was caught on the rebound, I guess. And he talked about equality. Not the old generalisation, a classless society, all that stuff. No, he talked about practical equality. Ways of achieving it. If secrets could be traded – arms, policies, subversive intentions – with or without the knowledge of the world's leaders then a balance of power could be established. Most of all,' Calder said, 'he talked about blowing the identities of clandestine agents in the seats of power. Blow those on both sides and the teeth of aggression would be pulled.'

'And your wife?'

'Let's not run ahead.'

It was the first time he had told the whole story. It was a haemorrhage.

He poured them both brandy.

'Ruth. She was beautiful. Straight. If you told a lie it hung between you and shrivelled. We met when I was at Harvard studying law and got married too soon.'

Reddish hair skipping in the salt breeze.

'Also from one of the first families of Boston. Then I graduated and through my father got this incredible job in Washington. If you can't beat them join them. And become an in-fighter. Can you imagine, a Harvard graduate, subverted by a Soviet agent – because that's what the bastard was – suddenly attached to the team of lawyers advising the Secretary of State? With access to classified material! What a chance to implement everything that lonely young man had said in between bites of king-sized sandwiches.'

He saw doubt in her eyes. He tried to wipe it out.

'That wasn't the whole of it. Revenge? Sure, that was there. Wounded ego? Maybe. The sense of clandestine importance that fuels every spy? No doubt about it.'

Katerina nodded, acknowledging human frailty. 'And did you supply the Soviet Union with a lot of information?'

'Nothing world-shattering. I was blown too soon. By my wife. I tried to keep up the pretence but with Ruth it was hopeless. One day I told her. I tried to make her understand, pleaded with her. She woke Harry and took him to her parents' house as though I were contaminated. Then she went to the FBI. I was tipped off and got out of the States just in time. That was five years ago and I haven't seen Ruth since. Or Harry . . . .'

Today was Saturday and Harry would be on a sailboat with his instructor. Other boys would be sailing with their fathers. What had Harry been told? That his father was a traitor? What did he tell the other boys? That was what terrified Calder: that his son had to carry his disgrace. The story had never broken publicly but on Beacon Hill they would know.

'I've lost you,' Katerina said.

'I was on a boat.'

'Come back into harbour.'

He stood up and walked to the window. Although it was dark

93

the day's heat was still rising from the ground. Galaxies of stars looked down.

Katerina said: 'I don't understand why you're a privileged defector. This apartment, a dacha in the country, a director at the Institute . . . . If you didn't pass on any important secrets why are you so important?'

But he couldn't tell her. From the moment you were suborned you were wedded to deceit.

She was standing behind him. He turned and kissed her.

She lay naked on the bed and he slid into her so easily. They moved together and he knew that this had been sealed long ago with a smile on a cold winter day. Pausing, he looked into her eyes and saw that the challenge in them had been replaced by need. Momentarily it scared him, that nakedness of the mind: he felt as if he were looking into a holy place. They moved as one again, oiled and urgent, possessing, sharing, deeper, her hands clawing his back, breasts pushing at his chest, the need swelling . . . . He came first, then she cried out. They slept a little. Then she made him hard again and climbed upon him and sank upon him and this time the need had been replaced by pure and wonderful lust. When Calder next awoke it was a chiming, sunlit Sunday morning. She stirred beside him and whispered his name. Then she whimpered. And as she surfaced from sleep he saw a shadow of fear cross her face. Then she saw him and smiled and held out her arms and gathered him to her.

Chapter 12

The mushroom-hunters, led enthusiastically by Mrs Lundkvist, met in a birch forest twelve miles south-west of Moscow the following Saturday.

Calder brought Katerina. Dalby was there. Even Jessel who

occasionally rubbed shoulders with treachery in the line of duty.

'Beware the Death Cap,' said Mrs Lundkvist gaily as, ferreting in the dead leaves with a walking stick, she led her *gribniki* through sun-slatted glades.

Beside Calder and Katerina walked an English defector named Fellows who always carried with him a Bryant and Mays matchbox containing a specimen of his native soil. 'I may never stand on it again,' he frequently confided, 'but at least I'll die close to it.'

He was in his late seventies with wasted features and a tick in one eye. He had crossed the Great Divide in 1939, served in the Red Army in the Siege of Leningrad and been packed off to a labour camp for five years for his pains. He wore what appeared to be an Old Etonian tie but was in fact Thames Harriers, and he followed cricket as best he could on BBC World Service. He was always keen to make friends but no one took to him: he was the ghost of the future.

'It's good to see you young people taking part in group activities,' Fellows said.

Flattered, Calder lied, 'You're looking pretty sprightly yourself.'

'I lived in Suffolk. We used to gather mushrooms from the fields in the morning.' His faded eyes gazed across Europe. 'The fields used to be covered with dew. It sparkled like diamonds in the sunlight.'

Katerina said: 'Why did you defect, *Gaspadeen* Fellows? You seem to love England.'

He focused his eyes on her. 'I forget,' he said.

Dalby joined them. 'I wonder who will be the first to stop for refreshment.'

'Bennett,' Calder guessed.

Bennett, an Australian journalist, was the heaviest drinker among them. He was middle-aged with booze-bright cheeks and a small grey moustache stuck to his lip like a postage stamp. He and Fellows wrote to each other to make sure their letter-boxes weren't perpetually empty; other defectors had catalogues sent to themselves. Bennett was already nipping from a worn silver hip-flask.

The *gribniki* began to spread out, younger members pushing ahead in search of exciting fungi.

Mrs Lundkvist cried out: 'We'll remuster in two hours by the cars. At 1200 hours. Synchronise your watches.' She peered at her wristwatch. 'Don't eat any fruitbodies until you've checked them with me. And don't get up to any wickedness.' Laughing, she winked at Calder and Katerina; as she laughed her grey-blonde hair tied in a pony-tail bounced on her shoulders like the tail of a dog.

Dalby said: 'Do you two want to be alone?'

Calder shook his head. He liked people to see Katerina and himself together. And he liked to share people with her. Since they had first made love there was a sheen of satisfaction about her.

Accompanied by Dalby and Jessel they plunged deeper into the silver woods leaving Fellows behind in Suffolk. Heat was collecting under the fragile foliage. Calder took off his tweed jacket and hung it over his arm. He touched Katerina's neck above her white blouse. She smiled at his touch.

It was Katerina who made the first sighting. Three red-capped toadstools with white gills and stems straight from a nursery picture book. 'Careful,' Calder cautioned, consulting a photo-copy of Mrs Lundkvist's do's and don'ts.

'Fly agaric,' Dalby told them. 'Once known as Soma, the symbol of immortality. Siberians used to get stoned on them before they discovered vodka.'

Jessel said: 'Let's hope Bennett doesn't know that.'

'But there's nothing wrong with these,' Dalby said pointing with his stick at a clutch of mushrooms with brown velvet caps. 'B-brown birch boletus. They feed reindeer on them in the north. Fine for humans provided the maggots haven't got there first.' He picked one. 'No, these are okay,' plucking the others and putting them in his basket.

'You seem to know a hell of a lot about mushrooms,' Jessel said.

'Of course. Russians love their mushrooms. I'm a Russian.'

96

He folded a smile towards Katerina. With his longish grey hair and his basket Dalby looked almost matronly.

The birch trees thickened into sturdier deciduous trees. Calder found a growth of yellow fungi. They looked like seaweed with fronds upright in still water. 'Chanterelle,' Dalby said. 'Marvellous cooked with butter. But, of course, it's too early in the season for the best fruitbodies.'

They passed Russians foraging in the woods. In the late summer some of them would devote a whole weekend to the hunt and store their harvest and their memories throughout the winter.

Katerina was about to pick a mushroom with an olive umbrella-head growing under an oak tree when Dalby shouted: 'Don't touch.' When she had recovered he said: '*Amanita phalloides*, better known as the Death Cap. Deadly. Responsible for most fungi deaths.' He kicked the mushroom. They could smell its honeyed breath.

They walked out of the wood into a field where mushrooms grew in enchanted circles. 'Horse mushrooms,' Dalby said. 'Delicious,' and began to gather them. Calder and Katerina filled their baskets; the chocolate-coloured gills smelled of aniseed.

They left the basket in a shady corner of the field for a while and explored an almost deserted village built around a water-pump; then they headed back to the cars.

Bennett was sitting on the grass with his back to his car, a little Zaparozhet; Fellows was fiddling with a radio trying to find out how England were faring against the West Indies – 'Badly,' he prophesied; Fabre was breathing into an asthma inhalant. Mrs Lundkvist, basket brimming with fungi, was talking animatedly to two of the younger defectors; she liked the company of younger people because, she was wont to say, they kept her young; of Mr Lundkvist there was no sign.

Dalby produced a bottle of Ukrainian pepper vodka, Barzhomi mineral water, black bread and red caviar. 'Half p . . . peasant, half prince,' he said.

They tossed back the firewater, doused its flames with Barzhomi and swallowed lifebelts of red-smeared black bread.

Calder lay down to take the sun; Katerina lay beside him; their hands touched and were still.

Jessel wandered into the forest. Dalby slept. Bennett sang songs from the outback. Insect noise was sonorous around them.

An hour later Calder and Katerina drove back to Moscow in the new, slightly chipped Volga. Jessel dropped into Calder's apartment for a beer, stayed five minutes and left. Then Calder and Katerina made love.

Katerina left at five just before Lidiya, who had volunteered for the specialised job of preparing the mushrooms, arrived.

When Katerina arrived home Sasha was watering the geraniums on the narrow balcony and her mother was preparing dinner.

Sasha, dripping watering-can in his hand, asked: 'Is everything all right, *dochka?* You seem to have been troubled lately.'

'Everything's fine.'

'The American?'

'A good friend.'

'Be careful, *dochka*. We are different people.'

'Then we shouldn't be,' Katerina said with spirit.

He looked at her with the ancient wisdom that occasionally sobered his exuberance. 'Perhaps one day you will tell your mother and me the truth about *Gaspadeen* Calder.'

She went to her room and lay on the bed. She could still feel Calder inside her. She had never believed that love could be so sensitive and so raw. And as for loving a foreigner, a middle-aged man, a defector . . . it was absurd.

But the lines on his face were finding direction again and he moved with purpose and now he appreciated this city of hers and his strong hands were tender.

And she was betraying him.

Soon I will tell him.

She gazed at her possessions. Dolls, a painting of poppies in a wheatfield, a balalaika, a champagne cork slotted with a kopek, posters of Lenin and Yuri Gagarin and the Rolling Stones, a photograph of Svetlana and one of her boyfriends, *samizdat* tracts on feminism bought in a park not far from the Kremlin, one of Sasha's recordings, a poem from a boy long ago.

All pre-Calder.

And the strange thing was that if she had ever been asked to describe the man she would one day love he wouldn't have looked unlike Leonid Agursky.

She turned her head into the pillow; it smelled of lavender and cleanliness. And she consoled herself: 'I haven't told Spandarian anything that could have harmed Calder. Never will. Just snippets of useless information. Such as the time and place of the mushroom hunt. How could that hurt anyone?'

Calder's contact from the Second Municipal Hospital arrived while Lidiya was cleaning the mushrooms in the kitchen before cooking some of them for Calder's supper.

He was a student pathologist named Talin who intended to specialise in forensic investigation. He was the brother of a Russian in Calder's section at the Institute and Calder had paid him fifty roubles to examine the flakes of paint from the chip in the Volga.

Calder nodded towards the kitchen, put his finger to his lips and led Talin into the living room. Talin, bearded and precise, said: 'You needn't worry, it's all here,' handing Calder a buff envelope.

The analysis was exhaustive. Composition of the paint, number of coats . . . . The gunshot came at the bottom of the sheet:

Faint traces of lead, steel and nitrocellulose compatible with client's theory that indentation was made by a bullet. If estimates of indentation and restricted range are correct impact was probably caused by a 7.62 mm bullet.

Talin was going to go far.

Calder handed him twenty-five roubles, the balance of his fee.

When Talin had gone he sat on the sofa.

Why had the attempt on his life been bungled? As Dalby had pointed out the KGB would have employed a pro. Perhaps

99

lightning had struck as the marksman pulled the trigger. They would make sure there wasn't any threat of a thunderstorm next time!

Now? He stared through the window across dusty tree-tops.

He drank some vodka and, when the bottle was half empty, went to sleep in the coffin that was his bed leaving his supper untouched.

Lidiya, Calder learned later, became ill seven hours after she left the apartment. She had stomach pains and vomited but assumed that she was suffering from gastro-enteritis to which she was prone.

She died three days later in Golitsin Hospital from irreparable damage to the liver and kidneys caused by cytolytic poisoning.

There was absolutely no doubt, the casualty officer told Calder, that she had died from eating *amanita phalloides*, the Death Cap mushroom. The KGB, he confided, had asked him to falsify the cause of death 'but I told them to get fucked.'

Calder remembered the curls at the nape of her neck and her patient ways and her love for the little boy who wore his red Young Pioneer scarf with the pride he inherited from his mother and, knowing that he was the cause of her death, wept.

The following day he drew ten thousand roubles from the Bank for Foreign Trade on Neglinnaya Street and handed it to Lidiya's stricken parents who shared her apartment. 'For the boy,' he said and left.

He asked Talin to analyse the untouched mushrooms in the refrigerator. They were mostly *arvensis*, horse mushrooms, he reported, but *amanita phalloides* was there in small but deadly quantities.

Most peasant women would have spotted the lethal interloper which was the same height as the horse mushroom but not Lidiya: she was city.

Accident? Calder didn't even consider the possibility. It was the second attempt on his life. The killer fungi must have been put into the basket when he and Katerina had left it in the field. And Mrs Lundkvist, occupied with the younger generation, had only made a cursory inspection of its contents.

For a while Calder fatalistically accepted the inevitable. He had caused Lidiya's death. Let the assassins get on with it before any more innocents died.

Then two unrelated events occurred which irrevocably changed his character.

'He knows,' said the Estonian. He was blond with a weight-lifter's physique and a high-pitched voice and he irritated Spandarian.

'How do you know that?' Spandarian ran his hand through his glistening hair; when he withdrew it his fingers were dressed with oil and spices.

'A student pathologist named Talin visited him twice. I stopped him the second time.'

'Why not the first?'

'After the incident with the sniper you warned me to be careful.'

'Incident! Anyone would think you bumped into him in a crowd, not kicked him off a cliff and half killed him.'

'He's dead now,' the Estonian told Spandarian. 'Complications set in.'

'How unfortunate,' said Spandarian who knew this to be true because he had arranged for the life-support machine to be disconnected from the marksman in the Golitsin, the same hospital where Calder's woman had died. They had been unlucky there: if Calder had eaten his supper as he normally did at 8 pm he would be dead now. 'What did this Talin tell you?'

'That Calder knows someone tried to shoot him. That he also knows that someone tried to poison him.'

'So he'll be ducking.'

But not, Spandarian thought, scented fingers toying with a 1980 Olympics cigarette lighter on his desk, from accident or natural causes. You couldn't duck the unseen, the unsuspected.

If Katerina Ilyina could be persuaded to lure Calder to some little love nest in an apartment high enough to ensure death on impact with the ground . . . multiple injuries . . . .

They said that Bertoldi seemed to have floated. Spandarian

101

saw Calder floating, death snarl on his face. Not as subtle as he would have wished but time was running out.

As Kirov had pointed out when he had summoned Spandarian to his office in Dzerzhinsky Square. Staring at him across a battery of coloured telephones on his desk, the Chairman of the KGB had said: 'You have three days left. If Calder isn't dead by then I shall hand the contract to the Executive Action Department.'

And I, brooded Spandarian, will never be head of the First Chief Directorate. Or reach the Politburo for that matter.

As usual Jessel, wearing earphones, swept Calder's apartment with a bug detector. He paused beneath the painting of mauve flowers growing in Siberia and, without speaking, pointed at the wall. From his executive briefcase he took an electronic microphone eliminator and, placing it beneath the painting, switched it on.

'So,' he said, 'our friends really are interested in you. Are you going to tell me why?'

'Because they want me dead,' Calder said. He told Jessel about the positive ballistics test. And about Lidiya's death.

'That could have been an accident . . . . But no, I guess you're right. But why do they want to kill you?'

Calder didn't reply.

'It's odd,' Jessel said. He sat down and lit his pipe. 'One botched shooting, one poisoning. It's as though two different brains were at work.'

Calder remembered the smell of Lidiya's *borsch* wafting from the kitchen. The sparrow that had flown into the apartment, an omen. He shrugged. 'Maybe, maybe not. There's not a lot I can do about it either way.'

'A sitting target? That's not like you, the re-born Robert Calder. What about Katerina?'

'A dream. I'm twice her age.'

'Bullshit. In twenty years you'll be fifty-eight. Young if you keep jogging.' The sparrow's claws guarding his eyes were sheathed. 'And she'll be forty.'

'Last time we met I was her grandfather.'

'Go to her,' Jessel said. 'You're going to need her . . . .' His soft voice trailed; he stared at the bowl of his pipe. 'I'm afraid I haven't brought good news.'

'Harry?'

Jessel nodded. 'He was hit by the jib of a sail. He's in hospital. A fractured skull.'

Calder began to shiver. 'Is he going to be okay?'

Jessel said carefully: 'His condition is critical.'

And I don't even know him.

But Jessel was right: he needed Katerina.

He drove blindly towards the second occurrence that was to change him.

As he cut the engine in the parking lot on Leningradsky he noticed Katerina talking to a man at the entrance to the apartment block.

Who was the man? Wavy hair, luxuriant moustache . . . for one ridiculous moment he reminded him of Spandarian, the KGB officer whom the Twilight Brigade knew to be their real but little-seen general. Calder had seen him once climbing into his black curtained Volga outside the Institute.

Whoever he was he was talking animatedly to Katerina. Until, abruptly, he turned on his heel and walked towards the parking lot.

A driver opened the door of a *black curtained Volga* for him.

When Spandarian had gone Calder drove, more calmly this time, to a bar near Red Square called the Chaika. It wasn't unlike the public bar of a British pub. Workers from a building site were guzzling beer, snapping at shrimps and tiny crabs and dropping the shells and scales on the floor.

Calder ordered a beer.

So that was how the gunman had known he would be at the used car mart.

That was how a killer had known he would be on the mushroom hunt.

So simple. He should have guessed.

In America his own people were against him. In Russia the one person he had trusted was against him. That was equality for you.

103

A terrible exhilaration overcame Calder.
He finished his beer and strode out of the bar.
Calder was running.

Chapter 13

Calder had for some time been vaguely aware of a blur in his
vision while driving. As dormant instincts for survival surfaced
the blur came into focus in his driving mirror. A battered cream
Volga.

After finishing his beer in the Chaika he parked his own
Volga near Manezh Square. His freshly kindled intuition told
him that he could never drive it again – they might even put a
bomb under it. He walked across Red Square and went into the
Government Department Store, GUM.

Lunchtime shoppers and tourists thronged the arcades and
galleries linked by bridges beneath vaulted glass roofs. He
walked casually, paused beside a woman wearing a rainbow-
hooped dress and a small boy with cropped hair staring at the
fountain.

Accelerating, he elbowed his way to a flight of stairs, climbed
them three at a time and ran along the second-floor gallery of
shops. Half way down it, before any pursuer could have
reached the gallery, he turned abruptly onto a wrought-iron
bridge and jumped onto the ground-floor arcade.

Startled shoppers jumped aside.

He ran for the exit leaving outrage in his wake. In Razin
Street he hailed a taxi with a green light on its windshield and
told the driver to take him to Gastronom No. 1 on Gorky
Street.

He approached his apartment block warily on foot. He
needed documents, ID, money. Another taxi, identifiable by
the chequered pattern on the door, was parked near the arch.
The militia used souped-up cabs. Two men sat in the back;

they both wore lightweight topcoats; only policemen wore coats on a day stunned with heat.

He continued down Gorky Street. Without ID – workpass and internal passport – he was impotent.

He took a cab to Komsomolskaya metro station and telephoned Jessel.

Jessel arrived at Komsomolskaya – with its ornate ceilings and chandeliers, more like an underground cathedral than a subway station – half an hour later. Calder met him, as arranged, under the third chandelier from the foot of the escalators.

When he heard what Calder had to say he said: 'You must be out of your skull.'

Calder said: 'Bring me temporary ID and cash. I'll meet you in two hours.'

Beside them two women remonstrated with a youth who had thrown an apple core on the marble floor. Heads lowered, crowds streamed towards escalators and trains.

Jessel said: 'Don't you understand? We can't help you. You betrayed your country. You aren't wanted back there.'

'In Sokolinki Park,' Calder said. 'By the fountain.'

'You're crazy. Give me one good reason why Washington should help you to re-defect.'

Calder gave him six.

If I were Calder what would I do?

First go to ground in Moscow until the heat dies down, Spandarian decided. But just in case Calder reasoned differently he put a cage round Moscow.

He spread a map of the city and its environs across his desk. Then he telephoned orders for all airports, railway stations, and militia road patrols on the 40-kilometre limit for visitors to be alerted. He also requested militia assistance to watch all exits where the metro burrowed outside the cage.

He replaced the receiver and lit a cigarette; the smoke made devious grey patterns in the afternoon sunlight. *The most dangerous man in the world*. What the hell had Kirov been talking about?

105

The phone rang. Kirov. He already knew that Calder had made a break for it. His words dropped in Spandarian's ear like pellets of ice. Spandarian had failed . . . forget the time limit . . . the Executive Action Department had now been ordered to liquidate Calder. But if Spandarian killed him first? Then, Kirov conceded, there was still a remote chance that he might become head of the First Chief Directorate.

Spandarian put down the telephone and gazed through the window towards the Kremlin. Then he applied himself to the inside of the cage.

He summoned a deputy to the office and told him to alert all KGB informants in hotels, hostels, restaurants, cafés, bars, thieves' kitchens, cinemas, parks, sports stadiums, anywhere that *stukachi* were planted.

The Executive Action Department would be doing the same but in the case of Calder he had the edge because he had his own informants within the Twilight Brigade. He called his driver and told him to take him to Dalby's apartment on Prospect Mira near the Ostankino television tower.

Although it was long past lunchtime Dalby was still wearing a dressing gown, once rich and red but now threadbare. Like its owner, Spandarian thought, accepting a glass of Armenian brandy and settling himself in a punished leather chair.

To the rest of the defectors Dalby was a mentor, an idealist who had found fulfillment in jaunty retirement. But not to Spandarian who made it his business to confront him before he had donned his mask. Dalby had one of those faces that invited you to peel back the years. Erase the slanting lines, re-texture the flesh, restore the pigment of the hair and there was the young Dalby quick with hope. Not many older faces encouraged this transition, only those on which a knowledge of waste had settled.

The living room was a mirror of the man. Crumbs of toast beneath the broken teeth of the gas-fire; a leaning pile of copies of English magazines *Country Life* and *Private Eye*; on the wall a speckled photograph of a family group staring defiantly through the passage of time and a black and white sketch which, according to Dalby, was an Aubrey Beardsley original. It was as though Dalby had tried to recreate the rooms in which he had lived when he was at Cambridge.

Spandarian had often wondered why Dalby had renounced his sunny heritage in favour of the haunted realism of espionage. Had he truly hoped to promote an alternative to fascism which, when he was young, was enslaving Europe? Hadn't he realised that the Soviet Union was also enslaved? Or had he believed that there was still time for true Marxism to arise from the ashes of the Revolution?

Unlikely – Dalby would have been too shrewd to accept such generalities. What had happened, Spandarian believed, was that a grand deception had been staged: Dalby, troubled by his own irresolute character, had deceived himself into accepting such beliefs. The Cause had become a substitute for moral fibre, intrigue the drug that sustained the deception.

But when the dosage had stopped – when Dalby had been forced to escape to Moscow – he had experienced withdrawal symptoms. And when he had traced them to their source he had seen only the grand deception. His reward for a life of deceit? Pensioned exile in an alien land.

'So what can I do for you?' Dalby asked. 'I don't imagine this visit is purely social.' He stood at the window where, on the sill, a dying fly buzzed intermittently.

'Calder. He's on the run.' As always they conversed in English.

'I'm n . . . not surprised. I warned you that he was becoming restless.' Just the same Dalby looked a little surprised, for him an extravagance.

'You didn't know?'

'Why should I? He would hardly seek refuge with me.'

'He might get in touch if he's desperate. If he does call me. And he may have confided in other defectors. Sound them out.'

'If you wish. You're very sure of me, aren't you?' The fly buzzed despairingly beside him.

'I'm not very sure of anyone. But I do know you regard it as your duty to report any traitors to The Cause. Very commendable.' Spandarian stroked the wings of his moustache.

'Traitors? That's a laugh. We're all traitors.'

'On the contrary, you're idealists, a cut above patriots.'

'Idealists? My dear fellow you're too kind. What am I, after all, but a g . . . grass. A super grass I believe they call them in Britain. Idealists? Is Fellows an idealist wearing a spurious Old Etonian tie, warbling about cricket and carting a matchbox full of English soil around with him? Is Bennet an idealist searching for his convictions at the bottom of an ever-empty glass? Is Fabre an idealist listening to his lungs wheezing with guilt and acting like an emaciated Maurice Chevalier, God rest his soul? Is idealism seeking justification for your actions and saving p . . . pressed flowers from the land of your birth?'

'But surely you all had ideals. All that's happened is that they've aged, like all values.'

'What you're saying, my dear chap, is that age merely contradicts our expectations. That maturity is only a clouding of vision. Or is age truth?'

Spandarian said abruptly: 'As you're in such a cynical mood tell me – why did you turn on your own kind?'

'Ah, there you have me. I would like to profess belief in equality, or some p . . . platitude. But that wouldn't fool you for one minute would it, Comrade Spandarian? You're far too clever. You know something? I envy you: you've never doubted. You're no more a communist than I am but you accept the society into which you were born and you intend to prosper in it.'

Spandarian lit a yellow cigarette and blew smoke in the direction of a vase of spent carnations. 'What bothers me at the moment,' he said, 'is why, after all these years, you've suddenly become indiscreet.'

'Isn't it obvious? One of our flock has flown the nest. It makes me restless, rash.'

'Does that mean you envy him?'

'A difficult question, comrade. Calder is a younger man than I am. If he has found his convictions then, yes, I envy him. But if he is merely running because circumstances dictate it then he's welcome to his freedom.'

108

'Freedom? You make Moscow sound like a prison. And don't forget, Comrade Dalby, that one of the reasons he's running is that he fears for his life because of information laid by *you*. Why did you tell me about Calder's doubts? Did you envy those? Did all those who died because of information laid by you lose their lives because you envied them?'

The fly buzzed for the last time as, with a rolled-up copy of *Pravda*, Dalby swotted its upturned body. 'What is true is that you need have no fear that I will renege. No need for anyone to grass on the grass. For better or worse the c . . . corkscrew that has been my life has straightened out.'

'I'm glad to hear it.' Spandarian finished his brandy and stood up. 'Now tell me, where in Moscow would Calder arrange to meet a contact before making the real break?'

'Sokolinki Park,' Dalby told him.

From a call-box outside the apartment block Spandarian called the Estonian who had lost Calder in GUM. He told him to change his car and drive to Sokolinki. If he caught Calder, there was just a chance that he wouldn't be posted to Yakut in Siberia, the coldest territory in the northern hemisphere.

What Calder had forgotten was that there was a Japanese trade fair at the exhibition site in Sokolinki. The Japanese pavilion, deceptively fragile with silk screens and water gardens, stood near the American hall, a geodesic dome that had lingered there, spanning more than a quarter of a century of Russo-American suspicion. Businessmen in lightweight suits from Comecon and capitalist countries thronged the site near the entrance to the park.

Calder waited at the fountain where he normally met Dalby. He had considered calling Dalby. But no, Dalby was devious – and honest about it. 'Everything is a deception,' he had once told Calder. 'We deceive ourselves: we are our most gullible enemies. Values, ideals, aspirations – all fraudulent.'

Despite the crowds, despite the grey lightweight that made him look like a foreign buyer, Calder felt conspicuous. If it was true that one in twelve Soviet citizens had KGB contacts then

109

he had twenty million enemies!

Jessel said: 'Okay, let's walk. And talk. And it had better be good.'

'You brought cash and ID?'

'First the proof.'

Calder guessed that Jessel had been in touch with Washington otherwise there wouldn't have been any documents or money. He shook his head. 'That isn't the deal.'

'We don't have a deal yet.'

'We will,' Calder said.

He set out across the park where falcons once plundered. A military band was playing chirpily on a bandstand. Calder looked for a place to talk. The birch wood where he and Dalby had once kept indiscretions in deep-freeze was now sighing with lovers. He scanned the amusement park and shooting gallery, finally settled on the open-air theatre; they were showing a mime about the Great Patriotic War but on this balmy summer afternoon not many Muscovites had any stomach for it. Calder and Jessel sat in a wilderness of empty seats at the back of the theatre.

Calder said: 'Okay, give.'

Reluctantly, Jessel handed over the ID and a wad of used ten-, five- and three-rouble bills. Calder examined the forged internal passport complete with Moscow registration. He was Ivan Yacob, a computer hardware specialist from Irkutsk in the Far East of Siberia. Height, weight *et cetera* were accurate as near as dammit; the head-and-shoulders photograph was too young but that was a common discrepancy in Soviet documents.

'It will do for now,' Calder said.

'Now your side of the bargain.'

In a quiet voice Calder spelled it out, fleshing the skeletons he had dangled in Komsomolskaya metro station.

The brief of KGB agents such as Fuchs, Philby and Blunt, he told Jessel, had not been merely to pass on secrets: they had been charged with recruiting successors before retiring or defecting.

But not junior league successors: they had been ordered to steal the souls of young men who looked as if they were going

110

places. Steal enough and you were assured of a clutch of spies ultimately walking the corridors of power in the West.

Jessel said: 'And you're saying these sleepers were established?'

'What I'm saying is simply this: the West is blown. If a nuclear war broke out tomorrow the Soviet Union would win it.'

On stage six Red Army soldiers wordlessly counter-attacked the Germans outside Moscow. Ten empty rows in front of Calder and Jessel an old man snored.

'And you know the identities of these high-flying spies?'

'I know the codenames of *all* of them. They're the days of the week. I know the real names of six.'

'Who's missing?'

'The Man Who Was Saturday,' Calder said.

'And you want to trade the real identities in return for an assisted passage back to the States?'

'You'll have to get authority first.'

'You can say that again.'

'I want you to contact Washington again.'

'Who in Washington?'

'The President,' Calder said. 'Who else?'

The Estonian entered the park as the Red Army recaptured Kharkov.

He gazed uncertainly at the Japanese and their customers swarming round the trade pavilion. Then, picking his way through sun-reddened families sprawled on the grass, he made his way towards the birch woods.

Sweating beneath his jacket hanging awkwardly over his gun-holster, he explored the park through a pair of binoculars.

Hopeless. Siberia here I come.

He made a last, cursory sweep of the amusement park and, far away, the open-air theatre. He steadied the binoculars on the third row from the back.

And began to run.

Jessel said: 'Give me one name and I'll do it.'

Calder thought it over. He could hear the crackle of gunfire from the rifle range and piped music from an old-fashioned carousel. 'Okay,' he said after a while. 'It's a deal.'

'The name?'

Calder gave him one.

'Holy shit,' Jessel said.

'What I don't understand,' Jessel said, as they left the theatre, 'is why the comrades have allowed you to stay alive for so long.'

'I can only guess. The KGB always look after their servants. I had spied for them, defected when I was blown. Why would I try to destroy their network?'

'But all those deaths from natural causes, accidents . . . . You thought the defectors were being liquidated. You must have wondered if you would be next.'

'I suspect that Spandarian assesses a defector's breaking point. If he displays symptoms of reneging then he is killed in a way that won't alarm potential turncoats. Logical, I guess: they found evidence that both Maclean and Burgess were contemplating back-tracking.'

'Then,' Jessel said, dodging a small boy with a dripping ice-cream, 'I'll re-phrase my first question. Why are they so keen on killing you *now?*'

'A change at the top of State Security. Andropov was an honourable guy, so was his successor. But Kirov is a hard-liner. He can't see any justification in keeping alive the one man who could destroy the Soviet initiative in the West.' Calder smiled thinly. 'He has a point.'

Calder glanced behind him. He remembered the blur that had become a Volga. But in the windshield there had been a smaller blur. It cleared now. A blond head.

Calder dived through a game of volley-ball. The blond head followed. Calder ran down a path – into a gaggle of cyclists. Some wobbled onto the grass, a couple stopped abruptly tipping onto front wheels, three fell in a heap of threshing legs and spinning wheels; but Calder was through them.

He reached the amusement park. A children's ferris wheel rotated slowly beside the carousel. Cocoons of pink candy-floss floated around him. A girl with pigtails holding a goldfish in a plastic bag of water stared at him.

He looked back. The fair-haired man was gaining on him, parting the crowds with the pistol in his hand. Calder stopped by the shooting gallery and grabbed an ancient rifle from a youth about to take aim. The rifles were loaded with lead pellets; the object was to cut out the heart from a man-sized target. One burst could do the trick.

Calder swivelled and squeezed the trigger.

The blond head turned crimson.

Calder dropped the rifle and ran to the exit of the amusement park. A bicycle lay on the grass beside a man asleep beside an empty half-litre vodka bottle. He mounted it and pedalled towards the tiny outpost of Japan at the entrance to the park.

ADJOURNMENT

Chapter 14

The first part of Calder's message was relayed to President Gary Holden as he sat at the bedside of his dying father in Boston.

Holden rose, walked to the window and stared into the past. Games of chess, sandwiches at Elsie's, words like shining coins, treasure troves of them. But the words had been an indulgence of youth and, being older than Robert Calder, he had realised that first.

To give substance to those shining coins you had to manoeuvre, to compromise. And he had succeeded: like another young president before him, John F. Kennedy, he had given the American people a new resolve.

But while he had climbed, Calder had sunk. Calder's defection had disgusted him. But was I partly responsible? he asked himself as he gazed across the lawns where he had played as a boy.

It was possible. He had been a surrogate brother and, although he had been older, he hadn't been mature enough to understand how easily he could disillusion Calder. Hardly grounds for betraying your country but where would I be today if my brother had been killed in Vietnam?

And now Calder wanted to come back. The shadow on my conscience for the past five years.

The old man lying on the bed sighed, a rustling like wandering autumn leaves. Holden turned and smiled at him, but his father hadn't recognised him since he had arrived: he had returned to a past more real than the present. Holden watched two golden retrievers chasing each other across the grass; the garden reminded him of the Rose Garden outside the Oval Office – boxwood hedges, anemones, delphiniums and roses beneath crab-apple trees.

Not only was Calder hellbent on returning, he was proposing to bring with him the means to negate Soviet penetration in the West. *At the highest possible level*, according to Jessel.

Holden lifted his father's arm which was hanging beside the bed and placed it on the blanket. The old man looked at him through faded blue eyes and said: 'Most goals in one season? Easy one, Charlie. Phil Esposito, Bruins, 1970-71.'

In the corridor the nurse in crackling white said: 'He could stay like that for a long time, Mr President. But he's happy enough.'

Holden laid his hand on her shoulder. 'He's in good hands,' he said and walked down the great curve of the staircase to the hall. On a rosewood table he noticed a photograph of himself as a teenager standing in the stern of his father's yacht; the photograph had stood on his mother's bedside table until she had died three years ago. Holden picked it up. The young man, dark-haired and bold, smiled winningly at him, an electioneering smile even then. The smile had become more professional over the years and the dark hair had thinned but Holden was still a crusader, or so he believed.

Another similar snap had been taken at the same time. Calder in the stern of the boat. The photograph had been destroyed five years ago.

President and traitor. What extravagantly different directions their lives had taken. But whereas I knew where I was going, Calder had only wanted to be a successful lawyer. I changed all that.

Holden replaced the photograph on the table and admitted to himself that there was another reason why the prospect of Calder's re-defection perturbed him: Calder knew about those adolescent flirtations with communism and a youthful indiscretion could easily blight a re-election campaign.

He saw a newspaper headline. PRESIDENT ADMITS HELPING SPY TO FLEE RUSSIA. A gift from the gods for the Opposition. He shrugged. It was a risk he would have to take.

He summoned an aide standing in the corner of the hall and headed for the door. But what had made Calder renege after

118

five years in Russia?

He paused at the door, turned to the aide and said: 'Do me a favour, Dick, find the unlisted phone number for a Mrs Ruth Calder in Boston and get her on the line.'

He took the call in the living room and heard the splinters of anxiety in her voice.

'Gary? What do you want for Chrissake?'

'Bob wants to come back. I thought you might know why.'

A pause, a sob. 'Harry's been hurt. Maybe Bob knows.'

'Bad?'

'He got hit on the head boating. He's in intensive care. Fractured skull . . . .'

'Jesus, I'm sorry. Is there anything . . . ?'

'Nothing.' Another pause. Then incredulously: 'He wants to come *back?*' Holden imagined her distractedly combing at her short red-gold hair with her fingers. 'Are you going to help him?'

'Maybe.'

He could hear her breathing. 'He's got something to trade?'

'A lot. Would you have him back if he put the record straight?'

'Harry came out of his coma for a few moments last night. He asked after his father. After all those years . . . . Strange, isn't it? You know, old people when they're dying return to their youth.'

She began to cry.

For a moment it was his own wife, Helen, crying, his son, Tom, hurt. 'I'm sure he'll be okay,' he said inadequately.

He heard her trying to control the sobbing. Then: 'You know you were one of the reasons Bob did what he did.'

'I know it.' And gently: 'I asked you a question just now.'

'Would I have him back? I can't answer that, Gary. But if Harry regains consciousness again and asks about Bob can I tell him he's on his way?'

'Tell him,' Holden said.

He beckoned the aide and they walked down the marble steps to the black Mercedes.

Two Secret Service limousines shepherded the Mercedes to

Logan airport where Holden boarded the executive jet, which he used when he was travelling unofficially, to fly back to Washington to take delivery of the second half of the message from Moscow – the name of one high-flying spy.

The meeting of the nucleus of the National Security Council was held in the Cabinet Room in the West Wing of the White House.

Holden sat at the head of the mahogany table facing a portrait of Harry S. Truman. Appropriate because it was Truman who in 1952 had approved the formation of the NSA, the grey eminence of American Intelligence.

The Director of NSA, Howard Zec, sat two chairs away with his back to the blue drapes framing a window overlooking the Rose Garden. Zec was an admiral in the US Navy who had sailed into NSA via post-Pearl Harbor cryptology and Washington intrigue; white-haired and weatherbeaten, he looked expansive although he was in fact taciturn and reclusive.

Opposite him sat Louis B. Thurston, Director of the CIA, Yale and Justice Department. Scholarly-looking, in his mid-thirties. When most people remove spectacles they look nakedly vulnerable: Thurston looked calculating.

Even today, Holden reflected, most people believed that the backbone of US Intelligence was the CIA. Wrong. NSA, the National Security Agency which from its HQ at Fort Meade off the Baltimore-Washington Parkway kept watch over a global and spatial empire, was in charge.

Not that Thurston would have agreed. Animosity between him and Zec crackled across the long polished table bought for the Cabinet Room by Richard Nixon.

On Holden's right sat Secretary of State Howard Fliegel, a plump and affable diplomat who spent his leisure hunting game and retained his predatory instincts at the negotiating table.

On his left, Defence Secretary Martin Duff, beaky and wary, young for the job but aged prematurely by a workload of suspicion.

Farther down the table, next to Thurston, sat Donald Shoemaker, Holden's Assistant for National Security Affairs.

120

He was only thirty-eight and he was Holden's lifeline in clandestine waters. His fair hair was slicked down and he wore an aide's grey suit and a button-down collar but he still looked like a Californian lifeguard. Twice a week he and Holden played squash: Shoemaker always won.

Holden unbuttoned the jacket of his navy mohair and picked up the decoded print-out relayed by satellite from Moscow to the microwave tower at NSA headquarters and transferred by teletype to the Communications Room at the White House.

The name of a high-ranking defector was promised but it still hadn't been decoded at Fort Meade.

Holden began to talk. 'I'm sure everyone present here today remembers Robert Calder.' He glanced at Zec: the Director of the NSA probably knew already what was coming but his weatherbeaten features were expressionless. 'He was a KGB plant in the State Department and when he was blown he defected to the Soviet Union. With what we shall never know. Luckily the media never got hold of the story. Anyway, within the past few days Calder has been in touch with our Embassy in Moscow.'

'And he wants to return?' Thurston asked, taking off his spectacles and polishing them. Perhaps he knew too.

'Wouldn't you?' Zec said.

Holden went on: 'Naturally such a request wouldn't be considered unless Calder had something to trade. And he *claims* he has. The identities of six Soviet agents operating in the West. But not just any agents. According to Jessel, Calder has told him that hundreds of students were approached by KGB agents posing as knights in shining armour. The usual procedure?' Holden looking inquiringly at Zec and Thurston.

Zec said: '*Were* approached? Still are.'

'And in this particular operation the selection was made with great care. Only students with potential in public life were chosen. Students who could be turned – Vietnam was manna from heaven for the persuaders. Some were subsequently blackmailed. A hell of a lot of these young people were turned but the Soviets struck real 22-carat gold with seven of them.'

'I thought,' Duff remarked, 'that you said six just now.' He

121

crossed his legs and swung one nervously.

'Seven. Calder only knows the identities of six. Claims he knows,' Holden corrected himself.

'And we're supposed to believe him?' Fliegel asked incredulously. 'With respect, Mr President, when I go bargaining with a Head of State I take more persuasive weapons with me than that.'

Shoemaker said quietly: 'Maybe we haven't heard it all yet.' They should have been playing squash about now, Holden remembered.

He said sharply: 'I can assure you, gentlemen, that I wouldn't have brought you here today if I hadn't anything more concrete than a Judas promise. Calder has sent us the name of one of these agents. If he checks out then in my opinion we have to get Calder out of Russia.'

'I assume,' Fliegel said, drumming the table with his trigger finger, 'that all this information is reaching us by satellite. Can't the Soviets break the codes?'

'No way,' Zec told him. 'One-time pads. Unbreakable. An old trick in a new pack of cards.'

A jet crayonned a white line across the blue sky outside. A clock on the mantelpiece beneath Harry Truman began to chime.

Holden said: 'If you, Louis,' to Thurston, 'and you, Howard,' to Zec, 'find out that Calder's levelling then a whole lot of decisions have to be taken. What has to be done to this guy, whoever he is . . . .' The clock stopped chiming – 11 am. 'What we do with Calder *if* we get him out.'

Duff, the only smoker in the room, lit a cigarette, caught Holden's eye and crushed it in a silver ashtray after one drag. 'What I don't understand,' he said, 'is why Calder's changed direction.'

According to Jessel there was a contract out on Calder. There was also a girl. And Harry. Holden liked to think that the three factors had only been catalysts, that Calder now wanted to help his country.

Thurston gave his spectacles a final polish, replaced them and said: 'This is what I reckon happened. Calder escaped to

122

Russia with the identities of six high-ranking KGB agents under his belt. Right? The KGB were aware of it but what the hell, why would he blow them? More than his life was worth: if these six sleepers were blown the culprit would obviously be Calder. Bang.' Thurston put two fingers to his temple. 'Then the leadership of the KGB changes. A real hard bastard named Kirov takes over. He doesn't buy this theory. Once a traitor always a traitor. Why risk the whole Soviet intelligence operation in the West by keeping one miserable defector alive? At the same time the section of the KGB's Second Chief Directorate responsible for defectors steps up surveillance on Calder just as we do on Soviets granted asylum when they're getting restless. Calder is reported to be unhappy, disillusioned, whatever. Kirov's worst fears are realised. Calder has to be liquidated but he gets to hear about this. There's only one option left for him – he's got to get out.'

Zec said: 'My guess is that an attempt has already been made on his life.' He had a knack of sealing Thurston's theories with his own stamp.

Shoemaker asked: 'Do we know how Calder got these names in the first place?'

Holden shook his head.

'Obviously through Soviet contacts when he was spying in the State Department,' Thurston said.

'Obviously,' Zec said.

Holden said to Shoemaker: 'Why don't you go to Communications, Don? See if they've come up with this name yet.'

When Shoemaker returned he handed Holden a sealed buff envelope. Holden opened it. 'Well I'll be a sonofabitch,' he said.

The one possibility that hadn't occurred to him was that Calder had named a woman.

Shoemaker stayed to lunch. Ham salad, sorbet and half a bottle of Sancerre in the living quarters of the executive mansion. The dining area was informal – untidy, according to indignant servants; the morning newspapers were still piled on a marble-topped coffee table, rose petals spilled onto the bright

123

mahogany between the serving mats on the luncheon table; the room was a capsule of imprisoned summer.

When Helen, blonde and chic, had departed for a Third-World fund-raising rally, Holden said to Shoemaker: 'So, what do we do?'

'Wait till Calder's first offering is checked out, I guess.'

'And if it checks out?'

'Figure a way to get Calder out of the Soviet Union.' Shoemaker spooned raspberry sorbet, sunlight shivering on his hand.

Holden, sipping white wine, was, as always, re-assured by Shoemaker, the voice of sanity in the paranoic ambience of intelligence agencies.

He had been one of those gilded Californian young men who had inherited so many of life's bonuses that, in the search for variety, he had joined a set with a life-style verging on the decadent. But on the campus of UCLA he had found direction and, with a formidable scholastic record behind him, moved to Washington where he had become a leading authority on national security, believing, as Holden did, that world peace could only be preserved through strength.

His influence in clandestine circles in Washington was often resented. So, Holden suspected, were his age, looks and popularity with society hostesses.

Holden said: 'And what about the woman? What shall we do if Calder's information is correct?'

Shoemaker leaned back in his chair so that the sunlight quivered on his fair hair. 'Kill her,' he said.

At 4.30 that afternoon Marion Stacey Shannon, fifty year-old President of a multinational oil company, member of the Center for National Security Studies, a director of the Fund for Peace and frequent guest at Bilderberg conferences where, so it is often asserted, the champions of Western clout meet to devise economic strategy, received a call at her vacation home on Long Island summoning her to Milwaukee where her daughter, aged twenty-four, was said to be seriously ill.

The report proved to be false, the sort of cruel hoax, Marion

124

Shannon decided, to which a multi-millionairess in the public eye is vulnerable.

While she was away her mansion was burgled and harmonica bugs controlled by frequency-signalling devices installed in her telephones.

Three days after NSA and CIA operatives had studied the harmonica tapes and photographs of documents found in her safe Marion Shannon was involved in an accident while taking her afternoon dip from her private beach. She was struck by a power-boat and cut to death by its propeller.

MIDDLE GAME

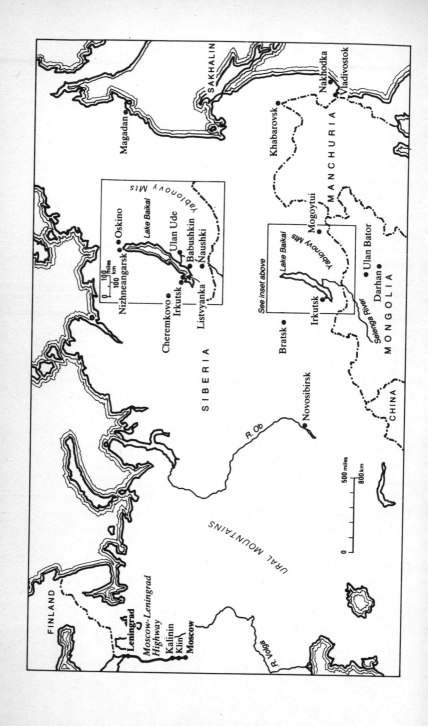

Chapter 15

In London beleaguered males escape to the pub. In New York they retire to dark bars. In Moscow they run for the bath-house.

Calder paid his seventy kopeks at the entrance to a *banya* in the Arbat and, holding his towel, made his way down a flight of stairs the colour of old piano keys to the changing room, spartan and mustily decadent. A chandelier hung from the ceiling – a torch glimmering from the Czarist past; metal lockers clung to walls.

Calder hung up his clothes and walked naked into the steam-room carrying plastic-sheathed money and ID rolled up in his towel. He sat on the lowest tier to escape the rising heat; even so the pine-scented steam scalded his nostrils and throat.

Beside him two plump Muscovites beat each other with birch twigs for the crime of living. They were both as pink as prawns.

Conversation expanded in the steam. Sex as crude as a ploughshare. *Blat*. Graft. The lottery. Chess. Horse-racing at the Hippodrome. An apartment to be exchanged on the open-air market near the *banya*. The Dynamos last night – 'Played like spare pricks on a honeymoon.' The family. The *babushka*.

Cameraderie and concern but no politics: the dead hand of the ideologist wasn't welcome in this exuberant place.

A newcomer sloshed weak beer on the hot bricks and for a while the chamber smelled like a cage in a zoo; then pine re-asserted itself.

It was the second *banya* Calder had visited in two days. From the Japanese pavilion in Sokolniki Park he had cycled to Komsomolskaya metro station hoping that Jessel would follow. Ten minutes later Jessel had arrived under the same chandelier.

'Let's get the fuck out of here,' he said.

They took the escalator to ground level, turned down a side

129

street and walked briskly towards the disciplined buildings of Lefortovo, home of the Military.

Jessel said: 'If that guy in the park recognised me we're in trouble.'

'We?'

'The Embassy.'

'Isn't he dead?'

'You don't kill people with pop-guns.'

'The KGB know you used to contact me.'

'That was before you were running.'

They crossed the Yauza, a capillary of the Moscow River, and strode past the Red Barracks.

Calder said: 'Make sure you send that message.'

'It will take them a couple of days to check out the Shannon woman. I don't want you to contact me for three days. And don't call my apartment.'

'I wouldn't want to soil the American dream.'

Jessel said: 'Let's get this straight. I've never liked you. Why should I? You shopped your country. I've kept in contact with you because it was my duty: you were one of my ears. Now it looks as though I may have to help you, again in the line of duty. But don't think for one goddam moment that I like the idea.'

A platoon of soldiers marched past; they looked dishevelled and exhausted.

'So until we get confirmation from Washington keep your head down. I can't get you into the Embassy because the militia will be waiting for you outside, and the same applies to all staff quarters. And don't book into any hotels or hostels. You might be Ivan Yacob but you sure as hell look like Robert Calder.'

Calder said: 'And find out about Harry. Please,' he added.

'I'll do what I can.' Jessel consulted the calendar on his watch. 'I'll meet you in three days. That's Tuesday. At the Foreigners' Cemetery. 1600 hours. Okay?'

Calder said it was okay.

He spent that night in a sobering-up station after acting drunk when a van drove along a stretch of the Sadovaya Ring picking up bodies. He was hosed down and strapped onto a bed next to a black-bearded Ukrainian. The night was a heaving

130

nest of unfettered dreams. In the morning he was given a hunk of black bread and a mug of cocoa – by tradition Russian drunks have to be protected rather than penalised – and dispatched into the new day.

He took the trolleybus to Serebriani Bor river beach, stripped off his shirt and lay in the sun. White steamers pushed their way along the river rocking the row-boats; the voices of sun-worshippers around him picked up the slow eddies and currents of the water; ping-pong balls on the sagging tables at the rear of the beach tapped out SLEEP.

Calder was awoken by two uniformed militia. They looked as tall as trees. They asked for his papers.

One of them prodded him in the chest with his foot. 'You don't say much, comrade.'

'You haven't asked me anything.'

'Where are you from?'

'Irkutsk.'

'A long way, comrade. What brings you here?'

'Work,' Calder said. 'There's a shortage of computer specialists in Moscow.'

'Irkutsk . . . that accounts for his accent,' the second militiaman said.

His colleague was still studying Calder's forged ID. 'The number of your *propiska?*'

Calder sat up. Sweat trickled down his stomach. 'Does it matter?'

'Of course. You should know that. In any case the number giving you the right to live in Moscow should be printed on your heart.'

Calder's saviour was a thin youth running through the sprawling bodies carrying a cassette recorder. Behind him, streaming with water and wearing black trunks that sagged alarmingly at the crotch, was twenty stones of enraged Muscovite. 'Stop thief!' he shouted.

'Shit,' said one of the militamen dropping Calder's papers beside him. And 'Enjoy Moscow,' as they gave chase. Near the table-tennis tables the militiaman drew his pistol and shouted: 'Stop it right there,' but the youth continued to run until the militiamen aimed his gun at the sky and fired.

As the militiamen drove away with the youth Calder put on his shirt and made his way to the refreshment hut. He ordered blinis, bread, hard-boiled eggs and sardines and drank beer from a fluted brown bottle.

He slept that night in the Silver Wood behind the beach. The following morning he went to a bath-house near the zoo and then to another beach at Rublevo, spending the night in the pine forest there.

Six hours before he was due to meet Jessel he was sitting on the bottom rung of the *banya* in the Arbat.

As he shed ounces he shed years. He felt liberated. He had purpose. He had a positive enemy who wanted to kill him. And when you had an enemy you had a cause. Calder wanted to save the West. He might even have been happy if it hadn't been for Harry.

A small naked man with a monk's fringe nudged him with his elbow. 'I am a happy man,' he said. 'Are you happy, comrade?'

'Content.'

'Ah, but that's not the same. Contentment implies the passive state. Happiness is an active experience.' He began to thrash his back with birch twigs. 'It is the development of contentment. You see I, too, have contentment. I get a fair wage, my rent and food are cheap, I have cheap holidays, I go to work when I feel like it. Today I should be at work but I thought what the hell, I won't get fired, why not go to the *banya?* And then perhaps a visit to the apartment of a girl who works in my office. A lively one that.' He stood up and flailed his stomach. 'Knows a trick or two. And when I get home my wife will have my dinner waiting for me. That, comrade, is happiness. Do you play chess?' And when Calder said he did. 'Come, my friend, let us play.' He led the way into an ante-room where men wearing towels as skirts or mantles were drinking beer and chewing salted fish, gherkins and black bread and playing chess or cards.

With a mug of beer in one hand and the dried skeletal body of a fish in the other, Calder summoned the spirit of Bobby

Fischer. US *v.* USSR. They played two games. He won one, lost the other.

'Not passive as I expected,' commented the little man pouring beer down his throat. 'Quite the opposite. And now the decider.'

But Calder declined: in one hour he had to meet Jessel. Invigorated, he walked into a summer heat which, after the *banya*, was as cool as mountain air. He walked with purpose and caught a bus to Lefortovo.

Jessel was waiting for him beside a gravestone honouring a French airman who died in the Great Patriotic War in the cemetery where the dead of 1812 were also buried.

Jessel had a plan.

Katerina walked down Gorky Street singing silently. She had defied Spandarian, she had won a thousand roubles on the Russian Republic lottery and she intended to take Calder, absent from the Institute for a couple of days with, according to Lev Koslov, a summer cold, to dinner in the Aragvi Restaurant. After that they would make love in his apartment: that would cure his cold.

She swung her handbag, her skirts swirled. A sailor whistled, healthy music. How squalid Spandarian seemed on this fragrant evening. Asking her to entice Calder to a high-rise apartment. Why? To photograph them, compromise them? Never. The brave future, shared equally between men and women, was no place for such seedy plots. But she would warn Calder.

Her summer-short black hair bobbed, her thighs thrust, her blouse felt taut across her breasts. Observing these phenomena, the driver of a small and dusty Zaparozhet drove across a red light and was stopped by two militia.

She turned into the arch leading to Calder's block and took the wheezing elevator to his apartment. Outside the door stood a bulky man wearing a rumpled blue suit and punished shoes.

'Excuse me,' she said. She tried to ring the bell but he held her arm and the sunlight drained from the evening. 'I want to

133

see *Gaspadeen* Robert Calder,' she said, 'and please take your hand off me,' but he didn't.

He said: '*Gaspadeen* Calder doesn't live here anymore.'

'I don't believe it.'

'I don't care whether you believe it or not. He's gone. And now you must go.'

'What right . . . ?'

'Every right,' he said, leading her to the elevator. He thrust her inside, closed the gate. The elevator descended slowly to the ground floor where a man with a thinning crew-cut was waiting.

He said: 'You would be well advised not to call here again,' and led her outside.

She walked like a woman at her lover's funeral. When she finally raised her head she went to a public call-box and telephoned Leonid Agursky.

The face of the Estonian lying in bed in Medsandtrud Hospital was a battlefield. Black and yellow, pitted with craters, black-stitched with barbed wire. Two eyes stared from the trenches.

'You were lucky,' Spandarian said. 'Unlucky to have your face scatter-gunned with lead but lucky to keep your eyes. Was Calder with anyone?'

The Estonian nodded, blond hair crusted with dried blood.

'Did you recognise him?'

The battlefield shifted from one side to the other.

'Any of these?' Spandarian showed him photographs of defectors currently in No Man's Land between their beliefs, Jessel, two CIA fieldmen at the Embassy, a visiting NSA agent posing as an adviser on wheat production and a chauffeur at the British Embassy.

A shell crater at the bottom of the battlefield opened. Spandarian bent to catch the words. '. . . don't . . . know.'

Spandarian straightened up, stroked his moustache above the smile on his lips. 'I'm afraid I haven't bought any grapes but I have bought good news: your transfer to Siberia has been confirmed.'

134

As he walked away listening to his footsteps sharp on the floor of the old hospital he thought: 'Calder is near, I sense it. Sense? Know. Because it is what I would have done. Kept my head down before making a break. Now there is only one man to catch this American renegade. I, Spandarian.'

He drove back to his office to transfer himself to the chase.

The principal hit-man of the Executive Action Department of the KGB was a veteran named Maxim Tokarev, a distant relative of the Tokarev who designed so many of the Red Army's guns in the 'twenties and 'thirties. In fact he still carried a 7.62 mm Tula-Tokarev pistol, CCCP erased from the walnut grip and replaced with MT.

Only Tokarev would have dared to make such a treasonable erasure. But Tokarev was Tokarev. Death.

He was a big untidy man in his late fifties with loose black hair laced with grey, and strangler's hands. He had no known vices – unless you considered killing to be one – and, a true Muscovite, hastened to the country when he wasn't working.

It was in the hunting grounds of the Caucasus that he had learned his trade, stalking boar and bear in forests guarded by snow-crested mountains. He regarded human quarry as animals believing that there was little to choose in the behavioural patterns of the doomed. Especially when the prey was aware that it was being hunted; then he put himself in the position of an animal and anticipated its flight.

He killed dispassionately. His favourite weapons were his hands but he was equally proficient with knives, guns and explosives.

The Chairman of the KGB summoned him to his dacha at about the same time that Spandarian was standing at the Estonian's bedside.

As Kirov limped towards the river glinting through the birch trees he said to Tokarev: 'I suppose you're wondering why I'm briefing you instead of your own director.'

'Because the last wet job was fouled up?'

'And I want the best man there is so that it doesn't happen again.'

'I am the best.'

'And I want to make sure personally that you understand just how important this hit is.'

'It doesn't matter,' Tokarev said. 'A job's a job. You needn't worry: I'll kill him.'

Tokarev, the Chairman reflected, was probably the only man in the Soviet Union who would address him so casually.

Tokarev was watching a squirrel looping through the trees. They reached the stretch of river where Kirov had conferred with Spandarian. *What a difference between the two men. But if one assassin fails I have a back-up, an elementary precaution.*

A river-smelling breeze ruffled Kirov's silver hair. Anglers still stood thigh-deep and motionless in the water, Japanese print undisturbed.

But what if both fail? Then Soviet penetration in the West is castrated – the Shannon woman had already been blown and murdered – and I am doomed.

A fish leaped, flashed in the sunlight and splashed back home. A blue dragonfly hovered over the water. The squirrel sat on a branch looking inquisitively at the two men.

'He knows I don't want to hurt him,' Tokarev said pointing at the squirrel. 'If he sensed that I did he would be round the other side of the trunk like that.' He snapped finger against thumb.

'And what would you do then?'

'Nothing. I would have killed it already.'

Kirov took a document from the inside pocket of his jacket. 'Here's everything you need to know about Calder. What he looks like, characteristics, habits . . . .'

'And he's on the run?'

Kirov nodded.

'Good,' Tokarev said.

The squirrel darted to the other side of the trunk.

'So far you've omitted to tell me one thing,' Jessel said. 'How you got these names.'

He and Calder had moved to a tombstone marking the grave of one of Napoleon's officers, Lieutenant Paul de Rougement

136

who had died at the age of twenty-six.

'It wasn't difficult,' Calder told him. 'I was at a conference in London and I met a KGB colonel there. He knew I was working for the Soviets, naturally I didn't know about him. Anyway he got very drunk and started hinting that we were both on the same side. I said, "I don't think so," and he got angry. You know, every spy yearns for recognition.'

'Do you?'

'Not right now . . . . Anyway he invited me back to his hotel room for a last drink and I went along because I was curious. When we got there he really flipped. Did I think all he cared about was material success? Position? I of all people, he said, should understand. And then he spilled the lot – because we were both working for the same great cause.'

'But no Saturday?'

'He didn't know who Saturday was. I doubt if anyone apart from Kirov and maybe a couple of his deputies know. He's the key to the whole Soviet operation. Their whole policy if you like.'

Finally, Jessel delivered his plan.

The Soviets, he told Calder, would expect him to take the shortest and easiest escape route i.e. west. And Calder would oblige them by doing just that. But not for long. Just as far as Kalinin, a hundred and fifty miles away on the Moscow-Leningrad road on the banks of the Volga.

What the Soviets would NOT be looking for would be a fugitive *returning* to Moscow. Calder would confound them by doing just that.

Nor would the Soviets be looking for an American tourist. Calder would be just that.

'I don't understand,' Calder said.

'You will go to Kalinin as Ivan Yacob. There you will become William Stephenson from Milwaukee making the journey of a lifetime across the Soviet Union. Here's your passport.' Jessel handed him an envelope. 'And biographical details and documents. And don't forget to carry a camera if you want to look authentic.'

'What about travel papers, hotel reservations? They can only

137

be obtained through Intourist.'

'We have a man at the Travel Office in Sverdlov Square. Your tickets and reservations are also in the envelope. And dollars. And while you're on your way to Kalinin start growing a moustache, you've got one in your new passport.'

'Are you out of your mind? I can't grow a moustache in a couple of days.'

'Ten days,' Jessel said. 'You're going by river-steamer.'

Chapter 16

The river-steamer *Tobolsk* was an old lady, a faded dowager. Her lines were sagging, her cosmetics rusty. But at night she recaptured the graces of youth, prow noble in the moonlight, portholes the eyes of trysts, lifeboats and masts her jewellery.

She was a three-decked, diesel-powered vessel that had once cruised the Irtysh and Ob, part of the Soviet Union's vast network of connecting waterways, before receiving the summons to Moscow.

She now sailed the Volga, leaving the Moscow River by the 128 kilometre-long canal which enabled ships to ply from the capital to Russia's five seas – Baltic, Black, White, Azov and Caspian.

Older Muscovites preferred the new boats but young couples preferred *Tobolsk* because she was slow and there was plenty of time to enjoy each other in her cabins. *Tobolsk* understood.

Calder took a bus to Khimki River Port where she was berthed. It took him down Leningradsky, past Katerina's apartment. He wondered if Sasha was singing. He hoped Sasha never knew the truth about him: trust was rationed. He looked the other way at the Bolshevik Sweet Factory: he didn't want to see a light in her window.

He was relieved he had come by bus when he alighted because uniformed militia were waiting at the metro terminal.

He went to a dockside café and ordered a beer; no one took any notice of him, least of all the barman, all interest aimed at the Spartak *v.* Tbilisi football match on the television. The pitch was psychedelic green and the players' faces were sweating strawberries.

When the last bus and subway train had departed, Calder joined a stagger of drunken river-sailors and, showing his forged pass to the dock militia at the gates, walked into Khimki.

At night stationary ships seem more alive than during the day and this was certainly true at Khimki: cabin lights beckoned, hulls trembled impatiently, engines throbbed.

At each gangway stood a militiaman.

Calder, shrinking from the quayside lamps, skirted the dock offices and their spire, said to resemble the spire of Leningrad Admiralty, and made his way to the wharf from which the passenger ships departed. There was *Tobolsk* at the end of the line and there, sitting on a capstan and smoking a cigarette, was a militiaman wearing a peaked cap. He smoked indulgently, long drags with the burns lighting a young face: fugitives didn't escape on dawdling old pleasure boats like *Tobolsk*.

Calder, wearing a blue reefer jacket, soiled white vest and rubber boots over blue jeans, hid his battered suitcase in the darkness, took out a bottle of Jubilee vodka, opened it and, whistling, approached the militiaman.

The young policeman threw away his cigarette and jumped to his feet, hand on his gun-holster. 'Who the hell are you?'

'A friend,' Calder said. 'I felt sorry for you: I've got a son your age in the militia in Khabarovsk.'

'ID.' He held out his hand. 'Irkutsk, huh? That accounts for your accent. What are you doing here?'

'Sailing for Rostov in the morning. Apparently the Rostselmash factory needs my expertise. I'm on loan for a couple of weeks.' He handed the militiaman the bottle of vodka. 'Here, take a nip.'

The militiaman took the bottle. 'Jubilee? The best. How did you get hold of this?' He took a two-gulp swig and handed the bottle back to Calder.

'From the skipper of the ship. I've got a crate. I can let you have half a dozen bottles for a song. Interested?'

'Because I remind you of your son?' He licked his lips.

'Because I can get another crate from the skipper. You see, I've got dollars. A lot of Americans come through Irkutsk on the Siberian Railway.' He handed the bottle back. 'Here, have another snort.'

When the bottle was almost empty and the militiaman was dramatically drunk Calder retrieved his suitcase. When he returned the young man was lying beside the capstan snoring at the stars.

The distance between the quayside and the deck of the *Tobolsk* was about six feet. Calder threw his suitcase first, then leaped. He slipped back, grabbed the rail and was on board.

He went down two flights of stairs into *Tobolsk's* womb. The door of his cabin, No. 13, was open. Two bunks, locker, washbasin. Calder chose the one at floor level; beneath the mattress he found a red rose, pressed and dried, and a pink packet contained one unused feather-light condom manufactured in Los Angeles. Therein lay a tale.

He locked the door, stripped off his clothes and lay down. The air was like soup. Outside the water talked and far away a ship's siren broke the night with sadness. He closed his eyes and the note of the siren was Harry calling to him from Boston.

When he awoke *Tobolsk* was making her arthritic way down the canal. Water threshed past the porthole but, despite the commotion, you could feel the dawn, milk-quiet.

Calder washed and shaved and put on the black trousers and white shirt he had packed in the suitcase. Then he went to look for the steward.

He had intended to slip him twenty-five dollars, paper gold, to leave him in peace in the cabin but the steward, a long-faced Kazakh with opium eyes, anticipated him.

'You want to be left alone, comrade. I understand.' He became a conspirator. 'Our friend with Intourist made it quite clear. A passport and a *probiska* aren't always what they seem . . . I, too, worked for State Security in Alma Ata. If there's anything I can do . . . .'

140

'You can get me some breakfast,' Calder told him.

The Kazakh brought him singed bread, two runny fried eggs, a slice of goat's cheese, lemon tea from the samovar at the end of the corridor, an orange and a 500-gram carafe of brandy. I must be at least a colonel, Calder thought.

For two days he confined himself to his cabin and the lowest of the three decks which wasn't popular because the view was limited. But he could see that the Volga was crowded, August holiday traffic buzzing the freight barges and getting out of the way of the 60 mph hydrofoils. The beaches were also crowded; behind them small hills climbed gently to the horizon. The air smelled of mud and oil and heat.

He spent much of this time sitting in the rest area in the stern furnished with rickety cane furniture that imparted a faint air of decadence. He drank cold beers, ate *zakuski* and read *samizdat* paperbacks provided by the steward – Harold Robbins and Agatha Christie. Occasionally he was joined by exhausted lovers who were quickly lulled to sleep by the churning propellers.

On the morning of the third day, while trying to concentrate on the deductions of Hercule Poirot, he became aware from the creaking of cane behind him that another visitor to the lower deck had joined him.

He glanced over his shoulder.

'G . . . good grief,' said the newcomer. 'What on earth are you d . . . doing here?'

Calder jumped ship that night at a pier on the south bank of the Volga, ordering the Kazakh not to mention his disappearance.

He found himself in a wooden village. Televisions flickered behind lace curtains moving in the river breeze in fretwork windows. He walked towards the silhouette of a church; it was also made of wood with two button-mushroom cupolas growing from its roof.

He pushed the door. It opened with a sigh. The nave, lit with dusky light by dying candles, was empty. Calder made his way to the vestry; in one corner was a pile of vestments. He lay down on them, sinking into incense-smelling depths.

141

He wondered when Dalby would report his presence on the *Tobolsk*. He should have remembered that Dalby had been engaged in a long love affair with Mother Volga and frequently visited her. Perhaps Dalby had even been anticipating that he would escape by riverboat.

He closed his eyes. For the first time since he had been on the run he didn't feel alone. He wasn't a religious man but it was comforting.

He was awoken by rain. He looked up from the vestments into black undergrowth. It took him a few moments to identify it as the beard of a priest, a fine square beard knitted in black and silver.

His explanation – he had missed the boat – was stark and unembroidered and the priest, stout and fleshy-nosed, didn't believe a word of it. It was hard to lie in a House of God.

'You are on the run?' the priest asked.

Calder said he was. But from what? He could hardly tell the truth; but half-truths were more difficult to muster than swashbuckling lies.

'Have you done anything of which you're ashamed?'

'I did once,' Calder said. 'Now I'm trying to put the record straight. My son is ill,' he added.

'Where are you heading for?'

Kalinin, Calder told him.

'You want to leave immediately?'

The last thing he wanted to do: he wasn't due there for three days. 'Not immediately.'

'You want sanctuary?' Brown eyes regarded him knowingly. And when Calder said he did: 'On one condition. Do you play chess?'

Calder nodded.

'Then you can stay.'

In Moscow, Spandarian, sensing that Calder had escaped from his cage, asked himself: 'Where would I go?'

West.

'By what route?'

That depends on how I got out of the cage.

142

He stared at a map of the Soviet Union.

'How?'

Ask the computer.

Spandarian was wary of the computer: he knew that sooner or later it would tell him where he had fucked up.

The phone rang. It was evening and in the empty office the shrilling was a dentist's drill touching a nerve.

Kirov. 'Have you traced him yet?'

'Don't worry, Comrade Chairman, he's still in Moscow. He'll surface any time now.'

The lie stood up and took a bow.

'I hope for your sake, Comrade Spandarian, that you find him before the Executive Action Department.' Click.

That bastard Tokarev. The best.

Spandarian consulted the computer in the communications room adjoining his office.

An hour ago the last militia and *stukachi* reports covering the period since Calder escaped from Sokolniki Park had been fed into it.

He pressed a button. Predictably the tremulous green letters repeated the routes that Calder could have taken.

What am I missing? Spandarian poured himself a brandy. Brandy! Booze! Spandarian snatched a telephone and called the central number for the sobering-up stations.

Names of the customers? The voice on the end of the line was plaintive. 'In three days there are so many . . . .'

'The names,' Spandarian said amiably, 'or you will spend the rest of your life strapped to a bed in one of your own stations.'

He listened attentively to the dreary recital. Not that he expected CALDER to leap over the line but names had a way of giving themselves up.

Yakhimovich, Yakir, Yacob . . . .

His senses bristled. He cut short the weary monologue. YACOB. He concentrated. Then he activated his accomplice, the computer. He had seen the name trembling on the screen. When?

Incidents involving militia . . . . He re-cycled the incidents. Plenty of them. Robbery, mugging, hooliganism, attempted rape . . . . *No*, as the green letters flickered, *this had been different*. How different? Spandarian sipped his brandy.

Booze!

He sought confirmation from the computer: MILITIA-MAN OLEG VOLOKOV ARRESTED FOR BEING DRUNK ON DUTY . . . .

Where?

At the quay at Khimki Port from which passenger ships depart, Spandarian remembered without further recourse to his accomplice. Three nights ago. Guarding the *Tobolsk*. Shit! So Calder had got away on a riverboat. He should have thought of that – *had* thought of it but only by checking passengers as they boarded the ships.

But with luck Calder would assume that he had got away with it. Spandarian called the port authority. 'Where does the *Tobolsk* sail to?'

He heard paper rustling. A woman's voice read a list of ports.

Spandarian hung up. What would I do? I certainly wouldn't chance my luck by staying too long on a geriatric steamboat . . . .

He returned to the map. I would jump ship and pick up the Moscow-Leningrad highway, that's what. And try and cross the border into Finland.

Over the phone Spandarian issued orders to watch all points of disembarkation visited by old *Tobolsk*. In particular the obvious port at which to pick up the Leningrad highway, Kalinin.

Tokarev, feeling relaxed, fondled the ears of his cocker spaniel in the garden of his dacha near Peredelkino, the writers' colony eighteen kilometres south of Moscow. The spaniel drooled.

Why should I make a move yet? Tokarev asked himself. Spandarian lost Calder: let him find him. Take the flak if he fails.

He threw a stick for the spaniel. Resignedly, the dog fetched it and, quivering, waited for another fondle.

The telephone rang inside the wooden house. Tokarev took the call in the conservatory.

144

His assistant's voice said: 'Spandarian's moving.'

The spaniel watched sadly as Tokarev climbed into his black Moskvich and, tyres spitting gravel, took off for Moscow.

Just before Spandarian left his office to drive to Kalinin the phone rang.

'Calder's on a riverboat called the *Tobolsk*,' Dalby told him.

'I know.'

Unperturbed, Dalby said: 'There's one thing you d . . . don't know – he's growing a moustache.'

Chapter 17

The priest drove a fawn Zaparozhet. The tiny cars manufactured in the Ukraine were sometimes given to invalids; in the priest's case the car was the invalid – the brakes squealed, the exhaust pipe grazed the rutted road and the windshield wipers switched the warm rain when the mood took them.

They drove first to Klin, once the home of Tchaikovsky, where the priest had ecclesiastical business at the Uspensky Monastery. While he was gone Calder waited in the Zaparozhet. Tchaikovsky, according to the priest, had written his sixth Symphony, the Pathètique, here and you couldn't get much nearer the soul of Russia than that. Nor could you escape the fact that today was Construction Workers' Day: a red-on-white banner stretched across the street invited workers to BUILD FOR THE ULTIMATE TARGET, THE GLORY OF THE SOVIET UNION.

When the priest returned, shaking rainwater dog-like from his beard, he said: 'We have a long drive ahead of us; let's hope that my little *dochka*,' patting the car's dashboard, 'makes it.'

Tobolsk and the priest's *dochka*, unconventional vehicles for a fugitive but effective. So far. 'You'd better pray, Father.' He smiled at the burly cleric. He warmed to him; not once had he

145

asked why he was on the run. He had also beaten Calder five times at chess, one draw when the priest had interrupted the game to pray.

But what moved Calder most was his spirit: his church, it materialised, was used in winter for storing beet and the only Russian Orthodox church in use in the area was in Kalinin. It required a sturdy faith to survive. He asked the priest about it as the Zaparohzet made its unsteady way past fields of vegetables, deserted hamlets and villages secretive in the rain.

The priest was surprised by the question. 'Don't you understand, I'm taking part in a crusade? What can be more exhilarating? You see Russians are the most religious people in the world and I'm helping to bring their love of God into the open once more. All the Bolsheviks did was burn the trappings of religion. The phrase God-fearing is often misused but in the case of the Communists it's apt: they do fear his influence over the Russian people and secretly most of them also believe: that's why God has never been banned from the land: the *Party's* soul is in torment. And a great revival is taking place.'

Something dropped off the Zaparozhet and rolled into a ditch; the car went faster.

'As you're a man of God does that mean you're anti-Communist?'

'On the contrary. You must never forget that, despite inefficiency, miracles have been worked in this land after a war in which twenty million died. A decent wage, a roof over their heads, enough food, cheap holidays . . . . Can you say that about America?'

The equation.

'We have freedom,' Calder said.

'Not much of a meal for the family when you've just been laid off work.'

But today Calder had no stomach for the equation. 'So you can reconcile Communism and religion?'

'Why not? They have the same aims.' He pulled at his formidable nose. 'And there's plenty of room in heaven for Communists.'

146

Five hours later they drove through fields of flax on the approaches to Kalinin. Calder alighted by the Lenin Monument in Sovietskaya Street, the urban stretch of the Moscow-Leningrad Highway, and shook the priest's hand.

'May God go with you,' the priest said. 'And teach you to play a better game of chess.' He pulled at his beard as though trying to re-adjust it and drove away, leaving behind a bolt which fell off the chassis and rolled into the gutter.

Calder made his way to the Tsentralnaya Hotel on Pravda Street to await the party of American tourists breaking their coach journey from Leningrad to Moscow to have lunch and tour the city on the Volga considered by Catherine the Great to be 'the most beautiful in the empire.'

He asked the receptionist if he could use a room in which to bath and change and was given the key to No. 23. The room was functional, decorated in pastel colours with a painting of Mikhail Kalinin, the venerated Bolshevik and one-time President, on the wall.

He ran a bath and, before shaving, examined his face in the mirror above the washbasin. No doubt about it, younger. The lines had filled out, the black hair was glossier. That was what came from being loved and betrayed and hunted. He stroked the moustache with his fingertips: it worried him.

When he had shaved he dressed in the grey lightweight suit he had brought in the suitcase and rehearsed his Milwaukee heritage. Beer, of course – he would make a point of comparing it favourably with Soviet brews – and German ancestry and fishing for coho salmon and eating kielbasa sausage with the Polish community.

And what are you doing in Kalinin? 'Writing a history of the Soviet Union, ma'am, at the request of Marquette University. And any historian worth his salt has to visit the city where Ivan the Terrible slaughtered ninety thousand of its inhabitants because there was some doubt as to whether they supported one of his campaigns. And did you know, ma'am, that in White Trinity Church blood from victims killed in secret rooms trickled down the pillars into the nave?'

'Ugh.'

'And that Kalinin was once as powerful as Moscow? Why, we're even suggesting twinning Kalinin with Milwaukee. We might even teach the Russians how to brew beer . . . .' Laughter.

And he would explain that, having researched Kalinin, he was joining their party on the journey to Moscow. 'Why I might even be persuaded to show you round the Kremlin; guess I know more about it than the guides.'

He went downstairs to the bar handing the receptionist the other half of the twenty-dollar bribe to use the room.

Spandarian arrived in Kalinin half an hour after Calder and went straight to the offices of State Security at the rear of the militia HQ close to the Regional Executive Committee building on Sovietskaya. Militia and plainclothes officers, he was told, were already combing the city; all vehicles leaving the boundaries in the direction of Leningrad were being searched. He demanded the services of two officers experienced in *apprehension and search* and concentrated on the places where he, Spandarian, would take cover before making a dash for Leningrad and the Finnish border. Bus and train stations, parks, cafés, bars, even hotels.

Tokarev followed Spandarian and the two officers in a taxi.

'Why I might even be persuaded to show you round the Kremlin . . . .'

Mrs Sundlun said: 'I don't think Intourist would take too kindly to that, Mr Stephenson.' She had a wise, sun-browned face, a blue rinse and fingers that seemed too fragile for the rings on them.

She was an archaeologist from San Diego. In fact the party eating lunch in the Chaika Restaurant on the banks of the Volga were all archaeologists from California. Jessel hadn't told him that: it wasn't going to be easy to be a convincing historian.

'Where are you from, Mr Stephenson?'

'Milwaukee. Did you know that more popcorn is consumed in Milwaukee than any other city in the world?' Popcorn was safer than history.

148

'I stayed there once,' she said.

Why couldn't Jessel have kept him in Boston?

Mrs Sundlun picked up her heavy coffee cup; her fingers made a jewelled clasp of the handle. 'I don't know about popcorn,' she said, 'but I do know about the Joan of Arc Chapel at Marquette University. You know about it, of course?'

'Of course.'

'Joan of Arc prayed there before being burned at the stake in 1463. The chapel was brought to Milwaukee from France. They say the stone she kissed before leaving the chapel is colder than the others. And do you know something, Mr Stephenson, I rather think it is.'

'I haven't touched it,' Calder said.

'And do you know something else?'

Calder spread his hands.

'You're a fraud, Mr Stephenson.'

It had to be Kalinin, Spandarian thought. According to the steward Calder had been on board the *Tobolsk* until it docked that morning: he wasn't there now.

It shouldn't be difficult to find him; Kalinin was built on a grid-system, almost an island lodged between the Volga and two of its tributaries, the Lazur and the Tmaka. The riverboat station was on the other side of the Volga, opposite the Chaika Restaurant, but to reach the highway Calder would have to cross one of two bridges.

A taxi-driver outside Party Headquarters on Sovietskaya gave him his first lead. He had seen a man answering Calder's description get out of a Zaparozhet driven by a bearded priest.

'Wearing?'

'White shirt and black trousers.'

'Heading in which direction?'

'I was cruising. I think he went down Pravda Street towards the Tsentralnaya Hotel.'

'Did he have a moustache?'

The cab driver nodded.

But the receptionist at the Tsentralnaya hadn't seen anyone answering Calder's description. The only visitors had been a

149

party of American tourists. They were lunching at the Chaika.

'Joan of Arc was burned in 1431. Not much of a historian, Mr Stephenson. KGB?'

He shook his head. 'I *am* American. I've got to get back to the States. My son's ill. It's a long story . . . .'

'You're on the run?'

'Have been for a long time. I'm in your hands, Mrs Sundlun.'

She lit a cigarette and stared across the Volga, dancing with shoals of light, at the riverboat station. 'What I don't get is why you're heading for Moscow. Shouldn't you be going that-a-way?' jerking her thumb west.

'That's the way they expect me to go.'

'Okay,' she said. 'I'll buy it. But give me a call back in the States. If you make it' she added.

Calder saw Spandarian as the party spilled down the steps of the restaurant to the waiting Intourist coach. He was talking to the driver.

Calder, who had shaved off the moustache in the Tsentralnaya – Dalby might report it – swung round to Mrs Sundlun. 'Would you do something for me? Drop one of your rings on the ground and shout.'

The ring bounced off the steps and she shouted, a robust noise for such a fragile lady. Archaeologists scrambled for it as though it were a find. Calder slipped into the coach and kept his head down behind a seat half way down the aisle.

He sat up for the head count before the coach departed. Mrs Sundlun, holding the errant ring, said: 'You know something? This sure beats the hell out of digging for pottery.'

Spandarian watched the red and white Moscow-bound coach take off. At least he could rest assured that Calder wasn't on it: he wouldn't be trying to go back into the cage.

Tokarev watched it more thoughtfully.

Chapter 18

Every footstep was a contradiction of logic. He knew that but he continued to walk.

And as he waited in the darkness across the street from the apartment block on Leningradsky he thought: 'Madness.' But he stayed. Despite the fact that others would be keeping watch on Katerina Ilyina. That was elementary: to catch a fugitive watch his woman. And they, too, would know that Katerina walked the brown-nosed dog – puppy no longer – at eleven every night.

Unless Spandarian is convinced that I've left Moscow. Dalby my saviour!

The dog came out first dragging Katerina behind it. She was a silhouette a hundred yards away but he could feel her. A light shone inside him.

She turned right. Calder walked ahead of her on the opposite side of the broad thoroughfare knowing that she was going to the small park near the Dynamo stadium. He hurried ahead, scanned the street and sidewalk behind Katerina's briskly moving figure. No shadows, no dawdling cars.

Calder entered the park.

Madness.

He called from behind a tree and, gasping, she was in his arms.

They held each other until the dog, overcome by jealousy, began to jump.

He looked at the moonlit intensity on her face. The flower-scented park rustled.

'Why?' she said. 'Why did you go?'

He told her but the explanation sounded worthless. He had seen her talking to Spandarian, that was all.

'But you knew I would never betray you. He asked me to

151

make you come to another apartment. I refused. Of course I refused,' incomprehension in her voice.

He stroked her face with his fingertips. 'They want to kill me,' he whispered.

'Who? Who wants to kill you?'

He told her as much as he dared. He also told her about Harry. 'I have to go back,' he said.

'For ever?'

He kissed her.

'How will you go?'

'To the east,' he told her. Truth was a luxury.

'I have friends on Lake Baikal. The Petrovs. Remember? I told you about Yury Petrov, a friend of my mother . . . . Yury hasn't any love for the KGB: he used to be a gold thief! Here.' She took a ballpoint pen from her coat pocket and wrote the address and a message – *Please help this man, Kata* – on the back of an envelope.

The dog began to bark.

Calder made a heart with his hands and held her face in it. 'I love you,' he said.

She nodded her head slowly, solemnly.

He kissed her and turned towards the gates to the park and sank into the ocean of the night.

'It seems to have worked,' Jessel said, soft voice carrying as though it were on a wavelength of its own. 'The heat's off in Moscow: the KGB is convinced you're heading west.'

They had met, as arranged, outside the Metropole Cinema on Sverdlov Square. Crowds hurrying to catch the last house at 10.45 pm swept past them. The film, Calder noted, was Tarkovsky's *Stalker*.

They walked round the big, theatrical square presided over by the imperial bulk of the Bolshoi.

'And now,' Jessel said, 'you're going to make your third and last identity change. How does Grainger grab you? Franklin Grainger, chess freak.'

'A master?'

'Not quite. But no slouch. Not anymore, though.'

152

'Dead?'

'He collapsed a couple of weeks ago playing in a tournament in Chicago. He was going to play with me in Vladivostok. Remember I told you about the tournament? I had written him off: when the contract was put out on you I resurrected him. He'd got his visa, the works. I told Washington to get hold of his documents and send them over in the bag. Here they are. And dollars, lots of them.' Jessel handed Calder a copy of *Evening Moscow*. 'Read the biog. and destroy it. You're well-heeled, a bachelor, a fan of the Chicago Symphony and a wow with the Marshall Attack.'

'I've never played it,' Calder said.

'Then read it up. It can't be all bad: Spassky used it in the world title eliminator against Tal in '65.'

'Very neat. But supposing the Russians know that Grainger died?'

They were outside the cinema again, beginning their second circuit of the square. Cinema-goers who had been shut out prompt at 10.45 pm stood in disconsolate groups.

'A calculated risk,' Jessel said. 'But it's doubtful. Grainger wasn't big enough to figure in their chess calculations and his death wasn't reported in the media.'

'But they knew he was coming here.'

'He was taken ill, that's all. We didn't cancel any of his bookings.'

'Not even when he died at the tournament?'

'He died much later in hospital. We were just about to make the cancellations when you cropped up.' Jessel paused to light his pipe. 'The bookings for Grainger and me were made weeks ago. Too late to change them now.'

'Any reason why you should?'

'Not if you like trains. We're going on the Trans-Siberian Express.'

'When?'

'Tomorrow morning. Don't be late. The Trans-Siberian never is.'

The modernist Hotel Rossiya is a monument to the statistics

153

Intourist scatter like confetti. It has 5,738 beds and if you can't sleep there are ten miles of corridors in which to pursue Morpheus.

Close-by stands another awesome pile, the Kremlin. From some of the Rossiya's rooms you can see its illuminated red stars thrust into the night sky staking a claim to the heavens.

From Room 308 Calder stared at one of the stars. It was the colour of power. In movies fugitives in hotel rooms were lit by blinking neon lights. But they were only hunted by a police force – 'We know you're in there, come out nice and easy . . . .' I'm pursued by twenty million KGB contacts.

But not, he remembered, Franklin Grainger. Which was why, Jessel had reasoned, it was preferable to occupy Grainger's room in the Rossiya: in the Soviet Union a neglected booking was suspicious.

'How,' Calder had asked, 'did I get into Russia?'

'By air. You broke your journey in London. Arrived in Moscow this evening on British Airways Flight 710 which landed at Sheremetievo at 16.45 hours.'

'What happened to me then? I presume I wasn't a ghost.'

'Your look-alike was taken to the United States Embassy on Tchaikovsky Street in a car bearing CD plates to meet me.'

'And where the hell am I now?'

'Still in the Embassy. We haven't worked out how we're going to get him out again yet.'

'You'll manage,' Calder said. 'But what about his passport? I suppose he looked like me – and Grainger.'

'Not a bad likeness. His passport is forged, yours is genuine. What happened to your moustache?'

Calder told him about Dalby.

'He'd pick his own pockets,' Jessel said.

Calder drew the curtains and, lying on the bed in the clinically clean and comfortable room, studied Intourist brochures on Siberia and its railway.

In the first place Siberia – forget the rest of the Soviet Union – would swallow all of the United States plus half Canada. Traversing seven time zones and 5810 miles of track he would arrive in Vladivostok on the Sea of Japan in 170 hours and five

154

minutes on the eighth day of his journey.

If he arrived. Sooner or later the KGB would realise that he hadn't gone west. And the Trans-Siberian was an obvious escape route east. Hopefully they were still looking for Ivan Yacob with a moustache. Hopefully they would assume that if he was on the train he would change at Khabarovsk in the Far East for Nakhodka, the exit port for Japan.

Or was he under-estimating State Security? He suspected he was.

He undressed and lay in bed, head cradled in his hands. Lenin returned his gaze from the white wall. He remembered the Robert Calder who had once lived in Moscow. He had been a flabby-minded fellow. This Calder, this Grainger, was different.

He uncradled his hands and touched his temples. A head full of secrets. They could change the balance of the world. A far cry from the simple ideas of equality he had once nursed in his youth. He frowned.

Then he switched off the light. Through the drapes he could still see the glow of the red star. He slid one hand under the pillow and touched the pistol he had taken from the militiaman on the quayside at Khimki River Port.

Everyone was looking at him. Receptionist, cashiers, porters; the cab driver, through his mirror, on the way to Komsomolskaya Square, site of three of the city's main railway stations; a grey-uniformed militiaman as he paid off the cab outside the Hans Andersen extravagances of Yaroslavl station. He felt as though he had a sticker on his forehead WANTED. Had the KGB discovered the deception? Were they waiting for him at the ticket barrier?

He dived into the ethnic adventure that is Yaroslavl. Shoals of minorities – Mongolians, Tartars, Moldavians, Yakuts, Kazakhs, Tajiks – swarmed around him like startled fish. He was the shark, hunted.

He glanced at his watch. He was fifteen minutes early. He made for the waiting room. It was a refugee camp. Almond eyes beside Slav cheekbones. Babies at the breast. Vodka passing

155

from hand to hand. A game of cards. Guitar strumming. Mounds of parcels and battered suitcases. They looked, Calder thought, as if they were there to stay. He stood beside a couple of lounging soldiers with cropped hair and dusty boots.

He waited seven minutes then shouldered his way past the black pillars of the chandelier-lit station to the platform where Train No. 2, maroon coaches pulled by a green electric locomotive with a serpent's nose, was waiting.

'Grainger!'

He swung round.

Jessel.

Together they walked down the platform and boarded the train to the other side of the world.

Chapter 19

It was at this stage of the chase that Tokarev drew marginally ahead of Spandarian. It was, after all, his time, the time for instinct. Animal instinct.

Instinctively he knew that in Kalinin the trail had gone cold. But where would I, a hunted animal trapped in a city, have hidden before breaking cover?

In a substitute for forest depths. In a cool hotel room in the heart of the city.

Big hands bunched in his trouser pockets, shaggy head low and questing, Tokarev went first to the Siliger Hotel where he terrified the receptionist. Blank.

The receptionist at the hotel Tsentralnaya, a pale young man with a sharp Adam's apple, was abrasive and Tokarev sensed that he was lying: no call for truculence with the KGB if you have nothing to hide. Tokarev, his own lie-detector, looked for proof. Rapid throat pulse, any nervous mannerism – in this case flicking thumb against finger as though squashing aphids – that

156

long, unwavering stare that is supposed to beam honesty. 'You're lying,' he said. 'When was he here?'

'One of your people has already . . . .'

Tokarev leaned forward, placed his thumbs on the receptionist's Adam's apple, fingers round the back of his neck, and squeezed gently. 'When?'

'Yesterday. Room 23.' He coughed as Tokarev released his grip.

Tokarev held out his hand and the receptionist gave him the key.

In the room he could smell Calder. The faintest traces. Aftershave, sweat, hotel soap – TSENTRALYNAYA was slightly worn on the red bar – camphor . . . a change into clothes stored with a preservative? He would know Calder's smell in the future.

He examined the plug-hole in the washbasin where the vortex of escaping water usually left a deposit. A few black and grey bristles, longer than the normal residue of a shave. So Calder had grown a moustache. Did Spandarian know? Quite possibly. What he didn't know was that Calder had shaved it off. Calder grew in his estimation.

He got times of arrival and departure and a description of Calder from the receptionist. 'Did anyone else see him?'

The receptionist told him about the party of Americans.

Think like an animal.

Herd instinct!

Tokarev was hunting bear in the Caucasus. What did bears do? Why, they turned back on their tracks . . . .

The red and white Moscow-bound coach.

Spandarian, you stupid prick.

Tokarev made his way calmly but purposefully to the nearest call-box.

Spandarian's secretary Yelena answered the phone when he made a check call to Moscow from Kalinin.

She said urgently: 'Comrade Kirov wants to speak to you. He has been very insistent.'

'What did you tell him, Yelena?'

157

'That you were looking for the American Calder.'

'In Kalinin?'

'I didn't specify . . . .'

'Thank you, Yelena. What would I do without you?'

He called Dzerzhinsky Square. Swat – straight through to the chairman's office.

'Progress report please, Comrade Spandarian.'

'We have Calder in our sights.'

'We?'

'I do. And the Executive Action Department operative.'

'According to my intelligence you haven't been in contact with the Executive Action Department.' A pause, an intake of breath – the old wound. 'Let's not play games, Spandarian. Are you in Moscow?'

Kirov knew perfectly well that he wasn't: Tokarev had told him. You're lagging, Spandarian. 'No, Kalinin.'

'Calder's there?'

'Was.'

'You lost him?'

'We'll get him, Comrade Chairman. You have no cause to worry . . . .'

'He's back in Moscow,' Kirov said.

'We know that. Kalinin was a diversion,' Spandarian said quickly.

'We?'

'It looks as though he's going to strike east.'

'As from now,' Kirov said, 'you and Tokarev will collaborate. Closely. Georgian cunning and a huntsman's instincts. Together you should be unbeatable. Get back to Moscow. Meanwhile surveillance on *all* exits from Moscow has been re-imposed. And Spandarian . . . .'

'Comrade Chairman?'

'No arrests. I want him good and dead.'

On one point Georgian cunning and animal instinct coalesced: Calder, like a dog after a bitch on heat, might have tried to see Katerina Ilyina.

Spandarian and Tokarev faced each other across mugs of

coffee in the canteen of the KGB building on the Sadovaya Ring.

'I'll interrogate her if you like' Spandarian offered.

'I'm sure it's an art in which you excel.'

Hostility condensed in the steam from the coffee.

'I'm sure you excel in other arts, comrade. How do you like to kill? With your hands?'

'How do you interrogate comrade? With *your* hands?

'Or a knife perhaps?'

Tokarev regarded him patiently. 'It depends on the hit. The circumstances in which he's run to earth. If he were a wily customer, dangerous when cornered, then he would die with a bullet through his eyes. The quicker the better. You see I don't enjoy killing; it's the hunt that absorbs me.'

'You must be having one hell of a time at the moment.' Spandarian sipped his coffee; it tasted like a third pressing.

'I'm lucky. Ninety per cent of the people on this earth do jobs they dislike. Clock-watchers all. What a way to waste your life. Do you enjoy your work, comrade Spandarian?'

What I shall enjoy most, Spandarian decided, is authorising your execution when I become head of the Second Chief Directorate.

He finished his foul coffee. 'If you'll excuse me, comrade, I will go and interrogate the bitch.'

Apart from a few unfortunate stains on the walls, the room on 25th October Street that Spandarian used for occasional interrogations wasn't unwholesome. With its khaki filing cabinets, tubular steel chairs and pinewood table, all covered with a patina of dust, it was more like a spare room whose function had yet to be decided. There was even a threadbare carpet on the floor; beneath this was a floor safe in which Spandarian kept the lives of those who could assist him on his ascent to pre-eminence – copies elsewhere in case the owners of any of those lives took it into their heads to search the interrogation room.

Prowling the room, addressing her from all angles, Spandarian questioned Katerina skilfully, hot and cold, lies

159

and facts, benevolence and menace, and hit her only once.

'At what time did he come to your apartment?'

'He didn't.' She moved her legs from the cold steel of the chair. Good legs, Spandarian noted. He saw her for a moment naked.

'It was dark?'

'He didn't come.'

Spandarian picked up some papers from the table. 'I see you held a feminist meeting near the firemen's barracks on Kropotkin Street yesterday.'

'What of it?'

'Rowdyism, hooligan behaviour . . . . It really won't do Katerina Ilyina.' He clucked disapprovingly. 'In fact you're going to be confined to your apartment. Unless . . . . Was Calder there when you got back from the meeting?'

'I told you, I didn't see him.'

'Did he screw you?'

'No . . . .'

'In the park?'

She didn't reply but her lips trembled.

Spandarian stood behind her and placed one hand gently on her shoulder. 'He's going west, isn't he? Going to cross the border into Finland.'

'Yes.'

The blow knocked her from her chair. As she knelt on the carpet he noticed that the rings on his fingers had stamped an instant bruise on her cheekbone.

He helped her back to the chair and said amiably: 'Please stop lying, Katerina Ilyina, we know you saw him, we know he's going east, and there's no way he can escape. Every railway, every road, every airport is being watched. But it would help if we knew his destination. Nakhodka, I assume . . . .'

'I don't know,' she said.

He lit one of his yellow cigarettes and blew smoke into a shaft of exhausted sunlight.

'Perhaps your good friend Svetlana might refresh your memory.'

She was on her feet. 'You keep her out of this. It's nothing to do with her.'

'Such spirit,' he said and opened the door and the glory that had been Svetlana stood there, eyes slitted, hair matted, lip split.

In the room adjoining his office Spandarian conferred with his computer. From time to time Tokarev, sipping a glass of tea, glanced in.

Once he said: 'Calder isn't in Moscow; you must know that. He used the time we wasted in Kalinin to make his real break. And if I were him I would lose myself in the *taiga* in Siberia.'

Spandarian ignored him. But he had been right on the first point: Calder must have returned to Moscow – with the party of archaeologists. He consulted the computer: they had been given accommodation in the Metropole, Rossiya and Minsk hotels.

He called the hotels on the phone. Only one guest answered Calder's description. Franklin Grainger in Room 308 at the Rossiya. Moustache? Not as far as the receptionist could recall.

Where had he gone? The receptionist hadn't the faintest idea: all he knew was that he hadn't returned although he had been booked for three nights.

Spandarian thought like a Georgian, like Lazishvili, like Beria, like Stalin. What chance did animal instinct stand against such distilled cunning?

So, Katerina Ilyina had virtually confirmed that Calder was heading east. By air? Impossible. Surveillance had never been lifted from airports. Road? Not across Siberia! River? Not again, for God's sake. Train . . . .

Spandarian summoned the latest Intourist programming on the computer – sub-dividing it into FOREIGNER ARRIVALS/DEPARTURES MOSCOW and then again into TRANS-SIBERIAN RAILWAY.

Jessel. The name leaped at him. Why was the United States intelligence chief in Moscow who used Calder as his Twilight Brigade informant travelling across Siberia?

He picked up the telephone, dialled 52 00 11, the US Embassy and, posing as an official of UPKD, the State agency that caters for diplomats' needs, asked to be put through to Information. Jessel, he was told, was playing in a friendly chess tournament in the Far East and had a special permit to visit the closed city of Vladivostok.

So the Foreign Embassy Department of the Second Chief Directorate was laying on a misinformation junket for Jessel.

'Is he travelling alone?'

The voice on the other end of the line sounded surprised as though UPKD should have known. 'No, he's been joined by a guy named Grainger. Another chess fanatic.' Franklin Grainger the American who had vanished from the Rossiya! Names were hammer blows today.

'How's it going?' Tokarev asked from the doorway.

'Coming together.' He wished he could double-cross Tokarev here and now; but in Moscow that would be suicide – Kirov would get to hear about it and break him. He would have to fix him later.

Grainger. Green letters as tremulous as leaf shadows in sunlight appeared on the screen. *Arrived BA 710 at 16.45 hours yesterday*.

Calder would have got back from Kalinin yesterday. Spandarian telexed Immigration at Sheremetievo and asked for the KGB extension. How had Franklin Grainger been transported to the city centre? A pause. Then: 'By US Embassy limousine.'

Spandarian made his penultimate call to the militia post outside the American Embassy. Another pause while the NCO consulted ARRIVAL and DEPARTURE records.

Arrived 18.42 hours. Departed 19.37. And yes, the figure in the passenger seat had been indistinct.

Of course it had. An embassy official with a coat-collar turned up. An imposter had been flown to Moscow from the United States and taken to the Embassy. Grainger, alias Calder, had booked into the Rossiya after the limousine had left at 19.37 hours. The man who had flown the Atlantic via London was still in the Embassy.

162

Spandarian made his last call – to the radio compartment on the Trans-Siberian. He ordered round-the-clock surveillance on Jessel and Grainger. 'No positive action until I arrive unless an escape bid is made.'

Smiling, Spandarian returned to his office and took a railway time-table from a shelf. The obvious place to join the train was Novosibirsk, an easy flight from Moscow. Train No. 2 arrived there at 15.50 Moscow time, 19.50 local on the third day of its journey.

He was about to pick up the phone to reserve two flights when Tokarev said: 'Let's not over-book. I made the reservations a couple of hours ago.'

Chapter 20

From the window of the train the *steppe*, black-earth and birch-wood, reached for the horizon and beyond. A hamlet of wooden cottages wearing fretted pink and blue bonnets drifted past. A girl in a gypsy skirt standing in a field of lush grass waved.

Calder yawned. It was 5 pm. In fifty minutes they would be in Novosibirsk, the Chicago of Siberia, more than two thousand miles from Moscow. Jessel was asleep on his bunk in the two-berth, soft-class compartment. It wasn't difficult to fall asleep lulled by the slow rhythms of the Trans-Siberian – *express*, never. But even in sleep Jessel, thin hair undisturbed, seemed watchful, compact.

Calder left the grey-walled compartment to get a cup of tea from the girl with the blonde, sugar-spun hair in charge of the samovar at the end of the corridor.

She handed him a cup and he gave her five kopeks for the lump of sugar. He made a joke about the concrete-hard cube but she didn't smile. Was it his imagination or had her attitude changed? As the train passed through the Urals crossing from

163

Europe to Asia she had been a flirt: now she seemed possessed by spirits of the doomed legions of exiles who had once trekked across Siberia to die in the gold, silver and coal mines.

To encourage her to talk Calder said: 'What time are we due at Novsibirsk?'

'There are eighty-three stops on the line,' she said. 'I can't be expected to know what time we arrive at each of them.'

Once she would have pouted her bosom and replied: 'Time to get to know each other,' with a flash of steel teeth deep in her smile. She *had* changed.

He glanced down the corridor. A man in a blue track suit was leaning against a compartment door gazing out of the window. Calder felt as though he were suspended on a thread held by the girl and the man. Stupid. The girl had quarrelled with her boyfriend, one of the cooks on the train, and as for the man – the train was full of Russians in blue track suits. But what was he doing here? Few Russians, Red Army generals or influential *apparatchiki* mostly, travelled soft-class. He had developed a persecution complex: the man, lean and dark and unshaven, was probably Party Chairman of the Novosibirsk Oblast.

A train coming from the east raced past startling him. A troop train by the look of it. Burrowing through rustic tranquillity, you forgot that the border with China was only five hundred miles to the south. In the Far East it almost hugged the track.

Calder walked along the corridor of a hard-class coach of four-berth compartments; three samovars later he reached the dining car. He bought fruit and plain chocolate from a girl wearing a paper tiara at the glass cabinet at one end of the car and sat at a table next to a man in a red T-shirt reading a book about bridge construction. He bit crisply into a green-skinned apple.

The samovar girl had depressed him. He felt like one of the *brodyagi*, the convicts who had managed to escape from their manacles after they had said farewell to their families at the Monument of Tears in the Urals. Escaped in the winter into desolation so cold that the permafrost never melted and trees

164

exploded. Millions of convicts had been dispatched and many had helped to carve the Trans-Siberian through the wilderness.

Staring out of the window Calder saw an old woman feeding geese beside a pond.

The man in the red T-shirt snapped his book shut and produced a half-litre bottle of vodka. 'A little nip, comrade? They don't sell it on this train – the peasants might start a riot.'

Calder declined; his companion tilted the bottle down his throat and gave a deep, hot sigh. 'Mother Russia's milk. The fuel of the Soviet Union.' He slid the bottle back into his travelling bag; it chinked against another bottle. 'So you're not superstitious, comrade?'

'No, why?'

'Because in the good old, bad old days it was considered unlucky to take the Trans-Siberian on a Monday and we did just that . . . .'

Calder looked over his shoulder. The unshaven man in the blue track suit was sitting four tables away. A coincidence, of course. Why shouldn't he come to the dining car?

The train pulled into a small station with pink and white petunias growing in beds of soot-fine soil. Two women wearing headscarves were selling meat pastries, bowls of raspberries and ice-cream from a canvas-covered pushcart. Eagles watched from the high blue sky.

As the train moved away Calder stood up and continued his journey towards the engine. Four samovars later he was in one of the cheap dormitory coaches. Fifty-seven bunks arranged in tiers. The aisle was a back street of a New York ghetto at the turn of the century. Dripping laundry strung between bunks; blankets on the floor laid with bread and cheese and beer; babies crawling on nut-shells and sunflower seeds among chess players lost in their gambits.

The woman attendant for the dormitory confronted him. 'What are you doing here?' she demanded.

'Just looking.'

'You don't belong here. Out.'

'I thought this was a classless society.'

She pointed a stubby finger at the door. Shrugging, Calder

turned and walked into the man in the blue track suit.

The attendant beamed at him. 'Comrade Ragozin. Welcome back.' The man in the blue track suit lay down on a bunk and closed his eyes.

When he got back to soft-class Jessel was arranging the chess-pieces on a magnetic board that folded in the middle like a small, chequered briefcase.

'We'd better get in some practice,' he said. 'Especially if you're going to play like Marshall. He was a real bruiser on the board except that he sometimes led with his chin. A boozer, too. Died in '44.'

'I know,' Calder said sitting at the table, 'I once played at the Marshall Club in New York on West Tenth. Even though I don't know much about the Marshall Attack I don't figure I have to change my style too much.'

He chose white and they moved into a Dutch Defence, Staunton Gambit. He played purposefully, cheered by the man in the blue track suit's indifference.

Jessel resigned on the twenty-ninth move. He stared out of the window. 'Siberia,' he said, 'the biggest treasure trove in the world. Six million square miles of it. Gas, oil, uranium, diamonds . . . . These days a young man goes east. Have you ever been to any of the new cities?'

'Boston is the only city I want to see.'

'Well right now you're about to see Chicago.' Jessel pointed out of the window. Factory chimneys trailing thick banners of smoke fingered the sky. Train No. 2 passed over a bridge spanning the Ob and they were in Novosibirsk station.

Calder and Jessel went into the corridor. Another man in a blue track suit was standing at the end of the corridor. This one had shaved.

As they alighted from the coach a clerk from the radio compartment handed Jessel a cable. He scanned it and said: 'I'll go back to the compartment to decode. You take a walk.'

Calder bought a plastic cup of *kvas* and, sipping it, queued for a copy of *Krokodil* at a magazine stall. Down the platform passengers clustered round a food-stall like ants trying to drag a crumb of cake back to their nest.

Clutching his magazine, the only one that dared to satirise Authority, Calder walked the length of the train to the green serpent that was hauling it. He wondered what the cable said. Before they left Moscow he had asked Jessel to find out about Harry.

The train stayed in Novosibirsk for twenty-two minutes. There were still twelve minutes left. He sauntered back past the maroon coaches embossed in gold with CCCP and hammers and sickles and, underneath, Moscow-Vladivostok in Cyrillic.

From one of the windows a small boy thumbed his nose at him. Calder glanced up and down the platform. Blue track suits everywhere.

When he got back to the compartment Jessel was staring at the decoding. Light from the window shone through the original cable paper and Calder could see the outlines of the strips of ticker-tape; there were a lot of them.

Jessel folded the two sheets, original and decode, with nimble fingers and slid them into his wallet.

'Good news?'

'Not bad, not good.'

Jessel's attitude had changed. The sweet coating had been licked from a pill and he was tasting the kernel.

'Harry?'

Jessel nodded. 'Just a one-liner – he's still unconscious, as well as can be expected.'

He was lying: there had been several strips on the cable. Why was he lying?

'Anything else?' Calder asked to give him a chance.

Jessel shook his head.

Spandarian and Tokarev boarded Train No. 2 one minute before it was due to depart and went straight to an empty hard-class compartment reserved for them four coaches from the soft-class car bringing up the rear.

Spandarian lay on a bunk and watched Tokarev as he checked the fittings. There was a certain heavy grace about the man. And those hands – he could pull your head off with them.

But at last they were in accord. On the plane from Moscow they had agreed that it was stupid to compete for the privilege of killing Calder. Much more practical for Tokarev, the professional assassin, to do the job.

Smiling at Tokarev, he thought: 'And then I will kill you.'

In the days of doubt, before he had met Katerina, Calder had taken strong sleeping tablets. He palmed one now as, with his back to Jessel, he poured their nightcaps – bourbon which Jessel had brought from Embassy stock. The tablet fell into Jessel's glass and stayed there insoluble as a tooth. Calder swirled the whisky.

Jessel, sitting at the table reading an old copy of the *Wall Street Journal*, said 'Hurry up, I don't want it with my breakfast coffee.'

Calder dipped one finger into the bourbon and pressed the tablet. It broke up; the fragments hesitated then they, too, dissolved. Calder handed the glass to Jessel.

Jessel, wearing pyjamas and a blue towelling robe, raised his glass. 'Here's to Saturday.' He held the glass high. 'Why the days of the week? You never told me.'

Drink!

Calder tossed back half his whisky. 'There were seven of them. It was an obvious way to codename them.'

'I guess so.' Jessel sniffed his drink, held it up to the ceiling light. 'How much water did you put in this? It looks as though it could pole-axe a Siberian tiger.'

Calder topped up the drink with water from a plastic jug.

Jessel sipped it. He usually tossed his liquor back like cowboys did in Westerns. 'When we get to Vladivostok,' he said, 'you'll have to play a couple of games. Then we'll smuggle you on a boat to Yokohama. It's all been arranged.'

Calder finished his whisky in one more gulp.

Jessel drank his in slow swallows; but down it all went. Then he took off his robe and climbed into his bunk.

Calder lay on his berth on the other side of the compartment and waited.

168

Jessel rustled his *Journal* a lot. Finally he stroked the long strands of his hair and glanced inquiringly at Calder. 'Okay?'

Calder nodded. Jessel turned down the ceiling light to a dim, ghostly blue. 'No jogging in the morning,' he said. He slept.

Calder gave it half an hour. Jessel's wallet was under his pillow. Calder edged his hand underneath. The wallet slid out easily.

Calder read Jessel's decode.

The words were bullets.

MARION SHANNON LEAD FALSE STOP MUST ASSUME THAT CODENAMES MONDAY TO FRIDAY ALSO FABRICATIONS AND SUBJECT ATTEMPTING ELABORATE DECEPTION STOP HANDLE WITH UTMOST CAUTION AND AWAIT FURTHER INSTRUCTIONS EN ROUTE VLADIVOSTOK.

The signature in Jessel's decode was garbled so presumably it was in the original. But obviously it didn't matter to him: he knew who had sent the cable.

Calder made a note of the scrambled signature, replaced encode and decode in the wallet and replaced it beneath Jessel's pillow.

Calder returned to his bunk. But he didn't sleep. Instead he wrestled with the anagram of the garbled signature because he knew it had to be the name of The Man Who Was Saturday.

Chapter 21

By morning the blue sky had vanished and the *steppe* with it. Rain fell mistily dribbling rivers and tributaries down the windows of the train, and the *taiga*, pine and swamp and mist, crowded the track on either side.

Tokarev, planning Calder's death over a boiled egg, tea and toast in the dining car, loved the predatory atmosphere of the *taiga* and was grateful to the American for leading him here.

He sensed animals watched the train from dark depths and the prospect of returning to Moscow depressed him. Perhaps, after the killing, they would be allowed to continue the journey to the east, the domain of shaggy tigers, wolves, mink, sable, squirrel and elk. To trap a Siberian tiger, *felis tigris*, now that would be something.

Thank God Spandarian, who had stayed in the compartment in case Calder spotted him, wasn't sitting at the same table spoiling the mood. Tokarev detested the narcissist Georgian, and the stink of male cosmetics and stale tobacco smoke in the compartment turned his stomach.

And what conceit! Did Spandarian really believe that his concession had been accepted? That I don't realise he intends to murder me after I've killed the American?

Tokarev finished his tea and, pushing his way past sleepy passengers queueing for tables, made his way to the compartment where the Director of Train No. 2 ruled.

The Director, plump with soap-shined cheeks and gold-chain looped across a tight waistcoat, stared woefully at Tokarev's red ID and asked without enthusiasm how he could help.

Tokarev sat opposite him at a table and told him. He wanted Jessel and Calder to be told that tonight their meal could not be served in their compartment: they would have to eat in the dining car with the less privileged passengers.

The Director made a note with a fractured ballpoint pen. 'No trouble. Is that all?' he asked hopefully.

No, Tokarev told him, there was more, much more. He pointed at a wall map of the Trans-Siberian greased by many prodding fingers. 'We arrive at Irkutsk at 05.12 hours?'

'On the dot,' the Director said.

'So when we stop at Cheremkovo two hundred kilometres this side of Irkutsk it should still be dark?'

Surprised, the Director said: 'Of course. But you don't want to get off there, surely. There's nothing there but coal-mines.'

'I don't want to get off there: I want someone else to stay there. There are sidings?'

'Naturally.'

170

'Good. Now while the two Americans are having dinner I want all soft-class passengers evacuated to hard-class.'

The Director was appalled. 'I can't do that. We have very important passengers in soft-class.'

'How important?'

'The Deputy Director of the Soviet Academy of Sciences from Akademgorodok . . . .'

'Not very important. The top scientific brains went back to Moscow years ago.'

'A cosmonaut.'

'He's only important up there.' Tokarev jerked his thumb skywards.

'A Red Army general . . . .'

'Get them all out,' Tokarev said, bored.

'I'm afraid I can't do that,' the Director said with nervous importance. He pulled a gold watch from his waistcoat pocket and spun it on the chain.

'You'll do what you're told,' Tokarev told him.

'I'm in charge of this train.'

'Not anymore. Now let's go to the radio car and call Moscow.'

'Moscow?' The Director grimaced; cracks appeared in his shining cheeks. 'Why Moscow?'

'I want you to speak to someone there.'

'Supposing I don't want to speak to anyone in Moscow?'

'He'll want to speak to you. His name is Kirov, Chairman of State Security.'

The gold watch stopped gyrating. 'I'll clear the soft-class coach,' the Director said.

'We'll go to the radio car just the same. You will call the stationmaster at Cheremkovo. I want a quick turnaround and I want the soft-class coach uncoupled and shunted into a siding. Then I want the station cleared of all staff.'

On the way to the radio car the Director asked, 'May I ask, Comrade Tokarev, why all this is necessary?'

'You don't want a death *on* the Trans-Siberian, do you comrade?'

When Tokarev got back to the compartment Spandarian was washed, shaved and pommaded. He looked what he was, a

171

gangster with a beat between a barber's and a funeral parlour. These Georgians with their thick accents were all the same: they all thought they were Stalin.

'All fixed?' Spandarian asked.

'04.45 hours when it's still dark.'

'Calder *and* Jessel?'

'Of course. No witnesses, no complications. They both disappear in the *taiga*, simple as that.'

Spandarian said: 'Calder shouldn't present any problems. He's supposed to be Grainger and the Americans can't get too indignant about someone who doesn't exist. But Jessel . . . that'll have them howling for blood.'

Tokarev shrugged. 'So, he disappeared. What are we supposed to do about it?'

Spandarian lit one of his foul cigarettes. Tokarev coughed, opened the window and sat in a corner cleansed by rain-wet air.

Spandarian said: 'Have you any idea why Calder is so important?'

Tokarev shook his head slowly. In the depths of the *taiga* he saw a glint of water. Siberia, with its abundance of rivers and lakes, had once been compared to an ocean silted with *steppe* and *taiga*. Maybe when they reached Irkutsk and Lake Baikal he would be able to go duck shooting.

'Obviously,' Spandarian said, 'Calder has access to vital information. But he hasn't obtained it in the Soviet Union: I know that because he's been under surveillance ever since he arrived. Presumption: it must be some intelligence he brought with him. Conclusion: Calder knows the identity of top Soviet agents in the West and is running home to blow them. Doesn't any of this interest you?' he asked Tokarev irritably.

But Tokarev, eyes closed, was standing thigh-deep in rushes waiting for duck to come in from the dawn sun to join a decoy on silver water.

All night a blizzard of letters had swirled inside Calder's skull assembling in crazy names, unpronounceable names, a few possibilities that meant nothing to him. When he dozed he was agonising over crosswords. One across: *The day after Friday*.

172

Ten down: *The day before Sunday*. When he awoke the signature on Jessel's decode was still garbled.

Even now eating lunch in the compartment brought by the sullen samovar girl the letters presented themselves. His head ached with them.

'Don't worry,' Jessel said, spooning soup and rolling black bread into a pellet, 'Harry's going to be okay.'

How would you know? Care? Calder wondered if Jessel had received his 'further instructions' yet.

The girl brought them *pyelmeni*, meat dumplings, and white wine. She said: 'There is no service tonight, you will have to eat in the dining car.'

Jessel said: 'Maybe they've decided to bug the compartment. It's been clean until now.' He drank some wine. 'Of course when you get to the States there'll be one hell of a debriefing. You'll be taken to a safe house. And then they'll have to work on *you*.'

'How do you mean, work on me?'

'Plastic surgery, another identity. Our friends don't give up that easily. Look what happened to Trotsky.'

'And Ruth, what do you know about Ruth?'

'I know she's at Harry's bedside.'

Was. You don't know where the hell she is now; the cable said nothing about Harry.

Jessel said: 'Maybe she'll have you back. You're doing a great job for America.'

'You sound like a baseball coach.'

'It's true. No war-medalled hero has done more.'

'Don't give me bullshit. I didn't defect to help the States. Ruth isn't stupid.'

In any case, did it matter? He loved Katerina. But had loved Ruth.

He remembered Lidiya who had died because of him. He remembered the ordinary face and the innocent curls at the nape of her neck. He remembered the boy in his red Pioneers' scarf.

He drifted further back. His father's voice carrying down the dining-table picking up the silver tones of the candelabra on its

173

way. Chess. Names on the bases of the pieces. Everyone had always known Holden would go far. But not as far as he had gone. But Holden's character was blemished. Only I know about it.

Christ, how pompous hindsight could be. A glade cut from pines and embroidered with kingcups passed the window. A family were picnicking in it. Mosquitoes biting your ankles, ants in the sandwich spread . . . . If only we realised that one day we'd look back through a hole in the parchment of time – and wonder why we had eroded sunlight with complaint.

'Don't worry,' Jessel said. 'Harry will be all right.'

MARION SHANNON LEAD FALSE . . . . Someone was trying to stop him getting back to Harry. *Saturday*. The letters were snowflakes fluttering coldly in his skull.

At 9.30 that evening when Calder and Jessel had gone to the dining car Tokarev set in motion the evacuation of the soft-class coach. Although they had been forewarned the passengers still protested, but the red ID backed by Kirov's reputation held sway.

What Tokarev proposed to do was tiresomely elaborate but necessary because he couldn't risk a shooting match on the Trans-Siberian – with so many foreigners on board the reverberations could easily reach the West.

When everyone had been transferred to hard-class compartments, all demanding fare rebates, Tokarev entered the Americans' compartment. Entered their lives. He smelled the fading camphor from Calder's clothes, his after-shave; the oil Jessel used to keep his hair in place, his deodorant. He also smelled hostility.

The magnetic chess board was lying on three paperback books stacked at the rear of the table by the window. He opened it, removed the pieces nestling inside and dropped them into his jacket pocket. In their place he packed sticks of 808 gelignite and in the hinged space that had separated the white and black camps he inserted a pencil time fuse fitted with an acid bulb; he squeezed the end of the fuse to arm it.

The fuse was set to detonate the gelignite when the soft-class coach was in the siding at Cheremkovo. According to surveillance reports Calder and Jessel didn't play chess after dinner. But just in case they did Tokarev booby-trapped the board with a flash fuse and release switch that would blow the gelignite immediately the board was opened.

An explosion on the Trans-Siberian would be messy and complicated but the two Americans would be good and dead. The stock explanation would be offered: saboteurs killed by their own weapons.

Tokarev replaced the chess board on top of the paperbacks and, swaying with the motion of the train, made his way back to the hard-class compartment where Spandarian, his next target, was waiting for him.

At 2.30 am Calder, hearing a metallic click, opened his eyes and in the dim blue light from the ceiling lamp looked into the barrel of an automatic pistol fitted with a silencer.

Jessel, prodding the gun, an American High Standard, at Calder said: 'I'm glad you woke up. I've wanted to tell you what an asshole I think you are for a long time.'

'I never doubted your views,' said Calder who hadn't been asleep.

'No one likes a traitor. Not even the Russians.'

'Nor me.' Calder felt under the duvet for the butt of the TT pistol he had taken from the militiaman at Khimki Port.

'Did it ever occur to you that the KGB and the CIA sometimes collaborate?'

Calder's fingers found the butt of the pistol. He shook his head.

'I think you should know a few home-truths before I kill you. I wouldn't want you to die thinking your values were clear-cut. Them and us . . . .'

The train was slowing.

'Cheremkovo,' Jessel said. 'No sweat.' He backed away a little as though he had seen danger in Calder's eyes; he stood between the table and Calder's bunk. 'A two-minute stop.'

Calder's hand closed round the butt of the TT. Now he had to aim it under the duvet. 'How do you mean collaborate?'

'The CIA help to kill your kind in Russia; the KGB do the same in the West. It's easier that way. An American defector in Moscow being approached by a nice friendly diplomat from the United States Embassy. A Soviet dissident in New York meeting a kindly Russian from his hometown with news of his family. An accident, natural causes . . . .'

A summer day. Mrs Lundkvist's jolly voice. Baskets of mushrooms. Jessel wandering back into the wood.

'You killed Lidiya! You went back to the wood and got the Death Cap. You dropped by for a drink later and slipped it into the basket of mushrooms . . . .' Astonishment momentarily eclipsed fear.

The train stopped with a jolt.

'I also killed Kreiber acting on information supplied to the KGB by Dalby, of course. Like you he had begun to doubt, to think about reneging. But the West doesn't want traitors back. Why should it? Nor does Russia want to keep them if they want to re-defect. So at decent intervals they are dispatched as inconspicuously as possible.'

'Trying to put a bullet through my head in my car . . . inconspicuous?'

'An Executive Action Department fuck-up.'

Another jolt. The train seemed to be moving backwards.

'So why did you stop collaborating with Spandarian?'

'Because you came up with this crap about blowing the KGB godfathers in the West. Suddenly you were valuable to Washington and I had to help you escape.'

'Like the good scout you are.' Calder raised the barrel of the pistol a fraction.

'Even the President believed you. And why did you suddenly decide to re-defect? Because you knew there was a contract out for you, that's why. The only reason. And do you know when I knew you weren't going to get away with it?'

'When you got the cable telling you that my information was bullshit?'

Jessel paused.

The train stopped again.

'You read the decode?'

176

'Sure I did. Have you received "further instructions" yet?'

Jessel smiled. 'I didn't need further instructions. *Handle with utmost caution*. A pre-arranged code within a code. It means go ahead, kill the bastard.'

'Then why haven't you?' Calder asked.

'Because I want to kill you quietly while everyone's asleep within commuting distance of Irkutsk. By the time your body has been discovered in the luggage rack under the bunks, I'll be boarding a plane back to Moscow. And in any case the KGB will thank me for doing their job for them. Vladivostok? I didn't stand a goddam chance in the chess. And as for gathering intelligence – they would have produced every World War II warship they can find just for my benefit.'

'Reti was right,' Calder said. 'A chess player's style *is* a contradiction of his character. You're a pirate, Jessel.' The TT was now aimed at Jessel's heart.

'A sophisticated pirate. For instance I took the precaution of unloading that pistol you're aiming at me under the duvet.'

A train crept away from the station; then there was silence except for the night breathing.

Jessel's finger tightened on the trigger of the High Standard.

Calder, preparing to make a hopeless leap, said: 'You realise we're still in the station.'

'So? The gun's silenced.'

His trigger finger tautened, as the magnetic chess board exploded behind him projecting him, a human shield, at Calder, snapping his head forward and scooping a hole in his back that left the knuckles of his spine bare.

The blast buffeted about the compartment breaking things. Blood sprayed the mirror and the shards of window. Calder, lying beneath Jessel's body, felt him die. He pushed the dead-weight from him, prising the slippery butt of the pistol from his fingers. His ears ached and he was screaming silently but the blood on him was Jessel's not his.

Dressed in vest and pants, he waited inside the door that had been kicked out by the blast. Footsteps, toe and heel the way a hunter stalks, cracking glass on the floor of the corridor.

You didn't wait any longer for the sort of man who had made

a bomb out of a chess board, for a man who approached with such a professionally tentative tread. Calder leaned abruptly into the corridor and shot Tokarev in the head.

Tokarev dropped his gun, brushed at the blood and bone with his big hands and came at Calder. Calder shot him again in the chest. The hands reached for Calder's throat. Another shot in the belly. But Tokarev was an inexorable bear squeezing the life out of the tormentor in the green depths of the forest, his forest.

Calder's gun-arm was pressed impotently between their two bodies. He cried out hoarsely like a bird warning the forest that a predator is on the loose. Hearing the cry, Tokarev released his grip, gazed into the branches and fell onto the soft bed of leaves.

Spandarian watched the door of the soft-class coach through the sights of the AK 47 assault rifle he had drawn from militia HQ at Krasnoyarsk half way between Novosibirsk and Irkutsk. He had lodged the gun with the driver of the locomotive because Tokarev would be on his guard.

But Tokarev, absorbed with the results of the explosion, wouldn't be anticipating the executioner's bullet quite so soon; nor would he know of the existence of the AK 47.

Spandarian heard three shots, Tokarev making quite sure that Calder and Jessel were dead. Smiling, he caressed the trigger of the rifle with his forefinger: one bullet to make him Director of the First Chief Directorate. And then . . . .

Calder stood quite still for a moment to allow his instincts for survival, honed by pursuit, to re-assemble. It was probable, those instincts told him, that Tokarev would have had a back-up.

He dressed quickly, found Jessel's briefcase in the darkness and slid it into his suitcase. Then, using a corner of his duvet as protection, he pulled the daggers of glass from the frame of the window. He swung one leg over the sill, then the other, and disappeared into the rain-powered night.

He had no idea where he was going. Just away from the station and the gunman who, according to his sharp new instincts, would be on the other side of the train.

He didn't run: kicking up noise was death. He saw railway lines gleaming faintly with the polish of night and stepped over them. Ahead the saw-edge of pine forest against the sky, sprawling hills of coal and the skeletal outline of a bridge. From the station came movement, the sound of voices; he assumed that the staff had been dismissed for the killing but had been called back by the explosion.

He reached the bridge spanning a river and crouched behind a steel support pillar. In Russia rivers were used day and night for moving raw materials and there would be a steady stream of barges taking coal from the rich fields of Cheremkovo to Irkutsk.

He waited. The rain thickened. A movement near the abandoned coach. In the distance the muted roar of an approaching train. Up river a throb – a tug. Behind it three whale-like shapes.

The tug passed under the bridge as the train, swaying and rattling through Cheremkovo station, howled into the streaming night.

As Calder stood up a bullet hit metal beside his head.

Suitcase in hand he jumped.

When Spandarian reached the bridge all he could see through the rain was the grey breadth of the river, a channel of the night washing away the detritus of the day.

By which time, the coal barge carrying Calder, one leg broken, had rounded a curve of the river, and was proceeding on its elephantine but majestic way to Lake Baikal, the deepest lake in the world.

Chapter 22

When Katerina was released from house arrest she assumed that Spandarian had either caught Calder or knew where to find him.

Despairing, she went to see Svetlana in her apartment on Gruzinsky Bank Street. Svetlana had already shed the husk of her beating and, apart from a few fading bruises, was magnificent once more.

Wearing a brown and saffron kaftan, she made coffee in the kitchen. The apartment was only a studio and bathroom but Katerina envied her the smart little home with its trailing greenery and avant-garde pictures, furnished by pilots and architects and, once, the centre-forward for Zenit Leningrad.

'So,' Katerina said, sinking into a black-leather armchair. 'How's the architect?'

'He's doing marvellously,' Svetlana said sitting opposite. 'He's had a great incentive to work. When the KGB worked me over he was so worried about being contaminated by my wounds that he applied himself whole-heartedly to designing a new block of flats. I haven't seen him since.' She bit sharply into a chocolate biscuit. 'And Calder?'

'They must have got him.'

'Maybe.' Svetlana's voice became more gentle. 'I wondered why they stopped redesigning me with rubber truncheons. But don't give up hope: he's not stupid, your American. He'll give them a run for their money. Has anyone heard anything at the Institute?'

'I wouldn't know; I've been suspended.'

'Because of Calder?'

'According to the Director because of my association with the feminist movement.'

'Good.' Svetlana swept blonde hair from her forehead

revealing a cut with two spider stitches in it. 'Because we're having a rally next week. Are you game?'

'Of course.'

'Because, pussycat, we have to carry on whatever happens.'

'You don't have to tell me,' Katerina said, frowning.

'Ah, but you don't know everything: the rally has been banned. This is it, Kata, time to see what sort of stuff we're made of. Precocious infant doomed for a premature death or resilient youth.'

The phone rang; Svetlana picked up the old-fashioned receiver, the only antique in the room. She put on her telephone-voice-for-males; Katerina knew it well – firm but loaded with suggestion. Yes, she would love to go to the Bolshoi. *Giselle?* It always seemed to be *Giselle* but, no matter, she would look forward to seeing it again. She hung up and said to Katerina: 'The replacement.'

'A quick turnaround,' Katerina remarked.

'You've got to be quick to catch them. He's a little on the old side but distinguished.'

'And influential?'

'Naturally. And do you know something? When I really fall it's going to be for some little guy with a mother fixation instead of *blat*. It is written.' Svetlana picked up a copy of *Family* magazine. 'Here, listen to this. *Single man, 23, with one-roomed apartment and car with good prospects as a teacher seeks older woman with a view to marriage.* Older, that's the giveaway. A wet-nurse is what he wants. Maybe I should reply . . . .'

'So you're not going to tell me who this devastating octogenarian is.'

'I don't know how you're going to take this. But first I want to point out that he's going to be very useful to us.'

'Spit it out,' Katerina said.

'Okay. He's a colonel in the KGB. The one who stopped the beating.'

Katerina was on her feet. 'For God's sake, Svetlana!'

'I thought you wouldn't like it. But before you stomp out of the apartment *think*. We need someone on the other side, someone with influence, someone who can tell us which way the

181

wind's blowing, someone who can tip us off it they're going to raid us . . . .'

'Have you . . .?'

'Slept with him? Not yet.' She tried a smile. 'Sleeping with – I always thought that was a contradiction in terms.'

'I don't like it,' Katerina said.

'And you can stop being a prig, Katerina Ilyina. Did I criticise when you were *sleeping with* your American defector?'

'That was . . . .' Different? No, don't bother with the platitudes. Where was he now? Facing a firing squad? She put down her coffee cup. Her eyes burned.

She said: 'So where's this rally?'

'Red Square,' Svetlana told her.

Today, despite its intimidating aspect, Red Square was a wistful place. September sunlight lingered and, although there were heady days yet to come, a chill breeze fanned the broad expanse of cobblestones like the first sniff of a gathering cold.

On one side foreign newsmen had assembled opposite the red walls girding the Kremlin, close to the Christmas tree baubles of St Basil's Cathedral, as though seeking their blessing. Women's Lib, although old hat in the West, was news in Russia, especially when a couple of the protagonists could have graced *Playboy's* centrefold, especially if the militia mounted on pawing horses in the side streets were ordered to charge.

So far only a few women had arrived but there were still ten minutes to go before rallying time, advertised in *samizdat* newspapers and spread by word of mouth.

Militia were already doing their best to break up the gathering, employing *druzhniki*, part-timers wearing red arm-bands, to fool the snapping cameramen. A party of Cubans in shabby military denims bringing up the rear of the queue leading to Lenin's Tomb watched nervously.

But not as nervously as the officer, wearing the blue epaulettes and collar tabs of the uniformed KGB, sitting in the grey Volga on the corner of Kuibychev Street. His name was

Shevchenko and, like the nineteenth-century poet of that name, he came from the Ukraine. Shevchenko, thirty years old with, so he had been told many times by adoring women, Paul Newman's blue eyes, was nervous – shit-scared, he confessed to himself – for several reasons.

Firstly, he hated the authority of Moscow, yearning for the wind-rippled wheat-fields of Little Russia and the leisurely graces of the Kreschchatik, the Champs-Elysées of Kiev, and you couldn't get much closer to Authority than Red Square.

And then, although he was KGB, infiltrated there by his father who worked in the Procurator's Office in Kiev, he secretly admired defiance and had been known to tip off members of the OUN, the Organisation of Ukrainian Nationalists, who believed – rightly in his opinion – in an independent Ukraine, that a police raid was imminent. He suspected that it was these sympathies that had resulted in his transfer to Moscow. Siberia next, he thought gloomily as re-enforcements reached the women gathered opposite the Redeemer's Gate.

Moreover, although rebellious by nature, he was scared of women – a Ukrainian failing, according to Muscovites – and here he was charged with the destiny of God knows how many mutinous females. Although, he admitted, he wouldn't mind sharing the destiny of the blonde with the heart-breaking legs.

And finally, his briefing had been outrageously ambivalent. His Director didn't want the rally to succeed. 'We can't allow any form of dissidence to prosper; it would spread like wildfire throughout the Soviet Union.' (Didn't he realise that the Soviet Union was spawned on dissidence?) But at the same time he didn't want the Western media to witness force being used to disperse female belligerents. 'You must use your discretion,' that popular injunction for passing the rouble.

Behind the Volga a horse reared on its hind legs. Shevchenko recalled pictures of sabre-wielding Czarist cavalrymen cutting down mobs of peasants. Imagined the photographs in the Western newspapers of his own horsemen charging a mob *of women*. He glanced at a copy of *Pravda* lying on the seat beside him. It contained an article advising men not to waste time over

183

the kitchen sink, to untie their apron strings and hurry back to the assembly line where they were needed.

The article attacked the Western idea of sharing housework. 'The worth of the husband, his prestige, should be the prime thing in the moral code of a family. There should be a strict hierarchy in a man's home. He is the provider of the family, the builder, the keeper of the foundations. Women should always feel the strong hand and kind strength of the man.'

And an extraordinary case was quoted. A housewife had caught her 'hapless' husband washing the dishes. She was quoted as remarking: 'I saw my man had changed – even his voice wasn't what it used to be.' And then, realising what she had done to him by demanding equality, she had thundered: 'Take off that apron. I don't want to see you bent over the kitchen sink again. Be a man!'

It didn't help, Shevchenko brooded, on this day of days.

He looked at his wristwatch. In five minutes it would begin. A few rabble-rousing speeches, a petition at the Redeemer's Gate and a march twice round Red Square. Really it was unthinkable. So what are you going to do, Shevchenko? Behind the cavalry, militia armed with water cannon and rifles loaded with rubber bullets were awaiting his orders.

The blonde tapped on the window; he wound it down. 'Are you Shevchenko?' Stacked as well.

'How do you know my name?'

'Bykov told me.'

'Bykov?'

'First Chief Directorate.'

That Bykov! That bastard. The lingering spectre of the execution chambers that had once existed in Lubyanka in Dzerzhinsky Square.

'You know him?'

'I was with him last night.'

Doing what? he wondered. 'So, what do you want?'

'He told me that Kirov is quite adamant there shouldn't be any violence. Did you know that?'

'I have my instructions.'

'My God,' she said, 'those eyes.'

184

'Eyes?' He was becoming confused.

'Cornflower blue. I suppose lots of women have told you that.'

'A few,' he admitted.

'I've got tickets for an Agursky concert tonight. Would you like to come along?'

'Will Bykov be there?'

She shook her head. Her smile was devastating. 'It's a date,' she said. 'See you at the ticket office.' She strode across the square and began to address the suffragettes.

On the fringes of the gathering a few scuffles broke out but the *druzhniki* stood no chance: every time they manhandled a woman a cameraman took a picture.

Shevchenko bleeped the cavalry to be at the ready and radioed his Director.

'The rally's started,' he said.

'So?'

'Permission to move the horses in?'

'You have your orders Shevchenko. Use your discretion.'

'But . . . .'

But the Director had cut the connection. Shevchenko stared at the mausoleum where Soviet leaders stood to review the military parades. Were the old men of the Politburo even now watching him from above the swallow-tail battlements of the Kremlin wall? Was Kirov there?

He bleeped the horsemen to move onto the square, water cannon and rubber bullets to stand by.

The blonde was well into her stride now. He could just hear her over her microphone. 'Equality is all we seek. We have it in the office, in the factory. Oh yes, the equality of which the founder of this glorious nation of ours, Vladimir Ilyich Lenin, was so proud is well established in our workplaces. But is it elsewhere? The answer, comrades, is no. And I have here the organ of the Communist party to prove it.' She held aloft the copy of *Pravda* urging Russia's manhood to undo its apron strings.

Shevchenko admired her with a terrible perversity. He would put on an apron for her any time. But the way events were progressing he would soon be chipping ice from tin plates in a labour camp.

The blonde's place was taken by a girl with shining black hair and a face full of suffering. Beautiful but not his type: she lacked the arrogance of the blonde.

Cameras clicked. Foreign tourists disobeying Intourist shepherds stopped and gazed curiously at this display of feminine defiance on the Kremlin's doorstep. Whatever I do, Shevchenko thought, I am doomed.

He was saved by the arrival of a procession of Young Pioneers, the boys in black trousers, white shirts and red scarves, girls in black dresses under white aprons, rehearsing for November 7th, the anniversary of the Revolution. They were led by a goose-stepping boy and girl carrying the Red Flag and it was a safe bet that, as they must have come from a school close to the Kremlin, some of them were the sons and daughters of the privileged.

At any rate his subsequent explanation that he couldn't send in the horses or fire the water cannon or rubber bullets in front of the children was accepted, albeit without enthusiasm.

'You know something?' he whispered to Svetlana that evening while Leonid Agursky wooed his audience in a concert hall near the Botanic Gardens. 'I wouldn't be surprised if Kirov's own grandchildren weren't among those kids.'

'And do you know something? You could go down in history as the man who established Women's Lib in Russia.'

'I am not sure I want that,' he said.

'What's that got to do with anything?' She took his hand and patted it. 'Now be quiet and listen to Agursky.'

When Katerina got home Spandarian was waiting for her. But he was different; the gloss had gone.

Sasha was at work at the Operetta Theatre and her mother had been dismissed by Spandarian. They were alone.

Spandarian, pacing the floor, said: 'I want you to think very carefully: I want you to remember where Calder said he was going.'

Joy expanded inside her: Calder had eluded them.

186

'I told you before, he didn't say where he was going.'

'You knew he was going east. You lied to me. You told me he was heading west.'

She didn't care what she had told him: she wanted to dance. Outside children's kites, red and blue and yellow, flew high in the September sky.

Spandarian grasped her shoulder and spun her round. 'You will remember!' he said. The gloss had left his voice too.

'There's nothing to remember.'

He raised his hand to hit her, changed his mind. He said: 'You remember what happened to your friend Svetlana?'

'She's going out with a Colonel Bykov in the KGB at the moment.' She was also going out with a very junior officer with cornflower-blue eyes but that wouldn't help. Katerina was amazed at the instincts aroused by the realisation that Calder was free: she was in the ascendancy. 'Do you know this Colonel Bykov?' Bykov was undoubtedly very junior to Spandarian. Or had been? The new instincts were racing.

'I know of a Colonel Bykov. Why?'

'He wouldn't like to see his fiancée' – another inspiration – 'hurt in anyway. Or her best friend for that matter.'

'What do I care what a colonel thinks?'

Katerina appraised him: he had a beaten air about him. 'I think you should care,' she said. And then: 'Have you been sacked, Comrade Spandarian?' Masterly.

Spandarian didn't reply. He walked to the door leaving a slipstream of brandy fumes behind him. 'I'll give you until tomorrow. Think hard, Katerina Ilyina. In the meantime you will remain under house arrest.'

Not quite beaten. Still dangerous.

But he didn't return the following day. And three days later Katerina made her move. She packed a bag and took the money she had won on the lottery from Sasha's safe under the linoleum covering the kitchen floor.

When Sasha and her mother were out she undid several buttons of her blouse and opened the front door. The plainclothes militiaman standing outside was middle-aged, bored and untidy. Leaning forward so that he could see the slopes of her breasts, but not quite the peaks, she asked him if he would like some tea or some beer, or even a little vodka.

She led him straight to her bedroom. 'You must be hot,' she said, and helped him take off his jacket, and, 'You make yourself comfortable while I get a drink. Vodka?' and when he nodded and sat on the side of the bed, 'Then we can both make ourselves comfortable,' breasts brushing his face.

In the living room she picked up her case and went into the corridor locking the door behind her. Then she ran.

She caught a taxi to the apartment of Leonid Agursky who, she remembered, was embarking on a tour of Siberia and asked him if he could help her to get there because her new and wonderful instincts told her that Calder would make for the address she had given him on the shores of Lake Baikal.

ADJOURNMENT

Chapter 23

The White House. December.

First snowflakes of winter hesitating outside the long, blue-draped windows of the Cabinet Room. Beyond them the Rose Garden in hibernation.

Holden, addressing select members of the National Security Council, said: 'So that's it, gentlemen, it looks as though we lost Calder.'

He stared down the long mahogany table at Harry Truman warming himself on the wall above the fire.

'How long since we lost contact?' Secretary of State Howard Fliegel asked. Being a part-time huntsman he could never give up a chase.

'Nearly three months.'

And not a whisper from the *steppe* about his fate. Or the fate of Jessel. All the passengers in the faulty soft-class coach of the Trans-Siberian had been moved to another car; all, according to the Soviet authorities, had arrived at their destinations except the two Americans.

'But they can't just have disappeared off the face of the earth,' the US Ambassador in Moscow had protested. To which the Russians had responded: 'We agree. We demand to know the nature of their mission in Siberia.'

'So,' NSA Director Howard Zec said, 'we've lost a heaven-sent opportunity to bust the Soviet operation in the West.' He rumpled his soft white hair and stared accusingly at Louis Thurston, Director of the CIA.

Thurston removed his spectacles, his disguise, and said: 'Unless they got lucky it looks to me as if our friends were tipped off by someone that Jessel's chess-playing buddy was Calder.'

'Monday?' Defence Secretary Martin Duff suggested. He stroked his beaky nose. 'Or Tuesday or Wednesday.'

'Or Saturday,' Zec interrupted. 'Not even Calder knew who Saturday was.'

'*Knew?*' Thurston queried.

'Sure. To disappear in Siberia is to be dead. Wasted.'

Shoemaker, Holden's Assistant for Security, said: 'It figures, I guess. If the six agents left, now Marian Shannon is dead, are as influential as Calder suggests, then one of them might have heard about the Trans-Siberian escape route.'

Shoemaker, Holden thought, looked damp, as though he had just struggled into his grey suit after saving someone from drowning off Malibu beach. A bead of water from the shower slid off his slicked blonde hair.

Silence as the snowflakes peered in.

Finally Zec, still staring at Thurston, said abruptly: 'Has it occurred to anyone in this room that Jessel may have killed Calder?'

'And why in the hell would he want to do that?' Fliegel asked, predatory instincts aroused.

'Yes, why?' from Duff.

'Supposing he was a double-agent working for the KGB as well as us. Supposing he was Saturday. What better place to be installed than the American Embassy in Moscow?'

'Then he would have killed him a long time ago,' Thurston said. 'As soon as he knew that Calder was going to renege. Let's not get too convoluted just because the NSA hasn't got too many fingers in the pie in Moscow.'

'In any case,' Duff remarked, 'Jessel is missing too. Presumed dead. Unless, of course, they killed each other . . . .'

Holden intervened. The situation was serious enough without intelligence directors infecting the meeting with their own paranoia. 'All that need concern us,' he said, 'is the disappearance of Calder and the names he was bringing with him. If Calder is dead then we have to think about tracing their identities without his help.'

Dead. And in a way I killed him. It was as if the chess games all those years ago had been the opening moves for the gambit – the betrayal – with the final check-mate somewhere in the wastes of Siberia. Holden remembered how, after giant sandwiches at Elsie's, they had tabbed the names of personalities they would like to have eliminated under the major pieces. The name he should have written under Calder's king should have been CALDER.

The previous day he had spoken to Calder's ex-wife. Harry who had surfaced from his coma back in September had made a good recovery physically. But the neurologist wasn't over-optimistic about his progress mentally. Apparently it was difficult in the formative years to assess whether brain damage would be permanent.

'Wouldn't it be ironic,' Ruth had said on the phone, 'if he came under my care at the school?' Her voice was taut.

What do you say? *Don't worry, he's going to be okay*. He said: 'These things take time.' Worse.

'No news of Bob?'

'None.'

'They got to him, didn't they?'

'I don't know, Ruth. He vanished. Maybe he escaped . . . .'

'A few hours after he regained consciousness Harry was asking about his father again . . . after all those years.'

Maybe, Holden thought, the children of Bostonian high society had never let him forget that his father was a traitor. His defection had never come into the open but it would be discussed in the *cul-de-sacs* of élite gossip.

'. . . according to the psychiatrist,' she was saying, 'it might help if Harry could see his father.'

'We're still looking,' Holden said.

'In Siberia? Don't insult my intelligence, Gary.'

'If there's anything I can do . . . .'

'You did enough,' she said. 'A long time ago.'

Click.

'And how do we go about doing that?' Fliegel asked. Holden returned to the Cabinet Room. 'How the hell can we trace the identities of six days of the week? Computer print-outs on every VIP in the Western world?'

'We're working on it,' said Zec who never elaborated on his platitudes.

Thurston, face naked but calculating, was more expansive.

'*We*,' CIA not NSA, 'got a few leads from Marion Shannon's effects. It was her function to promote disarmament. You know, disarmament in the West but not in the Soviet bloc. She funded peace rallies, got to the kids, even turned a few heads at Bilderbeg. She was doing a good job. Given a few more years she might have fashioned "a world fit for our kids to grow up in" – and the Communists to occupy. Peace perfect peace and freedom a whisper from the past.'

'The leads,' Duff said lighting a cigarette. 'You were going to give us the leads.' He coughed, confirming everyone else's worst fears about smoking. He stubbed out the cigarette.

'Nothing specific but we're making progress,' Thurston told him and Holden knew he was lying.

Shoemaker said: 'It's my guess that the other six codenames operate in totally different areas from Marion Shannon. Each in a different section of the Western structure so that, co-ordinated, they could destroy us. One in NATO maybe, up there at the top.'

'Maybe one in the European Economic Community,' Fliegel said thoughtfully. 'A government minister even.'

'A Secretary of State?' Duff suggested, smiling.

Thurston said: 'If Calder was – is,' he corrected himself, 'right then the traitors of the 'fifites and 'sixties were minor league. Their job was to establish and maybe train the major league of the future. Get them primed for the final takeover. And if, in their own fields, they're as influential as Marion Shannon was in disarmament then they could make it.'

'Unless we find Calder,' Holden said.

'Yes, Mr President, unless we find Calder.' Fat chance Thurston's tone said.

It was Duff, one crossed leg swinging, who put the words to the notion that had been crystallising in everyone's minds. 'I think we've got to accept,' he said slowly, 'that at least one of these influential sleepers operates in Washington. Maybe two or three. Who knows, maybe Saturday.'

A breeze sprang up in the Rose Garden and blew away the inquisitive snowflakes.

★ ★ ★

194

Thwack.

The small rubber ball hit the white wall of the racquets squash court hard and low at an awkward angle. But not awkward for Shoemaker; he lobbed it softly into a corner and Holden didn't even try to reach it; that was the difference between them – he played to try and keep fit, Shoemaker *was* fit and played because he enjoyed it.

'Okay,' Holden said, 'you win. Let's take a break.'

'You played well,' Shoemaker said.

'For an old man.'

'Come on,' Shoemaker said. 'You're one of the youngest presidents in the history of the United States.'

True. But at the moment he didn't feel young. He was weighted with Calder's wasted years.

They adjourned to the soft-drinks bar adjoining the squash court in the grounds of the White House. Holden poured them orange juice.

'So,' he said, leaning on the bar, 'as Assistant for Security what do you think?'

'About Calder? I don't know. He's been gone a long time. The Soviets may have got him. Or he may have escaped.'

'Everyone else figures he's dead.' As always Shoemaker's optimism appealed to Holden. The optimism of youth? Not quite. Shoemaker was thirty-eight but young by Cabinet standards. And uncomplicated by Security Council standards.

Shoemaker said: 'You've got to admit it's the most likely explanation.'

'I don't happen to think so.'

'Oh?' Shoemaker frowned.

'But maybe it's because I'm involved personally . . . . Did you know Calder and I were friends?'

'A long time ago? Yes, I knew that.'

'What you didn't know, at least I hope you didn't know . . . .'

And Holden told Shoemaker about his betrayal.

'It goes without saying,' he finished, 'that this is between the two of us.'

'Of course. We're both on the same side.'

195

Holden sipped his juice; the ice tinkled like wind chimes. 'I've got a job for you,' he said at last.

Shoemaker waited. The falling snow had melted and rain spattered the window.

Holden said: 'I want you to go to Russia,' and when Shoemaker looked startled: 'You see I've given this a lot of thought and you're probably the only man who can find out if Calder is still alive.'

'Why me?'

'Because if the Soviets allow the American President's Adviser on Security into Russia it means there's still hope.'

'They will assume I've come to get him?'

Holden nodded. 'Which in its turn means that he's escaped, gone to ground.'

'I still don't understand. Why me?'

'Who else? The Soviets have to be impressed by the importance we attach to finding Calder and there are only a handful of people in high places who know what's going on. I could hardly send the director of the CIA or the NSA . . . .'

'I'm to be used as bait?'

'What I'm saying is that, one – we need confirmation that Calder is still alive. Two – we need someone in the area in case he makes contact with our embassy in Moscow. Three – there's always a chance that, if the KGB get a lead, you'll be able to beat them to it.'

'Chance would be a fine thing,' Shoemaker remarked.

Holden poured himself more juice, thick with fresh pulp. 'The first two points are the important ones. If Calder makes a break for it he can't go it alone. Who knows, he may be injured.'

'So I fly to Moscow observed by a brigade of KGB and then fly to Irkutsk. Isn't that a little obvious, Mr President?'

'I'm not suggesting that anyone is fooling anyone. We and the Russians will be using each other to get a lead on Calder's whereabouts. But I agree, we have to make a pretence of deception. Which is why you'll enter the Soviet Union through the back door. California, Japan, Nakhodka and then the Trans-Siberian Railway to Irkutsk in Siberia. Luckily Irkutsk is one of the stopovers allowed by Intourist.'

'With respect, sir, you have a devious mind.'

'Why is it,' Holden asked, 'that whenever anyone says *with respect* they mean the opposite? Devious? How about subtle? You see I'm a chess player and I have to consider every nuance of an opponent's move.'

'So I'm a move in a game of chess?'

'You're a gambit,' Holden told him.

'I don't know a great deal about chess,' Shoemaker said, 'but isn't there another ploy called a sacrifice?'

END GAME

Chapter 24

By December the annual battle between General Winter and Old Man Baikal had reached a crucial stage.

All over Siberia, from the Arctic to China, from the Urals to the Pacific, the lakes had surrendered to the cold and were manacled with ice. With the exception of Baikal. With its home-brewed hurricanes and earth tremors that shook its bed, a mile deep in places, it would resist until the middle of the month. It always did. And even then it would carry on guerrilla warfare: a thunderous clap and a crack wide enough to swallow a truck would fizz across the ice like black lightning. Respect winter by all means, but revere Baikal.

But in September when Calder jumped onto the coal barge on its way to the lake, hostilities were only tentative. A few fogbanks rolling up the four-hundred-mile-long crescent moon of the lake, the occasional breeze testing its winter sinews on the glass-clear water.

For a few moments Calder didn't realise that he had been hurt. Then the pain knifed him.

He sat up on the coal, powdered rain washing his face, and reached for his leg. He touched a sharp stick and when he realised that it was his shin-bone protruding from his flesh, passed out. When he regained consciousness the sky was glowing green, the rain had spent itself and a man was looking down at him.

'And who might you be?' He wore a spade beard and a leather hat with ear-flaps tied under his chin.

Calder sat up again. He could see the shin bone sticking through his trouser leg like the prow of a model boat. He wanted to vomit. He said: 'There was an escape . . . . I'm one of the *brodyagi* . . . .'

'With a suitcase? Wearing a raincoat and a suit? If you're a convict I'm Grandfather Frost.'

'I had just arrived in the camp,' Calder told him. 'From Moscow.'

'I thought you had a foreign accent.'

'I was at reception when they broke out. I joined them. What would you have done?'

'What you did. What camp?'

'Volokon.'

'Political crimes, isn't it? Dissidents? What did you do, comrade?'

Remembering the legendary Siberian independence from Moscow, Calder told him that he had foolishly indulged in a vendetta with a highly placed bureaucrat – 'A Muscovite, of course' – and accused him of corruption.

'Foolishly?' The bargemaster tugged at his square beard. 'I don't think so, comrade. You showed spirit; you should have been a Siberian. Those pricks in Moscow . . . *na levo* is their password: they don't know what it is to do an honest day's work.' He sat on a rock of coal shining in the dawn light and saw the shaft of bone. 'Shit! What are we going to do with you, comrade?'

'In the old days they used to put food out for the *brodyagi* so that they didn't have to steal.'

'You need more than food, my friend. If you don't get treatment you'll get gangrene. And you can't run far on one leg.'

'If you take me to a hospital I'll lose more than a leg.'

'Your life? Maybe. They'd certainly move you north to a camp where you piss ice-cubes.'

The green light above the pencil-points of the pines on top of the looming river-banks was turning pale blue. It was going to be a beautiful autumn day.

Pain ran up Calder's leg in ripples.

The bargemaster said: 'You've got money?'

'I've got something better than money: I've got dollars.'

The bargemaster was impressed. 'They didn't take them away from you?'

'They were about to. How much?'

202

'Not for me, you understand. I'm a Siberian: Siberians don't hustle for money. We have a saying: "In Siberia only the bears steal." Have you heard that?'

From every Siberian I've ever met, Calder thought, and reached for the suitcase lying in the coal.

The bargemaster said: 'I know what you're thinking because you've been corrupted by Moscow, but I don't want a kopek. Now my mate who I've left in charge of the old tub towing the barges, he's different. He's Siberian but he's a Buryat and he'll want money to keep his mouth shut. And the medic who fixes your leg, he'll have to be paid off.' He watched Calder release the catches on the suitcase. 'Where do you want to get to?'

Calder found the address Katerina had given him. 'To a village at the north-east tip of Baikal.'

'Your lucky day. We're taking this coal to the top of the Old Man. But it's going to be tricky. We pass through Irkutsk to get to the lake and if there's been a break the militia will be checking anything that moves. But still, you have dollars . . . .'

Calder handed him a wad. The bargemaster pulled a tarpaulin over his body, making a tent of it over the exposed bone, and made his way back along the rope gangways connecting the four barges to the steamboat, the *Ulianov*, Lenin's real name, butting against the current.

Five hours later the bargemaster anchored off Angarsk thirty miles from Irkutsk on the banks of the Angara, the only one of Baikal's 336 waterways to drain rather than feed it. He rowed to one of the wharfs. He returned with a man with sagging cheeks and sad eyes who hissed his s's when he spoke. The medic.

When he saw Calder's leg he hissed like a punctured football. 'Bad, very bad. The bone is dirty. Where can I work?'

'Here,' the bargemaster told him. 'We can't get him onto the *Ulianov*. Even here's dangerous.'

A militia helicopter clattered over the docks and wheeled away to the north before reaching the *Ulianov* and its barges.

The medic pointed at a plank. He told the bargemaster to insert it under the broken leg and fetch a pail of boiling water.

The medic handed Calder a bottle of vodka. 'Here, drink this.' *And bite on the bullet!* He began to cut away the trouser leg with a pair of kitchen scissors. Calder put the neck of the bottle to his mouth; the vodka, oily moonshine, scalded his stomach. 'This is some mess,' the medic said. Calder looked away from the naked bone and drank more moonshine; this time it didn't burn so sharply. From his black bag the medic took yellowing cotton wool and, with the water the bargemaster had brought steaming in a galvanised bucket, bathed the edges of the wound. 'More vodka,' he said. 'Drink more, get good and drunk. Maybe I'll have a shot.' He took the bottle and swigged. 'Good stuff, I know a chemist . . . .' He handed the bottle back. Calder poured more moonshine down his throat; this time it was salve. The medic poured hydrogen peroxide on the bone and the wound. It frothed. He took a plaster bandage from his bag, dipped it in the boiling water and stood it upright on the plank. Then he washed his hands with carbolic soap. He nodded at the bargemaster and whispered. Calder picked up the whisper: 'Hold him, this is going to hurt.' The medic needn't have worried: the pain was receding, flying away with the arrowhead of ducks passing overhead. The medic placed the heel of his hand on the bone and pressed down and Calder's scream rose into the pale blue sky; his body bucked but the bargemaster held him. Holding the bone in place with one hand, the medic poured orange mercurichrome onto a piece of lint and placed it on the wound above his hand. 'Now you hold it,' he said to the bargemaster, pulling the lint over the bone. Deftly he wound the plaster bandage round Calder's shin. When he had finished he said to the bargemaster: 'That's the best I can do.' And: 'Ten more dollars please – for the vodka.' *And only bears steal*. Calder almost smiled, then the sky turned black.

Militia boarded the *Ulianov* at Irkutsk, city of gold and furs from which Russians once journeyed to settle in California and Alaska, but the bargemaster persuaded them with vodka and dollars, manna from heaven, that there was no point in searching the barges. Look, he said, and they looked and all they could see was coal and a couple of tarpaulins.

With high-rearing hydrofoils skimming past, they made their way down the last forty miles of the Angara to Baikal. Calder came to as the *Ulianov* pulled its barges into the low curve of the crescent. The evening sky was cooling but his body was hot with fever.

He peered over the side of the barge. He had visited Baikal long ago with an Intourist guide and he remembered her claims. Seventeen hundred types of fauna and flora . . . freshwater seals – 'Yes, seals,' irritably – that had made their way down river from the Arctic aeons ago . . . and, triumphantly, containing more water than all the Great Lakes of North America put together.

North America. Was Harry dead? He burned inside; outside his sweat was iced. His leg pulsed with pain.

The *Ulianov*, churning water, turned in an arc and, like a duck with coal-black chicks, headed north-east.

At 1 am they were stopped by a patrol boat. A searchlight swept the barges turning black carbon into silver; the beam lingered for a few moments on the two heaps of tarpaulin, then swept back to the *Ulianov*. The skipper and mate of the patrol boat boarded her in the blue-white glare but were also persuaded with vodka and dollars that there was no point in searching the barges. 'A convict on a barge as slow as a porpoise heading back in the same direction as the break? Stupid,' the bargemaster said.

'Who said anything about a convict?' the skipper of the patrol boat asked. 'Who said anything about a break?' He took a gulp of firewater but didn't elaborate.

The following morning, as they passed the island of Olkhon, the lake brewed a storm. Brimming waves punched the barges and rain sluiced from sagging clouds. The wallowing of the barge woke Calder from a feverish sleep. He peered inside the canvas. Blood was seeping from the bottom of the plaster-cast; the cast was streaked with coal-dust.

On a storm-tossed lake with a broken leg and every KGB operative and militiaman in Siberia looking for him. Hopeless. The futility of his life since those bold years on the campus washed over him with the rain.

The *Ulianov* pulled into the shelter of a grey cliff and anchored. Here the waves slouched. Shivering, Calder closed his eyes. So he would submerge from life – he heard the water lazily slapping the hull of the barge and there was foam in his brain – and the Soviet sleepers would continue to undermine the West in their seats of power.

Why hadn't Western intelligence been more zealous in pursuing the proposition that agents such as Philby and Maclean had been instructed to recruit youth? That their brief had been to establish a hierarchy of awesome power in the 'eighties.

Too late now: the illustrious sleepers were above suspicion. But Holden should have acted on the information I sent him about Marion Shannon. And yet she was in the clear. Why? Has everything I've done been a waste?

The engine of the *Ulianov* thumped into life and the bursting foam bubbles in Calder's skull became louder and more rhythmic.

The village of Oskino, lazily wooden but gritted here and there with cement outhouses, lay the width of a grey beach from the water. Behind it green hills covered with brush climbed timidly to crests of pine and larch. On either side granite and basalt cliffs stood guard.

A few years earlier Oskino, which depended for its survival on fishing, had nearly died. Chemical and cellulose plants had begun to poison the lake and its fish, but the protests had been so passionate that Moscow had thrown in its hand.

The village's main catch was *omul*, the salmon of Baikal, but today as the *Ulianov* hove to half a mile offshore, transparent fish sucked from Baikal's depths by the storm and tossed onto the shore were being harvested. So fat were the ugly little fish that they provided fuel for lamps. The women also collected bright green sponges, fruit of the storm, with which they scoured their pots.

The bargemaster waited until nightfall before rowing Calder, quiet now but breathing as rapidly as an exhausted dog, to the shore. He moored the row-boat to a wooden jetty on the opposite side to the fishing boats and went looking for the family Petrov. He found them in a wooden dacha on the edge of the village.

Yury Petrov, prematurely grey hair a crown of fulfillment rather than age, read Katerina's note, handed it to his wife, dark and feline-sleek with Mongol cheeks and eyes, struggled into a coat and followed the bargemaster to the jetty.

Together they carried Calder through dark streets made from upturned logs to a wood-panelled room in the dacha where Petrov's wife had already made up a bed. The bargemaster went back for Calder's suitcase. 'I don't know whether you want money,' he said. 'Our friend has plenty of it. Dollars,' watching for an animal-twitch of interest.

He was disappointed. 'We have enough,' Petrov told him and the bargemaster returned to his coal without knowing that Petrov had once filled barges with gold.

In the morning Petrov's wife brought Calder *omul* steaks and tea and black bread as rich as cake. 'I think,' said Petrov, sitting beside the bed in a room overlooking the now-placid lake, 'that you'd better tell us all about it.'

When he had finished, Petrov, wearing a white bathrobe and looking uncommonly urbane for a member of a fishing community, said: 'We'll help you, of course, but it's going to be tricky. The militia have already searched the village and they'll be back.' He toyed with a gold St Christopher medallion hanging from his neck. 'Do you realise they're probably searching every village, every town, in Siberia. Unless . . . .'

Calder, unshaven and wracked with spasms of shivering, said: 'Unless what?'

'Unless they got the name of the village from Katerina. And the name of Petrov . . . .'He lit a cigarette; he looked, Calder thought, like a certain Russian film star who had always seemed just a little too suave for Soviet movies. 'So it might be even trickier than I thought.' St Christopher flashed in the reflected light from the lake. 'So what are we going to do, Raisa?' he asked his wife who was replenishing Calder's cup from a samovar.

'You know perfectly well,' said his wife. She was wearing a

red silk robe embroidered with Chinese dragons. Her blue-black hair hung in night-dishevelled tresses and beneath the silk her body moved sinuously with the dragons. She smelled faintly of lemons.

'I suppose I do. You see,' he said to Calder, 'I used to be on the run. I worked in the gold-fields in the north and I used to transport the rock south to Irkutsk for crushing and milling.'

'You don't look like a trucker,' Calder said.

'He was a thief,' Raisa said fondly.

'I believe you have a word in America: scam. Well believe me there are scams here that would make the Mafia die of shame.'

'What was yours?' Calder asked.

'I had my own refinery. You know, Siberia's so vast you can get away with things like that. It was supposed to process ferrous rock. And it did, millions of tons of it. But it also processed gold-bearing rock creamed from the trucks. A little cyanide, a little zinc dust and we had gold to refine in the furnaces.'

Raisa poured steaming tea into Calder's cup – he couldn't eat the food. As she bent down he saw her small satin-smooth breasts. Straightening up she said: 'By the time Yury was in maximum production so many high-ups were involved in Irkutsk that no one could touch him.'

'Goldmail,' Yury said in English. 'Much more grand than blackmail. But in the end,' reverting to Russian, 'we had to do a deal because rumours of *apparatchik* weighted with gold were reaching Moscow. So I agreed to abandon my scam and the authorities in Irkutsk agreed to forget the whole thing. And here I am, living off my golden opportunities.' St Christopher winked at Calder. 'But you're probably wondering what all this has got to do with you . . . .'

'In the old days,' Raisa explained, 'Yury was always anticipating getting caught. So he bought this place – we lived in Bratsk in those days – and he built a secret room in it.'

Calder raised himself on one elbow. 'How secret?'

'Secret enough to hide most of my gold in it,' Yury told him.

'Katerina's a wise girl.'

'Are you in love with her?' Raisa asked.

208

Thinking: 'I don't look much like an object for love,' Calder said: 'Yes, we love each other.'

'And you're going back to America?'

'I have no choice.'

'Will she go with you?'

'I don't know,' Calder said.

'She's a beautiful girl. Not just her looks,' Raisa shrugged and the dragons shrugged with her. 'But I suppose she knows what she's doing. If any of us do when we love a man.' She stretched out and touched the arm of her robber-baron husband.

'I knew her mother years ago,' Yury half-explained. 'Before she met Sasha. Ah, that Sasha. What a voice. What a man. When things got really tough in Moscow Kata came to stay with me. When she was a little girl, that is. Then I met Raisa.' He shared a smile with her. 'Then Sasha came on the scene and Kata didn't come here anymore. There wasn't any need for it, I suppose.'

'Whatever Kata says,' Raisa said, 'is all right by us.'

'As soon as my leg mends,' Calder told them, 'I'll be on my way.' He lay back on the pillow again and, as he moved so the blankets moved, and a faint smell of putresence reached him.

Raisa pulled the blanket from his legs. 'Oh God,' she exclaimed. Calder, craning his neck, stared at his leg. The blood oozing from the bottom of the cast was streaked yellow.

Yury whistled softly. 'We'll have to get a doctor.'

'Then I'm finished.'

'In Siberia?' Petrov shook his head vigorously. 'We don't hand *brodyagi* back to Moscow that easily.'

'I hope,' Calder said, managing a smile, 'that you aren't going to tell me that in Siberia only bears steal.'

'Only bears and truckers.'

Petrov stood up. He crossed the room and pressed the base of a light-fitting fashioned like a dripping candle. A panel of wood opened on the other side of the room. A rich metallic gleam came from within.

The bars of gold were stacked beneath an aperture in the wall –

fitted with a wooden shutter if the hunt for the occupant of the room grew near – that overlooked Baikal.

Calder, lying on an iron bed, stared at them as the doctor from Nizhneangarsk thirty miles away across the lake cut through the plaster cast. He continued to stare as the doctor exclaimed: 'Mother of God, who treated this?'

'A medic at Angarsk,' said Calder thinking how strange it was that God was invoked so often in a country ruled by atheists.

'A butcher,' the doctor, scrubbed and studious, said, 'not a medic. We'll pump you full of antibiotics and clean the wound and give you some painkillers.'

He covered the wound with lint, patted Calder on the shoulder and, ducking and beckoning to Petrov, returned to the living room.

Calder stared through the aperture. A fishing boat was becalmed on the blue and white sky reflected on the smooth water. I shall get to know this lake, Calder thought. Already it was his guardian. To the right, on a hard-rutted lane leading to the grey beach, he could see a man pouring vodka, makeshift anti-freeze, into the radiator of an old Moskvich.

The doctor, smelling of carbolic, returned and began to clean the wound. As he worked he talked. 'Don't tell me who you are, how you got here, I don't want to know . . . The Petrovs, wonderful people . . . . If they'd known you were coming they would have had bread and salt waiting for you . . . . You can trust them as you would your own hands . . . .' He stared at his own; the fingers were blunt and strong. 'And from Baikal you'll get strength, we all do . . . . Superstitious? Perhaps . . . nothing wrong with a little respect for your elders . . . . They say the Old Man is twenty-five million years old, the oldest lake in the world . . . . My God,' plucking a sliver of bone from the wound with a pair of tweezers, 'what a mess.' He sprinkled powder on the wound and dressed it loosely; then he strapped a metal splint to Calder's leg. He gave Calder some tablets, shot antibiotic into his buttock and was gone.

By midday Calder felt better. The pain had shrunk to an ache, like muscle fatigue after exertion, and his brain had cleared. He even felt hungry.

210

Raisa brought him borsch and black bread and sat beside the bed while he drank the purple soup floating with islands of cream.

'How is Katerina?' she asked. 'Still fighting for us poor underprivileged women?'

Calder couldn't imagine anyone less underprivileged than Raisa dressed now in a red track suit, polished hair coiled. 'As long as they allow her to fight,' he told her.

'The women will win,' she said. 'One day they'll win; it's part of evolution.' She spoke Russian with what Calder decided was a Han Chinese accent, rippling her r's prettily into l's. 'Katerina is merely a catalyst of change. Some people are born like that; without them we would still be in the Stone Age.'

'Tell me,' Calder said, spooning borsch, 'with all this gold,' pointing the spoon at the ingots, 'why do you live here?'

'Many reasons. We've come under Baikal's thrall for one. For another Yury can carry on his love affair here. You see I have a rival – gold. Yury is trying to manufacture his mistress.'

'Crazy?' Yury, in black, grey hair healthy against his tan, came into the secret room; he reminded Calder of a fashionable New York psychiatrist. 'You think it's crazy?' as though everyone else did. 'Not so. It can be done. You didn't know that?'

Calder shook his head wondering if Petrov *was* crazy. Raisa left the room to get more food; Yury took her place and began to lecture.

'You can make gold from platinum. It's been done. But obviously it's very expensive, more expensive than natural gold and therefore pointless. But if you can make gold from platinum why not other metals?'

'The alchemists didn't succeed.'

'They didn't succeed with platinum either. Today we have harnessed science to help us. In my laboratory I have lasers . . . .'

'But surely if you manage to manufacture gold you're debasing your mistress. Making a whore out of her.'

Yury shook his head. 'I only want to learn the secret. I won't make a big production of it.'

211

'Won't other people?'

'Maybe they already have: it doesn't matter: the formula will be kept secret by the gold barons. They don't want to kill the golden goose . . . . As a matter of fact,' pointing vaguely north, 'there's enough ore-producing rock in Siberia to make the world's gold as cheap as tin. To bankrupt the Bank of England and Fort Knox. Come to that there are enough gem-stones there to make shoe-shops of every jeweller's on Fifth Avenue. But, of course, the Russians aren't stupid: they've no intention of ruining their own market. Unless one day . . . .' He didn't finish the sentence.

Raisa returned with a plate of stewed bilberries sprinkled with powder. Calder pointed to the powder and asked what it was.

'Gin-seng, the herb of youth . . . .'

'And virility,' Yury said, smiling man-to-man. *We old men with young women*.

'It grows in the *taiga*. Where the shaggy tigers roam – or so they say.'

'So,' Yury said, 'you eat gin-seng in Siberia and go to Georgia and live to be a hundred and fifty.'

When Calder slept he dreamed golden dreams of youth and love.

For a while it seemed as though the fracture and wound would heal.

And while bone and flesh were knitting Calder, walking with crutches, leg in plaster except round the wound, lurched round the house watching winter assemble its forces round the last pocket of resistance, Baikal.

He saw the first blizzards attack the distant mountains leaving them imperiously white – but the sky was so blue and the sun so bright that they only menaced in the evenings. He saw the dawn tissues of ice on the fringes of the lake and he saw them melted by banks of fog advancing across the water. When the ice grew thicker overnight the ground trembled and dispersed it.

212

'They say,' Petrov confided proudly, 'that if we had another earthquake like the one a hundred years ago the Old Man would wipe out Irkutsk.'

Since the cold had pushed its way into the village Yury had exalted. Sitting at the living room table, examining a ten-tola gold ingot, he said: 'Siberia means Sleeping Land, you know, but it only sleeps in the summer. In the winter it comes to life.' He rubbed his hands together. 'The snow and ice talk and out come the skis and the sky is full of eagles . . . .'

'And you freeze to death,' Calder said fingering the beginnings of a beard.

'Not here. It's warm here. Thirty degrees – below, that is – nothing more. But in the north, Yakut, that's the real Siberia. Seventy degrees sometimes and permafrost as hard as concrete. That's cold,' Yury said with relish. He reached for a bottle bearing a red label. 'Here, let's drink to winter.' He poured two shots of crystal-clear liquid. '*Spirt*. Grain alcohol, 192 proof. Makes vodka taste like mother's milk.' He tossed the spirit down his throat as the KGB Border Guard cavalry arrived at the other end of the village.

The horsemen, green piping on their grey uniforms, had been brought by train from the eastern border with China. They were the élite and they rode arrogantly on their fine chestnut horses, AK 47 assault rifles strapped beside their saddles, pistol holsters unbuttoned.

While a dozen of them dismounted and began their search, heels of their leather boots crisp on the wood-log streets, the others blocked all exits, even the beach. The horses' breath smoked on the frosted air; from time to time a cavalryman would lean forward and pat the sleek neck of his mount.

The streets emptied. Dogs, the door-knockers of Siberia, barked. Far out on Baikal a school of seals played boisterously.

One by one the dismounted horsemen searched the fretwork cottages. They were bored but they treated the occupants courteously. They didn't hold out any hope of finding anyone, their attitude implied, but orders were orders even if they did

213

come from Moscow. They didn't even bother to consult the KGB informant in the village: in Siberian villages informants were a joke.

Finally, not quite as soberly as when they arrived, Siberian hospitality being what it is, they reached the Petrov dacha. There, because it was so grand, they stopped and conferred. Then, with the slightly aggressive swagger of a horseman without his horse, the officer in charge knocked loudly on the front door, and dispatched two of his men to the rear.

Petrov was on his second glass of *spirt* when the officer hammered on the door.

'Quick,' he said to Calder. 'Only the police knock like that. Once. Then they knock the door down.'

Picking up his crutches, Calder lurched towards the secret door. But one of the padded rests wasn't fitted snugly under his armpit. As he negotiated the step he lost one crutch. For a moment he stood like a stork in water. Then he fell sideways.

Behind him the panel closed. Darkness except for a bright shaft of light from the aperture in the wall. Imprisoned dust sparkled in the beam.

His leg was agony. Remote from him. Someone else's agony. He dragged the agony towards the aperture. It was heavy. A concrete encumbrance.

Supporting himself on his good leg, he pulled himself up to the aperture. He saw a uniform. Green piping. He shut the wood slats across the opening.

Then he slid to the floor.

The officer was young with close-cropped hair and a small, fierce moustache. He was very correct and held his cap under his arm.

He said: 'With your permission, comrade, we want to search the house.'

'Permission? Since when did you need permission?' Petrov poured himself another *spirt*. 'Will you take a nip to keep out the cold?'

The young officer stared at him without expression. 'I don't drink on duty.' Behind him two cavalrymen swayed slightly.

214

'Suit yourself.' Petrov drank the *spirt*; he should have been eating something to soak it up. 'What are you looking for, *brodyagi*?'

'That needn't concern you.'

'You're very correct, young man. What did you do when the Chinese showed their bare asses across the Amur?'

'I wasn't there; I was too young. And now if you'll excuse me . . . .' He nodded crisply to the two cavalrymen. When they had gone clumsily about their business he asked: 'Are you alone?'

'My wife is in Nizhneangarsk stocking up for winter.' He remembered the second glass on the table. 'She likes to take a shot before boarding the ferry.'

'The ferry left half an hour ago,' the officer said. He picked up the glass. 'Doesn't she wear lipstick?'

'She doesn't have to. A natural beauty from Mongolia. Not like city women. Are you from Moscow, comrade?'

'Leningrad. Tell me, how do you manage to look so prosperous in a village like this?'

'Furs,' Petrov said promptly. 'Barguzin sable. The finest in the world.'

'Everything in Siberia seems to be the best, the biggest, the oldest.'

'We cannot lie,' Petrov said.

After a while the two cavalrymen returned and reported that there was no one else in the dacha.

The officer took a silver case from the pocket of his tunic and, with neat movements, took out a cigarette and lit it.

Crossing long, leather-booted legs, he regarded Petrov speculatively. 'Irkutsk and Baikal,' he said removing a flake of black tobacco from his bottom lips. 'They've always had, shall we say, a *golden* reputation . . . .'

'Historically? They taught you well in Leningrad. Many a governor has been hypnotised by gold. Governor Gagarian, wasn't it, who was hanged for 'unheard-of theft'? His horses were shod with gold . . . .'

'The associations are much later than that. In the Civil War. When the Bolsheviks captured Admiral Kolchak and shot him.

215

That was when *we* recaptured our gold from the Czechs who were supporting the Whites. Twenty-nine truckloads of gold, I believe. According to rumours some of it's still at the bottom of Baikal . . . .'

Petrov poured himself another shot of *spirt*. 'Really? I hadn't heard that. But I wouldn't argue with the pride of the Chief Border Guards Directorate.' He really should have eaten something with the grain alcohol.

'Well, we must be on our way.' The officer stood up and Petrov rose from his seat a little unsteadily. 'You dress very well,' the officer observed.

'Really?' surprised. 'That's very kind . . . .'

'But you should see your tailor about the jacket – it really doesn't fit too well.' The officer leaned forward and lifted the ten-tola bar of gold from the inside pocket of Petrov's jacket. 'Meanwhile you'd better come with us.'

Like a periscope the tip of the bone protruded from the dark blood and pus filling the cavity in the plaster. And beneath the plaster the flesh swelled so that, two days after Calder had fallen, the doctor had to cut it away.

When he saw what lay beneath he sighed. He shot Calder full of antibiotic but by now Calder's body had built up a formidable resistance.

He told Raisa he would return from Nizhneangarsk in two days. Before he came back Yury Petrov returned having 'goldmailed' the authorities in Irkutsk.

'You should have seen the face of that cocky little whippersnapper from the Border Guards,' he said but Raisa didn't smile and said: 'One day, Yury, you will be weighted to the bottom of Baikal by gold,' and 'I'm worried about Calder.'

'Don't worry,' Yury said, full of golden optimism, 'he'll pull through,' and of the Border Guard officer, with true Siberian feeling: 'May he have ulcers on his soul.'

When the doctor returned and examined Calder's leg he shook his head. Later that day he operated.

Calder was in Fenway Park discussing the latest Red Sox

triumph over Cokes and hot dogs with Ruth and Harry and Dalby and Yury Petrov.

Casually he slid his hand down his thigh towards the fracture.

His hand reached his knee. After that there was nothing.

Chapter 25

Sometimes youth departs in a moment. Dispatched by the lack of interest in a pretty girl's eyes, a lost game of tennis, a snapped tooth, a young boss. Thirty years of making it and, click, middle-age.

With Spandarian it took a little longer than a moment but it was abrupt just the same. Click, he was sacked from his job with the Second Chief Directorate and assigned to Registry and Archives. Click, he was thrown out of his smart apartment and given a one-roomer overlooking Danilovsky Cemetery. Click, when he tried to hit the slut with the pouting lips she drew a knife on him and left the view of the gravestones for ever.

To seek rejuvenation Spandarian took a vacation in Georgia, keeping in touch with his former secretary, Yelena, who had taken an instant dislike to her new boss, a dull Slav who kept count of the number of cubes of sugar she used in the tea and told her to remove the rouge from her thin cheeks.

From Yelena he learned that, by the end of October, Kirov had dismissed Calder as 'missing, presumed dead.' Spandarian didn't believe that. Calder had jumped — the image of the American silhouetted against the framework of the bridge at Cheremkovo was printed on his vision — and disappeared. If he had dropped into the river his body would have been swept north before sinking or becoming snagged. Before his disgrace and recall from Siberia, Spandarian had supervised the dragging of the river and dropped body-weight objects from the bridge to see where they went. He had found nothing.

217

Reluctantly he had concluded that Calder must have jumped onto a passing ship; he should have considered the possibility earlier. He had checked all shipping movements on the night Calder had vanished and found that an old steamer named the *Ulianov* towing coal barges had passed through Cheremkovo at about the time Calder had jumped.

He had interviewed the skipper, a spade-bearded river-sailor who had struck Spandarian as being suspiciously honest. But even in the interrogation room in Irkutsk, spitting out teeth, he hadn't remembered anything untoward on that dark, rainswept night. Spandarian would have continued the interrogation – electrodes on the testicles had a way with defective memories – but the summons to Moscow had cut short his investigation.

Then on top of everything the bitch had disappeared. And all he had to show for his efforts were the corpses of Jessel, who had once co-operated in the liquidation of restless members of the Twilight Brigade, and Tokarev.

'And I thought Georgians were supposed to be cunning,' Kirov had said as he sacked and demoted him and Spandarian had thought: 'Fuck your mother, I'll be back.'

But as the November days shortened and snow dusted the Georgian Military Road so the prospects of a comeback dwindled: the intrigues and vendettas of Tbilisi weren't exerting their therapy and, middle-aged, he was beginning to accept that the seats of power had been kicked from beneath him. Not even flying in his old Lavochkin fighter plane with the aero club had any effect.

What he needed was an incentive. A lead that would resurrect the drive of his recently departed youth.

He got it one evening early in December.

He was seated in a café near the foot of the funicular leading to the summit of Holy Mountain drinking Armenian brandy, smoking a thin cheroot and playing *Zhelezhka*. But the serial numbers on the rouble notes with which they were playing were not co-operative and in five disastrous minutes he had lost two hundred and fifty roubles. In the old days when he had revisited Tbilisi from Moscow, the living proof that an astute Georgian could outwit those dolts in the capital, he had usually managed to pick the highest digits. But now he had lost his confidence – and the respect of his countrymen.

In fact he suspected that his old cronies would have liked him to return to Moscow. What was he doing back here behaving like a whipped cur? Spying? An *agent provocateur*?

In one corner of the smoked-hazed café a group of tailors were singing songs from the crumpled peaks of the Caucasian Mountains. In another a bevy of barbers and shoemakers were conspiring. A girl with tortoiseshell combs in her seal-sleek hair and flirtatious eyes peered into the café; she recognised Spandarian but looked away. He couldn't blame her: his face was blotched with brandy, his moustache a ragged memory of its former splendour.

'Sixteen,' said his friend Lazishvili, related to the still-venerated Godfather. 'Can anyone beat that?'

No one, least of all Spandarian. He paid up another fifty roubles. Thank God he had salted away a few thousand when he ruled at 25th October Street.

The telephone rang behind the bar. 'It's for you,' the barman shouted to Spandarian. Once, before Calder, he would have presented himself at the table. 'Moscow on the line, Comrade Spandarian. Are you here?' As though Moscow were no more important than a predatory wife.

He picked up the receiver. It was Yelena. 'I may have something for you,' she said. 'Is it safe to talk?'

It was generally safe enough with Yelena: the information she imparted was so innocuous that it didn't matter a monkey's toss if the wire was tapped. But he was touched by her loyalty; the flowers on Women's Day had been a good investment.

'As safe as it ever will be,' he said as the barman moved away. These days he didn't even try to eavesdrop. 'What have you got for me?'

'I don't know if it's important . . . .'

'Let me be the judge of that,' trying to keep the irritation out of his voice.

'The Americans are sending a new man to their Embassy.'

'So?'

'It looks as though he's taking over from Jessel.'

219

'Someone has to.'

'But apparently Comrade Razin, head of the First Chief Directorate, doesn't think he's career CIA.'

'That happens, Yelena. They dispatch a decoy to take over the position of the departed Company man. The real operator fills a vacancy in another section.'

'But the new man is or was a member of the National Security Council.'

Spandarian held the receiver away from his ear for a moment. Dormant instincts awoke. He put his lips closer to the mouthpiece. 'Are you sure?'

'Comrade Razin seems to be sure,' a suspicion of a sniff over the line.

'What's this new man's name?'

A pause. She was consulting a note. Then: 'Shoemaker.'

Shoemaker was the President's Personal Assistant on Security. Spandarian frowned, uncertain of the implications; but his instincts surged and in the past they had seldom been wrong.

'And another thing, Comrade Spandarian?'

'Yes, Yelena?' A clincher, please make it a clincher.

'He's coming to Moscow via Japan on the Trans-Siberian Railway.'

'Any stops?'

'Just one. Irkutsk.'

So Calder *was* alive: Moscow was sending a man to make contact with him. Spandarian's heart thudded.

'Yelena?'

'Yes, Comrade Spandarian?'

'I love you,' he said and hung up.

The following morning he caught a flight from Tbilisi to Moscow.

Spandarian was young again.

He had more than twelve hours to kill before the night flight from Domodyedovo Airport to Irkutsk. He decided to find Dalby and put out feelers among the Twilight Brigade.

From his apartment he telephoned Dalby but there was no

reply. He then called Koslov, head of Personnel at the Institute, and asked him where Dalby was.

A pause, a gritty clearing of the throat. 'Ah, Comrade Spandarian . . . I don't know . . . you see things have changed . . . .'

Spandarian said pleasantly: 'Did you hear about the recent case in Murmansk in which a man was executed for large-scale dealing in *definsitny* goods? How's the caviar business, Lev?'

'He's at his dacha,' Koslov said.

Dalby's dacha lay twenty kilometres outside Moscow. Spandarian put on a sable hat and sheepskin coat and, leaning into the falling snow, went looking for a taxi.

As they drove east along Enthusiasts' Road, the route along which exiles banished to Siberia had once tramped, the snow fell in soft Christmas flakes. By the time they reached Izmailovo Park it was faltering; when they reached the old wooden house it had spent itself and cross-country skiers were already pushing their way across tranquil white fields.

Small grubby cars were parked on the roadside and the dacha, grey with a single onion dome perched on the roof, was full of light. Dalby was throwing a party.

Spandarian banged the brass knocker on the door and when Dalby opened it pushed past him and was gratified to observe the effect his intrusion had upon the guests. He was a switch: for a moment all noise stopped.

In the past he had heard about parties like this from informants. Dismal occasions by all accounts. Disparate individuals forced by exile to seek each other's company. A few drinks and they embarked on their incestuous quarrels, intrigues and affairs.

As they started to talk and move again, as though their puppeteer had returned, Spandarian, accepting a brandy from Dalby, appraised his erstwhile flock.

The Canadian Langley, fading stud, seeking sexual re-assurance with the young wife of a Belgian electronics expert, practising for the occasion with railway station whores; finding locker-room innuendo in the most innocent remark. At the moment he was drinking beer from a can and winding up a

221

story, probably about his days as an ice-hockey player and sexual athlete, to Mrs Lundkvist who, although plainly perplexed, was smiling gamely.

Lundkvist himself, the owner of a small wagging beard and a hoard of moth-eaten secrets about Swedish submarine surveillance, was standing at the window staring at the snow-covered garden, seeing, perhaps, the abandoned past. Lundkvist wasn't really a party-goer; he collected postage stamps.

Spandarian scanned the room with theatrical deliberation. A log fire was burning in a cavernous grate; beads of aged resin shone from timber walls; the Christmas card collection had begun to assemble on the bookshelves – Twilight Brigade members sent each other cards early to make sure they were reciprocated – even though the birth of Christ wasn't celebrated in the Soviet Union.

In one corner, apart from the other guests, van Doorn, the Dutch homosexual, was talking wistfully to a muscular German who pumped iron. Even in this enlightened age homosexuals were still vulnerable to blackmail; therefore they were numerically high in the espionage stakes. In Moscow, despite the lenient view taken by the KGB, they also seemed more vulnerable to loneliness. Unless ordered otherwise by the KGB the gays outside the Bolshoi and elsewhere took them to the cleaners.

There was Fellows, rewarded for fighting with the Red Army with five years in a labour camp, using one of the lines on his old face to fashion a smile, boring the arse off a KGB plant in the UPDK with a description of a cricket match. Cricket! What had made this archetypical Englishman leave his serene pastures at a time when Hitler was threatening to trample all over the cricket pitches? According to his dossier, Spandarian remembered, it was a distaste for patronage; what they called in Britain The Old Boy System. Rebellion against the old order: Spandarian could understand that: what he couldn't understand was the abandonment of one's country. No Georgian could, no Russian for that matter.

Then there was Bennett, the Australian, face already

burning with booze, spouting dogma. At least he still believed in the dreams of equality that hadn't quite materialised in the Soviet Union.

Spandarian sipped his brandy. Outside there were trailers of night in hollows in the snow. Inside the Twilight Brigade were picking up the strands of their village gossip, glancing at him surreptitiously, wincing like sea-anenomes when he fielded the glances.

Spandarian wondered if any of them had found justification for their actions. Certainly some of them worked at seeking fulfillment, enthusiastically promoting the benefits of the system. Full employment, cheap holidays, cramped but adequate housing, good education . . . and, eyes fluttering with Cyrillics, did battle with the Russian language. But even they remained in the twilight.

Of the defectors who had tried to find purpose Calder had been outstanding. Unlike the others who, like retired businessmen, invented incentives, he had possessed a secret fuel.

Glass in hand, Spandarian approached van Doorn and the ageing, over-muscled German. 'So, what's the latest gossip?' he asked. 'Who's sleeping with who? Wife-swopping must become a problem when you run out of swops. But of course that wouldn't concern you two gentlemen.'

Not quite true: the German was ambidextrous, frantically seeking any sexual diversion as his virility waned.

The German, already a little drunk on beer and schnapps imported from Finland, asked: 'What brings you here Spandarian?' rasping his awful Russian with intrusive vowels and consonants.

'I thought you might be able to help me.'

'Help you Spandarian? We thought you had left us. Rumour has it that you have been demoted.'

'I want to know if you've heard anything from Calder,' Spandarian said pleasantly.

'Ah, the one that got away.' The German moved some muscles in his grotesque chest. 'What does it feel like to be outsmarted, Spandarian?'

Spandarian stroked his ragged moustache. Then he said: 'I understand you two have been seeing a lot of each other recently.'

Van Doorn said eagerly: 'We have a lot in common.'

'I'll bet.'

'No,' van Doorn said, 'you don't understand. We're playing a lot of chess.'

'Your move,' the German said to Spandarian.

'My move? Not too subtle I'm afraid. You are both aware that under Article 121 of the criminal code homosexual acts between males are punishable by a maximum of five years imprisonment?'

'You haven't got any proof.'

'Oh yes I have,' Spandarian lied. 'And in your case,' to the German, 'there is always the possibility of an eight-year sentence if minors have been involved.'

Van Doorn, touching the German's arm, said: 'Of course we'll co-operate, won't we Ernst?'

The German nodded briefly and flung schnapps down his throat.

Spandarian, still smiling, moved purposefully towards Langley and Mrs Lundkvist. Mrs Lundkvist, he recalled, had a penchant for young men and indeed a willowy KGB gigolo had been startled by the exuberance of her matronly passion. But within the parish of defectors young people were thin on the ground and, as Langley still retained some green sap, he was, Spandarian supposed, the next best thing to rampant youth.

She said gaily: 'How wonderful to see you, Comrade Spandarian. I always hoped that one day you'd join our little circle,' and Langley, interrupted in full flood of some raunchy memoir, said: 'We thought you'd left us,' hopefully.

'A vacation,' Spandarian told them. 'Siberia. Hunting. I'm going back.' And to Langley: 'Calder, have you heard from him?'

'Me? Why the hell should I? We weren't close.'

'He's got to get in touch with someone. If he calls you call me.'

'Any reason why I should?'

'Many,' Spandarian told him. 'The illegal exchange fifteen months ago of Canadian dollars for roubles at three times the official rate on the black market at Katilnikovskaya Street . . . . How's that for an introductory offer?' and before Langley could answer returned to Dalby who was remonstrating with a Dane for feeding a Bing Crosby tape into a battered recorder.

'Do I g . . . gather you're making a comeback?' Dalby asked pouring himself a Stolichnaya vodka.

'What makes you think I ever left? I never made a point of intruding into your activities.'

Dalby shrugged. Inside the recorder Bing Crosby began to dream about a white Christmas. In their corner van Doorn and the German were arguing furiously.

'So what do you want?' Dalby asked. 'Calder?'

'He's alive. Gone to ground. He's going to need help and if he contacts anyone it will be you.'

'Do you really think so?'

All around him defectors were immersed in Christmases past. In the untrammelled snow of childhood. Spandarian wondered what Dalby's childhood had been like. Lonely, he suspected. The loneliness that only the English upper class knew how to inflict upon their offspring.

'They always come to you,' Spandarian said. 'You know that.'

'Pathetic, isn't it?'

Why did Dalby still betray? To buttress the betrayal that had been his life, Spandarian assumed. To honour his frayed ideals. At least he remained true to his long-ago visions.

For a moment Spandarian saw a small boy with bitten fingernails sitting alone at a desk staring through the window at sunlit playing fields . . . .

If the Georgians have one weakness it's sentimentality. He said to Dalby: 'If or when Calder contacts you call me on 4 60 64 – the Angara Hotel in Irkutsk.'

Spandarian turned abruptly and walked into the dying afternoon that was already bladed with cruelty.

★　★　★

225

As the jet flew over the pastures of cloud covering the Urals and the dawn sun splintered orange on the horizon, Spandarian studied a map of Siberia.

If I were going to make a break, he asked himself, what escape route would I take? Siberia's ten million square and rugged kilometres were daunting but in a way they made his task easier: with the rivers frozen and the roads, what few there were, blocked with snow, Calder's choice was limited – air or railway.

Air? Spandarian doubted it. Although Kirov had officially pronounced last rites on Calder the KGB, according to Yelena, were still watching all airports. You could jump off a train but a plane . . . . Spandarian gazed down at the cotton-fields of cloud.

The obvious ports to make for in the extreme south-east, were Vladivostok, his destination with Jessel, or Nakhodka. From either of those he could use his dollars to buy an illegal passage to Japan. But Vladivostok, a naval port, was clamped tight with security at the best of times, and Nakhodka, the tourist exit, would be crawling with militia and KGB.

Spandarian's finger hugged the coastline to the north. Magadan? A possibility. But how would he get there? There was only a tiny stretch of road linked with the Chelomdzha River and that would be crammed with pack ice. In any case it was God-knows-how-many miles to Japan and any ship sailing there would have to negotiate patrol boats from Sakhalin Island to the west and the Kuril archipelago to the east. Air? Spandarian shook his head. Magadan airport was small and every passenger would be photographed and identified before his feet touched the ground.

Ambitiously Spandarian vaulted over the northern limit of wooded country to the point where Russia and the United States almost nudged each other across the Bering Strait, and the International dateline – Monday in the USSR, Sunday in the USA.

A submarine from the Soviet mainland to the Seward Peninsula of Alaska? So simple. Perhaps Shoemaker was travelling to Irkutsk to make the arrangements with Calder. Spandarian's excitement flared and died: the Bering Strait was nearly five thousand kilometres from Irkutsk and not a sign of a road or railway in the northern extremity, only reindeer trails.

The President's Assistant for Security. Shit, Calder must be important. So important that Kirov had never elaborated. But Spandarian had confidence in his own guesswork – Calder was a reneging defector with the names of the KGB's spymasters in the West in his skull.

Kill Calder, produce the corpse, prove that Kirov's face-saving assertion that he died back in September is false and you're back in business, Spandarian. Back on the stepping stones to the Politburo.

A plump but passably pretty stewardess dumped a tin tray in front of him. Narzan mineral water, tea, black bread, anonymous fish and a shiny red apple. Spandarian shuddered and pushed the tray to one side.

The stewardess said: 'You must eat.'

'Give it to the pilot,' Spandarian said.

'You eat.' She progressed down the aisle waking sleeping passengers.

He sipped the bubbling water with distaste. Hadn't Aeroflot heard of the spring waters in Borzhomi? Well, they soon would when the Georgians infiltrated the Kremlin.

He air-freighted his finger back to Irkutsk. Back west? No, Calder wouldn't be stupid enough to attempt that. There was only one railway and one main highway west: Europe was infinity and he would be picked up like a vagrant on Gorky Street.

North? Never. It was gripped with ice, it led nowhere.

Which left south. Spandarian sent his finger on patrol half way round the world. The Black Sea and Turkey, the Caspian Sea and Iran, Afghanistan – if you could call that a border anymore – the Sinkiang Province of China, Mongolia, then China again with the disputed areas of Manchuria.

Spandarian favoured the south. True it was impossible to

227

guard all the boundary, true many of the KGB Border Guards had been deployed inland – originally at his behest – but really you only had to consider a relatively short length of demarcation. If, that was, Calder was near Baikal. And Spandarian had every reason to believe he was: the *Ulianov* had been towing its barges up the lake, Shoemaker was heading for Irkutsk.

Mongolia.

A road led from the eastern banks of the lake to the Mongolian capital, Ulan Bator; sometimes passable, sometimes not. The Selenga River flowed from Mongolia into Baikal. Better, the Peking Express which left Moscow every Thursday at 17.30 and passed through Irkutsk *and* Ulan Bator.

Mongolia. It had to be. Perhaps! Spandarian stared at the map until it blurred into a vast snow-field. On this snow-filled waste two black spots hardened. It has come to that – Calder and me. No one else matters. One will survive, one will perish, to be found in the spring thaw, a snow flower.

He closed his eyes. When he opened them there was only one black spot on the white expanse.

Who?

The west-bound Trans-Siberian pulled into Irkutsk at 6 am local time.

Shoemaker was met by an Intourist girl with stiff blonde curls and taken in a green minibus to the Angara Hotel, smart and white and square.

After breakfast he dodged the blonde and walked the tree-lined streets of the graceful city. Holden had told him to be on the lookout for intensive surveillance – 'more than you would normally warrant.'

Thurston had described a high-ranking KGB officer named Spandarian. 'If you see him then Calder's alive.'

Babushkas were abroad, shovelling the night snow from the sidewalks. Shoemaker, ears hidden beneath the flaps of a fur hat he had bought in Yokohama, walked past old wooden houses with fanciful eaves tucked between the straining flanks of modern blocks.

On Stepan Khalturin Street he came upon Kirov's house. Sergei Kirov had been a luminary in the abortive 1905 revolution; but the Kirov whom Shoemaker knew about was currently the head of the KGB.

A little later he stopped outside a mansion with six Corinthian columns. It had once been the home of the Governor-General and it was called the White House.

Apposite, Shoemaker thought. Ironic, too, that the city should contain the grave of Grigori Sheleknov who in the eighteenth century founded the first settlement in Russian America – Alaska – which was subsequently bought by the United States for less than two cents an acre. He watched a snowmobile race through a snow-covered park. Very Alaskan.

Parts of the city reminded Shoemaker of Anchorage which he had visited during a winter vacation from UCLA in Los Angeles. That had been at the time of his re-assessment and the snowy challenge of Alaska, The Great Land, had helped to hone his new values.

Sated with the easy pleasures of his circle in California, he had determined to insert some meaning into his life. And what better place to buckle up the armour of a crusade than Washington?

It was a professor of economics at UCLA who had suggested the field of his endeavour: the clandestine background to security. With his honest, all-American looks he was, the professor pointed out, a natural candidate for undercover activities.

So from UCLA he had graduated to the intelligence agencies quartered in Washington. To the Pentagon. To the White House.

Shoemaker crossed the bridge over the river and headed for the Angara Hotel on Sukhe Bator Street. It was quite possible, he reflected, that a very formidable Russian had walked down this same street: a young revolutionary named Joseph Stalin had once been exiled to Irkutsk.

She kissed Calder on the lips above his new, grey-stitched beard. 'Just once more,' she said. 'Then you can take a rest.'

229

Obediently, Calder toured the house again. The padded rests of the crutches chafed his armpits and occasionally a pain like an electric shock darted through the emptiness below his left knee. But by and large he was making good progress and the doctor was delighted with the amputation – no sepsis, flaps healing well.

When finally he sat down awkwardly Katerina brought him salted mushrooms and a dish of bottled bilberries and a shot of vodka.

Outside dusk was settling. Baikal had conceded defeat early this year and already the ice was thick enough to take a truck and small fir-trees had been frozen into it to mark a safe road; safe, that was, unless a fissure suddenly ripped it open.

She sat opposite him beside the log fire flickering with butterfly wings of flame. The room smelled of pine. The Petrovs were in Nizhneangarsk and the atmosphere enfolded them. At moments like this they never spoke about the time when he would have to leave.

A finger of ash fell thickly like snow from a branch. She smiled at him and thought: 'We've come a long way in nine months, we two products of rival creeds.' Both fugitives now. To what extent had each crafted the other's fate? If he hadn't believed that I betrayed him he might not have made a break for it: if he hadn't made the break the KGB wouldn't have turned on me.

And now she had involved a third person, an innocent, Leonid Agursky.

She had stayed in Agursky's apartment in Moscow for two weeks. During that time he had obtained permits for her to join his entourage on the Siberian tour. It hadn't been difficult: Agursky was Agursky, Spandarian had lost all his power since she had escaped and the KGB were delighted that a feminist firebrand should defect to a pop star's bed. Personal secretary . . . . That was mistress, wasn't it?

In fact, although she knew he was attracted to her, Agursky hadn't even kissed her. And yet they looked good together and when girls tried to touch him or stroke his silky beard on the train journey east she noticed how they envied her. And at night as the wheels of the Trans-Siberian ground sleepy rhythms on the track she saw herself with Agursky in a photograph on the piano in her step-father's apartment, his hand on hers.

Perhaps that was the way it would have been if she hadn't met an American who wanted to believe in something.

'What are you thinking?' Calder asked.

'About what might have been.'

'If I hadn't eaten redcurrants at a funeral?'

'I'm glad you did,' she said. 'You should have seen your face.'

'They would make a hell of a mess now.' He combed his beard with his fingers. 'Some people grow impressive beards. Like Leonid Agursky . . . .' His eyes searched her face. 'Others grow thickets. Maybe I should shave it off.'

'Don't do that,' she said. 'It's a disguise. That and . . . .'

'The absence of half a leg? Don't you think Long John Silver would have been a little conspicuous in the middle of Siberia?'

'This is beard country. Siberians wear them to keep warm. I always thought they made men look older; you're the exception.'

'You're sweet,' he said. 'You're also a terrible liar.'

'I love you,' she said.

He smiled but the smile was infinitely sad. As he stared into the glowing caverns of the fire she wondered fearfully what he saw.

When Yury Petrov returned he had found a way for Calder to escape from Russia.

Standing in the bubble of cold air he had brought in from outside, he said: 'You wait, it's pure genius,' and for the first time Katerina hated him. 'But first the essentials.'

While Raisa took off her arctic fox coat bought with gold, Yury returned to the *gazik*, the jeep, to fetch ice cut from the lake, blocks of milk bought in the market and hunters' vodka so cold that it would pour like oil from the bottles.

He took off his *shapka* and long sheepskin coat and, while Raisa cut wafers of raw fish, deep-frozen on the window ledge, and prepared the mustard dip, he poured them each a slug.

Then, standing in front of the fire, hands behind his back,

231

the feudal baron, he said: 'China.'

When the Trans-Siberian was first built at the end of the nineteenth century, Petrov said, the trains were carried across the lake on two British-made ferries, the *Baikal*, a great white cliff of a ship with a stateroom and chapel, and the *Angara*, a demure sister. But in deep winter they were both ice-bound and passengers were hauled across on sledges.

In 1900 work began on a loopline round the southern shore through impassable terrain. In hurricanes, blizzards, fog and temperatures of minus 40 Fahrenheit teams of Russians, Persians, Italians and Turks, licked into shape by Circassian guards, built two hundred bridges and bored thirty-three tunnels into the cliffs.

'It took thirteen years and four months to build the whole railway from west to east,' Yury Petrov said as though he had personally laid the track. 'Can you imagine what it was like when the permafrost thawed on the surface and they walked knee-deep in mud?'

'What none of us can imagine,' Raisa said, poking the log fire, 'is what any of this has got to do with escaping to China. His first love,' she said to Calder and Katerina, 'is gold. Second Baikal. Third the Trans-Siberian. Fourth – I think – me.'

'Fourth? I suppose so,' Yury said. 'But I'm very fond of vodka.' He drank some. 'What I'm getting at – indulging myself a little, I grant you – is that the railway is the *only* route you can take.'

He fetched a map of Siberia and laid it on the coffee table in front of the fire. 'Railways, rivers and a few roads. You,' stabbing his finger at Calder, 'have to get to Ulan Ude four hundred kilometres from here.' He transferred his finger to the Buryat capital to the south-east of the lake. 'And you're in luck, because the road is close to the lake and still passable.'

'I thought you said I had to take the railway,' Calder said. His hand reached for the long stump of his thigh; there were times when he couldn't believe that a part of him had gone.

'Right. From Ulan Ude. You can't get there by railway from

here because there isn't one.'

Katerina said: 'Still passable? Are you suggesting he's got to go now? Before his leg has healed properly?'

Petrov said sombrely: 'I'm afraid so. For two reasons. One, a blizzard could close the road any day now. Two, the enemy is closing in. The Border Guards have never left Baikal – I saw a platoon of them in Nizhneangarsk today. And there's nothing better that bastard with the moustache would like than to nail me to the door with his bayonet.' He paused. 'You,' to Calder, 'must be *very* important, my friend.'

'I wish I could tell you about it,' Calder said. Would Petrov help him if he knew the truth? He was a brigand but he was a Soviet.

'Do *you* know?' Petrov turned to Katerina.

'I only know they want to kill him.'

'A good enough reason to help him.'

Raisa said: 'Get on with it, Yury. Why China?'

'Don't hurry me; we've got a long way to go yet.' He prodded Ulan Ude again. 'There you pick up the railway south to Mongolia and its capital, Ulan Bator.'

'But the KGB will be watching every train,' Calder objected.

'But not every automobile.'

'Stop talking in riddles,' Raisa said. 'You're not on television.'

'Robert will *drive* along the railway,' Petrov said triumphantly. 'And here, my darling, we return to my third love, no my fourth,' kissing his wife on the cheek, 'the Trans-Siberian. You're lucky,' to Calder, 'that I know every sleeper of its history.'

Petrov tossed back a shot of vodka and chewed a slice of frozen fish. 'This part of the line was ruled during the Civil War by Grigory Semyonov, a Cossak paid by the Japanese to cause havoc. And he did that all right – he swooped up and down the line in an armoured car killing and torturing as many locals as he could lay his hands on. In five days his men killed eighteen hundred. They strangled them, shot them, poisoned them or burned them alive. In winter they poured water over them so that they could break off a limb or two as souvenirs.'

233

Raisa, lovely slanting eyes narrowed, said: 'Is this really necessary, Yury?'

'The next bit is. Have you heard of the Peking-Paris automobile race?' And when they shook their heads: 'Well, Prince Borghese decided that as the road was so bad he would drive his car on the railway.' Petrov paused, timing perfect. 'He got permission from Irkutsk, not Moscow of course, and drove his car on the track as though it were an autobahn. He even left instructions on how to do it – left wheels between the rails, right on the outside where the sleepers protrude.'

Deftly he countered their objections.

'But Robert can't drive in his condition,' from Katerina.

'No problem with the *gazik* – hand-controlled clutch.'

'If he can drive why not go by road?' from Raisa.

'There's only one road and it's probably impassable. If not the Russians will stop every car.'

'But if I go on the railway,' Calder said, 'they'll pick me up in Ulan Bator. Mongolia is as much part of the Russian empire as Siberia.'

'You won't go to Ulan Bator. You see, my beloved comes from Mongolia.'

'Always beloved when he wants something.'

'And her home is just across the border. Robert will drive off the railway there. No one will have seen him leave Siberia, no one will see him arrive.'

'But why Mongolia?' Calder asked. 'Isn't that one hell of a way to go to China?'

'The only way, my friend. The KGB will be watching every border crossing into Manchuria. It would be relatively easy to get across in summer – the locals do it every day – but not in winter when the exits are limited. So what you do is abandon the jeep in Mongolia and pick up the Peking Express. No one will be watching it over the Chinese border because there is no way you can have got on it. Not even the KGB will anticipate a stroke of genius like that.'

Raisa said: 'It was his modesty that first attracted me to him.'

Katerina said: 'But what makes you think the Chinese will let him cross the border from Mongolia?'

'Because anyone trying to escape from the Russians can find sanctuary in China.'

It was left to Raisa to ask the obvious question. 'And what happens,' she asked with theatrical innocence, 'if he happens to meet an oncoming train when he's driving along the railway?'

Petrov had been waiting for that. He was triumphant. 'There won't be any oncoming trains,' he said. 'We're going to blow up a bridge.'

That night Katerina made love to Calder for the first time since she had arrived on the shores of Lake Baikal. She kissed him and stroked him and then, sitting astride him, lowered herself onto him and, moving urgently, brought them both to a climax.

Afterwards he said: 'So that's what they mean about women's equality,' and, lying beside him, still feeling him inside her, she said: 'You didn't look as if you had any complaints,' and he said: 'None, because that's the way it's got to be from now on,' and she thought: 'But for how long?'

He switched off the light and opened the wooden slats on the wall to let the cold moonlight in. They could hear the waves on the beach, the wind in the hills.

He said: 'Yury's right, you know that, don't you?'

'I wanted us to have an American Christmas,' she said. 'And a Russian New Year.' And, with tears in her voice: 'Will I ever see you again?'

'Life is now,' he said.

'Now? That's the future and the past, even as you speak.'

'Now,' he said. 'Only now,' and with one hand he stroked her breasts and her belly and the moist hair between her thighs.

'We were meant to be together.'

'Others don't want us to be.'

'We're us. No one should be able to interfere. Politicians, police . . . no one.'

'We slipped by them in the first place,' Calder said.

'Then we can do it again.'

'You forget, I am the enemy now.'

'No, not you.'

'Me. You don't understand . . . .'

235

'I can guess. It doesn't matter.'

'It matters. I'm doing . . . .'

'I don't want to know what you're doing,' she said fiercely.

'When I was a kid I had naïve dreams about equality.'

'And you're about to destroy them? Don't make me your conscience.' She turned away from him and stared at the hard-glittering stars. 'In any case people like you misinterpret equality. It has nothing to do with material possessions.'

'It has to do with the sexes,' Calder said slyly, slipping his arm round her waist.

'Don't worry, I'll see to that. While you're away in America. For ever?' The tears were wet on her cheeks as she pressed herself against him. 'If you ever get there. It's crazy, this idea of Yury's.'

'It's all we've got.'

'I could come with you,' and when he didn't reply: 'Just to the border,' and when, still without speaking, he kissed her shoulder: 'I wish we'd never met.'

'It was the most beautiful thing that ever happened to me.'

Then, feeling him hard behind her, she turned and knelt above him and guided him inside her again and the moonlight was warm on their bodies.

Failure garbs a man like an old and shabby suit. Seeing it on Spandarian people questioned his authority, asked to see his ID. This didn't aggravate him: it merely emphasised his aloneness, sharpened his singleness of purpose. Calder and me. In the wilderness. One or the other.

Even the medic on the docks at Angarsk treated him indifferently. 'Who are you? What right have you to question me?'

'None,' Spandarian told him. 'But I do have this,' producing a Georgian stiletto with a jewelled handle from the pocket of his squirrel coat.

They stood on the wharf in the privacy of softly falling snow. Ten feet below ice-flows drifted past on dark waters.

'You tricked me,' reproachfully. Spandarian had told the

236

sad-eyed medic in the dockside bar that he wanted to buy cocaine.

'How astute.' Spandarian grabbed the medic's black bag. 'How much cocaine have you got in here? A thousand roubles worth?'

'Give it back.'

Spandarian held the bag over the edge of the wharf. 'Splash goes a week's pickings. Unless you answer my questions.'

The medic tugged at the ear-flaps of his moulting *shapka*. 'He had a broken leg, I put it in plaster, that's all I can tell you.'

Spandarian, who had been told by a docker that the medic had treated some sort of fugitive on a barge on the day that Calder had disappeared, said: 'Describe him.'

The medic described Calder.

'How bad was his leg?'

'A bad break. But I fixed it. He'll be walking now. Running even. Now, please give me the bag back.'

'Where was he going?'

'How should I know?'

Below them two blocks of ice collided ponderously, joined each other and spun away.

'To the lake?'

'Perhaps.'

'In fact,' Spandarian said, lowering the bag to his side, 'I know the *Ulianov* was sailing to the northern tip of the lake.'

'Then why ask me?'

The medic made a grab for the bag but Spandarian stepped aside like a bullfighter and pushed the medic into the snow.

He stood up slowly. The fall had knocked the defiance out of him and his white, drug-addicted face had collapsed. 'The skipper did mention a village.'

I should have made that skipper swallow his teeth, Spandarian thought. 'Which village?'

'I don't know. That's all I know. The bag . . . please.'

'In the north?'

'I suppose so.'

'No mention of dropping him off on the way?'

237

'No mention.'

Spandarian who knew from experience when a subject had been drained of the truth, when he was approaching that dangerous time when he began to lie to please his interrogator, slid the stiletto back into the sheath in his pocket. Then he dropped the black bag into the water.

The medic screamed thinly and, as Spandarian walked away into the falling snow, screamed obscenities after him.

At the met. office on the dockside at Irkutsk where experts attempted, with varying degrees of success, to anticipate the moods of Baikal, Spandarian checked the weather on the day Calder escaped. There had been a storm.

Today? 'Cold and clear – as far as we can make out,' a young meteorologist told him. 'We're better at forecasting the weather on the moon; that's the trouble with this country . . . .'

But Spandarian had gone. From the Angara Hotel he called the coastguard on Olkhon Island. The spectre of failure didn't extend along a telephone line and the coastguard was suitably awed. Yes, there had been a storm that day. Yes, he had seen the *Ulianov* and its barges; in fact they had sheltered beside the island.

Any passengers? Funny Spandarian should have mentioned that. He had scanned the barges through his telescope. From beneath a tarpaulin he had noticed what looked like two feet; but he had assumed Baikal was playing tricks.

'You know, the Old Man is a great deceiver. Sometimes I see what looks like a monster . . . .'

But Spandarian had hung up.

So Calder *had* reached the northern shores of Baikal.

He left the hotel by a rear entrance. Although Shoemaker's presence in Irkutsk confirmed that Calder was alive it had soon become obvious that he didn't know where he was. So I must lose Shoemaker.

At the next exit he darted through the double doors, slammed them behind him, sprinted through long corridors, emerged at the front entrance and ran across the car park to his rented Volga.

As he gunned the car past a red and white Intourist coach he saw Shoemaker appear on the steps. Too late, comrade: go back to the beaches of California where you belong.

Spandarian drove along the road running parallel to the Angara to the port of Listvyanka. From there he took the car ferry across the lake, kept navigable by icebreakers, to Babushkin; then he drove north.

The action that Calder took that evening was foolhardy. He knew it but he persevered. He had heard nothing about Harry for a long time; if the journey ahead was abortive then he might never hear again. It had to be done even though the line might be tapped. A terrible, calculated risk.

While Katerina and the Petrovs were at a cottage at the end of the village trading caviar from a 245-lb Baikal sturgeon for provisions for his journey he picked up his crutches and made his way in the dark to the call-box beside the beach wall.

The fresh air smelled of cleanliness. The cold stung his nostrils. The call-box was encased in ice.

He splintered the ice round the door with a slab of granite from the wall and squeezed inside. Then he telephoned Moscow five time zones away. Moscow 52-00-11. The United States Embassy on Tchaikovsky Street.

He had no idea who had replaced Jessel so he asked for his old extension. 'Who's calling please?' It could have been an operator in New York or Boston.

'It doesn't matter, just put me through.'

A Texan drawl answered the extension. 'Sorry, Mr Jessel isn't here right now.'

Calder spoke urgently. 'My name's Calder.' An intake of breath. 'I haven't got much time, no time. I want you to do something for me.'

'Sure, but . . . .'

'No but's. I want you to call Washington. The White House.'

A pause. The Texan was patching other extensions into the call. The CIA bureau chief. The Ambassador. Pressing buttons, waving his hands at some flustered secretary. His call would have exploded in the Embassy.

'Okay, Mr Calder. Shoot.'

239

'Get through to the President. No problems if you give my name.'

Another pause. Faintly Calder heard: 'Jesus.' Then: 'Okay, got it. What do we, ah, tell the President?'

'You don't tell him anything. You just ask him how my son is.'

'But . . . .'

'He'll understand. Tell him no names unless I get a progress report. He'll understand that too.'

'Just hold the line a minute, sir.'

'You just hold the line a minute. Call me back on this number 4-93-20 in eight hours. On the button. Got that?'

'Sure I've got it. Eight hours. But . . . .'

But what Calder never knew. Ice fell in daggers as the door of the call-box shut behind him.

Shoemaker made his routine call to the Embassy at midnight. The duty officer put him through to Jessel's replacement, Wade, a one-time FBI agent in Los Angeles, in the consular section.

Wade snapped short any preliminaries. He said: 'The subject has surfaced. He gave us a number to call. We checked it out. It's a village called Oskino on the north-east shore of Lake Baikal. You know what to do . . . .'

'I'm on my way,' Shoemaker said.

The call was picked up on a KGB line-tap on the third floor of a 22-storey block of apartments in Vosstanaya Square close to the US Embassy. When its import registered a call was made to Dzerzhinsky Square. A few seconds later the late-night duty officer, voice twanging with nerves, telephoned the Chairman of State Security at home. Calder's name dispatched the sleep from Kirov's voice. He told the duty officer to contact the unit of Border Guards nearest to Oskino. 'And keep me posted, whatever time it is.' 'Yes Comrade Chairman.' The duty-officer's voice broke like a schoolboy's, this time with relief.

240

Chapter 26

While Katerina, who didn't know that he was leaving next morning, prepared an evening meal Calder packed his bag. Clothes, roubles and dollars, ten-tola gold ingots the size of small chocolate bars stitched into the lining.

Thoughtfully he picked up Jessel's empty briefcase. When had Jessel been ordered to kill him? Even as they jogged along the banks of the Moscow River was he debating the manner of the execution?

Calder was still bewildered by the duplicity of the soft-spoken spy who returned every evening to an oasis of American respectability. Drink in hand, pipe drawing nicely. 'Dinner nearly ready, dear?' and with joyful inspiration: *Why don't I poison the bastard?*

Calder fingered the smooth swelling inside his bag where, beneath canvas, gold gleamed shyly. It was then that it occurred to him that Jessel's bag might contain secrets. He ran his fingertips along the pigskin lining on the bottom of the black executive briefcase. There was a swelling there too.

He took a clasp-knife from his own bag and slit the pigskin. A brown notebook. Calder picked it up.

Five pages of code. But given time any code except a one-time pad arrangement can be broken. And by the look of the spacing, the keywords were names. Then probably addresses. And then numbers. Telephone numbers.

53-75-47. That was familiar. Calder frowned. The Czech Embassy in Moscow. Another number jangled in Calder's brain. The Institute! And another – Tyuratam, the Soviet space centre.

His mind must have slowed up with his incarceration in the dacha because it wasn't until he had isolated a few more familiar numbers that he realised the significance of the book.

His fingers slackened, the book fell to the floor. He retrieved it, ripped out the pages of writing, undid the almost-invisible, spider-web stitching round one of the ten-tola ingots in his own bag and slipped them beside the gold.

The gold, he reflected, was worthless compared with the contents of those pages. So, it could be argued, was all the gold in Fort Knox.

Chapter 27

Calder waited until the second bottle of Georgian red before he told them about the phone call.

'You're crazy.' Petrov's anger was distilled. Across the table Calder glimpsed the menace beneath the sophistication.

'I know. It was just something I had to do. I'm sorry. You see some values are more important than material considerations.'

Petrov said coldly: 'You left it a bit late to reach that conclusion. You abandoned your wife and kid in the States, didn't you?'

'I had no choice. But a kid . . . sick . . . maybe dying . . . maybe dead . . . . I can't explain,' and he stopped because he could feel the strands of his voice parting.

'Why the hell couldn't you have waited until we got to Ulan Ude?'

'I wanted to know before I set out. I might not get too far . . . .'

Katerina said softly: 'Yury and Raisa had a child once. I think they understand.'

Calder said: 'I'm sorry, I didn't know.'

Raisa said: 'He died on Baikal. An accident when the ice was thin. I can't have any more children.'

Petrov said to Calder: 'Okay, so you were stupid; we'll just have to adapt.' He poured Khvanchkara wine while Raisa went to the kitchen to fetch the dessert. 'We've got to face the fact that the KGB will have traced the call. But there's no way

242

anyone can get here until daybreak.'

Katerina stared at Calder: 'You were going tomorrow anyway?'

He touched her hand. 'Before the weather makes me a prisoner.'

'You didn't tell me.'

'It was better that way.'

'To go, just like that?'

'I was going to tell you this evening. You knew it had to be soon . . . .'

She took her hand away from his; she stared into her wine.

When Raisa returned with the *stakan kiselya*, stiff with cranberry sauce, she said to Yury: 'Now perhaps you'd better explain the *we . . . . until we got to Ulan Ude.*'

At last Petrov smiled, little-boy-caught-out. 'You guessed, didn't you? I couldn't let Hoppalong Cassidy here try and drive the jeep. Impossible. I lied about the clutch.'

'I suppose I knew,' Raisa said. 'Even though I can't drive.'

'One thing's for sure,' Petrov said. 'They'll take this village apart. You,' to Raisa and Katerina, 'will have to take the Zhiguli across the ice to Nizhneangarsk and then head north to Bratsk while we go south. And now,' wiping cranberry dessert from his lips with a napkin, 'I have work to do.'

Although he was waiting for the call the ringing of the telephone in the call-box startled him.

Heavy with foreboding, he picked up the receiver.

The Texan. 'Mr Calder, sir?'

Harry was dead: he could hear it in the Texan's tone.

'How's my son?'

'As well as can be expected, sir.'

Calder pressed his head against the side of the call-box, breath melting the frost patterns on the inside of the windows.

'Mr Calder, are you there?'

'I'm here. What the hell do you mean, "as well as can be expected"?'

'That's all I'm authorised to say, sir.'

'Authorised to say? It's my son we're talking about you

sonofabitch. Where is he? Is he still unconscious?'

'I'm sorry, I don't know anything more. But I do have some urgent questions.'

Calder replaced the receiver. Eleven thousand miles severed.

He elbowed himself into the iced night and retrieved his crutches. But Harry was alive. There was hope.

Making his crutches run he returned to the dacha.

2 am.

At the time Calder was talking to the Embassy, Spandarian was driving off the end of the main highway at Mogoyto high in the mountains to the east of Lake Baikal.

To reach the northern tip of the lake two hundred kilometres further on he had to drive through second-class roads and unmade tracks sheeted with ice and clotted with snow. The wind pushed him to the edge of precipices, gusts of hard snow scooped from granite pockets machine-gunned the double-glazed windscreen of the black Volga.

2.10 am.

Shoemaker, in a six-seat Chaika hired with magic dollars without the knowledge of Intourist, was leaving the late-night ferry at Babushkin in the south. Ahead, lay Spandarian and Calder. As he stared into the diamond-hard stars glittering in the sky he remembered soft stars over Malibu beach and the slurred call of the waves and the feel of a girl's body still warm from the day's sun.

2.20am.

The young officer who had arrested Yury Petrov began to round up his men based temporarily in Nizhneangarsk. So this very important American *was* in Oskino. With Petrov. The officer had no doubt about that.

They would leave for Oskino, he decided, at first light.

When he returned to the warm nest of their bed Calder asked Katerina to come with him to America.

Holding her from behind, hands cupped round her breasts, loins curving beneath her, he whispered. 'We could disappear together . . . I could still see Harry.'

244

He felt her heartbeat quicken beneath his hands. She pressed herself against him and said: 'These are our last hours. We haven't time for dreams. I shouldn't have suggested going with you before. That was just dreams, too.'

'Why?' although he knew.

'It has nothing to do with America: it's here. I don't think anyone in the West really understands how we feel about our country. It has nothing to do with Communism, just Russia.'

'But they'll arrest you. Put you in prison. Maybe expel you.'

'I don't think they will arrest me. You see Spandarian is in disgrace; he doesn't have any power anymore. And the movement is on the march. Ever since that day in Red Square.'

'Ah,' he said, 'the movement.'

'I'm part of it. Part of progress. I can't leave. I can't desert people like Svetlana.'

He stared into the darkness looking for truth. Then he said: 'I know. You can't escape from what you are. I tried. Now I'm going back.'

He opened the panels of wood and a bar of cold moonlight fell across the blankets. She turned to him.

'Robert,' she whispered.

'You never did call me Bob.'

'To me you're Robert.'

'What will you do?'

'Go north with Raisa. Wait. Then come south to Irkutsk.'

'Leonid?'

'He's in Khabarovsk. But he will go back to Moscow through Irkutsk.'

'And you with him. You know, I think that was always written. I was just an interruption.'

'An interruption?' She kissed him. 'You are life.'

He looked at his watch in the bar of moonlight. Time was accelerating.

He held her more tightly. He had never intended to make love in this final time but suddenly he was inside her and, as the minutes and seconds pulsed away, they were one.

First light apricot above the mountains, shafts of it finding the frozen lake and polishing it with dawn. Snow on the kneeling foothills ermine soft, tufted with leafless brush like barbed wire on a deserted battlefield. Ice dust sparkling in the night-cleaned air.

Jeep packed. Zhiguli panting beside it, facing the opposite direction.

Raisa clinging to Yury beneath his sheepskin coat. 'You will come back . . . .'

Tilting her face: 'Like a boomerang – *you* know where the gold is.'

Katerina helping Calder into the jeep and not knowing what to say except '*Dasvidanya*' and wishing that he'd never eaten those redcurrants and rejoicing that he had and knowing that they were losing everything and knowing that they weren't because it would always be with them and giving him the small parcel she had wrapped for him, and as the jeep moved away with part of her inside it, turning and facing east where the light was strengthening over her land.

Spandarian saw the horsemen as he was driving the black Volga between the small pine trees marking the track gritted on the ice. At first he thought they were an ice mirage. Then he saw the green piping on their uniforms and realised that they were the KGB Border Guards he had deployed inland when he had still exercised authority. With luck they wouldn't study his revamped credentials too closely: Moscow, Dzerzhinsky Square, that should be enough on a bitter morning like this.

As he stopped the car a young officer with a Prussian moustache alighted. Spandarian flashed his ID; the officer was unimpressed but not suspicious. 'What can I do for you, comrade?' the officer asked.

Spandarian explained that he was looking for the American named Calder. He understood he was at the northern tip of the lake.

'North-east,' the officer corrected him. 'At a village called Oskino. Turn round and follow us.'

Half way along the snow-blown road overlooking the lake

246

Shoemaker passed a Russian jeep coming in the opposite direction. The driver was grey-haired beneath his fur *shapka*, his companion bearded. Shoemaker put his foot down. When he next glanced in his driving mirror the jeep was no longer to be seen.

'So,' the officer said, 'they've got a six-hour start.' He had just finished questioning a villager who, peering through the blinds, had seen the jeep take off. He had seen nothing until the officer had threatened to turn him into an ice statue by hosing him down with water.

The officer, who seemed more interested in Petrov than Calder, said: 'There's no way we can catch them unless . . . .'

They both looked at the black Volga.

'All right,' Spandarian said reluctantly. 'Do you know where he's heading for?'

'Irkutsk?' The officer shrugged.

'Only if Calder's crazy which I've discovered he most certainly isn't.' Spandarian opened the door of the Volga, took a road map out of the glove compartment and pointed east of Baikal. 'Ulan Ude. Then south to Mongolia by rail. That's the way I would do it.'

The way a Georgian would do it. God these Slavs were unimaginative. Irkutsk! One phone call and the place would be one vast ambush. Calder – or Petrov – had cut the telephone lines from Oskino but there would be others.

On the way, Spandarian thought, I should alert Ulan Ude. If I didn't want Calder to myself . . . . 'What the hell are you doing?' he asked the officer who was dousing Petrov's dacha with gasolene.

The officer didn't reply. He struck a match and applied it to the wall. Flames splashed over the wood. Horses reared and whinnied.

'Why?' Spandarian asked.

'He tried to outsmart me.'

Not difficult, Spandarian thought as they drove away.

When Shoemaker reached Oskino villagers were still hosing

water onto the smouldering ashes of the Petrov dacha. With dollars he discovered that Calder had departed nine hours earlier, Spandarian three hours ago. He must have missed Spandarian's Volga when he stopped for gas at Barguzin. Wearily he spun the wheel of the Chaika; at least they were strung out in some sort of order now; that was something but not much.

Chapter 28

The old part of Ulan Ude, the Buryat capital a hundred miles north of the Mongolian border, is still a frontier town.

Wooden houses cling to each other in the side streets; men with gooseberry chins support each other outside open-air beer stalls; Buryats with eyes like smiles and polished black hair stride down the poplar-lined Leninskaya Street arm-in-arm with Muscovites and Cossacks; in the foyer of the Selenga Hotel a long-dead bear glassily appraises new patrons.

After a few vodkas or *spirts* the sound of Cossack cavalry which once enslaved the peaceful Buryats can be heard and you must take a streetcar to the new town where Lenin rules benign in bronze to escape them.

Petrov stopped the jeep on a spur overlooking the town built on the junction of the Selenga and Uda Rivers. He told Calder: 'We'll have to hide in the old town. I've got friends there, we'll be okay.'

He wiped frost from the inside of the windshield. It was late afternoon; the temperature outside the sealed panels of the jeep was minus 20.

On one side of them pine forest, harbouring bear and boar and wolves; on the other permafrosted scrub studded, according to Petrov, with Siberian topaz, beryl, aquamarine and garnet.

Petrov put the jeep into gear and drove towards the city.

On the way they passed a group of Buryat girls who smiled flirtatiously from the fur frames of their hats. 'Beautiful, aren't they?' Petrov said. 'And we've got Genghis Khan to thank for them. He decided to tame the tribes and of course pretty soon they got around to mating. Result: the Mongols of the Soviet Union.'

'How did you meet Raisa?' Calder asked.

'On a gold run. I used to take my bullion through Mongolia to China – that's how I came up with your escape route. One day the Border Guards got too close for comfort and I took refuge in a Buddhist lamasery. The Guards came in of course – Buddhism is discouraged in Mongolia – but they didn't find me. Do you know where I was hidden?'

Calder who was untying the parcel Katerina had given him shook his head.

'In a drum as big as an elephant. When the Guards came in a lama began to beat it. I was deaf for a week but the noise got rid of the bastards.'

'And Raisa?'

'She used to take food to the lamas from the village. She came with a van one day – the only one in the village – and went back to her parents' home with me inside it. And then . . . . Well, I followed the example of Genghis Khan. I was very lucky . . . . What the hell's that?' pointing at the content of Katerina's parcel.

'A game I once played,' Calder said, feeling the soft black leather of the pocket chess-set. He opened it out like a wallet. The pieces were slivers of white plastic stamped with their names. He held it to his face and smelled Katerina.

'Kata?'

'A farewell present.'

'I didn't know she played.'

'We all play,' Calder said. 'We're all pawns.'

Petrov drove slowly through the darkening streets – 'No sense in upsetting the militia at a time like this' – to a warehouse bearing a faded sign: SOBENIKOV and MOLCHANOV BROTHERS, tea and sugar. He unlocked the doors and drove in.

The door of the wooden house next door was opened by a sinewy old man wearing smoked glasses and a white mandarin moustache. Petrov introduced him as the lama who had once saved his life in Mongolia.

'But what's he doing in the Soviet Union?' Calder asked when they retired, after a meal of soup and *blinis*, to their bedroom.

'Ah, there you have the strength and the weakness of the Kremlin. They're pretty useful at suppressing a faith in a satellite state: in their own country it's a different matter; they try to control it rather than extinguish it – you can't have dissenters five thousand miles from your capital. So the lama stays here, plays the Soviet game and pops back to Mongolia to practise it.'

'He's not coming with us, is he?'

'Don't worry. He's going before us.' Petrov opened a scuffed briefcase and put a newspaper cutting, maps and documents on the table between the two beds. 'Forget the lama and concentrate.'

He opened a map of the Buryat Autonomous Soviet Socialist Republic which included the northern regions of Mongolia. 'The last town on the Soviet side of the border is Naushki. But long before that, not far from here in fact, I discovered that God – or Buddha – is on our side.' He handed Calder the clipping.

Calder sat on the edge of the bed and read: 'Grave concern has been expressed by railwaymen travelling between Ulan Ude and Ulan Bator at the condition of a bridge ten kilometres south of Ulan Ude . . . .'

Calder looked up. 'The one you're going to blow?'

'If you read on you'd find that they're scared that the steelwork's defective and in extreme cold it might snap. You know, in climates like this a girder can break like an icicle. But apparently bureaucracy has decided in its wisdom – probably quite rightly – that there's nothing wrong with this bridge.'

'And you're going to prove bureaucracy wrong?'

'I figured that if we blew any old bridge it would stop all traffic. But at the same time it would alert Border Guards. This way it will just seem like another bureaucratic blunder.'

'When?' Calder asked.

250

'Tomorrow afternoon. That will give them plenty of time to stop all traffic from the north and south. When it gets dark we'll put the jeep on the track.'

'You don't think this is a little too . . . flamboyant?'

'You tell me another way. The road across the border is impassable, snow-drifts two metres deep. The airport is crawling with KGB. Every passenger on every train will be checked back to the moment he was conceived.'

'You know something?' Calder sat up and began to undress. 'You look like Omar Sharif.'

'The difference,' Petrov said, 'is that I'm not going to play bridge: I'm going to blow one up.'

When Calder finally closed his eyes it occurred to him that what he was doing, the information he was taking back to the States, was yet another betrayal. Of people like Yury Petrov. And Katerina.

But now, thanks to Jessel, there was a way to solve the equation that had plagued him since he had arrived in Russia.

The Siberian-Express from Moscow arrived at Ulan Ude at lunchtime the following day. And from it stepped recently widowed Mrs Betty Quarrick from Fitchburg, Massachusetts, USA.

Not for Mrs Betty Quarrick the leisured life of retirement in Florida which, with the collect on her husband's life assurance, she could easily afford. From the travel books that her husband, a librarian and fireside traveller, had brought home she had acquired an appetite for adventure that had been unrequited until that chair beside the fire had finally become vacant.

After a decent interval Mrs Quarrick, Visa and American Express to hand, had taken a package trip across Europe, London, Paris, Rome and Madrid, but, apart from an unfortunate interlude when a young Italian who professed himself smitten with older women had departed with her travellers' cheques and credit cards, there hadn't been much emphasis on adventure.

So a little nervously it must be admitted, she had elected to cross enemy territory. To fly to Moscow and take the train

251

across Siberia 'to see the other side of the coin.' One of the last volumes her husband had brought back from the library had been a *National Geographic* special about Russia; the Siberian sequences had conveyed an impression of civilised desolation in which adventure could be sampled without too much discomfort. Besides, she was fairly sure that no one within her circle in Fitchburg had ever been to Siberia of all places.

But by the time Train No. 2 reached Ulan Ude Mrs Quarrick was even more bored than she had ever been watching her husband turning the time zones of the world on the other side of their imitation log fire. So when a cripple with a grey-streaked beard approached her on crutches as she queued to buy a copy of a horrendously dull English newspaper, the *Morning Star*, she experienced a tremor of excitement.

The cripple said: 'You're American?'

A trifle disappointed – before she had left Fitchburg one of her friends had commented: 'With that hairdo you could be mistaken for a Parisian' – she confirmed that she was.

'Will you do something for me? It's terribly important. In fact – and I know this sounds crazy but you've got to believe me – the future of the United States depends on it.'

A nut. Just my luck, thought Mrs Quarrick. And yet there was something compelling about the intensity of his gaze, the refined wasting of his features above his beard.

'It depends what it is,' she said warily.

'I want you to deliver a package for me in the States.'

'What sort of package?' A bomb? From Yokohama she flew to LA and then to Boston. Did he have some grievance against American airlines in general?

He took a package from his pocket. A letter-bomb? 'This. You can open it if you like. It's only a chess-set.'

'A chess-set? Now why would a chess-set be so important? And why can't you post it? No one would dare to interfere with the US mail.' She hoped it wasn't just a chess-set.

'Please Mrs . . . .'

'Quarrick. Betty Quarrick.'

'Do you have children?'

252

'A daughter. Married with one child in Ladysmith, Wisconsin. Did you think I had a grandchild?' She really would have to stop being coy at her age. She wondered how he had lost his leg.

'Then for the sake of your daughter's future, your grandchild's future, the future of every young person in the United States, I beg you to deliver this package.'

She took it gingerly. It was addressed to a Mrs Ruth Calder at an address in Boston. 'Well, if it's that important . . . .' Even if it did only contain a chess-set its contents could, with a little innocent embroidery, become infinitely more intriguing when the incident was recounted in Fitchburg.

'By hand, please.'

'Well . . . .'

A voice on the loudspeaker was urging onward-bound passengers to return to the train. Intourist couriers were busily rounding up their charges. Mrs Quarrick turned her back on a proffered *Morning Star*.

'Here's something for your trouble.' He thrust some bills at her.

'That won't be . . . .'

'Take them.' She found the bills in her hand. 'Promise?'

'Promise.'

And he was gone. When she counted the bills in her hand as the train picked up speed outside Ulan Ude she found to her astonishment that he had given her one thousand dollars. Was it her imagination or was the package on her lap ticking?

The horses, high-stepping and breathing smoke, came into the old town of Ulan Ude first, causing more alarm than any tank or armoured car: Russians knew their sabre-slashed history. Then, in cars, militia wearing uniforms and plainclothes; soon you couldn't walk down a main street without dancing a few steps with some kind of policeman or another.

'How can you be so sure?' the young Border Guard officer asked Spandarian, doubt blunting the blade of his rule-book voice.

'That they're in the old town? Because that's where I would

253

be,' Spandarian told him as, sitting in the black Volga, they watched militia erecting a road block at the end of Leninskaya Street. Not that the officer would understand: he was a prisoner of military logic.

Once during the long and perilous drive from Oskino the officer had suggested telephoning Ulan Ude but Spandarian, accelerating, had told him the lines were down.

The officer, half a man without his horse, said: 'I'm going to call headquarters.' As he walked briskly towards a call-box, boots martial on the frost-sparkling sidewalk, Spandarian, knowing that he was intent upon checking him out, geared himself for retreat. When the officer's back was towards him in the call-box, he reversed the Volga round a corner and down a side street and took off.

He parked near a beer queue. Closed his eyes to clear Slav peasants and Buryat savages from his reasoning. Calder was close. He could feel him.

Shoemaker, whose Chaika had broken down at Turantayevo where the highway forks south-east to Ulan Ude, arrived in the old town at 1.30 pm when the manhunt had been stiffened by re-enforcements of militia from surrounding areas. If you wanted to pull a heist in Khorinsk now was the time.

He tried to call Moscow but all the lines were busy and were likely to stay that way, according to an English-speaking operator who appeared to derive considerable satisfaction from this state of affairs. Then he went looking for Spandarian. And Calder.

Petrov had risen at 5 am. Prepared the explosives, changed the plates on the jeep and driven it from the warehouse to a garage in the new town.

After handing the chess-set Katerina had given him to Mrs Betty Quarrick, Calder caught a streetcar driven by a woman with a potato face up the hill to the new town and rejoined Petrov outside the opera house where *La Bohème* was showing.

'*Your tiny hand is frozen* . . . . That must get a few laughs

254

with thirty degrees of frost outside,' Petrov re
problems?'

'No one seems to be looking for a one-legged n
beard.'

'Did you do what you had to do?'

Calder nodded.

'But you're still not telling?'

'You'll have to trust me.'

'You can say that again. You know something? Raisa's right,
I am crazy.' He began to walk towards the garage beneath an
apartment block.

'Why *are* you doing it? I've never really understood.'

'Just as I told you when all this started. Kata. Whatever she
says goes. We were very close. As you know Raisa and I lost our
son. I suppose I still regard Kata as a daughter.'

Abruptly, like a summer rainstorm, it began to snow. Within
seconds it was a blizzard, hard-grained flakes sweeping down
from the north, pasting bowed pedestrians instant white.

Militia, much in evidence but not as thick on the ground as
they were in the old town, shrank into doorways and stared at
their feet.

Petrov backed the jeep from the garage and Calder, having
thrown in his crutches, climbed in beside him. They drove
towards the outskirts of the town.

They were stopped once by militia with fur hats like iced
cakes.

Petrov showed them the documents that accompanied the
new registration number. 'And who's he?' A militiaman with a
frozen face pointed at Calder.

'He lost his leg building the BAM,' the new two-thousand-
mile Siberian Railway from Baikal to the Far East which had
taken ten years to build. 'He's got pains in the stump. I'm taking
him to hospital.'

'Ghost pains,' the militiaman said to Calder. 'Don't worry,
comrade, it's all in the mind,' pointing to his snow-capped head
and waving them on.

'So,' Calder said, 'where did those documents come from?'

'The old days. The gold run. I thought I'd finished with it.'
He winked. 'I'm glad I'm not. Does the jeep seem heavy to
you?' The wink still shuttered his eye. 'It should, I've got a load
of gold hidden in the back. I wasn't going to let that shithead
with the moustache get his hands on any more of it.'

'It's *all* in the back?'

'If it was the axle would have snapped like a matchstick.'
Petrov drove into a skid. 'Some of it's in the Zhiguli and the
rest's at the bottom of Baikal. I told you I had work to do that
last night – it took me an hour to cut a hole through the ice.'

They turned south, windshield wipers speed-swatting the
snow.

'After I've blown the bridge,' Petrov said, 'we'll wait a couple
of hours. That will give them time to stop traffic coming from
the south. By nightfall the whole track into Mongolia should be
clear. This time tomorrow you should be taking it easy in a
Buddhist temple.' He peered through the snow. 'Look, there's
the bridge,' waving at a blurred skeleton to the right of the road.
'It takes the track over a river which at this time of the year is
frozen solid from bed to surface.'

He changed down, braked and the jeep's chained tyres slid to
a halt on the side of the road running parallel to the railway.
Then he backed into a parking area screened from the road by
birch trees.

From the back of the jeep, between the provisions and the
gold, he took the detonating equipment he had stolen from the
gold mine before his retirement. The apparatus was old-
fashioned but adequate and, although he hadn't told Calder, he
still felt ill from handling the almond-smelling gelignite in the
garage.

Head down, warding off the buckshot snow with one arm,
holding the equipment in the other hand, he ran from the road
to the bridge. It was a beauty for blowing, a T-beam single span
high above the ribbon of solid ice. A partisan's dream. Thank
God the prudent railwaymen of Ulan Ude had decided it was
vulnerable to the cold.

Petrov crawled on the girders directly below the track. Wind

256

channelled along the river's gorge clawed him. A south-bound train thundered over him.

Half way across the bridge he found a demolition chamber. How decent of the constructors. What had they been anticipating half way across Siberia? An attack from the Japanese? A rearguard action against the Germans in the Great Patriotic War? By God, as he prised ice from the chamber, that gave you some idea of the Soviet potential for retreat: Hitler, and Napoleon before him, were lucky to have withdrawn when they did.

Into the chamber he packed a mixture of gelignite, plastic and ammonal; into another chamber on the other side of the two tracks a similar mixture. A junction box and two time pencils primed with ten-minute delays and Petrov was ready.

He squeezed the time pencils and ran back to the jeep. He and Calder kept low.

Five, four, three . . . . 'You need armoured-plated balls for this' Petrov whispered . . . two, one, zero . . . .

'Shit!' spat Petrov. 'I'll have to go back,' as the explosion veined the falling snow and pushed the jeep sideways. When they raised their heads they could still hear metal falling on the ice far below.

'Extreme cold has a curious effect on tired metal,' Petrov said.

'Supposing,' Calder said, 'that a train comes along?'

'It won't,' Petrov assured him. 'I checked. And in half an hour everyone from here to Moscow will know that bureaucracy was wrong about the bridge.'

'Supposing someone heard the explosion?'

'Trees explode in Siberia.'

Petrov flicked a switch and the windshield wipers thrust the snow aside.

'How far are you coming with me?' Calder asked.

'Until I get you on the train. You see with the bridge down and the road blocked no one will realise that you can get to Mongolia. When they've fixed the bridge then they'll check all trains at Ulan Ude and at the border. But you will be *over* the border: they won't appreciate that. You should have a clear run to China.'

'What about the Chinese border?'

'I know it well.' Petrov took a bottle of Jubilee vodka, the best, from beneath the dashboard, swigged and handed it to Calder. Somehow Petrov still managed to look composed, as though a stand-in had done the dirty work on the bridge while assistants daubed his long sheepskin coat with dirt and mussed his grey hair. 'The guards on this side are very fond of gold. Especially if it's wrapped in dollars. No problems on the other side.'

Half an hour later the blizzard stopped as abruptly as it had started. A fading sun was uncovered and the snow-white hills cushioning road and rail were tranquil in its light. To the east they could see the crests of the Yablonovy Mountains, creamed and sugared on the horizon.

A breakdown engine, a rusted antique, approached from the direction of Ulan Ude and stopped on the approach to the bridge. Three men in black coats and fur hats alighted and stared at the fractured girders. Even from a distance they looked mournful.

'Bureaucrats,' Petrov said happily. 'Already trying to blame the girl in charge of the samovar.' He put the jeep into gear. 'We'd better get out of here before a whole gang of them arrive by road.'

As he drove south, chained wheels still gripping the driven snow, the signal lights on the railway changed to red.

He stopped four miles south. The road ahead was blocked by a drift but the rail track on the bed of a shallow cutting had been regularly cleared and the snow from the spent blizzard was only a few inches deep.

'We'll give it a little longer,' Petrov said, 'to allow them time to move rolling stock stranded between here and the border.'

Calder shifted uncomfortably in his seat.

'You were lucky,' Petrov said. 'The doctor thought he might have to amputate at the hip.'

258

Lucky? Crippled. Part of your body cut away from you like a branch from a tree. Lucky?

'They'll fix you up in the States. I read about an Englishman named Bader who lost *both* legs in the war. A flyer. He played golf with tin legs.'

Lucky? He supposed he was.

Pain probed the emptiness where his shin had been. But it had lost its scalpel sharpness, just an aching reminder now of flesh and bone.

When the sunlight had faded to winter-pink and there were mauve shadows in snow-fields Petrov drove down a track leading to the cutting. He stopped on the lip of the shingle slope leading to the line.

'I hope Prince Borghese knew what he was doing,' he said.

'You forget to tell me – did he win?'

'I never found out,' Petrov said and engaged first gear.

The jeep descended ponderously. At the bottom of the slope it slid to one side, leaned to the right on two wheels, then settled.

Petrov drove over the outer rail, flush with the snow and shining in the last light. With one set of wheels on the sleepers linking the rails, the other on the stubs protruding beyond the outside rail, he began to drive south towards Mongolia.

Two people in Ulan Ude didn't believe that cold had wrecked the bridge on the railway.

For one thing it was too much of a coincidence, reasoned Spandarian, slugging his tea with brandy in a raucous café opposite the railway station. Calder makes for Ulan Ude . . . only possible escape route to Mongolia is the railway . . . bang, the railway is severed . . . .

For another it wasn't quite cold enough: it took a lung-freezing 40 degrees to make over-stressed metal disintegrate.

And the clincher: the trail had gone cold. *I* wouldn't be in Ulan Ude anymore. But how would I have got out?

Road? Out of the question. Air? Impossible – there was only

259

one airport in Ulan Ude and there they were even checking out the sparrows.

So it had to be rail. From the other side of the ruptured bridge? So Calder and Petrov were train drivers?

Spandarian stroked his sable *shapka* and thought like a Georgian. Isolated himself from the guzzling cretins around him.

Through the window he saw a Border Guard jeep . . . as there was only one route and as it was unlikely that either Petrov or Calder could drive an engine . . . a four-wheel drive . . . .

Spandarian rammed the *shapka* on his head, pushed his way through a group of indignant Buryats and ran to the railway station.

According to the Border Guard officer Petrov had once been suspected of smuggling gold through Mongolia to China. But such was his *blat* with the Irkutsk mafia that the investigation had been dropped.

Two call-boxes at the station were out of order. In the third he got through to militia HQ, identified himself as State Security from Moscow and gave a detective who spoke in apologies a hard time.

Who were Petrov's contacts in Mongolia?

'I'm sorry but . . . .'

'You're sorry but? The most dangerous man in the Soviet Union is on the loose and you're sorry but? Your name, comrade— I'm going to call Moscow.'

'I'm sorry . . . . Wait a minute, comrade.'

Impatiently Spandarian waited while the detective consulted Petrov's dossier on a computer, assuming that the technological revolution had reached Ulan Ude.

He heard breathing: it sounded as though the detective had run down to the archives and back. 'I'm afraid . . . .'

'Don't be. Petrov's contacts . . . .'

'All we know is that he used to hole up in a monastery at Darhan.'

'Where the hell's that?'

'Halfway between the border and Ulan Bator.'

'Near the railway?'

'On the railway.'

'I'll speak with Moscow about you,' Spandarian said ambiguously and hung up.

After consulting his directory of aero clubs in the Soviet Union he climbed into a taxi outside the station – he had abandoned the Volga because the Border Guard officer would have put out a stop-and-search on it – and told the driver to take him to the airport.

It was almost dark when he pushed his way through the passengers stranded by the snow to the office of the Airport Director who was also secretary of the local aero club.

The Director, plump with wispy hair and crinkled eyes, said he had his own small plane on the banks of the Selenga.

'Take me to it,' Spandarian said.

The Director's pet was housed in a small corrugated-iron hangar. It was a veteran. A red-painted biplane with a foraging nose and skis fitted to the undercarriage.

Spandarian the plane buff recognised it as an Avia 534. A Czech-made fighter which went into full production in 1935 and was flown against the Russians in the Great Patriotic War. But, as Spandarian remembered it, several Czech pilots had defected to Russia with their Avias. This, presumably, was one of them.

He patted its red fusilage. 'Hello beauty,' he said as though he were feeding sugar to a horse. And to the Director: 'Designed by Nowotny, wasn't it?' and when the Director, pleasantly surprised, confirmed that it was: 'Thank God it's the model with the closed cockpit. Plenty of juice?'

'Full up,' the Director said, 'but you can't take her out now,' anxiously, 'you'd fly straight into a mountain.'

'Unfortunately you're right. I'll stay with you tonight and take off at dawn.' He pointed at the Avia's 7.92 mm machine guns. 'Loaded?'

'Of course not.'

'But you've got ammunition?'

'Old stuff from the war. Useless I should think . . . .'

'Let's load her up,' Spandarian said.

* * *

261

Shoemaker didn't believe that the bridge had been wrecked by the cold because the possibility never occurred to him. He understood, after a lot of exasperated miming from a railway official, that there had been an explosion and he immediately thought: 'Calder.'

The road was impassable, the airport, which in any case was closed, was micro-meshed with security; somehow Calder, with Spandarian behind him, had got onto the railway beyond the bridge.

Shoemaker parked the Chaika outside the Univermag department store and considered the possibilities from an athletic standpoint. Cross-country skis, horseback, sled – all out of the question with a range of mountains to cross. Then he remembered his teenage expedition to Alaska. Up there everyone flew, even in the winter. Objection: 'I can't fly.' And what was the Alsakans' alternative to flying by the seat of their pants? Skimming through the countryside on snowmobiles, that's what.

Ignoring an outraged militia-woman pointing her truncheon at a No Parking sign, Shoemaker strode purposefully into Univermag.

Track pale-ribbed in the dimmed beams of the jeep's headlights. On one side a wall of mountain with stars perching on it, on the other a black abyss. Yellow wolves' eyes glowing. Snow-dust sparkling.

Petrov reckoned it was minus 40 outside. 'Enough to freeze your soul.'

Suddenly mountains and stars disappeared and the sound of the tyre-chains against snowless sleepers was as loud as the long-ago clank of convicts' manacles.

'A tunnel,' Petrov said. 'We're getting near the border.' He switched on the lights and the walls showed soot-black.

They heard the explosion as they emerged from the tunnel. Petrov cut the engine. They listened. The wind played melancholy music in the pines; small whirlwinds of snow skipped through the headlamp beams.

262

Petrov started the engine again, inching the jeep along the track.

'It sounded like a hand-grenade,' Calder said.

'If it was what I think it was it just goes to show you shouldn't cheat nature. I took time off from the mine once,' changing gear and accelerating slightly. 'I said I had pneumonia. What happened? I got pneumonia, double pneumonia.'

'You mean the bridge?'

'It's cold enough now for anything with a fault in it to explode. Like a tree,' he said, pointing at the pine lying across the track in front of them.

He stopped the jeep. 'Not as bad as it might have been,' peering along the headlight beams. 'Only the tip of it. But we'll have to cut it before we can move it.'

'You've got a saw?'

'Of sorts. A handsaw. For lopping branches.' Petrov put on a woollen face mask and gloves. 'Expose any flesh out there and it dies.'

He pulled a three-foot long handsaw with yellow-greased teeth from beneath some sacking. 'I always wanted to be a tree surgeon,' he said and jumped onto the track.

He sawed for ten minutes, sawdust spurting in the beams; then Calder, face masked and hands gloved, swung himself down the track on his crutches to relieve him.

'Think you can manage? I've got to take a break in case my lungs freeze up.'

Calder knelt on his one knee and slotted the saw into the wound Petrov had made. It was half an inch deep; the trunk was only three feet in diameter; in normal circumstances it wouldn't have taken long to sever it.

As Petrov, coughing, returned to the jeep he began to saw. His arms were strong from supporting himself on the crutches but he was out of condition. It was pathetic. His lungs begged for air, his sawing arm burned.

Five minutes later the wound was a quarter of an inch deeper, both arms were on fire and he was inhaling icicles.

They worked in shifts until, as dawn glowed green over the

263

mountains, they were within six inches of the break-through. 'Okay,' Petrov said, 'now we make a bulldozer out of the jeep.'

The fender of the jeep pushed the tip of the pine. The wooden hinge bent, frayed. Petrov backed up and drove at it again; the hinge broke. Petrov kept the jeep going, pushing the tip of the tree along the track; gradually it assumed an angle. He reversed across the oncoming track and hit the pine hard; it slid to the side of the track, crashed through a wooden fence and rolled down a white slope towards a belt of pines far below.

Petrov drove on through a valley to the border. The Russian frontier post was manned by one drunk in a fur hat and crumpled uniform. His colleagues, he explained frowning at the jeep, had taken off when all traffic from Ulan Bator had been stopped and the Peking Express had been diverted. 'No trains, no work,' he said defending his missing colleagues. 'But cars . . . .' He pressed his knuckles into his red eyes.

Petrov told him a part truth. They had mounted the track this side of the wrecked bridge because an avalanche had blocked the road. 'Ingenious, eh?'

The official agreed blearily. 'Papers?'

'Green ones,' Petrov said. He handed the guard a wad of dollar bills. 'And here's something to wrap them round,' handing over a ten-tola ingot.

He put the jeep into gear and they drove towards the Mongolian frontier post. 'I'll take a small bet,' he said, swigging vodka and handing the bottle to Calder, 'there won't be a soul there. Russia, Mongolia, one and the same.'

He was right.

They drove into Mongolia as the sun rose in a blue sky and a small red biplane entered the valley behind them.

Shoemaker, crouched at the controls of his electric blue snowmobile, noticed the biplane as he approached the border. But he didn't pay much attention to it: his numbed senses were concentrated on the quarry ahead, Calder with Spandarian in pursuit.

He wondered how far ahead they were now. When he had

bought the snowmobile he had assumed that he was hours behind them. But in these conditions the sleek little gasoline-propelled sled would make better progress than any other vehicle.

It was similar to the model he had driven in Alaska. Single-cleated caterpillar tracks at the rear and broad skis in front for negotiating deep snow and a 350 cc engine capable of speeds of around 50 mph. But he didn't go flat out because even at 20 mph at freezing point there would be a wind chill factor of around minus 40.

He wore the crash helmet, face mask, visor and black insulated suit he had bought at Univermag and, as he had driven through the night, some of the skills he had learned in Alaska had returned. Shift your weight on the turns, sit back to maintain track contact, take the bumps like a horseman . . . .

And there had been plenty of bumps as, gripping the handlebars and following the beam of the headlamp – with its broad windshield and sleek coachwork the snowmobile was like a luxurious motorcycle – he had plunged through the darkness.

He had twice hurtled off the track into snowdrifts but the worst stretches of track had been the tunnels – entrances like sharks' mouths with icicle teeth. If the moisture between the two sets of rails hadn't frozen he doubted whether he would have been able to navigate them; even with the ice he kept striking the track and slamming into the walls.

With the morning light came hope. He noticed the stump of sawn pine and sawdust on the track. It must have taken someone a long time to accomplish that. They couldn't be that far ahead.

They? If the fallen pine had stopped Calder then surely Spandarian would have caught up with him. Or perhaps the pine had fallen after Calder, before Spandarian. Or – in the new light he noticed that there was only one set of wheel tracks – maybe Spandarian is behind me!

When he reached the border a dishevelled guard waved at him vaguely. Shoemaker thought he noticed a flash of gold in his hand.

As he entered Mongolia he spotted the jeep about a mile ahead.

Oh no, Spandarian thought when he saw the snowmobile, Calder is mine. And the snowmobile was catching the jeep fast.

Spandarian, flying at 350 kilometres an hour – a little too fast for the veteran Avia judging by the shudders racking it – fingered the firing button of the machine-gun.

The gun was synchronised to fire through the propeller. According to the Airport Director there was enough ammunition for two or three bursts. If the belt didn't jam or blow up.

Spandarian kicked the rudder and pushed the stick forward. He breathed deeply, loving the hot-oil smell of the cockpit; as always it intoxicated him.

Maybe I'm a little crazy, he thought. Because of Calder. He had despised him: now he admired him: he should have been a Georgian. He adjusted the goggles of his flying helmet with a gloved hand and lined up the Avia with the snow-covered railway track.

Calder or me . . . you, you poor brave bastard. But first the other predator, Shoemaker. He felt no emotion about him: he should have stayed at his desk in Washington where he belonged. One burst should finish the snowmobile, two left for the jeep.

Finger on the firing button on the stick, Spandarian began his approach.

Snowmobile in the sights . . . tightness in his chest . . . two detonations . . . hardly a burst . . . the gun had jammed . . . but the two bullets had done the job . . . the snowmobile was plunging off the track . . . finger still on the button . . . firing again . . .

The bullets, synchronisation thrown by the misfire, chopped off the blades of the propeller and the Avia began its last descent to the white grave below.

266

Chapter 29

The Buddhist monastery was five kilometres from a railway halt reached by a track quilted with snow. The buildings, grouped in a prayer circle round a red temple, were built from wood and separated from the desolate white world by a stockade.

Black-printed prayer flags made from surgical lint fluttered in the breeze coming down from the mountains; Buryats, stamping a circular path of ice in the snow, pushed a prayer wheel; Siberian tigers moulded in stone looked on impassively.

Inside the temple lamas wearing saffron robes, hair shaven or cropped, intoned prayers in the light of yak-butter lamps. Drums throbbed, from time to time horns dispatched sonorous echoes into devout corners.

A Buryat wearing rimless glasses served Calder and Petrov with sugared yoghurt and yellow soup. Petrov, Calder thought, seemed popular although it was difficult to believe that he could be associated with peace.

When the Buryat had departed to fetch cheese Calder said: 'So do you think he's dead?'

When the biplane had disappeared behind a hill oily black smoke had billowed towards the sky. Petrov had decided that it would be foolhardy to investigate. 'The smoke didn't mean a lot. If he's a good pilot he could have made some sort of landing. There was plenty of snow away from the track, the plane was equipped with skis . . . . He could be out there waiting for us.'

'He wasn't strafing *us*,' Calder said. 'Just before he went out of control I saw something rear up on the ground like a shark . . . a snowmobile!'

The Buryat brought their cheese. 'A lama will be with you shortly,' he said.

He left them in the company of a statue of Buddha. Petrov cut the cheese with a long knife.

The lama was plump, butter-coloured and bald; he reminded Calder of Kruschev. He said some monks had gone to the scene of the crash and asked them what he could do to help them, looking warily at Petrov whom he knew of old.

Petrov told him.

When he had gone Petrov said to Calder: 'He doesn't realise what I'm going to do – may Buddha have mercy on my soul.'

Spandarian who had managed a soft landing in the snow limped clear of the Avia before, with a discreet explosion, it caught fire. He had two alternatives: to make for the snowmobile or the monastery where Calder and Petrov would have taken sanctuary. If he concentrated on the snowmobile he ran the risk of a shoot-out: it was a risk he couldn't afford – blood was dripping steadily onto the snow from a wound in his groin. Snow began to peel from a darkening sky; it would hide him as he made a run for the monastery.

Leaving a trail of red poppies behind him, he made for the temple. Snow closed around him, flakes as big as leaves. He pushed the goggles back from his face. His strength was seeping away. He opened his flying jacket and stuffed a balled-up handkerchief into the wound; the wound swallowed it and could have taken more. He gripped the walnut butt of the automatic in his belt.

When he reached the monastery he had only one option: he would have to gain admittance before he collapsed in the snow and bled to death. His ID should do the trick. If not, the gun. As he stumbled along he smelled coffee perfumed with brandy in a café near the funicular climbing Holy Mountain and smiled at a girl with green eyes and she smiled back . . . .

On the snow the red petals grew larger.

It took Shoemaker twenty minutes to fix the snowmobile. Nothing serious. A fractured petrol feed. But God knows how much gas he had lost. Following the red-splashed trail he took off towards the monastery through the thickening snow.

Standing at the door of the temple, one hand inside his robe, a lama with unevenly cropped hair said: 'And what can I do for you, my son?'

His voice was gentle but Spandarian heard flints in it. Spandarian said: 'I'm coming inside . . . you are harbouring an enemy of the State.' He could barely hear his own voice; he showed the lama his ID.

The lama was not impressed. He pointed at a wooden hut. 'Over there, you will be given food and shelter.'

As Spandarian produced his gun Petrov took his hand from inside the robe the lama had given him and leaned forward. The knife that he had used for cutting the cheese, an extension of his arm now, slid easily between Spandarian's ribs and into his heart.

Spandarian staggered back into the soft arms of the falling snow. Four, five paces and there was another face suspended in front of him. Shoemaker.

So Calder had won. A worthy opponent . . . should have been a Georgian . . . .

But at the end there can only be one of us. Raising the pistol he shot Shoemaker in the chest, throat and head.

What was it Shoemaker had shouted as he pulled the trigger? Stupid, meaningless words. As Spandarian died Shoemaker's words seemed to reach him from Holy Mountain: 'Don't shoot, I'm Saturday.'

Chapter 30

The travelling chess-set was handed to Holden while he was having breakfast with his wife in the west wing of the White House.

Although it had been electronically checked by security he handled it delicately. As though it was more precious than its intrinsic value.

It had been delivered half an hour earlier by special courier after a phone call from Ruth Calder the previous evening. According to Ruth, a Mrs Betty Quarrick from Fitchburg, Massachusetts, had brought a small parcel to her door; it had been handed to her on the platform of a railway station in Siberia.

When Ruth had opened the package she had found the chess-set and a note from Calder: *Get this to Holden urgently, he'll understand.* Signed: *Bob.*

'Did she describe the man who gave her the package?' Holden asked.

'A bearded cripple.'

'Nothing else?'

'Only that Siberia wasn't anything like the travel books.'

Holden felt the soft leather. Then he smelled it although he wasn't sure why. A trace of perfume.

His wife, efficiently pretty even at this hour, stared curiously at him across the small flower arrangement – roses and maiden-hair fern – which she changed every morning. 'You look like a guilty husband,' she said. 'Who is she?'

'I don't know,' Holden said. 'Guilty? Maybe . . . .'

She poured him more coffee. 'I'm being shut out, aren't I?'

He reached out and touched her hand. Breakfast was one of their best times. Sleepy and intimate in a room he had designed to look like a breakfast room anywhere from coast to coast. Even the table-cloth was red and white gingham.

He held up the slim leather wallet. 'I know this is important, vital, but I don't know why.' He opened it. White pawn to king four, no message there. Or was there?

'You used to play chess with Calder, didn't you?'

'Sure. We were chess freaks.'

His wife said: 'Think back: that's where the message is.'

Holden took the chess-set into their bedroom.

P to K4. That was the key, had to be.

He tucked a white shirt into charcoal grey pants. Security Council this morning. Sombre dress for a sombre occasion.

Whoever played white . . . . He froze teetering on the brink . . . .

Whoever played white . . . . PUT THE NAMES OF PEOPLE HE DETESTED UNDER THE MAJOR BLACK PIECES.

With clumsy fingers Holden slid the slivers of plastic from their leather slots. With the exception of the king each major piece was labelled with a name and occupation printed on a stick-on tab.

He laid them on the dressing table. The names made him feel faint. Sweat broke out icily on his forehead. He leaned against the wall. He heard rain against the window-pane on the other side of the drapes. He drew the drapes back, opened the window and breathed cold, rain-washed air.

Then he turned again to the names.

SUNDAY. A rook. Marion Shannon.

MONDAY. Knight. The chief adviser to the Secretary General of the North Atlantic Treaty Organisation, NATO, in Paris.

TUESDAY. Bishop. Director of Communications for NORAD, the American Defence system, buried in the Cheyenne Mountains in Colorado.

WEDNESDAY. No, there was no name under the king. There were only seven codenames and in any case the king wasn't primarily an attacking piece.

The name under the queen . . . . Holden frowned. A garble of letters. And printed under them in minute letters SATURDAY.

So the queen's bishop was WEDNESDAY. A vice president of the Commission of the European Communities, policy makers of the EEC, at their headquarters in Brussels.

THURSDAY. Queen's knight. How appropriate – Thursday had been knighted by the Queen: he was the deputy head of the British Secret Service.

FRIDAY. Queen's rook. The West German non-permanent member of the United Nations Security Council currently serving a two-year term of office in New York.

Jesus Christ! The Soviets were poised to colonise the West. Through Marion Shannon, deceased, they had won the minds of the young; through NATO they could manipulate the armed forces; through NORAD the early warning systems; through the EEC the policies of its European members – easy meat because they were always at each other's throats; through British Intelligence the entrée into clandestine operations; through UNO a pro-Soviet voice issuing from ostensibly pro-West lips.

SATURDAY? The garbled name was under the queen and the queen was the most powerful attacking piece on the board.

Holden stared at the letters. Ten of them. An anagram. With a ballpoint pen he printed the letters on a sheet of White House notepaper and, with a pair of nail-scissors, cut them out one by one.

As he snipped away he wondered what had happened to Shoemaker in Russia and when he started to shuffle the letters on the polished surface of the dressing table he subconsciously began with S H . . . fingers working busily . . . O E . . . praying: 'No, please, no,' . . . M A . . . .

Relief spread warmly inside him. No K. In any case Shoemaker was only nine letters. So what had he got left? ICRE. He pushed the I and the C together and they became a K and transposed the R and the E and there was Shoemaker and he knew whom SATURDAY had been briefed to manipulate.

272

ME.

He picked up the telephone and cancelled the meeting of the National Security Council.

Calder was escorted from the 747 at Boston's Logan Airport by two laconic FBI agents who had joined the flight from Tokyo at San Francisco. They were awkward but kind enough and they laid his crutches on the floor of the black VIP Cadillac gently as though they were brittle-boned.

Calder who had shaved off his beard on the last leg of the flight stared out of the window at the inquisitive-faced aircraft, the foraging trucks, the busy people. It was raining. America wet-nosed for his arrival.

He closed his eyes and said goodbye again to Yury Petrov in another world. Another life.

Together they had caught a train from Darhan to Ulan Bator, the capital of Outer Mongolia; there were no security checks – only two predators knew they had crossed the Soviet border and they were both dead.

At Ulan Bator Petrov put him on the Peking Express, the first across the frontier since the bridge had been wrecked.

On the platform before boarding the train Calder handed Petrov an envelope. It was addressed to the Chairman of the KGB in Dzerzhinsky Square, Moscow. 'I want you to post this in three weeks time,' he said.

Petrov, frozen faced but still raffish in his fur hat and sheepskin coat, held the envelope in his gloved hand as though weighing it. 'Am I allowed to know what's in it?'

'Better that you don't. You've never really known what this was all about. I'd like you to think of me just as a guy on the run. Someone you helped, trusted. Nothing more.'

A bitter dusty wind blowing north from the Gobi Desert narrowed Petrov's eyes and bowed the heads of a group of Mongols saying their farewells.

Shrugging, Petrov slid the envelope into the pocket of his sheepskin. 'Whatever you say.' He smiled piratically. 'I envy you, my old run . . . .'

Calder wanted to say: 'Then come with me,' but he knew

273

Petrov had to get back to Raisa. And . . . .

'Don't worry, Katerina will be all right,' stealing his thoughts. 'Probably back in Moscow by now chaining herself to the gates of the Kremlin. With Spandarian out of the way she won't have any problems. What did she do? Went on tour with a pop star, that's all – and probably got a good job with him into the bargain. She's better off than she was in that Institute of yours.'

The Institute . . . . Calder saw starlings trapped inside the dome of a disused church, the fluttering of their wings becoming more and more feeble. Mrs Lundkvist's hockey voice losing itself in echoes.

'What about you?' he asked Petrov.

'I'll always be okay. I have Raisa and I have gold. One to keep me warm, the other to warm the palms of greedy hands.'

'Where will you find Raisa?'

'In Bratsk. We have friends there.'

'You have friends everywhere.'

'And now one in the United States . . . .' The train shuddered. Petrov held out his hand. 'Goodbye. Maybe one day . . . .'

'Maybe.' Calder gripped Petrov's hand very hard. Then he threw his crutches into the carriage and followed them. When he reached his compartment and looked out of the window all he could see was Petrov's back at the end of the platform. Even at that distance he looked jaunty.

At the Chinese border he showed his American passport to the Russian officials who boarded the train. Inside it were the most valuable travel documents he had ever possessed – a wad of dollar bills. When the passport was returned it was empty.

Calder didn't attempt to bribe the Chinese. He was taken off the train, held at the border until the evening, then taken on another slower train to Peking.

After the President of the United States had been in touch with the Chairman and Prime Minister of the People's Republic Calder was officially deported, placed, under guard, on a charter plane paid for by the Americans and flown to Tokyo.

He was given to understand that the Chinese were not displeased by his anti-Soviet activities.

In Tokyo he learned from the US Embassy that Harry was out of hospital. That he had made a fair recovery – not good, Calder noted – and that it was hoped that eventually the effects of the fractured skull would clear up and he would be as normal as any other child. A bullet-nose of fear had lodged and stayed with Calder for the rest of the journey.

They were waiting for him in a small room at Logan Airport furnished with red plastic seats, a table heaped with magazines and a bar. Ruth looked as she had always looked in his thoughts, smart and soft at the same time, red-gold hair more businesslike than she was . . . . When she saw him her hand flew to her mouth.

And Harry was as he had known he would be except his hair was a little shorter, cropped where the fracture had been, and he was wearing jeans instead of the short pants he had worn in Calder's dreams, and his expression was searching, like a child assessing a new teacher.

'Hallo Harry,' Calder said. The moment he had unreeled so many times and he didn't know what to say, what to do.

He stretched out his hand. Harry looked past it.

Ruth said: 'We didn't know what to expect . . . .'

Then Harry spoke. 'Hallo dad,' he said. 'What have you done with your leg?'

'It's a long story,' Calder said. 'Want to hear it?'

And when Harry nodded he bent low on his crutches, his hand still outstretched and this time Harry took it.

Calder, walking with his crutches in the Rose Garden, said: 'They think Harry's going to be okay. I was therapy apparently.'

'And Ruth?' Holden walked quickly to keep up with Calder who used his crutches flamboyantly.

'We'll try,' Calder said. 'For Harry's sake.' He reined in his crutches. 'Maybe for our sakes.' His hand looked for the beard he had shaved off. 'Anyway we'll try . . . .'

275

Hedges and pruned rose bushes still dripped with rain but winter sunshine was making a fragile place of the garden. A bird sang in the crab-apple trees.

'She knows what you've done,' Holden told Calder. 'Not in detail, of course. But enough. You won't be the first hero to remain undecorated. But you won't want for anything.'

'Except a leg,' Calder said.

'Of course we'll have to give you a new identity. A new image. A little plastic surgery maybe . . . . How do you fancy the West Coast? San Diego maybe.'

'It's warmer than Siberia.' Calder started to swing himself along again. 'That cable to Jessel saying I was wrong about Marion Shannon . . . it was to convince him that he had to kill me?'

'As we both know Jessel worked for the CIA. But he had another employer, NSA, the National Security Agency. People don't realise they're more powerful than the Company.'

'Did you?'

'I realise it now.'

'What sort of an answer is that, for Christ's sake?'

'Evasive, I guess. Anyway the fact is that Jessel's real masters were NSA not CIA.'

'The CIA was a cover? I'll be damned. CIA versus NSA . . . With a set-up like that the KGB doesn't have too many problems in Washington. Or maybe they engineered it that way?'

Holden nodded wearily. 'That was part of Shoemaker's brief, to spread dissension. He worked with Zec, director of the NSA; not that Zec was a traitor, he was just a dupe. Shoemaker even got to sign coded cables. As *you* know – Jessel got one.'

'And Shoemaker never attracted a whiff of suspicion?'

'Partly my fault.' Holden turned away and stared at the colours trapped in the raindrops. 'I trusted him too much, just as you once trusted me . . . .'

'Just the same he must have been one hell of an actor.'

'Actor?' Holden frowned. 'I don't think so. They got to him so young that deception became part of his character. But he

276

was brilliant, I'll concede that – he even recommended the killing of Marion Shannon. But that, of course, was when she had been blown, when she no longer served any purpose.'

'Was he suborned on the campus? Like the others? Like me?'

'At UCLA. A certain professor of economics. I suppose that's where we make our mistake: we assume that traitors are spawned in the ranks of the deprived rather than the privileged. Shoemaker looked around, didn't like what he saw in his own circle and blamed the system rather than the individuals. As soon as he did that he was a soft touch for our comrades. I suppose the best we can say for him is that he had moral values.'

Calder stopped, dug the rubber-blunted tip of one of the crutches into the rain-soft grass. 'Moral values? Do you really believe that? Is that what you thought about me when I made a run for it?'

Holden said carefully: 'At first I had nothing but contempt for you. But,' hurriedly, 'then I realised that, to an extent, I was to blame.'

'Damn right.'

'So I guess I came to terms with fallibility. I was fallible, you were, Shoemaker . . . I suppose he believed what he was doing was justifiable.'

'More than that. He believed it was right. Right, right, right. Just as I did. And who knows, maybe it was. Treachery, what a melodramatic word! Like patriotism. And that surely is merely a geographical accident.'

'It's something to believe in,' Holden said.

'The Russians believe in it.'

'So why have you come back if the values there are the same as here?'

'For that reason I suppose. In the final reckoning we're individuals. They wanted to kill me, my son was hurt. What the hell is patriotism? It's where you're conceived, that's all it is, goddammit.' He skewered the crutch in the grass and faced the White House. 'Shoemaker never got to realise that.'

'Like you,' Holden said, 'he was side-tracked by ideals.'

277

'Ah, ideals. Elusive, aren't they? How can you say that the ideals preached in Washington are preferable to the ideals preached in Moscow?'

'I can't,' said the President of the United States of America.

As they walked towards the Oval Office Calder said: 'So what we have established is this: the enemy isn't in the Kremlin anymore: it's here, established decades ago.'

'Which is why, perhaps, the KGB has allowed the old men to linger in the Kremlin: they knew that in the world stakes the Politburo that matters is in the West. Here.'

'Well, you've nailed seven of them. But their vacancies will be filled. Their successors are in their teens, twenties, thirties but they'll get there. Who knows, maybe one is being recruited right now over a giant sandwich at Elsie's.' He paused. 'Remember the naïve views we had about equality?'

Holden glanced at him curiously. 'I remember.'

Calder took a sheet of typewritten paper from the pocket of his topcoat. 'Read it. The names are the key Western agents inside the Soviet Union. I found them in Jessel's briefcase among the names of other contacts.'

Holden scanned the names. 'My God, dynamite!' He folded the sheet of paper. 'Hell, supposing the KGB had found them before you.'

Calder stopped, turned and faced Holden, saw him for a moment looking up triumphantly from the chess board as he called check. 'Those dreams,' he said, 'they weren't so naïve.'

No muscle moved on Holden's questing features but suddenly there was a filter there. Calder remembered the expression, too, across the black and white squares. 'I don't understand,' Holden said.

'In the cause of equality,' Calder told him, 'you've got two weeks in which to warn everyone on that list that they're about to be blown. Two weeks in which to get them out. After that a good friend of mine named Yury Petrov is sending the list to KGB headquarters in Moscow. Stalemate, Mr President, a terrible trap to fall into.'

★　★　★

Later when he was Christmas shopping in Washington, Calder remembered Holden's last words in the Rose Garden. 'I never did think we were naïve. Maybe what we possessed was pure wisdom. Maybe sophistication is the only naïvety.'

Fingering the pocket chess-set which Holden had returned to him he thought: 'Katerina possessed that pure wisdom when we first met. No longer.'

Older people had told him that as the years accelerated their youth returned in vivid detail. Perhaps we journey back to a time of sublime innocence, the only truth.

Or am I merely trying to divert my own conscience? On the list he had given Petrov – but not on the one he had handed to Holden – he had included Dalby's name. Even now he could save him; but he knew he wouldn't.

Holding his purchases with difficulty, he swung himself out of a store with GOODWILL TO ALL MANKIND frosted on its windows and told the driver of the waiting limousine to take him to the safe house in Georgetown where Ruth and his son were waiting for him.

In the apartment on Leningradsky a rousing party was held to welcome the New Year. Sasha sang with unrestrained passion, a dog with a brown nose got under everyone's feet, twenty-three bottles of vodka were killed, a young man with brilliant prospects in the Soviet Foreign Ministry fell instantly in love with Svetlana and Leonid Agursky proposed marriage to Katerina.

'Give me a little time,' she said holding his hand. 'But if we do get married you know you will always be second?' and when he asked to whom: 'To the movement, of course – you'll even have to wash the dishes,' and when he asked: 'But not second to anyone else?' she turned away from him so that he couldn't see how damp her eyes had become and said: 'No, no one else,' and gripped his hand.

In the New Year a dozen Western diplomats, businessmen and advisers were recalled abruptly from the Soviet Union. Four others ignored the warnings they received and were summarily

279

executed in white-tiled cells with bullets in the backs of their necks.

Dalby died from a heart-attack although, as it was frequently pointed out in the Institute for World Economy and International Affairs, he hadn't had a history of cardiac trouble.

During the next six months five VIPs in the Western political and military structure also died. Also from natural causes. Or accidents.

WOLVERHAMPTON
PUBLIC LIBRARIES